Pamela Evans was born and brought up in Hanwell in the borough of Ealing, London. She has two sons and five grandchildren, and now lives in Wales.

Also by Pamela Evans

A Barrow in the Broadway
Lamplight on the Thames
Maggie of Moss Street
Star Quality
Diamonds in Danby Walk
A Fashionable Address
Tea-Blender's Daughter
The Willow Girls
Part of the Family
Town Belles
Yesterday's Friends
Near and Dear
A Song in your Heart
The Carousel Keeps Turning
A Smile for all Seasons
Where We Belong
Close to Home
Always There
The Pride of Park Street
Second Chance of Sunshine

PAMELA EVANS

The Sparrows of Sycamore Road

headline

First published in 200
by HEADLINE BOOK PUBLISHING

First published in paperback in 2005
by HEADLINE BOOK PUBLISHING

5

ISBN 978 0 7553 2147 6

Typeset in Bembo by Palimpsest Book Production Limited,
Polmont, Stirlingshire

Printed and bound by
CPI Group (UK) Ltd, Croydon, CR0 4YY

Headline's policy is to use papers that are natural, renewable and
recyclable products and made from wood grown in sustainable forests.
The logging and manufacturing processes are expected to conform
to the environmental regulations of the country of origin.

HEADLINE BOOK PUBLISHING
A division of Hodder Headline
338 Euston Road
London NW1 3BH
www.headline.co.uk
www.hodderheadline.com

To my sisters, Iris and Daphne,
with fond thoughts of all the laughs we have together

Chapter One

It was January 1941 and Paddington station was on a full wartime footing, which meant cancellations, delays and hordes of long-suffering passengers milling about in the public areas. A pungent mixture of engine steam and cigarette smoke permeated everything, rising towards Brunel's graceful roof arches in grimy clouds. It felt sharp and gritty in Nancy Sparrow's eyes as she marched purposefully through the banks of people on platform one, pushing a hand trolley piled high with luggage.

'Mind your backs, please, folks.' She was hoarse from shouting to make herself heard above the clamour of voices, hissing steam, whistles blowing, incomprehensible loudspeaker announcements and the bullet-shot slam of carriage doors. 'Make way there *please*. Thanking you. Ta very much.'

A train had just come in and the crowd pushed forward in a frantic tide, clustering around the doors and barely allowing the disembarking passengers to alight before scrambling in, servicemen heaving kitbags, civilians dragging cases. These people had been waiting a long time and were eager to begin their journey.

Having loaded the luggage, Nancy then assisted its owners through the jostling tangle of people and on to the over-crowded train. The compartments were packed to more than twice their capacity and the corridor was full, people squeezed together as closely as cargo on the goods trains. But still they smiled tolerantly at one another and moved up to make room for more. In this job, Nancy came across plenty of wartime spirit.

'Food, shells and fuel must come first. If your train is late or crowded – do you mind?' enquired a railway placard aimed blatantly at the nation's conscience. Most people realised that the inconvenience was inevitable and put up with it, recognising the value of the railway staff and treating them with civility, though they did take the brunt when frustrations proved to be too much.

Glancing at the platform clock now, Nancy saw with a great deal of relief that it was more than time she went off duty. She'd been on her feet since early this morning and was tired and cold to the bone, despite an extra layer of thick winter underwear.

A tall, blue-eyed woman of twenty-four, Nancy was plainly dressed in a dark serge uniform consisting of a jacket, a skirt and standard black lace-up shoes, her flame-coloured hair turned under into a pageboy beneath her cap. Eager to get home before the siren heralded an evening air raid, she hurried back along the platform, replaced the trolley in the bay and weaved her way through the masses on the concourse, towards the staff quarters.

A fierce-looking woman of about fifty, her ample

proportions clad expensively in a fur coat and elaborately feathered hat, had other plans for her, however, and gained her attention by planting a kid-gloved hand heavily on her shoulder.

'My suitcase is still outside,' she declared in a manner to suggest that Nancy had broken the law on several counts. 'Go and get it, will you, and be quick about it. Fast as you can now, chop chop.'

Taken aback by this breathtaking display of bad manners, Nancy didn't move.

'Don't just stand there gawping, you stupid girl,' she ordered. 'You're paid to serve the public so get on and do it. I don't have all day.'

Even Nancy, who was renowned for her kind and helpful nature, drew the line at rudeness. It wasn't as if she didn't understand how miserable the conditions were for wartime travellers. She knew only too well how difficult it was, especially for people in the services whose journeys were *really* necessary, but this tyrant seemed to think her journey was more important than anyone else's. Deeming it wise to be courteously assertive – since even the most difficult passengers must be treated with civility, according to the rules of the job – she said politely, 'I'm sorry, madam, but I'm off duty.'

'Oh, you are, are you?' She was clearly miffed by Nancy's effrontery, her greyish eyes gleaming like cold little marbles in her well-powdered face, cheeks glowing hideously with an excessive amount of rouge. 'So what, may I ask, am I supposed to do about my luggage?'

The same as every other able-bodied person when they can't find someone to carry it for them – bring it in yourself, Nancy was tempted to say, but actually suggested that she look for another porter.

'And where am I supposed to find one, you half-wit?' she snapped. 'There's not exactly an abundance of them on this wretched station, is there?'

'There are a few around.'

'I don't know what things are coming to, I really don't,' the woman complained, feathers sweeping the air as she shook her head in disapproval. 'There are no standards these days among you people, no standards at all.'

'It isn't that we don't have standards but—'

'This country is going down the drain,' she interrupted as though Nancy hadn't spoken. 'There's no such thing as decent service any more.'

Which was hardly surprising since the country was at war and London had been having the guts bombed out of it lately, thought Nancy, but she gritted her teeth and clung steadfastly to her patience. Off duty or not, if a complaint was to be made against her, however unwarranted, it would be positively relished by the bigoted supervisor. Mr Percy Wellington – irreverently known as Bootface or Perce by the female porters when he was out of earshot – was one of a group of men who still couldn't accept the idea of women doing men's jobs, even though they were desperately needed, and he leapt at any chance to throw his weight around. The main gripe among Nancy and her workmates was the awfulness of 'Perce'. They were of one mind about that.

'We do our very best for our passengers here at Paddington, but there isn't much we can do about the war or the lack of porters caused by the men being away in the services,' Nancy pointed out now.

'The train service is appalling.'

'The service is restricted, yes, and we're very sorry about that. But it can't be helped, I'm afraid. Moving troops, tanks and essential goods has to take precedence over ordinary passenger trains,' she explained reasonably, though this was common knowledge and the woman should understand that and do the same as everyone else – grin and bear it. 'Then there's the bomb damage and the blackout causing—'

'Don't waste my time with feeble excuses,' the woman cut in brusquely. 'I don't care if you are off duty, you'll go and get my case and no argument about it. So get on and do as you're damned well told.'

A willing heart was one thing but slavishness quite another and Nancy had too much spirit to allow herself to concede to the woman's unreasonable demands when she was off duty.

She was about to remind her of that fact when someone touched her lightly on the arm and said in a courteous but panicky tone, 'Sorry to butt in, porter, but can I just ask you quickly if the train to Reading has gone yet?'

Responding to this warmer, more reasonable attitude, Nancy excused herself from Lady Muck – who complained bitterly before storming off to find some other unlucky porter – and turned away to find herself looking at a young woman of about her own age dressed in a shabby brown coat and headscarf, gas mask slung over her shoulder. She was carrying a shopping bag in one hand and a small boy of about a year old in the other. She looked pale, weary and close to tears and Nancy instinctively wanted to help her, even though she wasn't on duty.

'No, not yet. It's been delayed.'

'Ooh, thank Gawd for that. I thought I'd missed it.'

'Well, there's a novelty,' Nancy grinned. 'We don't often please our customers with the delays and disruptions there are to the service these days.'

'No, I don't suppose you do,' said the young woman, making a rather unsuccessful effort to smile. 'The buses are just as bad. That's why I'm late getting here.'

Nancy nodded sympathetically. 'Your train won't be in for a while yet.' She made a face. 'It's an hour behind schedule apparently. Sorry about that.'

'It's not your fault. Anyway, I'd sooner have to wait an hour than miss it altogether.' She gazed affectionately at the child who was peering out from the hood of a blue siren suit which looked to be a triumph to 'make do and mend'. 'Gawd knows how I'm gonna keep young Stanley amused while we're waiting, though.'

'Perhaps some refreshment might help if they've anything left in the station buffet. Shall I go and see if I can get you something?' offered Nancy, her journey home now taking second place to this woman who looked in such dire need of support.

'That's kind of you. But are you allowed to spend time doing errands for passengers?'

'It depends on the circumstances. But it doesn't matter anyway because I've finished for the day, so I'm on my own time,' she explained. 'A cup o' tea for you and a bun for his nibs might help to pass the time while you're waiting. I'll keep you company if you like.'

'That's very kind of you, but only as long as it won't put you out.'

'Not in the least.'

The woman looked thoughtful for a moment, then said, 'Actually, I'm dying for a wee. Do you think you could look after Stanley for me for a few minutes while I pop over to the ladies?'

'Certainly,' Nancy agreed without hesitation. 'I'll take him with me to the buffet and get in the queue. Meet you over there.'

'Thanks ever so much.'

'A pleasure.' Just a little ordinary human respect was all it took to have Nancy bending over backwards to help. The hard-eyed harridan with the imperious attitude could learn a lot from this weary young woman.

Despite her concern about getting home, Nancy didn't leave until she'd seen the mother and baby safely on to the train. Over a cup of tea, Nancy had heard her companion's heart-breaking story . . .

Mary and Stanley had spent last night at a rest centre after being bombed out of their East London home, and were on their way to stay with a relative in the country because they had nowhere else to go.

Everything Mary now owned was in her shopping bag – just a few mementos she'd managed to rescue from the rubble, and her handbag, which had been with her in the shelter. She and her husband – who was away in the army – had had a room at her parents' house. Both parents and other members of her family had been killed last night when the house had taken a direct hit.

'Stanley and me had been out visiting a mate of mine who's got a baby of a similar age. We got talking and I stayed later than I intended and the siren went as I was walking home, so I went into a public shelter because I still had a long way to go.' She paused, lips trembling, red-rimmed eyes brimming with tears. 'When the all clear went, I carried on home.' She stopped again, mopping her eyes with a handkerchief. 'I turned the corner and half the street had gone. Family, friends, neighbours, all wiped out.' Huge tears meandered down her cheeks and she could barely choke out the words. 'All destroyed, as though their lives meant nothing. It's so cruel. I mean, what had they done to deserve it?'

Deeply affected, Nancy had tried to find some words of comfort, but she hadn't wanted to insult Mary with platitudes so she had just taken her hand, offered her a clean handkerchief and let her cry.

The baby had been sitting on his mother's lap, chewing messily on a sticky bun. Mary kissed the top of his head and wiped her eyes. 'Now it's just 'im and me until his dad comes home.' She paused and blew her nose. 'Please God that he does. I couldn't bear to lose 'im an' all.' She looked at Nancy. 'Is your ol' man away fighting?' she asked.

'I'm not married.'

'Boyfriend then?'

'I don't have one of those either.'

'Oh.' As usual, this admission produced a surprised, questioning look, almost as though an explanation was necessary. But Mary just said, 'Oh well, at least you don't have to spend your whole life wondering if he's alive or dead.'

'There is that.'

When it was time for Mary and Stanley to get their train, Nancy had gone with them. There was no shortage of assistance for anyone with a baby. A soldier took Stanley while his mother climbed aboard and an elderly man gave them his seat in the compartment. Such friendliness warmed Nancy's heart and was just the antidote she needed for the incident earlier with the passenger from hell.

But now Nancy was a passenger herself and was standing on the platform in the underground station at Paddington waiting for the train to Ealing Broadway, her thoughts lingering on Mary and her little boy whose sad case was all too familiar these days. She felt a pang as the thought of Stanley's sweet baby face and trusting eyes triggered off memories. Tears welled up.

Admonishing herself for dwelling on the past when so many lives were being lost every day, Nancy swallowed hard and looked around at the crowds of people who were already settled down for the night on the platform with their blankets and pillows, though it was still only six o'clock. Regular shelterers got here early to secure a place.

Having initially banned the use of underground stations

as a means of shelter, causing the public to overcome the restriction by simply buying a platform ticket and refusing to come up, the government had now conceded to demand and supplied temporary bucket lavatories and some bunks, though not nearly enough and many people still had to sleep on the floor. The raids had been slightly less regular since the beginning of the new year, after almost nightly heavy bombing through the autumn up until Christmas, but everyone still anticipated a raid every night.

It was stuffy down here and the odour of sweat and urine wafted around on the stale, underground breezes. Those halcyon days before the war when her working hours had been enjoyably spent selling women's clothes in a small dress shop in Oxford Street seemed a lifetime ago. It hardly seemed possible that it was less than a year and a half since they'd clustered around the wireless to hear Neville Chamberlain tell them that their country was now at war with Germany.

A few months after that, Nancy had gone to the labour exchange full of patriotism and eager to do something worthwhile for her country. She'd been told that workers were urgently needed on the railways so that was where they were sending her, for the time being anyway. She was to be a porter on Paddington station and no argument about it. She'd had something more exciting in mind, like the Land Army or the Auxiliary Territorial Service, commonly known as the ATS. But they'd been adamant. She was young and fit and they, apparently, were the main criteria for a job as a porter. Older female volunteers were directed towards clerical work.

Now that she was actually doing the job, she could understand why. Handling heavy luggage and goods, and being on your feet for hours at a time required a great deal of energy and stamina. Muscles she hadn't known existed had ached since she'd been working at Paddington.

But despite her initial reservations, she enjoyed the hard work and hustle and bustle. Doing something of national importance was a reward in itself. She wasn't making shells or nursing wounded soldiers, but she was playing an important part in helping to keep the railways moving.

Now her train came in and she was swept forward by the crowd and just about managed to squeeze in as the doors closed against her.

Initially blinded by the blackout when she came out of the station into the bitter night, Nancy waited until her eyes adjusted to the dark then went to get her bike from the cycle rack. She could make out the shapes of buildings, and just about see the white painted line on the kerb.

With her lights masked in accordance with blackout regulations, a coat over her uniform and her gas mask over her shoulder, she pedalled off towards West Ealing, glad she hadn't had to cycle all the way from Paddington as she did when there were no trains or she was on late turn and would miss the last one home.

She headed for the main road, rather than take the short cut through the backstreets, because it had a small amount of authorised diffused lighting. This emitted only a pale glow around the base of the few lampposts on which it was installed, but it was better than nothing in the crippling blackness.

Staying close to the kerb, out of the way of any trolley buses – otherwise known as 'silent perils' because of the number of accidents they caused in the blackout – she cycled hard, eager to be at home with the family.

She'd only been on the road a few minutes when the chilling air-raid siren warbled across the town. Here we go again, she thought, her insides twisting. Although she was, to a certain extent, resigned to the raids after so many, it was easier to be brave when you were with people inside somewhere than out on your own in the dark.

Turning off the main road towards Sycamore Road and home, her sense of isolation increased, though there were other people around. She could hear them blundering about trying to find their way home, and their extremely colourful language as they collided with walls, unlit lampposts and each other. There wasn't a chink of light anywhere at ground level, but there was a pale slice of moon and the stars were magnificent in the midnight-blue sky, the silvery beams of searchlights weaving across the heavens.

When the siren stopped, the streets seemed hushed, as though the whole of Ealing was holding its breath. Then came the unmistakable drone of German bomber planes and the loud crack-crack of anti-aircraft guns. Somewhere nearby a woman started screaming in terror.

The serried rows of terraced houses – so ordinary in daylight – were sinister shapes in the dark. Even though she was familiar with practically every paving stone in this area, having never lived anywhere else, for a moment Nancy lost her bearings and felt a flash of panic. There was a loud explosion that shook the ground beneath her, and the sky above the rooftops turned crimson, the air instantly filled with acrid smoke.

Realising how close the bomb had been, and now very frightened, she focused her mind on a prayer for the family and cycled on, frantic to end her journey now. There was another ear-splitting crunch which was so startling she swerved, hit the kerb and flew over the handlebars, landing with a thump in the road and seeing stars as her head hit the ground.

Dazed at first, she eventually scrambled up and dragged her bike on to the pavement, knees smarting, head throbbing. Touching her face, she felt a bump on her forehead. The ominous whoosh of a descending bomb sent her down again instinctively. Lying flat on her stomach, her hands clasped above her head and her eyes shut tight, she prayed hard then broke into a shaky version of 'We'll Meet Again'. Singing always seemed to help somehow.

'Flippin' 'eck, that was a close one,' said Lily Sparrow to her mother Gladys.

'Phew, not half. I thought our end had come,' replied Gladys shakily.

'It makes me wonder how much longer our luck will hold when they drop as near as that,' said Lily.

'It's no good thinking that way, love. You just have to tell yourself that we've got the luck of the devil and long may it last,' advised Gladys with a mother's natural instinct to reassure her child, even though her daughter was forty-one.

'Our good luck is someone else's misfortune,' Lily reminded her. 'Some poor devils around here will have copped it. It's awful, the way we're so glad that it wasn't us.'

'Everyone else is the same. Self-preservation is a natural instinct.'

'Except when it comes to your own kids. Then your own safety comes second to theirs,' muttered Lily, whose carrot-coloured hair was poking out of a blue woolly hat that was almost the same shade as her eyes.

She held a candle close to the clock on the rough wooden shelf they'd rigged up between them out of an orange box. An upturned beer crate served as a table, on which stood a teapot in a knitted cosy, some cups and a bottle of milk. 'All three of them will be on their way home from work now.' She emitted a shuddering sigh as she replaced the candle on the table. 'I do hate it when they're out during a raid. It turns my insides to jelly.'

'I'm none too happy about it either, but it can't be helped as they have to go to work. They've got their heads screwed on; they'll find a public shelter,' said Gladys, who lived a few doors down in a ground-floor flat. The local authority had provided a communal surface shelter for the flat dwellers, but Gladys preferred the company of her daughter and grandchildren during a raid.

Swathed in coats, scarves and blankets, the two women were sitting opposite each other on cushions on homemade plank benches in the candlelit Anderson shelter. Smudge, the

14

family tabby – who treated the raids with typical feline disdain, but fully exploited the extra care and attention that came his way from his loving owners – was dozing contentedly on Lily's lap.

It was dank and dismal down here, despite their efforts to make it more bearable with a coat of green paint on the corrugated iron walls and lino on the floor. The constant seepage of water through the cracks in the concrete floor meant that there was always an unwholesome smell no matter how often they got saucepans and buckets to it. Most loathed of all by the entire Sparrow family was the constant presence of beetles and spiders.

'The girls might have the sense to take shelter, but you know what Micky's like,' said Lily now in reply to her mother. 'The war is just a big adventure to him. He's probably outside somewhere watching the raid.'

'He's at the age to find it exciting, isn't he? Most teenage boys are like that.'

'He's hungry for action, I know that much,' said her daughter. 'He can't wait for his eighteenth birthday so that he can get out of the factory and go off to be a soldier.'

'I think all little boys grow up wanting to be heroes. It's how they're made.'

'I'm dreading him going, Mum,' confessed Lily. 'I can't bear the idea of my boy going to fight.'

'We'll all miss him, that's for sure,' Gladys said with fond thoughts of her grandson. 'He's always so lively and full of chat . . . and cheeky if he's got the devil in him.'

'Kids, eh? At least when they're little you know where

15

they are and can try to keep them safe. But now I spend my whole life in fear for them. Nancy's sensible enough to take care of herself. But as for Jean . . . She won't let the air raids interfere with her social life if she can possibly avoid it. So while we're sitting here worried sick about her, she's probably gone to the pictures straight from work, or out dancing or something.'

Lily was chewing her thumbnail nervously through a hole in her grey knitted glove. She could be strong when everyone was here. But not knowing whether her children were alive or dead just knocked the stuffing out of her. Thank God the youngest of the four, ten-year-old Leslie, was away from all this and safe in the country. She hadn't sent him on the first evacuation scheme of the war, but last summer, when invasion had seemed imminent, she'd felt duty-bound to register him. It was just as well she had, because the Blitz had started soon after that and it had been far too dangerous for a child to stay in London ever since.

'I think I'll go out the front to see if there's any sign of them,' she said.

'That won't bring them home any quicker,' was her mother's wise response. 'And what will it do to them if you get yourself killed?'

A plane droned overhead, followed by the whistle of a bomb on the way down. They clutched each other, eyes shut, nerves jangling, until after the explosion. 'I see your point,' agreed Lily with a quiver in her voice.

Outside it went quiet. 'Perhaps Jerry's going home early tonight,' suggested Gladys hopefully.

'They won't let us off that lightly.' Lily put her hands to her head in desperation. 'Oh, where are those children of mine?'

At that moment someone climbed down through the ground-level hole at the end of the shelter.

'Wotcha, you two,' she said.

'Nancy,' greeted her mother joyfully. 'Thank God you're here. I've been that worried.'

'I picked her up off the pavement,' said a voice behind her and Micky clambered in, a tall, thin young man with the same colour hair as his mother, more obviously ginger than Nancy's which was a deeper shade of red.

'I hit the kerb and came off my bike,' Nancy explained, sitting down beside her mother.

'Oh no! Are you all right, love?'

'I'll live,' replied Nancy cheerfully. 'I've got a bloomin' great bump on my head, though.'

'People trying to get about in the dark,' tutted Lily. 'The damned blackout will be the death of us.'

'The blackout is the least of our worries,' said Nancy with a nervous giggle which infected the others. It helped to release the tension.

'We'll be all right in here. These shelters have proved they can withstand anything except a direct hit, remember,' said Micky, who was a mine of wartime information. 'They're safer than people originally thought they would be. Got any nosh down here, Mum? My stomach's been screaming at me for hours.'

'There's some bread and cheese under the cloth on the

17

table and tea in the pot,' his mother told him. 'I'll pour you both a cup.'

'Good old Mum. I knew I could rely on you to look after my belly.' Micky hugged her then sat down next to his gran.

Another member of the family appeared from above. 'Ooh good, a picnic,' said Jean, a pretty brown-eyed brunette of nineteen whose colouring came from their father's side of the family.

'Looks like we've got a full house,' said Lily, smiling with relief that they were all here.

Enemy aircraft could be heard again. Nancy started a chorus of 'Ten Green Bottles' and they all sang at the tops of their voices to blot out the din.

'I'm going out dancing on Saturday night with the girls from work, bombs or no bombs,' declared Jean Sparrow over her porridge the next morning. 'I need a bit of pleasure after being stuck at a machine making shells all week.'

'You'll have to wait and see what the situation is with the air raids,' advised her mother.

'I'll take me chances,' said Jean, who had her curlers in under a turban but still managed to look attractive, with her small features and well-shaped mouth. 'We can't let Hitler take over our lives completely. He's won if we do that.'

'He's won if we let him kill us, too,' Lily pointed out.

'All right, Mum,' she sighed with emphasised boredom, and no thought for her mother's concern. 'But he's not stopping me from going out. I'm young and I don't wanna be stuck at home. There's nothing like a night out at the Palais to take you out of yourself. The war seems far away when you're in there. There's a magic about it – the music, the lights – ooh, how I love it.'

'The music and the lights, my foot,' teased Micky. 'It's the men you go for.'

'What makes a little squirt like you the expert on the way I live my life?' asked Jean, giving him a warning slap on the arm.

'I've seen all the different blokes who bring you home.' He paused, his blue eyes full of fun. 'I've seen you kissing and cuddling at the front gate.'

'Then you shouldn't be such a peeping Tom,' she rebuked. 'You should get a love life of your own, then you wouldn't get such a thrill from mine.'

'Me, get a thrill from your goings-on?' he said in disgust. 'Don't make me laugh.'

She gave him another playful slap. 'There's nothing wrong with my having a healthy interest in the opposite sex. I'm very choosy, you know. I only go out with the ones I really fancy.'

'Which is the majority of the male population of this country,' joshed Micky.

'Don't forget all the ones from overseas who are stationed here too,' she said, playing along with him. 'Canadian, Polish, Norwegian. Some of them are gorgeous, and such lovely manners too.' She was an outrageous flirt and made no apologies for it. 'A girl's got to find a husband somehow. Anyway, there's no law against having fun. Lord knows there's enough misery happening everywhere. Live for today, is my motto. We might all be dead tomorrow.'

'Thanks for cheering us up,' said her mother.

'Just being realistic.'

They were seated around the table in the spotlessly clean but cluttered living room of their end-of-terrace house, the dismal blackout curtains drawn back to the sides of the net-curtained window overlooking the street. The raid had gone on well past the small hours, so nobody had had much sleep, but they were all up early for work.

Jean turned to her sister. 'Fancy coming with us on Saturday night, Nance?'

'Not particularly.'

'Oh, go on. It'll be a laugh.'

'I'll think about it.'

'You ought to come.' Jean could be very persistent when she wanted her own way about something. 'It's about time you had a regular bloke.' She scraped the spoon around her bowl for any last vestiges of porridge. 'You'll miss the boat altogether if you don't find someone soon. I'd be really worried if I was twenty-four and didn't have a man of my own. Most girls are married with a couple of kids at your age.'

'Nancy's happy as she is,' put in Lily, who knew more about Nancy's past than Jean did and wished her younger daughter would be a little more sensitive to other people's feelings. 'She's still got plenty of time anyway.'

'Phew! I wouldn't say that. She's getting on a bit in terms of finding a fella.' Jean gave Nancy the once-over. 'I can't understand why you haven't got anyone. I mean, you're not all that bad-looking, apart from the awful red hair.' Jean was always having a dig at Nancy and Micky about them

20

inheriting their mother's colouring while she and Leslie were dark like their dad.

'She's got very pretty hair,' defended Lily.

'You would say that since you've got it yourself,' chuckled Jean.

'No I haven't. Nancy's is a different colour to mine,' said her mother. 'It's a beautiful shade.'

'Perhaps you need specs.'

'And perhaps you need to watch your tongue, my girl.' She gave Jean a warning look. 'All this talk of Nancy missing the boat; she's had boyfriends.'

'Never gets much further than the starting post with 'em, though, does she?' said Jean cruelly.

'Oh, for goodness sake,' protested Nancy heatedly. 'Will you please stop talking about me as if I'm not here.'

'Yeah, leave her alone,' put in Micky. 'Not everyone wants to spend their life chasing men.'

'Keep out of it, you.' Jean turned to her sister. 'You don't want to be an old maid surely, Nance?'

'If that's the way it's meant to be, I can live with it,' Nancy told her. 'Anyway, as we're all going to be dead tomorrow, according to you, there's no need for me to worry about it, is there?'

'There's no need to be sarky,' Jean objected. 'You'll be on the shelf if you don't do something about it. Eligible bachelors don't come knocking at the front door. You've got to get out there looking.'

'You can worry about it if you like,' said Nancy, who wasn't as immune to Jean's jibes as she pretended. 'But I'm

21

not going to. We're losing enough sleep as it is with the bombs raining down on us.'

'I thought you'd be glad to come up the Palais with me. I thought you liked dancing.'

'I love it, and the music and the atmosphere. It's the standing there like a prune waiting for someone to ask me to dance I'm not keen on,' she explained.

'There'll be plenty of partners, with all the servicemen in town.'

Nancy gave her a look. 'Why do you want me to come if you've already got people to go with? It'll be for your own benefit somehow.'

'I was thinking of you.'

'Oh, per-lease. This is me you're talking to. I know how your mind works.'

'All right, maybe it would help me if you came along. Some of the girls who are going are a bit pushy, and it would be nice to have you there as support,' she grudgingly admitted. 'But I was thinking of you as well.'

As fond as Nancy was of her sister, she had never seen any evidence of an altruistic side to her nature. 'If you say so,' she said with a shrug.

'I don't care what you say, it would do you good to go out dancing,' Jean went on. 'But if you wanna stay in on a Saturday night like an old spinster, get on with it.'

'I will, don't worry.' Nancy turned her attention to their mother. 'Come to think of it, Mum, you haven't been out of an evening for ages.'

'That's true,' agreed Jean. 'A night out would do you good.'

'I hope you're not suggesting that I go to the Palais with you,' chortled Lily.

'Not likely,' Jean was quick to assure her. 'I'm not so desperate that I'd want to go out dancing with my mother. That really would cramp my style.'

'You used to enjoy going to the pictures and the works socials with your mates, didn't you, Mum?' said Nancy, remembering.

Lily nodded.

'So why did you stop going?' Nancy asked.

'There hasn't been much going on in that direction,' she explained. 'Anyway, I don't like leaving your gran on her own during the raids.'

Not for the first time lately, Nancy noticed that her mother looked rather pale and drawn. She'd seemed a bit peaky for a while now, but when asked about it she'd brushed it aside and claimed to be fine. Nancy's filial emotions were much stronger towards her mother than her father since he was so rarely around. Nancy admired her mother enormously. She'd raised four children virtually single-handed and with such joie de vivre. She'd been no pushover when they were younger; she'd been firm and straight with them, but good fun too, her love for her children always so reassuringly obvious. Nancy hated to see her below par and guessed it must be the strain of the raids taking their toll.

'You never used to go out anywhere of an evening before you started going out to work, did you?' Nancy mentioned, looking back on it. 'Even though Dad's been away at sea so much.'

'I wouldn't have dreamed of it before the war. Most married women wouldn't,' confirmed Lily, who worked in the offices of a munitions factory. 'But with you lot grown up and Leslie being away, there seemed no reason not to join in when the women at work were going somewhere.'

There was a noise from the hall; the rattle of the letterbox. 'The postman's survived the night, then,' said Nancy and went to get the mail.

'It'll take more than Adolf to stop us getting our letters,' stated Lily. 'They might take longer but they get here in the end. Well, most of them anyway.'

'There's just one from Leslie,' said Nancy, handing her mother an envelope.

'Nothing from Dad, then,' mentioned Micky.

'Your father never has been one for letter-writing,' Lily reminded them to ease their minds. Her husband had been in the merchant navy for the whole of their married life and she was used to his being away and not hearing from him for months at a time. But she still missed him and was eager for news. Although she didn't worry the children with it, she was very concerned at present because goods ships were prime targets for the enemy and many British ships had been bombed at sea.

'What's Leslie got to say?' enquired Nancy.

'Nothing much. You know Les, he's not a boy much given to putting pen to paper. Takes after his dad in that respect.' Lily finished reading the letter and passed it to Jean. 'It just says he's fine and can I send him some pocket money.'

'That sounds like our Leslie,' smiled Nancy, who was very

fond of her kid brother and missed his chirpy presence about the house. An energetic and entertaining child, he was always up to something.

'I must get down to Devon again to see him as soon as I can,' said Lily, her brow drawing tight. 'I can't go as often as I'd like with having to work most Saturdays.'

'Don't worry too much, Mum,' encouraged Nancy. 'We know he's happy and being well looked after. You've seen that for yourself when you've been to visit him.'

'Oh yeah, he's having a whale of a time down on the farm,' Lily agreed. 'Such lovely people he's billeted with, as I've told you. They're kindness itself when I go there to visit. But I still hate not having him here at home.'

Jean finished the letter and handed it to Nancy.

'Well, I've got to go and get ready for work,' she said, rising and walking to the door.

'Oi! What about helping with the dishes?' Nancy called after her.

'I haven't got time,' came Jean's predictable reply.

'You're not the only one. We all have to go to work,' her sister reminded her.

'You're such a nag.' And with that she turned and sailed from the room, followed by Micky, who was already late.

'She's so damned selfish,' muttered Nancy.

'Don't let her get to you, and don't you worry about the washing-up, love.' Lily moved on quickly to avoid more discussion on the subject, seeming weary as she got up and began clearing the dishes. 'It won't take me a minute. You go and get ready for work. You've got further to go than me.'

'Nonsense,' said Nancy. 'You look all in. You go and sit down and I'll finish this off. It won't take long.'

'Thanks, love. I don't know what I'd do without you.'

Sycamore Road was an ordinary street of red-brick terraced houses, fronted by tiny gardens, some of which had privet hedges. The wind was biting as Nancy cycled towards the main road on her way to the station, progressing into similar backstreets where there were smouldering ruins from last night's raid, people standing around the debris that had once been their homes, looking bewildered, some of the women crying. Nancy herself wanted to weep at the terrible sadness these people were forced to endure.

The leaden skies were smudged with black smoke and there was a pungent smell of burning in the air. One house had had the front blown off so that the interior was exposed, people's privacy on show for all to see. West London hadn't suffered as much destruction as the East End, according to the papers, but they'd had their share of damage and loss of life around here.

It was a raw, dull day, the silver barrage balloons floating reassuringly above the rooftops like huge, overfed fish. Sandbags were very much in evidence, piled high outside a disused building which had become the Air Raid Precautions Control Centre. There were plenty of people about on the main road, most of them walking in purposeful strides, queuing at bus stops or cycling. To the majority, getting to work on time was a matter of pride, even if they had been kept awake most of the night by the bombing. Some of the shops along here had been damaged in the heavy raids last autumn. There was a notice on a boarded-up shop warning that looting was punishable by death or penal servitude for life. She'd never heard of anyone receiving these dire punishments or seen anyone committing the offence, but rumour had it that the demolition squads and rescue workers pocketed valuables from bombed houses.

Her thoughts turned to her sister's comments. Jean tended to be shallow and immature, but some of what she'd said about Nancy's single status had hit home. She wanted love; she wanted marriage and children, very much. But what had happened years ago had made her wary and afraid. Love had become synonymous with pain and she couldn't bear to go through that again. This was why none of her relationships had lasted. But Jean knew nothing of this.

Nancy felt a knot of worry as her thoughts returned to her mother and how strained she seemed to be. Maybe I'll suggest an outing to the flicks for the two of us at the weekend, she decided. That might cheer her up. Jean could manage perfectly well at the Palais without her. Mum needed her more.

Meanwhile, there were more immediate matters to be contended with, she thought, as she reached the station and chained her bike up. She had to fight for a place on the train, if they were running today. If not, it was back in the saddle for her all the way to Paddington. She headed hopefully into the station with the surge of other commuters pouring in.

* * *

Lily always called in on her mother on her way home from work and they usually had a quiet cuppa together if they could spare the tea. Lily arrived back earlier than the others, so could spare a little time for a chat with her mother on her own, and did so that same evening.

Born and bred in the area, sixty-three-year-old Gladys had moved to the flat near her daughter after her husband had died, thus being able to retain her independence while having Lily and the family close at hand.

Since rationing had begun to bite hard, they often pooled their rations to make them go further. As Gladys didn't go out to work, she cooked the evening meal at her place then carried it round to her daughter's so that the family could eat together. It was company for Gladys, and saved on fuel too.

'I've made a stew for tonight as we agreed.' A small woman with hazel eyes that shone warmly from a round, pink-cheeked face, she was wearing a crossover apron on top of her jumper and skirt, a hairnet keeping her white hair in place.

'Thanks, Mum. I don't know what I'd do without you now that I'm out working.'

'You'd manage. But you don't have to because I'm here. We work as a team, you and me. You're on war work and I help you out at home, which makes me feel as though I'm making a contribution.'

'You are, a huge one.'

'Anyway, the stew is ready and only needs the dumplings to go in, though Gawd knows what they'll be like with hardly any suet. Like ruddy golf balls, I should think.'

'No they won't. The meal is bound to be delicious, if I know anything about your cooking.' Her mother was an absolute whizz in the kitchen, and a mistress of invention since food had been in such short supply. What she couldn't do with corned beef and a few vegetables wasn't worth mentioning. 'As long as it's warm and filling, we'll be happy.'

Gladys nodded. 'Had a good day?'

'Yeah, pretty good, thanks. How about you? What have you been up to?'

'The usual things. Cleaning, cooking, queuing at the shops. I got lots of knitting done as well.' Gladys knitted tirelessly for the war effort. 'I was pleased about that, as warm things are so badly needed by the troops.'

'Yeah, I must try to do more.'

'You do what you can, given that you're out at work all day.'

'I knit while I'm listening to the wireless in the evening, but I can't seem to stay awake long enough to do more than a few rows lately.'

Gladys gave her daughter a studious look. 'You look worn out now, love,' she observed.

'No, no, I'm fine, Mum,' Lily said, trying to sound convincing. 'You know me. I've always got bags of energy. It's only later in the evening I feel a bit tired.'

'You look exhausted already tonight.'

'Everybody's tired, which isn't surprising as we're all being kept awake at night by the bombs, and turning up for work the same as usual.'

Going out to work for the first time since her marriage

had given Lily a new lease of life and freedom she'd never even dreamed of before. She had money in her pocket, new friends and, having discovered that she could actually do something worthwhile outside of the home, her self-confidence had soared.

Inspired to take the plunge and go to the labour exchange because war workers were so urgently needed, she'd volunteered her services. Prepared for gruelling work in a factory, she'd been surprised to be directed into simple clerical work at a munitions factory. Wherever possible, apparently, women over forty were being given lighter duties than the younger women. She enjoyed the job enormously and everything had been going swimmingly . . . until recently.

Now tension was drawing tight between herself and her mother as the unmentioned created a palpable barrier between them. They were both avoiding the subject.

But Gladys couldn't bear a bad atmosphere for long. So she peered at her daughter over the top of her spectacles and came right out with it. 'You'll have to tell the children sometime soon, Lily.' Her tone was kind but very firm. 'This isn't going to go away and they have a right to know.'

'Yeah, yeah, Mum, I know and I really will do it soon,' she replied, her face turning even paler. 'It's just that . . . well, it's going to be so hard.'

'It won't be easy, that's for sure, but it has to be done. It won't get any easier for putting it off.'

Lily's heart was full of dread. 'You're absolutely right,' she agreed with a sudden air of resolve. 'I will definitely talk to them in the next few days.'

'That's the spirit,' said Gladys, smiling, but her gentle eyes were clouded with worry.

Chapter Two

'Mind how you go now, girls,' said a railway worker of about fifty a day or two later, as he lifted an enormous trunk down to Nancy and a porter called Polly from the back of a horse-drawn cart piled high with suitcases, trunks and bags. The petrol shortage had brought the horse back into its own as a working animal and a much needed means of transport. 'Careful now. Have you got a firm hold on it? Don't go dropping it now.'

'We've got it, Charlie,' puffed Nancy, breathless from the sheer weight of it, shoulders aching with the strain.

'Phew, and don't we know it,' added Polly as the two women struggled to heave the trunk on to a trolley. 'Gawd knows what the toffs put into these things. Ten ton o' house-bricks, judging by the weight of 'em.'

'Still, look on the bright side, eh? All this lifting and carrying will do wonders for your muscles,' joked Charlie, who had a habit of speaking with a cigarette dangling from the corner of his mouth. 'You'll be as strong as boxers and well able to keep your old man in order when he comes home on leave.'

'You've got a good point there, Charlie boy. It'll come in very useful if I find out mine's been messing about with any of those foreign women.' Polly paused to catch her breath from the exertion.

'The poor bloke.' Nancy's tone was light-hearted. 'He's out there fighting for his country, and living under the most terrible conditions. How is he going to get the chance to go chasing after women?'

'Men will always find a way.' In her early twenties, Polly was a blue-eyed blonde with a cheerful disposition and a wicked sense of humour. 'I'm only kidding. Of course I trust him.' She regarded Nancy thoughtfully. 'That's one advantage of being single. At least you don't have to worry about what your other half's up to when you're not there to keep an eye on him.'

'Single?' Charlie immediately picked up on it. 'A smasher like you? Cor, what a shocking waste. Now . . . if I was twenty years younger . . .'

'Make that thirty and you might be somewhere near the mark,' teased Polly.

'You'd sweep me off my feet, would you, Charlie?' Nancy entered into the banter with good grace, but the frequent references to her single status did get rather irritating at times.

'Not half.' Tough and fit-looking, despite his greying hair, he drew on his cigarette. 'I used to cut quite a dash with the ladies when I was young.'

'You can give us the juicy details of your misspent youth while we're working,' suggested Nancy. 'Come on, let's have another suitcase down and get this job done.'

They were in one of the station sheds, unloading the luggage that had been sent on ahead under the Passenger Luggage in Advance Scheme, which enabled travellers to send their baggage before their journey, and was especially useful at this time of difficulties on the railways. As long as the luggage was properly labelled, the system worked well.

Having regaled them with stories of his life in London before the last war, Charlie said, 'It's no good, I shall have to go and answer a call of nature. I shan't be a minute. Don't touch anything until I get back. I've got my own system and I don't want you two messing it up.'

Complying with his wishes, the two women stood there chatting to pass the time. Polly sat down on a nearby trunk.

'I was hoping to get a letter from my Bill this morning.' Polly's soldier husband was stationed in the Middle East. 'But not a bloomin' sausage. I hope he's all right. I haven't heard for quite a while.'

'I'm sure you'll hear soon,' Nancy reassured her. 'I expect there are several letters on the way and they'll all come at once. We can't expect postal deliveries to be normal with chaos reigning everywhere.'

'That's what I keep telling myself, but it's worrying, even so.'

Another woman porter walked by, pushing a loaded station trolley.

'Wotcha, Ruby. How's it going?' called out Polly with a friendly smile.

'All right,' she replied in a surly manner, pausing and looking at them.

'You settled into the job yet?'

A rather unprepossessing woman of Nancy's age with dull brown hair and greasy skin, Ruby Green was fairly new here at Paddington station. 'Of course I have. I've been here for two weeks, so I ought to have done by now.'

'Well, don't be afraid to ask one of us if there's anything you need to know,' offered Polly.

She gave Polly a withering look. 'It's hardly brain surgery, is it? Any fool can do this job,' she stated categorically. 'So I won't need to ask anybody anything, thanks very much.'

'Polly was only being friendly,' put in Nancy, who had known Ruby Green distantly at school. 'There's no need to bite her head off.'

Ruby gave a careless shrug and went on her way without another word.

'Miserable bitch,' said Polly.

'Mm. She is a bit spiky, to say the least,' agreed Nancy. 'I knew her vaguely at school. Or, rather, I knew of her. She was in the same year as me, but not the same class. Everyone had heard of Ruby Green because she had a reputation as a troublemaker. A right little bully, if I remember rightly. Nobody liked her.'

'Can you wonder at it, if that's the way she treats people?'

'She must be quite unhappy, though, to behave like that,' suggested Nancy.

'She'll feel even worse if she carries on as she is,' was Polly's opinion. 'Friends keep you going in a job like this. She's doing herself no favours by treating her workmates like dirt.'

'I agree with you. I think I'll have a chat with her if the opportunity arises,' decided the warmhearted Nancy. 'See if I can bring her out of herself.'

'Why bother?' queried Polly. 'She's made her position perfectly clear. I should leave her to get on with it. You just said she was a right little horror at school.'

'Yeah, she was, but we're adults now,' Nancy pointed out. 'Old enough to know that there's usually more to these things than meets the eye. Anyway, it won't hurt me to make a bit of an effort.'

The conversation was cut short when Nancy spotted the supervisor marching towards them with a thunderous expression on his face. 'Look out, kid,' she warned. 'Bootface is heading this way, with the look of battle about him.'

'Ooh, blimey.' Polly leapt up as a short, stocky man of middle age stormed on to the scene, holding a clipboard.

'Oh, very nice too. Having a little rest, are we?' said Percy Wellington sarcastically, his beady little grey eyes seeming magnified as they glared at the women through the thick lenses of his horn-rimmed spectacles. 'A nice woman-to-woman chat. How very pleasant for you. Put your feet up, why don't you? Do a bit of knitting perhaps. Maybe I should have a tray of tea and biscuits sent over?'

'We're waiting for Charlie to come back, Mr Wellington,' explained Nancy.

'You're not paid to stand about doing nothing,' he said, glowering at her. 'You should get on with the job while you're waiting.'

'Charlie told us not to touch anything, Mr Wellington,'

Polly informed him, careful to use his proper title. He was very fussy about that.

'Bloody petticoat porters, stopping work every time the mood takes them,' he muttered, fiddling with his droopy moustache irritably. 'I don't care what anyone says, women aren't up to this job. It's men's work and always has been. You shouldn't be employed here when you're so obviously unsuited to it.'

'Tell the labour exchange, not us,' responded Nancy, standing her ground. 'We just went where we were sent. And you'd be in real trouble without us, seeing as there aren't enough men to work on the railways.'

'We'd manage.'

'It isn't exactly the job of our dreams, you know, Mr Wellington,' Nancy pointed out bravely, 'but we're here because we're needed.'

'That's right.' Polly backed her up.

'Don't talk back to me,' he bellowed, his face potholed and wrinkled. 'Have some respect for your superiors. I'm your supervisor and don't you forget it.'

'I doubt if we'll be given the chance,' riposted Nancy.

Most people had now got used to seeing women in jobs formerly thought of as male preserves, but Percy was still rattled by it. His face was dark with fury and he grabbed Nancy roughly by the arm and took her aside. 'You're a troublemaker, Miss Sparrow,' he said in a low voice, making sure he wasn't overheard. 'And I don't like troublemakers on my team.' His grip was tight and his hard eyes full of malice. 'Is that clear?'

38

'Perfectly clear.' She met his hostile gaze. 'Now can you let go of my arm, please, before I find it necessary to contact my union representative.'

That shifted his grip on her and she saw fear as well as fury in his eyes. He wasn't used to having anyone stand up to him, let alone a woman. Suddenly she could see beyond the bossy persona to a sad and ageing man – too old to fight for his country and too young to draw his railway pension – feeling threatened by the changing times. 'Any more trouble from you and I'll report you to the stationmaster. Tell that to your ruddy union rep.'

He could be a dangerous enemy, she was under no illusions about that. Women were too urgently needed as porters for her job to be under any serious threat, but he did have the power to make her life a misery while she was working here. At the same time, it wasn't in her nature to kowtow to bullying from anyone. 'You must do what you feel you have to, Mr Wellington.'

He gave her a long, cold look, then his gaze moved beyond her to the cart to which Charlie had now returned. 'Go and get on with your work before you try my patience too far,' he ordered, and swung round and walked away.

Polly was eager to know what had been said.

'He was just emphasising his authority, as usual,' Nancy told her, lifting a smaller suitcase off the cart and putting it on the trolley. 'You know what he's like.'

'Don't I just.' She appeared to be mulling something over. 'He always seems to be picking on you. Do you think it's because you stand up to him?'

'It could be. But whatever the reason, I'm not one of his favourite people, that's for sure,' agreed Nancy.

When Nancy was waiting for the train that evening after work, she spotted Ruby Green on the platform. Elbowing her way through the crowds, she went up to her.

'Hello there, Ruby.'

The other woman didn't look pleased to see her. ''Lo,' she said, turning away and staring straight ahead.

'Do you still live in Ealing?' enquired Nancy in a friendly manner.

Ruby nodded.

'Me too.'

Silence.

'Still living at home?' She was still Ruby Green so Nancy knew she wasn't married.

'Yes,' the other woman ground out with seething impatience. 'Not that it's any of your business.'

'I'm still under my mother's feet too.' Nancy was determined to persevere, because she had the suspicion that, deep down, Ruby wanted someone to take the trouble with her. Surely no one could really want to be isolated from their workmates, could they? 'I don't suppose there are many from our school year still doing that. I expect they're all married with kids.'

'Could be. I dunno.'

'Where is it you live, Ruby? It can't be that near to me or I'd have seen you around.'

'Highgrove Crescent. Near Haven Green.'

'Ooh, very nice too.' It was in a much classier part of the

borough than the Sparrows' humble abode. 'Lovely and handy for the station.'

Ruby stared disinterestedly ahead.

'I leave my bike at Ealing Broadway station,' Nancy went on chattily, still hoping to draw Ruby into conversation. 'It's quite a long walk for me and you can't rely on the buses these days, can you?'

Ruby swung round, her cheeks flaming. 'What is this, the third degree or something?' she demanded. 'Why can't you shut your trap?'

'Just trying to be friendly,' replied the indomitable Nancy, keeping a tenacious grip on her patience. 'I was thinking that as we both live in the same region of London, we might as well keep each other company on the journey home.'

Behind the spite in Ruby's nondescript eyes, Nancy could see something else. Regret perhaps? Sadness? Maybe there was even a hint of wishfulness.

'Look, you probably mean well, but I don't want company and I certainly don't want to be friendly, so you can cut out all the matey stuff.'

'But . . .'

'Spare me the bit about there being a war on and everyone being part of one big happy family, please. I don't buy that one at all.'

'They're a smashing bunch of girls at the station,' Nancy went on. 'It helps the day go by with a swing when you can have a bit of a laugh with your workmates. Helps you forget all the terrible things that are going on around you, too.'

'I don't doubt it, but I prefer my own company. I don't

41

run with the pack. I never have done.' She gave Nancy a close look. 'But you were at school with me so you already know that.'

'That's a long time ago. We've all done plenty of growing up since then.'

'I am what I am, so just leave me alone, will you?' Ruby's voice rose with temper. 'Find someone else to talk to on the train.'

'If that's what you really want.'

'I wouldn't have said it if it wasn't, would I?'

'All right, I won't bother you again. But I think you're going to feel awfully lonely, being outside of the group at work, turning everybody away.'

'It's the way I want it, thanks very much,' came the curt response.

With a shrug of resignation, Nancy turned and weaved her way through the crowds to another spot on the platform. She wasn't so much hurt by the rejection as puzzled by it. Why would anyone want to shun companionship from people they were working with all day? Ruby was obviously a very strange and complicated woman.

Mum seemed especially tense that evening, Nancy noticed. As soon as they'd finished every last morsel of the corned-beef hash, Gran disappeared into the kitchen to wash the dishes and Lily stayed at the table and said she had something important to tell them.

'I can't stop to listen now, Mum 'cause I'm meeting the girls and they won't wait for me if I'm late,' said Jean dismissively. 'You tell the others and I'll hear all about it when I get back.'

'It has to be now, Jean.' Lily was unusually firm. 'I want to speak to you all together while there isn't a raid on.'

'I'm in a hurry too, Mum,' Micky told her breezily. 'I'm going round my mate's house. He's had his call-up papers. So whatever it is, it'll have to wait as far as I'm concerned. You can tell me in the morning.'

With an uncharacteristic show of temper, Lily thumped the table with her hand, her face brightly suffused. 'It won't wait,' she announced loudly, but her voice was trembling slightly. 'I want to speak to you all *now*. So stay where you are – *please*.' She cleared her throat. 'There's no easy way to tell you this . . .'

Nancy's heart lurched. 'Oh God, it isn't Dad, is it?' she asked shakily.

'No, no, this has nothing to do with your father.'

'Phew, that's a relief.'

'Spit it out then, Mum,' urged Jean, still indifferent to the obvious gravity of the situation.

Lily looked around at them all, then swallowed hard and took a deep breath. 'I'm expecting a baby,' she blurted out, adding quickly, 'It's due in May.'

There was an appalled silence. The only sound was a creaking through the wall as one of the next-door neighbours went upstairs.

'But . . . how can you be?' asked Jean at last.

'I think you know how these things happen, Jean,' said her mother.

43

'But you're too old and . . . anyway, Dad hasn't been home.'

Lily moved her gaze slowly round the table.

'Oh, no. You don't . . . you can't mean it's someone else's?' breathed Jean incredulously.

'Well, it didn't get there by itself, love.'

'Ugh, that's disgusting,' responded Jean, looking at her mother with disdain. 'You dirty cow.'

'Jean,' rebuked Nancy, struggling with her own feelings of shock and outrage, but instinctively defensive towards her mother. 'Don't you dare speak to Mum like that.'

'How else am I supposed to speak to her when she's having another man's baby, not our dad's?' She stared at her mother with contempt. 'Ugh. Just the thought of it makes me feel sick. You shouldn't even be doing it at your age, let alone getting yourself in the club by some strange man.' Her voice rose hysterically. 'We'll be the talk of the neighbourhood. Everyone will be gossiping about us, staring at us every time we walk down the street. Oh, Mum, how could you?'

'People are far more interested in trying to stay alive and making the rations go round these days than gossiping about other people's business. Nearly everyone's out at work and far too busy to notice their neighbours' comings and goings like they used to before the war,' Lily pointed out. 'They will just assume that your father had a spot of leave and they didn't happen to see him before he went back.'

'Mum's right,' supported Nancy.

'Don't kid yourself,' roared Jean. 'People aren't stupid and there's nothing they like better than a juicy bit of scandal,

44

war or no war. And this one is a beauty. The tongues wag loudly enough when a daughter gets herself into trouble. But when the mother gets knocked up – not that I've ever heard of anyone's mum doing what you've done – they'll have a field day.'

'Stop thinking of yourself, Jean,' urged Nancy heatedly, putting her hand on her sister's arm to restrain her. 'Let Mum finish speaking.'

'That's all I have to say really,' said Lily in a small voice. She was so pale her freckles were as dark as mud specks. 'I know that you're all shocked, and I'm not proud of myself but—'

'I should damned well hope you're not . . .'

'Jean,' admonished Nancy again. 'Carry on, Mum.'

'But I'm hoping that, when you've had a chance to get used to the idea, you'll find it in your hearts to forgive me and welcome the child into the family as your sister or brother.'

'But it won't be our—' began Jean.

'Of course it will,' Lily cut in. 'It'll be your half-sister or – brother.'

Nancy looked at her mother. 'Who's the father, Mum?' she asked quietly.

'That doesn't matter.'

'It matters a hell of a lot to us.' Jean was shouting now.

'The man is dead now anyway,' Lily informed them. 'He was killed in an air raid without ever knowing that I was pregnant.'

'We still have a right to know who he is,' demanded Jean.

45

'As you've ruined the reputation of the whole family, I think we should be told his name.'

'His identity is irrelevant.' Lily was adamant. 'It's the child who matters. I made a big mistake and there's nothing I can do about that now. But there is going to be a new life soon. That's the important thing.'

'God only knows what Dad's gonna say when he comes home,' said the doom-laden Jean, her elbows on the table and her chin resting in her hands.

'You let me worry about that. I'll handle your father when the time comes.'

'Oh, I'm not listening to any more of this,' Jean burst out, standing up, her voice wobbling on the verge of tears. 'I might as well make the most of being able to go out without everyone staring at me while I can. Once you start flashing your big belly about, there'll be no chance of that.'

'Trust you to look at it from your own point of view,' reproached Nancy. 'It might come as a surprise to you, but people do actually have more important things to do with their time than stare at you.'

'Shut up, you,' she blasted and rushed from the room.

'She'll get over it, Mum,' comforted Nancy.

Micky hadn't said a word since Lily had made her announcement. He was sitting very still with his eyes fixed on the table.

'You're very quiet, son,' Lily observed. 'Don't you have anything to say on the subject?'

He didn't reply at once, just continued to stare at the table. When he looked up his eyes were hot with rage. 'I think it's downright disgusting,' he burst out, his voice ragged with emotion. 'You've let Dad down; you've let us all down. You're nothing more than a filthy old whore. And don't call me son ever again because I don't want to be a son of yours.' He gulped back the tears, his freckled cheeks scarlet. 'I've always thought you were the best mum in the world. I thought your family meant everything to you. And all the time you didn't give a damn about us. You went out enjoying yourself and were unfaithful to my father. You've betrayed us all and I can't even bear to be in the same room as you.'

With that he rushed from the room and thundered up the stairs.

Gladys appeared from the kitchen and slipped a comforting arm around her daughter's shoulders. 'We both knew it wouldn't be easy, love,' she said kindly. 'But the worst part's over. It'll get better now that it's out in the open, even though it probably doesn't seem like that now.'

Nancy stared at her grandmother. 'You know about it?' she asked in surprise.

'Of course I know,' replied Gladys, pulling out a chair and sitting down next to Lily. 'You kids might be too wrapped up in yourselves to notice your mother's thickening middle and the fact that she's been feeling a bit queasy lately, but not me. I've been nagging her to tell you children for ages.'

'I knew you'd be hurt, that's why I kept putting it off.' Lily turned to Gladys. 'Thanks for staying out of the way in the kitchen, Mum.'

'It was as much as I could do not to come in and give the other two a piece of my mind for the way they spoke to you. They've no right, no right at all,' she told her. 'But I'd promised you I'd keep out of it so I stayed out there until it was over.'

'What about you, Nancy?' enquired Lily warily. 'Aren't you going to storm off like the others?'

'You know me better than that, Mum,' she replied. 'I'm the calm one of your brood, remember.'

Lily reached across and took her hand. 'Thanks, love. I appreciate that.'

'I can't pretend I'm not shocked, though.' It wasn't so much that she thought ill of her mother, more that what had happened was so alien to her perception of her. 'I thought you seemed a bit off colour lately, and I've been worried about it. But it never even occurred to me that you might be pregnant. I mean, you don't think of your mother in those sorts of terms, do you?'

'Especially not when your dad's away,' said Lily, managing a wry grin.

'Exactly.'

'If it makes you feel any better, I was knocked for six by it as well. It was the last thing I wanted.'

'But you must have, I mean . . . was it a love affair or . . .'

'I was swept off my feet, that's the only way I can describe it,' Lily tried to explain. 'It was a thing of wartime, you might say. I was lonely, I suppose, and not used to a man making a fuss of me. It didn't take much to turn my head.'

'But Dad's been away at sea for long periods for as long as I can remember, and you never seemed lonely,' Nancy reminded her.

'I was always lonely, even though I didn't show it and I was used to his being away. It's only natural that I would be. When you were all little, I was so immersed in bringing you up, it didn't seem to matter so much. But you grew up and the war came and Leslie went away. Going out to work was very exciting for me. I'd never had a job outside the home in the whole of my married life and I took to it right away, especially as I wasn't needed here. I learned new skills, met new people.'

'Including this man?'

She nodded. 'He didn't work at the factory but I met him at a work social. He was friendly with someone on the management, nobody I knew. I don't move in those sorts of circles at work. Anyway, he asked me to dance and we hit it off right away. He was a real gentleman. At my age, it's very exhilarating to find that you're still attractive to men, especially when your husband's hardly ever at home. This man seemed very keen on me and I was flattered, I admit it. He was a great romantic, something your dad, bless him, wouldn't know how to be. He made a great fuss of me, even used to write little love notes, and give them to me when we met.' She paused thoughtfully. 'I hadn't been told I was beautiful for years and it went to my head. With everyone being terrified of an invasion last summer and those raids just before the Blitz, I suppose I just wanted to grab some pleasure while I was still around to do so.' She gave Nancy a grave look. 'I know you kids think I'm ancient and long past those sorts of feelings, but everything doesn't stop when you hit forty, you know.'

'So when you told us you were going out with your mates from work you were actually out with him?'

49

Lily looked shamefaced. 'Most of the time, yeah. I couldn't tell you where I was really going, could I? Anyway, sometimes I was with them.' She was very much on the defensive. 'I was riddled with guilt the whole time and kept trying to end it but . . . well, I just couldn't seem to let go. It was an escape. When I was with him I could forget the bombs and the rationing, and the fact that I sleep alone every night.'

'Where did you used to go with him?' Nancy enquired, feeling she had to know, but dreading the answer because it was all so painfully at odds with the woman she knew only as her dear, family-orientated mother.

'To a hotel in the West End mostly. We couldn't go out locally in case we were seen. Sometimes he would drive us out of London somewhere. He never seemed to have any shortage of petrol for his car – yes, he was well off enough to have one of those – and I was too caught up in it all to ask questions about that. We'd spend hours talking, and . . . well, you know. It all seems so cheap and tacky now, but at the time it was very exciting.'

'So his dying was the reason it ended, then?'

'Oh, no, I ended it before . . . just before, actually.' Her lips tightened. 'I found out he'd been lying to me. He had a wife who was very much alive even though he'd sworn to me that he was a widower. That soon brought me to my senses and I finished it right away.' She paused, looking sad. 'We were in a pub when I told him. He stayed in there, said he was going to drown his sorrows if he could get enough booze. Just after I left, the pub was bombed. There were no survivors.'

'Is that why you won't tell us his name? Because he was married?'

'Exactly. His wife could get hurt if I name him. If no one knows who he was, they can't go running to her with tales while in a fit of rage.'

'Dad, you mean?'

'Well, yes. Or Micky. Or anyone. If nobody besides myself knows, she can't possibly get to know, can she? The man is dead, so there's nothing to be gained from breaking the woman's heart. Ignorance is definitely bliss in this case.'

There was the sound of heavy footsteps on the stairs and the front door slammed.

'Micky will come round.' Nancy tried to cheer her. 'It's probably harder for him to come to terms with it, being a boy. He's always worshipped you. I'll have a chat with him later. As for Jean, she'll get over it. She knows which side her bread is buttered. But I don't know about Dad . . .'

'He'll probably throw me out, and he'll have every right,' Lily said, shaking her head. 'But I'm hoping that when he's calmed down he might be able to forgive me and let me bring the baby up in the family, as a Sparrow.'

'I shouldn't bank on it, Lil,' warned her mother. 'It's a lot to ask of any man.'

'Yes, I know that, Mum, but Arthur and I have been married a long time. Maybe he'll find it in his heart to forgive me this one mistake.' She turned to Nancy. 'For what it's worth, I do love your father. I always did. What I felt for this other man was more of an infatuation, a break from reality. I've never been unfaithful to your dad before.' She sighed. 'Still, I don't suppose I'll be the last silly old bag to have her head turned by some charmer before this wretched war is over.'

'Oh, Mum,' said Nancy, tutting. 'How could you ever be an old bag?'

'It's what the others think.'

'They're still trying to take it in, that's all. They'll feel differently when they've got used to it and had a chance to remember all the millions of good things you've done for us all over the years. What's happened now is a shock, I'm still reeling from it myself. But it doesn't alter the fact that you've been a fantastic mum, bringing us up on your own because Dad was never here, always finding the time to play with us, read to us, listen to our problems as we got older.'

'And then I go and do something stupid and upset the applecart altogether.' She was full of remorse.

'As you said, we were all grown up, Leslie was away. These are terrible times we're living in. You're only human.' Nancy tried to soothe her.

'Anyway, it's too late for regrets,' sighed Lily. 'No matter how much pain and trouble this pregnancy is going to cause, there's going to be a child and I shall do my very best for it. With or without the blessing of the family.'

Nancy felt an ache inside as her mother's plight triggered off memories of her own.

There was the sound of someone running down the stairs and Jean poked her head around the door. 'Can I borrow a bit of your lipstick, Nance?' she asked. 'I can't get so much as a smidgen out of my tube.'

'Since when did you bother to ask?'

'Since I can't find yours.'

'I daren't leave it where you can find it or you'd have the lot off me.'

'Please, Nance,' she wheedled. 'Just a little smear . . . please. You can use mine when I get some. I promise.'

'You shouldn't spread it on so thick,' tutted Nancy. 'But go on then. It's in my make-up purse in my handbag in the kitchen . . . and don't take much.'

'I won't. Thanks, sis.'

As they heard her going back upstairs, Lily said, 'Well, for all that she stormed off in a huff, my news doesn't seem to be upsetting her social life.'

'Nothing short of death would do that.' Anxiety was visible in her mother's eyes and Nancy was horribly aware that the hostile reaction of her siblings to the news was a mere trifle compared to the trouble that lay ahead for Mum. 'You know Jean. She's too busy looking after herself to bother to be angry with anyone for long.' Nancy covered her mother's hand with her own. 'You can rely on me. I'll do what I can to help.' She smiled suddenly, her sapphire eyes lighting up her face. 'Anyway, it might be rather nice to have a little baby around the place. Yeah, I'm beginning to look forward to it already.'

'I haven't even got around to thinking about that side of it yet,' said Lily, her voice quivering. 'But thanks, love. Your support means a lot to me.'

Nancy struggled not to show how desperately worried she was about what this would do to her parents' marriage. 'We'll stand by her, won't we, Gran?'

'Course we will,' replied Gladys. 'It's going to be a bumpy old ride though.'

As the air-raid siren was mercifully absent, Gladys went home and Nancy and her mother stayed where they were, talking for a long time. They were just settling down to listen to the nine o'clock news on the wireless when Micky came in. Nancy's spirits rose in the assumption that he'd come back to make his peace with the mother he had always adored. But she couldn't have been more wrong.

'I've come back to collect my things,' he announced gravely, looking at Lily from the doorway.

'Collect your things?' she echoed. 'What on earth are you talking about?'

'I should have thought that was obvious,' was his icy reply. 'I'm leaving.'

'Leaving!' Lily's voice was little more than a whisper. She got up and went over to him, wincing as he shrank back from her as though she were vermin. 'What do you mean, you're leaving?'

'I'm moving out of here and going to live with Uncle Wilf,' he explained in a dull voice, his cold stare resting on her. 'In three months' time I'll be old enough to go in the army so I'll stay with my uncle until then. He said I can sleep on his sofa.'

'Micky, calm down and stop being so hasty,' Nancy intervened. 'There's no need for all this drama. You're over-reacting to a ridiculous degree.'

'You might think so . . .'

'Oh, for goodness sake. Anyone would think Mum had murdered someone, the way you're carrying on.'

'Please don't do this to me, son.' Lily was pleading with him now. He was her eldest son and there had always been an especially close bond between them. She couldn't bear not to have him in her life. 'Please stay. I'm so sorry for what I've done. Please try to understand.'

'I can't stay, not now. Everything's changed.' He was very bitter. 'I can't live under the same roof as someone who's done what you have.'

'Micky—'

'Don't say anything, Mum,' he cut her short, 'because I really don't want to hear it. It tears the heart out of me just to look at you.'

'That's quite enough, Micky,' Nancy reprimanded. 'This is your mother you're speaking to.'

'Pity she didn't remember that she was a mother and a married woman when she was out having her fun.'

'You've no right to say these things,' Nancy told him furiously. 'After all she's done for you.'

'She won't have to do anything for me ever again because I want nothing more to do with her,' he stated cruelly. 'And don't come after me pleading her case, Nancy, because my mind is made up. Now, I'm going upstairs to pack.'

Fifteen minutes later, he was gone, leaving Nancy to comfort their mother.

'You're still awake, then,' said Jean, as Nancy sat up in bed when the light was turned on.

'Shush, and shut the door,' whispered Nancy. 'We don't want to disturb Mum.'

'We won't disturb anyone because I'll be asleep as soon as I hit the sack,' she said, yawning and pulling her jumper over her head as soon as she'd closed the door. 'I'm too tired for a chat.'

'Micky's left home,' announced Nancy.

'What!' Now Jean changed her tune and sat down on the edge of the big double bed they shared. 'For good, you mean?'

'So he says.'

'Blimey! Where's he gone?'

'He's staying with Uncle Wilf until he goes in the army.'

'Because of Mum being up the duff?'

'Of course it's because of that. He's being completely unreasonable in my opinion. After all Mum's done for him, too.'

'It is a bit of a shocker, though, Nance,' Jean pointed out. 'You must admit that.'

'Of course I admit it, but there's no need for her own children to turn against her. She's our mother, and she feels bad enough as it is,' said Nancy. 'You didn't have to be so rough on her, either.'

'What was I supposed to do? Congratulate her?'

'No, but you could have been a bit kinder.'

'After what she'd just told us?'

'Yes, even after that.'

'Don't try to pretend you approve, Nancy, because I won't believe you.'

'It isn't for us to judge her. It's for us to be there for her. She brought us up, loved us, taught us how to live.'

'All that morality she drummed into us and she goes and does this.'

'So she isn't perfect,' Nancy came back at her. 'But she's a human being as well as our mum, you know. She's entitled to have feelings.'

'She should have kept them under control,' disapproved Jean. 'I didn't think women of her age still did it with their husband even, let alone anyone else.'

'Well, you know different now, don't you?' Nancy returned. 'And it's up to us, her daughters, to give her some support. It's time for some female solidarity around here, seeing as Micky's selfishly turned his back on her.'

'Ooh, I don't know about offering support.'

'Don't you feel even the tiniest bit sorry for her?' asked Nancy sharply. 'It could happen to any of us.'

'Not when we're turned forty,' Jean stated categorically. 'It's *so embarrassing*.'

'Self, self, self,' Nancy blasted at her, still keeping her voice down. 'How can you worry about something as unimportant as embarrassment when your mother is in trouble?'

'Look, I can't help the way I feel,' her sister replied. 'The whole thing is disgusting to me.'

'Then you'll just have to get over it because Mum needs us.' Nancy was very firm. 'Not only now, but after the baby is born too.'

Jean didn't answer at once. 'Yeah, I suppose it is a bit rotten for her,' she finally conceded grudgingly.

'You can't expect her to put your meals on the table for you, do all your washing and ironing and the hundred other things she does for you in the course of a week, if you can't even be civil to her.'

That hit the spot Nancy had been aiming for. 'I hadn't thought about that side of it,' Jean said gloomily.

'I think you should apologise to her first thing in the morning for all the terrible things you said.'

Jean got up, finished undressing and pulled on her faded striped winceyette pyjamas. 'I'll patch it up with her in the morning,' she agreed.

'It would be nice if you were to tell her that you'll be supportive to her, and mean it.'

'As long as it doesn't include promising to change the nappy of some smelly brat.'

'Showing Mum some compassion and respect will do for starters,' Nancy told her. 'Now that that's settled, let's turn out the light and get some sleep in case the siren goes.'

'I've got to put my curlers in yet.'

'Don't take all night about it then,' said Nancy, lying down and turning on to her side.

'I'll freeze to death if I do,' she said, getting her dinky curlers from the dressing-table drawer and winding her hair into them, shivering so much her teeth were chattering. 'The North Pole can't be colder than this bedroom.'

For once, Nancy was in agreement with her.

'But I'm the boy's godfather as well as his uncle, Lil,' said Lily's elder brother Wilf the next day when she called at his flat on her way home from work, knowing that Micky wouldn't be in yet. 'I couldn't just turn him away when he wanted somewhere to stay, could I?'

'You should have sent him home. I'm your sister, for heaven's sake.'

'He wouldn't have gone home, the mood he was in.' He puffed on a Woodbine. 'If I hadn't taken him in, he'd have slept rough and that would have been even worse. At least he's still with the family. He isn't a kid any more, Lil,' he reminded her. 'He'll soon be old enough to fight for his country, so he's certainly old enough to live away from his mum.'

'That isn't the issue, Wilf,' she pointed out. 'It's his leaving this way, being at loggerheads with me.'

'Micky is determined not to stay at home at the moment because he's angry and upset,' her brother told her. 'But he'll soon change his mind when he gets fed up with sleeping on the sofa and misses the home comforts that you provide for him. He'll have to pull his weight here. I've no intention of spoiling him.'

'He's stubborn. He'll probably stick it out until he goes in the army just to make a point.' She shook her head. 'Oh, Wilf, I can't bear it if he goes away leaving things like this between us. Our boys are falling like flies out at the front. God knows what will happen to him.'

'You've enough to worry about in the present, without looking ahead. Let's wait and see what happens over the next few days. I'll do what I can to make him see things your way, but I can't promise anything.' Wilf looked grave. 'Anyway, the way I see it, Micky isn't your main problem. I dread to think what'll happen when Arthur finds out.'

Lily held her head. 'Oh, Wilf. How could I have got myself into such a mess?'

'I can't think what came over you. You're not that sort of woman at all.'

'You don't have to be a certain type of person to make a mistake.'

'There's mistakes and there's bloomin' great calamities.' He stubbed out his cigarette in the ash-tray. 'And yours is definitely in the latter category.'

'Don't rub it in.'

'Fancy getting yourself up the duff, at your age. You're old enough to know better. It's no wonder Micky's upset. I'm having a job coming to terms with it myself.'

'We're all only human,' she reminded him. 'We all have feelings, though I realise that men think those sorts of feelings are exclusively for them.'

'It's the way of the world.'

'And very unevenly balanced, if you ask me.' Her voice rose. 'You men go out and have your fun and walk away. A woman gives way to her feelings and she's left with the consequences.'

'I don't make the rules, gel.'

'You're so damned disapproving—'

'I'm not disapproving, so much as worried about you,' he cut in. 'You've got a good marriage and a smashing family. I'm your brother and I care a lot about you. I don't want to see you lose all that. Arthur's a good bloke, but there aren't many men who would be willing to forgive you straight off for what you've done, war or no war.'

'Oh, Wilf,' she said despairingly. 'If I could turn the clock back I would, but what's done's done and I have to get on with it as best as I can.'

His tone softened. 'Come on, Lil. You'll get through it and I'll be there if you need me.'

Wilf was three years older than Lily, with the same colouring, though his brylcreemed ginger hair was now heavily flecked with white. A hero of the last war, during which he'd received a bullet in his shoulder which was still there giving him pain to this day, he was tall and of a smart appearance, though his mode of dress tended to be flamboyant and his ties were enough to dazzle the dead.

After years of unemployment during the depression, he was now established as a barman and general dogsbody at the Rook and Raven pub in West Ealing Broadway, which was only a short walk from his flat. Exempt from war work because of his health, he put far more into the job than he was paid for. He would see people home in the blackout, comfort the bereaved and keep everyone's spirits up during a raid.

Always a man with an eye to make an extra shilling, however, he occasionally dabbled in goods of a doubtful origin, but only in a very minor way. No one asked questions because he was a useful man to know, especially in wartime with everything being in such short supply.

The fact that he was a war hero, added to his warm heart and keen sense of humour, made him a popular man and everyone turned a blind eye to the fact that he was a bit of a spiv.

He'd lost his beloved wife to tuberculosis ten years ago and had never shown any interest in remarrying, though he did have the occasional liaison with the opposite sex. He seemed happy enough living alone, Lily thought, and kept this little flat clean and tidy. It lacked a woman's touch, but the floor was always swept, the furniture dusted and everything in its place, though the living room was currently cluttered with Micky's suitcase, the corner of which was just visible underneath a pile of loose clothes and bedlinen in the corner.

The flat was in an old converted house and was just right for him. He had no children of his own, which was probably why he was so fond of Lily's.

'Why don't you sit down and I'll make you a cup o' tea?' he offered now. 'You're all of a twitter, woman. You need to calm down. I don't have to go to work for a few minutes yet.'

'No, I'd better go before Micky gets in.'

'Maybe you're right,' he agreed, after a moment's thought. 'He'll think you've come chasing after him with the idea of trying to persuade him to go back home if he sees you here. That wouldn't be a good idea at this stage. He needs to be left alone until he's had a chance to cool off.'

'Exactly,' she said, walking to the door. 'I'll see you again soon, Wilf.'

He took her arm, and kissed her on the cheek. 'You look after yourself now, sis,' he advised in a caring manner. 'I know

I had a bit of a go at you just now for getting yourself into a mess but it's only because I think a lot of you. While you're doing all this worrying about other people's view of the matter, don't forget about yourself. We don't want you getting ill on top of everything else, do we?'

'You know me, I'm as strong as a horse.' She gave him a peck on the cheek. 'See you, Wilf.'

He watched her from the window as she walked down the street, a sad and dowdy figure in a maroon coat and headscarf. Not at all her usual strong, exuberant self. He sucked in his breath, shaking his head. This was a right old carry-on and no mistake. Still – when you really thought about it – compared to the terrible loss of life and hardship this war was causing, it wasn't such a big thing at all.

Chapter Three

Leslie Sparrow stared out of the bedroom window at the rainswept countryside, the steady drizzle causing a mist to rise over the empty green fields so that they seemed to blend into the great dark dome of sky for as far as the eye could see. No houses; no shops; no people. No sign of life anywhere. Even the cows were kept in the sheds in winter, and the farm dogs and cats were taking shelter somewhere.

There was an ache in the pit of his stomach and his throat felt clogged. He struggled to hold back the tears, determined not to sink that low no matter how bad things got. Nobody was going to get the chance to call him a sissy! He wasn't the sort to blub when the going got tough.

But then he remembered saying goodbye to his mother at the station earlier this afternoon, after her visit. He recalled the softness of her skin when she'd hugged him and kissed his cheek, the homely, soapy scent of her and her achingly familiar voice assuring him that he could come home as soon as it was safe. It was too much for even the sturdiest resolve and he sobbed violently into his rag handkerchief, trying to stifle the choking sound for fear that Mrs Farley would hear.

He'd be in big trouble if she did. She would rant at him something awful, call him a snivelling baby who didn't appreciate her generosity in taking him into her home and looking after him, even though he was a bloody nuisance. 'You London kids are nothing but trouble, with your filthy habits, bad manners and downright wickedness. Heathens, the lot of you,' she was very fond of telling him.

When he'd been with Mum today he'd wanted to throw his arms around her and beg her to take him back to London with her; he'd longed to tell her that Mr and Mrs Farley hated him even though they pretended otherwise when other people were around. But he daren't. He knew for a fact that he wouldn't be allowed to go home until the bombing had stopped in London, and the Farleys would give him hell after Mum had gone if she so much as hinted that he'd said anything bad about them. He'd had it drummed into him that if he breathed a word to anyone about his working on the farm, or not being happy here, he would wish he'd never been born. Even his letters home were examined by them before they were posted.

The farm work he could cope with, now that he was used to it, though he did have trouble keeping awake during lessons at school, and he felt sick with the cold in the milking sheds at five-thirty in the morning, having already drawn water from the well and filled the oil lamps all around the farmhouse. As soon as he got home from school, he had to sweep the yard and help with the afternoon milking, but he got on and did it because he daren't do otherwise.

Mucking out the cowsheds had been the biggest problem at first because the smell had made him vomit and that had infuriated Mrs Farley. 'We'll soon cure you of that, you little weakling. You'll be used to the smell of nature as God intended by the time I've finished with you,' she'd said, and had made him stay in there for ages, until there was nothing left inside him to bring up. He still hated being in there, but managed not to retch so much now.

It wasn't the hardship or the work that upset him so much as the constant trouncings and the misery of knowing that his hosts couldn't stand the sight of him. He missed the company of other kids, too. There were some boys in his class that he hung around with at playtime, but he wasn't allowed to see anyone outside of school hours because he was needed to work on the farm. 'There's a war on, boy,' the terrifying Mr Farley was always reminding him. 'Farming is more vital to the nation than ever now because a lot of the ships bringing food from abroad are getting blown up by the Germans. Without us, people couldn't survive and that's why we have to work so hard. Anyway, when I was younger'n you I was doing a lot more on this farm than you have to. You town kids haven't got a clue. Sissies, the lot o' you.'

Now the distant drone of the wireless from downstairs made him cry even more because it reminded him of home. He missed his mum, his brother and sisters, his gran, Uncle Wilf, the cat, his pals in the street and even the shop on the corner where he used to run errands for Mum.

He mulled over Mum's important news, that he would

soon be having a baby sister or brother. She'd looked odd when she'd told him, sort of sad and worried. But then she'd smiled and said she was looking forward to having a little one about the place again.

A bolt of fear shot through him with the sudden thought that she might forget all about him once the new baby arrived, and leave him here for ever. His pal Eddie's mum had had a baby and he said it was a flaming nuisance, always screaming and getting all the attention. Eddie reckoned that his mum was too busy looking after it to bother much about anyone else.

Recalled to the present by Mrs Farley yelling for him to go downstairs, he wiped his eyes and took some deep breaths to try to ease the trembling. Just the sound of her voice made his mouth go dry and his stomach churn. Shivering with fear and also because his bedroom was so cold there was ice on the inside of the windows for most of the day, he headed for the door. Oh, how he hated it here!

'Mr Farley has got some jobs to do outside and he wants you out there with him to help,' announced Mrs Farley in her shrill voice with the broad Devon accent that Leslie had found so difficult to understand at first, so landing himself in more trouble. A large woman, wearing an apron over her clothes, she had brown hair drawn back off her face, a long nose and scary dark eyes that seemed to bore right into him. 'You've had enough time lazing about with that mother o' yourn this afternoon. It's time you made yourself useful around here.'

'Yes, Mrs Farley.' He'd learned early on to address her with respect.

'I hope you haven't been whining to your mother about wanting to go home,' she said, her awful eyes narrowed on him suspiciously.

'No, I haven't, Mrs Farley.'

'She's got enough to worry about now that she's having a baby, so don't you go upsetting her.'

'I didn't . . . I wouldn't do that.'

'One thing's for sure. She won't want you coming home and getting in the way with a new baby to look after.'

Leslie had the breath sucked out of him as she articulated his own fears. In that moment, he hated his mother for sending him away but, at the same time, ached with love for her and wanted her like never before.

'Get your boots and coat on and get outside, never mind the rain,' she ordered irritably. 'And you can take that sulky look off your face, too. You try my patience, you really do.' Then she aimed the most crushing blow of all. 'It's no wonder your mother doesn't want you at home. You're enough to give anyone the willies with that long face o' yourn. I wouldn't have you in my house if I wasn't such a public-spirited woman, willing to do her bit for the war effort.'

That was a hurt too far for a boy who had managed to retain a modicum of spirit despite his hosts' constant efforts to crush it out of him altogether.

'My mum does want me at home,' he stated with defiance. 'She had to send me away because of the bombing. It wasn't her fault.'

69

'Happen she was glad of the excuse.'

'No. My mum isn't like that.'

'Don't answer me back, you evil young tyke,' the farmer's wife snapped. 'Get outside and do your work, out of my sight. And don't expect any supper. I don't waste food on boys who give me cheek.'

Leslie went to the back porch and pulled on his boots and muddy old coat. The suggestion that his mother didn't want him at home froze him inside and pushed him to a point of misery that went beyond tears.

The Exeter to London train was crowded almost to the point of suffocation. People were squeezed into the compartment, some standing, others packed into the seats so close together they could hardly move, soldiers perched on their kit-bags the length of the corridor.

Lily Sparrow was squashed between a man with a rattling cough who smelled of stale pipe tobacco, and a woman with the sniffles who reeked of sweat. But Lily was far too preoccupied with her own concerns to care about the discomfort. At least she'd got a seat, and was grateful for that.

Thoughts of her youngest child filled her mind. He seemed to be in good health, but was quieter than he used to be, seemed to have lost that cheeky sparkle. He was a little thinner, too, but that was only to be expected with food being in such short supply. He'd assured her several times that he was fine, and Mr and Mrs Farley had confirmed this, telling her that he fitted in very well with their way of life and they thought the world of him. So maybe it was just that he was beginning to grow up.

It hadn't been a successful visit, mainly because of the rain. Being Sunday, everything was closed, so there was nowhere for them to take shelter. The landlady of the cheap boarding house in the town where Lily had stayed last night, because it was too far to come just for the day, had made it clear that she wasn't welcome there after breakfast, so she couldn't even take him in there out of the wet. In the end, she'd managed to get them both a sandwich in the station buffet and they'd sat there for as long as was acceptable. Then they'd hung around in the station entrance in their damp clothes until it was time for her train, when – as arranged – Mr Farley had collected Leslie in his battered old truck to take him back to the farm.

She'd been sorely tempted to bring him home with her. She missed him *so* much, and it wasn't right for a child to be away from their family, especially as the air raids had been less constant lately. She'd been on the point of telling him when common sense had prevailed at the last minute. The bombing had lessened, but it hadn't stopped. She had to put his safety before her own feelings. The government was still urging parents to leave their children where they were, in safe havens in the country.

The evacuation stories she'd heard were mixed. In many cases, the children were greeted with open arms and taken into the bosom of the family. But you did hear the occasional horror tale of unhappy foster homes. Many mothers of pre-school children – who'd gone with their offspring to

71

safety – had returned because they were even less welcome than the children. At least Leslie was with people who wanted him, and he always looked clean and well cared for when she saw him.

But knowing that she'd made the right decision didn't make it any easier to bear. She wanted her youngest boy back at home where he belonged.

When Nancy went into the toilets during her shift she could hear someone crying in one of the cubicles. She curbed her natural instinct to offer help, because whoever it was had obviously taken refuge in here to weep in private.

Washing her hands at the basin, however, and noticing that the sobs were accompanied by groans of agony, she couldn't hold back.

'Hello in there,' she called. 'Is there anything I can do for you?'

Silence.

'Can I get you anything?' she persisted.

'Bugger off and mind your own business.'

It was Ruby Green. Nancy would recognise those gruff tones anywhere. 'I respect your privacy, Ruby, but you sound as though you're in pain.'

'Of course I'm in bloody pain,' the other woman said thickly. 'I wouldn't be sitting on the lavatory seat doubled up if I wasn't, would I?'

'Oh dear.' Nancy was very concerned. 'Is it a pain in your stomach or what?'

'A bad dose of the curse, that's all.'

'Oh, I see. Well, I've got some aspirin.'

'Lucky you.'

Ignoring her sarcasm, Nancy said, 'They usually do the trick for me. Especially if you have a hot drink with them. A drop of gin is the best remedy, of course, but since we don't have any of that to hand, aspirin will have to do.'

The door opened and Ruby emerged looking heavy-eyed and grey-faced. 'It's a flaming nuisance,' she complained. 'I get these hellish ones sometimes and they floor me. I just can't concentrate on anything because of the pain.'

'That's rough. But why shut yourself away in there, for heaven's sake?'

'Because I don't feel up to being out there on duty and I can't go to the sick bay just because it's the time of the month,' the other woman said, her face twisted with pain. 'I should have thought that was obvious.'

'All right, all right, don't jump down my throat.'

'Well, can you imagine what Percy Wellington would have to say if I were to take a break just because I've got my period?'

'It doesn't bear thinking about,' Nancy agreed. 'But let me worry about him.' She decided to take control because – for all her talk to the contrary – Ruby seemed to need it. 'Come on. Let's go to the staff room where you can have a sit-down with a cup of tea and some aspirin.'

'I can't do that. He'll do his nut when he notices that I'm not out there.' Ruby's face was creased with agony and she was bending over, holding her stomach. 'I'll probably be all right before long. It sometimes lasts a while, though.'

'Why not stop arguing for once in your life and let me help you?' suggested Nancy.

Her face still screwed up with the pain, Ruby followed her from the room without another word.

Having administered aspirin and hot tea and leaving Ruby curled up in a chair in the staff room, Nancy went looking for Percy. Unable to locate him on the platforms, she eventually found him in his office. It was just a cubbyhole really; a space for him to do his paperwork with just about enough room for a desk and chair. He was usually too busy seeking out slackers on his team to spend much time in here.

'I've just come to let you know that Ruby Green isn't feeling too good so she's taking a short break in the staff room,' Nancy informed him in an even tone. 'Just in case you're wondering where she is.'

'What's the matter with her?' He was sitting at his desk but turned towards her.

Nancy gave him a look. 'She's strained her back from lifting a heavy suitcase,' she lied.

'Oh really,' he snapped, bushy eyebrows sliding up his forehead in disapproval. 'Well, you can tell her to get off her arse and get back on duty sharpish. A bit of backache doesn't warrant time off.'

'She really does feel rotten, Mr Wellington.'

'We all get aches and pains from time to time, Miss Sparrow,' he pointed out brusquely. 'But we don't make a song and dance about it.'

'Neither is she; she just needs a bit of a break.'

'There's a war on and this station is the busiest terminus in London. We can't have people going off duty and sitting about in the staff room just because they've got a twinge in their back. If she's ill she should go to the doctor and get a certificate.'

'That isn't necessary. She only needs a rest. She'll be back on duty in half an hour or so.'

'Oh she will, will she?' he said in a mocking tone. 'It's nice to know that she'll grace us with her presence, *when she's feeling up to it.*'

'She really does need a break, Mr Wellington.'

He stood up. 'You women aren't up to the job, I've said it all along. This station has gone to pot since you lot came on to the platform staff. If you're not standing about yapping, you're feeling peaky. The place is in a permanent state of chaos.'

'That's because of the war, not because there are women working here,' she pointed out. 'We work damned hard, and you know it, even though you would never admit it.'

He pushed his spectacles up his nose. 'As I've told you before, you're a troublemaker,' he stated categorically. 'You've got far too much to say for yourself.'

'I speak my mind when something needs saying, yes,' Nancy admitted.

'You're a stirrer,' he accused. 'You should concentrate on doing a fair day's work and minding your own business.'

'I earn every penny of my pay and I don't deliberately stir up trouble. I don't like bullying, that's all,' she told him. 'The girls and I do more than our fair share to keep this station running and all we get from you is abuse. Now shall I go and tell Ruby that she can stay in the staff room until she's feeling better? Or shall I contact our union representative and ask him to intervene on her behalf?'

'Get out,' he growled.

She did as he asked without another word. Despite her calm front, she was inwardly trembling with a mixture of rage and jangling nerves. Percy Wellington could be very intimidating, if you let him.

The locker room was crowded when Nancy went off duty. Staff on late turn were arriving, day-shift workers were getting into their coats ready to leave. Nancy and Polly were having a chat when Ruby came up to her.

'Thanks for helping me out earlier.' She was still heavy-eyed, but not quite so ashen-faced. She gave Nancy a wary smile and her plain features were transformed.

'A pleasure,' said Nancy. 'Glad to see that you're feeling better.'

'It was good of you to square things with Percy. I appreciate that.'

'That *really* was a pleasure,' smiled Nancy, wrapping her muffler around her neck. 'I'm always glad of an excuse to get up his nose.'

'Aren't we all?' laughed Polly. 'It isn't difficult to do, either. Just the sight of a woman working on his station gets his dander up.' She did her coat up and tied her headscarf under her chin. 'Are you coming, Nance?'

'Yep, I'm ready,' she said. 'Coming, Ruby?'

'No. I'm going out straight from work,' she replied after a brief hesitation. 'I'm meeting someone and we're going to see a film in the West End.'

'Lucky you,' said Nancy.

'Very nice too.' Polly didn't bear a grudge about Ruby's usual offhand manner. It wasn't worth the energy.

'See you tomorrow then, Ruby, and have a good time,' said Nancy, and she and Polly left with some of the others, talking and laughing as they went, all going their separate ways outside as they came from all over London and the suburbs.

On the underground station platform, Nancy picked her way past the shelterers and tried to get nearer to the front of the crowd waiting for the Ealing Broadway train. There was such a crush here she wasn't sure if she'd get on the next one. She did actually manage it, but was pushed in backwards and squashed to such an extent she felt short of breath.

Just before the doors closed, she saw something that astonished her. It was Ruby walking on to the platform, not ten minutes after she'd said she was going in the other direction. Nancy knew instinctively that it wasn't a sudden change of plan. She knew, too, that Ruby hadn't lied to impress her workmates with a fictitious social life. That wasn't her style. She'd made the story up as an excuse not to travel home with Nancy, though she wasn't normally afraid to come right out and say she didn't want her company. Maybe the fact that Nancy had helped her this afternoon had made her feel obligated to be less horrid. Whatever the truth of the matter, it was an awful lot of trouble to go to just to avoid a spot of casual conversation on the way home with a workmate. She didn't understand Ruby at all.

It was a Saturday night in March and the Rook and Raven was noisy, smoky and packed to the doors. A piano was being played in the corner and people were singing along to 'You Are My Sunshine'. Seated at the piano was Nancy, singing at the top of her voice, her long, slender fingers moving gracefully over the keys.

Although she couldn't read a note of music and knew very little about the technicalities of the art, Nancy was a gifted pianist and could play any tune by ear once she'd heard it once or twice. As a child she'd been sent to piano lessons – like most children of her generation – but the teacher had finally had to admit defeat because Nancy's ability to learn how to play properly was impaired by her natural instinct to do it her own way.

Her rare talent meant that she was often in demand at parties and events like this, which pleased her because playing the piano was one of the joys in her life. Since the Blitz she was sometimes asked to play in rest centres and community halls in the hope that she would lift the spirits of those who found themselves homeless.

Tonight's shindig was the brainchild of Uncle Wilf, with the intention of compensating the customers for the fact that they had to make every drink last for hours on account of the shortage of every kind of beverage. Nancy was very much in favour of the idea. Pubs – with or without beer – were a valuable meeting place in these dangerous times when people needed company more than ever. The warmth and friendliness in here tonight was almost a physical thing. She could feel it washing over her and lifting her heart.

They'd had a few quiet nights lately, and people were feeling better for it, though Nancy doubted if the sirens would stay silent for long. There had been a heavy raid on London the other night, during which Buckingham Palace had been damaged. That raid was rumoured to be the beginning of the Luftwaffe's spring offensive against British cities.

Everyone had been cheered by the news from America last week when President Roosevelt had made a heart-warming speech, promising aid to Britain and other countries badly affected by the war. He spoke of the 'vital bridge across the ocean, the bridge of ships' carrying goods and arms 'to those who are fighting the good fight'.

It was generally hoped that this would ease the food shortage, as with the bombing of ships and ports everything was in increasingly short supply. With all the recent talk on the news of goods ships being heavily bombed, Nancy and the family were worried about Arthur. Many merchant seamen had lost their lives to the Germans, and as he wasn't one for letter-writing, they had no way of knowing how he was.

Now, glancing around the bar, Nancy could see family, friends and neighbours. The community spirit was as evident as the cigarette smoke and smell of beer. Only after a great deal of persuasion had she managed to get her mother to come, though she'd been extremely reluctant because her pregnancy could no longer be hidden. Always a strong, seemingly invulnerable woman, who'd held her head high and taught her children to do the same, Lily's shame over this pregnancy went deep, exacerbated considerably by Micky's cruel attitude towards her. The actual pregnancy wasn't an easy one either. She hadn't felt well from the outset. Nausea had plagued her throughout, her face looked puffy and she had swollen ankles.

But with encouragement from Nancy, and a reminder that she couldn't hide away for ever since the baby would show itself in two months' time, she'd put on her best hat and coat, albeit that she couldn't do the coat up, and seemed to be enjoying herself. If there was gossip, Nancy hadn't heard it. The war had changed everything, even people's chattering habits. Mum had been right about that. In the frantic live-for-today climate, most people were too busy working and queuing for food to delve into their neighbours' business.

Mum and Gran were sitting together, singing their heads off. Gran – wearing an ancient fur coat and her best brown hat with a tall feather on the side – never needed coaxing into a night out, especially if there was a glass of stout involved. Jean had made her peace with Mum, but was too full of herself to take much interest in the baby. She wasn't here this evening, preferring the bright lights of the Hammersmith Palais where she was to meet a Polish airman she'd first met there last week.

Nancy's spirits took a dive as her gaze moved around to Micky, standing at the other end of the bar and talking to one of his mates who was now in army uniform. Micky would be wearing one of those in two weeks' time. Too impatient to wait for his call-up papers, he'd joined the army on his eighteenth birthday and was going to Aldershot for basic training.

Frankly, Nancy thought he was being selfish in the extreme for turning his back on his mother and she'd told him so and begged him to have some compassion. Gran had had a few sharp words with him, too, and Mum had been to see him several times. But all of their pleas had fallen on deaf ears.

Nancy had never seen this side of her brother before. He'd always been such a warmhearted and easy-going lad, generous and funny; the one family member who could be relied upon to lift your spirits if you were feeling a bit down. Mum's indiscretion must have had a profound affect on him for him to behave this way.

The song came to an end and there were rousing cheers, whistles and requests for a variety of popular songs, everyone shouting at once.

'I'll get to all your favourites eventually, folks,' Nancy called out to the crowd. 'But for now, let yourselves go with this one.'

She led the gathering in a cheerful rendition of 'Roll Out the Barrel'.

'I like this one, don't you, Lil?' remarked Gladys, taking a small sip of her stout, careful to make it last. 'Nice and lively. Gets your toes tapping. Nothing like a good old sing-song to make you forget your troubles.'

Lily nodded, but it would take more than a sing-song to banish her woes. She could endure this awful war, the bombing and the shortages, the worry of what her pregnancy was going to do to Arthur, but losing the love and respect of her eldest boy was too much to bear. She'd tried everything in pursuit of his forgiveness. She'd begged; she'd pleaded; she'd wept. There was no place for pride at a time like this. He'd be going away in a couple of weeks' time, and after basic training he'd be shipped abroad. She might never see him again.

On one occasion, she'd lost her temper and given him a thorough wigging, pointing out that it was his father's place to judge her, not his. She'd pointed out that she'd always done her best for her children and didn't deserve this. He hadn't been cheeky or argumentative. He'd just let her say her piece then said it made no difference to his feelings on the subject.

Now she looked at him through the pall of smoke to try to catch his eye, but he wasn't looking in her direction, was deliberately avoiding her, she guessed. She longed to go home and weep into her pillow, but that would spoil the evening for her mother, Nancy and Wilf. So she took a deep breath, opened her mouth and joined in the singing.

'Are you listening, Micky?' asked his friend, when the singing had stopped during Nancy's break. 'Oi! Micky . . .'

'What's that?'

'I was telling you about our sergeant,' said the mate, who'd finished his basic training and was full of it.

'That's right, so you were.'

'You're miles away.'

'I just drifted off for a minute. Sorry, mate. You've got my full attention now, so carry on.'

'I was just saying that the sergeants are all jumped-up little Hitlers,' he informed him. 'I'm just giving you a friendly warning about what you're in for.'

'I've heard they're rough.'

'Rough! They're ruddy psychopaths.'

'So people say.'

'All they want to do is belittle you, no matter how hard you try or how well you do. They try to break your spirit . . . it's all part of the training.'

Micky went off into his thoughts again, taking a surreptitious look at his mother, who was talking to Nancy and Gran. Mum looked different, fragile somehow, even though she was plump with some stranger's child. He'd looked forward to the day when he would join the army and prove that he'd finally grown up. That day was fast approaching and he felt no joy. Just a hard knot of misery inside him that he'd had ever since that terrible night when the red mist had come down and he'd fallen out with Mum. It was almost a physical pain. He'd tried to ignore it, had refused to acknowledge its existence, and hoped it would go away. But it hadn't, and in his heart he knew it never would. There was an enormous void in his life without his mother.

He remembered once seeing her cry after an argument with his father. He had the same feeling now as he'd had then, only a thousand times worse. He'd wanted to hit Dad then in defence of Mum. Now he wanted to kill the man who'd done this to her, but as he was already dead, all his anger was directed towards his mother. He reminded himself that she'd been a willing party; she'd freely admitted it. How could she do such a thing to his father? To all of them?

'What is the matter with you tonight, Micky? I might as well be in here on my own for all the notice you're taking of me.' His pal was narked.

'Sorry. I've got things on my mind.'

'Course you have, you're going in the army in a couple of weeks, aren't yer?' said his mate, making the wrong assumption. 'That's enough to put the fear of God into anyone. I'm just trying to help you by giving you a few tips. Believe me, you'll need 'em when you get there, so why not do yourself a favour and listen.'

'I'm all ears.'

'It's no good now because your sister's going back to the piano, so the singing'll start up again and we won't be able to hear ourselves think, let alone talk.'

'Tell me later on, then.'

'You're a right misery tonight. The army ain't that bad, you know.'

Micky didn't bother to correct the misunderstanding. He had far more important things on his mind.

They were in the middle of 'The White Cliffs of Dover' when the air-raid siren went. Nancy stayed where she was and carried on. She decided that she should continue to play until everyone else had gone. As the entertainer, it was up to her to do what she could to keep things calm. Expecting a rush for the door, she was surprised when only a few trickled out. Some headed for the cellar at the landlord's invitation. But there was a defiant element here tonight who stayed and sang even louder than before.

She played 'Bless 'em All' and 'Little Brown Jug'. There were still quite a few punters in the pub and the vigour and volume of the singing stirred the blood. It almost drowned out the sound of enemy aircraft, though it ended abruptly when there was an explosion nearby.

People threw themselves on the floor. Nancy was down there with them. There was silence in the pub in the imme-diate aftermath, though the clang of fire engines and ambu-lances could be heard outside. When the sound of enemy aircraft receded, Nancy went back to the piano and launched into 'There'll Always Be an England'.

Slowly people got to their feet, and stayed there. A cheer went up for Nancy. Then they took their seats and joined in the song; she'd never heard a more rousing rendition. It was just as well she didn't need music, because she wouldn't have been able to see it through the blur of tears.

When the all clear sounded, Uncle Wilf came over to the piano and called for silence.

'Three cheers for my niece, Nancy, who's done us proud tonight,' he shouted. 'Hip hip hooray.'

The response was unanimous. They were shouting and stamping their feet. Never had Nancy been more grateful for her talent than she was at that moment.

*　　*　　*

85

'Well done, sis,' praised Micky, coming over to her at closing time just as she was putting the lid of the piano down.

'Thanks.'

To her utter astonishment, he put his arms around her and hugged her. 'You made me dead proud tonight, Nance, do you know that?'

As they'd been at loggerheads ever since he'd fallen out with Mum, Nancy was extremely heartened by this unexpected show of affection. 'That's nice to know.' She threw him a look. 'But what's all this? Praise instead of ribbing from my little brother? You must be ill.'

'No, not ill. Just seeing things more clearly.'

This sounded very promising. 'Really?' she said.

'You're quite a woman, you really are. Not bad at all for a sister.'

'I just happen to be able to play the piano, that's all.'

'It was more than that tonight. You were strong, and very brave.'

'Was I?'

She drew back slightly and looked into his face, surprised to see that his blue eyes were moist with tears.

'Yeah, you were. Very,' he confirmed. 'You must take after your mother.'

'Oh, Micky, that's the nicest compliment anyone could give me, and very special indeed, coming from you.'

He made a face, looking very ashamed. 'I've been stupid, haven't I?' he said.

'To say the least.'

'I'm sorry.'

'It isn't me you need to say sorry to, is it?'

'No, of course not.'

'Go on, then. Get on with it. This whole thing has gone on for long enough.'

She watched him walk across the pub towards their mother, a tall, well-built figure, the gangling look of adolescence no longer visible.

'Hello, Mum,' he said, his voice quivering with emotion.

'Hello, son.'

'Sorry, Mum,' he said simply. 'I . . . I don't know what else to say.'

'That'll do for me, son.' She stood up and looked at him, tears rolling down her cheeks.

'Come on,' he said gently, helping her on with her coat and handing her her scarf. 'Let's get out of here so that we can talk. I'll walk you home.'

With his arm around her, he led her towards the door and together they walked through the smoky streets towards Sycamore Road, deep in conversation. Nancy and her gran kept their distance behind them, realising that these were very private moments for mother and son.

Micky moved back home that same night, much to the relief of the whole family. The altercation had cast a dark shadow over everything. Mum was like a new woman with her eldest boy back in the fold, even though he wouldn't be at home for long. The fact that they were back on their old footing made his imminent departure seem more bearable somehow, and in the meantime the family atmosphere was a happy one.

Then, about a week later, there was a knock at the front door at breakfast time.

'It's Saturday morning, so it'll be the milkman come to collect his money,' said Lily, getting up and grabbing her purse from the sideboard.

As her mother left the room, Jean started complaining about having to go to work on a Saturday. 'It's a bloomin' nuisance. I'm tired. I need a lie-in at the weekend.'

'It's the same for all of us,' Nancy reminded her. 'We'll just have to put up with it until after the war.'

'Whenever that'll be,' Jean said gloomily. 'There doesn't seem to be much sign of it ending, does there? It just goes on and on.'

'They need me on the job,' joked Micky, introducing a lighter note. 'You wait till I get out there. Those Jerries won't know what's hit 'em.'

'Oh yeah. I suppose you think you're gonna win the war single-handed then,' said Jean.

He gave her one of the wicked grins that they'd all missed so much during his absence. 'That's the plan,' he joked, his eyes sparkling with mischief. 'Though I might need a little help from the rest of the British army.'

'You fool,' laughed Nancy. It was so good to see him behaving like his old self again.

Lily quietly re-entered the room.

'Mum?' said Nancy, observing her mother's ashen face and the yellow envelope clutched in her trembling hands. 'Mum, whatever's the matter?'

'It wasn't the milkman, it was the telegram boy . . .'

Three pairs of eyes were fixed on her face. Silence vibrated through the room.

'Dad . . .' said Nancy at last, her whole body frozen. 'Oh no, please not Dad.'

'It was from the shipping company,' Lily told them, looking dazed. 'His ship was hit. He was lost at sea.'

Jean collapsed into tears and cried loudly and theatrically; Nancy and Micky went to their mother, who looked about to collapse.

'Come and sit down, Mum,' said Nancy, easing her into an armchair and putting her arm around her.

'I've been trying to prepare myself for this ever since war broke out,' said Lily in a shaky voice. 'He's been in the thick of it, even though he wasn't in the military. I should have been prepared, but I kept praying that it wouldn't happen . . .'

'Bloody war,' sobbed Jean, her voice rising hysterically. 'Bloody Hitler and his thugs.'

'Language, Jean,' admonished her mother, trying to retain a degree of normality despite her grief. It seemed to help somehow. 'You know how your father hated to hear you girls swear.'

'But he can't hear, can he?' The girl's voice rose to a shriek. 'He won't hear anything ever again, and all because the politicians let this rotten war happen. Sods, the lot of 'em. Let them go and do the fighting, that's what I say. Get them off their arses in parliament and out to the front. That'll stop them letting wars happen.'

'Don't be so stupid,' argued her brother. 'Someone has to run things and they're doing what they can.'

'Surely they could have stopped it?'

'Oh yeah, and let Hitler rule the world,' said Micky, who was also reeling from the blow of knowing his father was dead.

'Calm down, the pair of you,' admonished Nancy. 'We're all upset and it's putting our nerves on edge.' She looked meaningfully towards their mother, who was sitting in the chair with her head bowed.

'Oh yeah, sorry, Mum,' said Jean, dabbing at her eyes with a handkerchief.

'Me too,' added Micky.

Nancy was fighting to hold back the tears. It seemed important that she stay strong for the others. Their father hadn't been around much and none of his children had been close to him. He'd been more like a jolly uncle who came home from time to time with presents for them from exciting foreign places. But he had been their dad and his death cut deep, though Nancy was acutely aware that her mother was the one who would feel it most. She was going to need plenty of looking after, especially in her condition.

Lily also had her condition very much on her mind. It seemed wicked to even have such thoughts, and her grief was no less for having them, but she couldn't help thinking that at least her poor, dear Arthur had been spared the pain of knowing about the child she was carrying. She was even more ashamed now, though, as the full impact of the facts registered. The truth was that while Arthur had been away risking his life, she had been creating a new life, with someone else.

'Could you call at Uncle Wilf's on your way to work, please, Micky, and ask him to come round here as soon as he can,' she requested, her voice breaking. 'He and Arthur were good pals, so he's going to be shattered.'

'Sure,' said Micky in a subdued tone.

'You need a cup of hot sweet tea for the shock,' suggested Nancy. 'I'll go and put the kettle on.'

'Don't worry about me, love,' Lily said bravely. 'You'd better get yourself off to work. And that goes for all of you.'

'We can't all just go off and leave you on your own; not today.'

'I'll be all right.' Lily wanted to be alone with her thoughts in the aftermath of this devastating news. She'd been forced to stop work because of the late stage of the pregnancy so could stay at home with her sadness and shame. Somehow she had to come to terms with it.

'You need us with you today.'

'If everyone stayed at home because they'd lost a loved one these days, the country would come to a standstill,' she pointed out wearily, her face and neck suffused with nervous red blotches. 'There is one thing I'd like to suggest before you all go off, though. I don't think we should tell Leslie yet, not while he's away. It'll probably be best to break the news to him when he's back at home with his family around to give him some support. What do you think?'

'No point in upsetting him while he's away from home,' said Nancy.

Her siblings nodded.

'We're all agreed on that, then,' said Lily sadly, stroking

Smudge the cat, who had jumped on her lap with perfect timing, almost as though he sensed that his comforting presence was needed.

Chapter Four

As Leslie walked home from school in the pale spring sunshine, he perceived a slight difference in the air today. Everything seemed lighter and smelled nice. The hedgerows were dotted here and there with wild flowers and there were patches of the purple stuff that grew on the bombsites at home.

An invitation from some boys in his class to play football with them on the village green on Saturday afternoon had cheered him up no end. He doubted he'd be allowed to go, but he was going to push his luck and ask Mrs Farley anyway. If he could pluck up the courage.

Just the fact of being asked had lifted his spirits; made him feel included; a part of things. He remembered feeling like this all the time back home in London where having pals had been an ordinary part of his life. Weekends on the farm, with no escape from the grim atmosphere or the fearsome Farleys, seemed to drag on for ever; hour upon hour of hard work and tongue lashings. It would be such a treat to be with people of his own age, as he used to be in

Sycamore Road where the street was a playground outside of school hours.

Perhaps the Farleys might let him go if he promised to make up the time by working harder for the rest of the weekend, and offered to do extra. It wasn't as if he'd be out for long. Yes, that was definitely worth a try. A surge of optimism lightened his step and he was smiling as he went into the yard.

'And where the hell do you think you've been?' demanded Mrs Farley, marching towards him with a fierce expression.

'School,' he replied, inwardly trembling from the viciousness of her scowl.

'Don't you dare be sarcastic to me, boy.' Her voice went right through him, making his nerves jangle. He didn't even know what the word meant, let alone how to do it. 'I've got a full set of brains in my head and I know you've been to school. I'm talking about after that, as you well know. You should have been here more than half an hour ago.'

He moistened his dry lips with his tongue, realising that he must have stayed longer than he'd intended, chatting about the football game. 'Sorry, Mrs Farley,' he said meekly.

'Sorry isn't good enough. I want to know where you've been all this time.'

'I was only talking to some boys,' he explained. 'I didn't realise I was late.'

'Talking to some boys!' So great was her disapproval, he might have just admitted to murdering the teacher, at least. 'You've no right to be hanging around with boys outside the school when there's work to be done here. You know perfectly well that you're supposed to come straight back after school. That's the rules on this farm.'

'Sorry, Mrs Farley,' he said again.

'You will be if you do it again,' she threatened. 'I can promise you that.'

Desperately keen to go to the football game, and not having sufficient guile to choose his moment, Leslie blurted out, 'The boys were asking me to play football with them on Saturday afternoon.'

She stared at him coldly. 'I hope you told them you can't go,' she said.

'Well, no, I didn't,' he began warily. 'I sort of wondered if I could go . . . please? I'd really like that and I'll make up for all the time that I'm not here.'

The look the farmer's wife gave him was enough to wither Tarzan himself, let alone a boy of ten. 'Of course you can't go,' she rasped. 'You're needed here. There's a lot to do on a farm at this time of the year. You've got to help Mr Farley finish mending the fences and a million other jobs around the place.'

'Oh please, let me go,' he begged, longing for a brief respite at the weekend. 'I wouldn't be gone long, I promise, and I'd work twice as hard when I got back. I'll do extra jobs, anything you say.'

'Well, I've never heard such cheek in all my born days. You're asking if you can go out enjoying yourself, when there's work to be done here and there are people dying in the war every minute of the day.' Her eyes were dark with accusation. 'That's downright selfish.'

A remaining spark of determination wouldn't let him admit defeat on this one. 'I'm very sorry about all the people dying, but my going to play football won't make any difference, will it?' He really was pushing it.

'Don't be so damned cheeky. You're not going and I don't want to hear another word about it. You ought to count your blessings, young man,' she lectured, cheeks flushed with anger, eyes hard and cold. 'You're a very lucky boy. You're living here in the peace and safety of the country because Mr Farley and I have taken you in out of the kindness of our hearts.'

The frustration and disappointment finally proved too much for Leslie. 'You're not kind,' he burst out, cheeks flaming. 'You're cruel and horrid and I'm gonna tell my mum that you're a nasty old witch.'

Her eyes widened, momentarily. 'Oh, so that's what you think, is it?' she said sharply, almost immediately regaining her composure. 'Well, well. I think you need straightening out about a few things. Oh, yes. You need a bit of time on your own to get all that silly nonsense out of your head and learn to respect your elders.'

He turned to run away, but she was too quick for him and grabbed him roughly by his shoulders and marched him across to the coal shed. Opening the door, she pushed him inside, snapping the padlock shut.

'You'll stay in there until you've learned some gratitude,' she called in to him. 'You're not coming out until you've realised how good me and Mr Farley are to you and promise not to tell your mother lies about us.'

Courage wasn't so easy to come by on this side of the locked door, especially as there was barely room to stand up. 'Let me out,' he pleaded with a sob in his voice. 'I won't say anything to Mum.'

'I can't trust you, boy. It'll take longer'n this before I can,' she told him. 'You'll come out when it's time to help Mr Farley with the milking and not before.'

'It's dark in here, and I don't like being shut in. I never have done.'

'All the better. Perhaps that'll teach you to behave,' she said triumphantly. 'If you breathe a word to your mother about anything that goes on at this farm, you'll be spending a lot more time in there.'

Inside it was black, the only light coming through the crack under the door, and the smell of coal dust stuck in his throat. He was shaking and sweating, his heart thumping. It was as though everything was closing in on him and squeezing his chest so hard that he couldn't take a deep breath.

'I'm sorry I was rude to you, Mrs Farley. I didn't mean it and I promise I won't say anything to anyone.' His words were uttered between gasps. He needed air. He'd agree to anything to get out of here. 'I'll tell the boys I don't wanna play football with 'em and I won't say a word to Mum.'

'There's nothing *to* say to your mother, is there, Leslie?' she said meaningfully.

'No, no, o' course not.'

'You're enjoying your life here at the farm with Mr Farley and me, aren't you?'

'Yeah, yeah, anything you say. But please let me out.'

'Ooh, that don't sound very convincing to me,' she disapproved. 'You obviously haven't had long enough in there to be sure about it.'

'Please let me out. I can't breathe.'

'You know what happens to people when they can't breathe, don't you?' she taunted. 'They die.'

'Please . . .'

'You can whine all you like and I won't hear you because I'll be inside with the door shut, having my tea,' she told him. 'Cheerio for now.'

As her footsteps faded into the distance, panic burned to the roots of his hair. He sank down on to a pile of coal with his head in his hands, shivering and heaving. He kept his eyes closed to avoid seeing the locked door, because he hated the sensation of being shut in. He would do anything, *anything at all* to avoid being locked in here again. He would obey them totally if that's what it took. Eventually the gasping subsided and he sobbed into his hands, cold, hungry and terrified. He had never felt so lonely.

Because all the London mainline stations were prime targets for the enemy, many of the subways and rooms under the Paddington station complex had been turned into shelters for passengers and staff. A store formerly used for staff uniforms was now a crèche for the children of mothers waiting for trains. A qualified nurse was on hand to look after them if their parents wanted to snatch some sleep in a nearby subway shelter provided for passengers.

The staff shelter was for those who couldn't get home due to working a late turn and those starting very early. Each bunk was equipped with a carriage seat, a cushion and a pillow. Nancy always found it a very cheery place with a strong sense of community. The shelterers came from all departments and grades, equal and united against the enemy, everyone mucking in.

One night in April there was a particularly long and vicious raid that went on into the early hours. Nancy and her workmates were forced to spend the night in the shelter because, although they weren't on late turn, the bombing had already been so heavy at the end of their shift, they hadn't been able to leave the station.

'Gawd Almighty,' said Polly now. She was sitting on the bunk with Nancy, while Ruby was lying on the one opposite with her coat over her, turned away from them. 'Hitler's thugs are really letting rip tonight.'

'They seem to have been at it for hours,' responded Nancy miserably. 'Sounds as though they're right overhead now.'

Those people who'd been trying to sleep were beginning to talk amongst themselves as the tension increased. Someone started a chorus of 'I've Got Sixpence' and people joined in to calm their nerves and drown out the noise above. Then, suddenly, the whole place shook from the impact of a deafening explosion, producing a shocked silence. No one moved or spoke. Nancy and Polly clung together. Ruby sat up. Nancy's whole body reverberated with the thump of her heart.

'The station must have been hit,' said Percy Wellington

from further down the shelter, making his way towards the door. 'I'm going up to see what's going on. There might be a lot of injuries, and they'll need help.'

People tried to deter him, suggesting that he wait for the all clear, but he went anyway, saying that he couldn't stay here and do nothing while people might be dying up above. Nancy and Polly didn't even discuss it. They went after him, with Ruby behind them.

'It was a bomb in the departure roadway, apparently; part of the offices, the boardroom and the waiting room have gone,' said a member of staff to Nancy as she emerged on to the platform and tried to take in the carnage all around her.

Almost the whole of the side of the station adjacent to platform one was affected by the blast, and there were broken bricks and concrete everywhere, clouds of smoke and dust hanging over everything. Several of the station shops were damaged, including Boots the Chemist, Lyons and Wymans. One of the booking offices was wrecked, as well as one of the station buffets. People were screaming in terror, crying and coughing from the acrid smoke.

'Oh, there you are, Nancy,' said Polly, reunited with her friend after being separated in the chaos on the platform. 'Blimey, what a mess.'

Nancy nodded.

'Isn't it terrible about the passengers trapped underneath what's left of the waiting room?'

'Oh my God! I didn't know about that,' gasped Nancy, clutching her throat. 'I saw the waiting room had been damaged, but I didn't realise there was anyone in there when the explosion came.'

'With it being left open all night, people were sheltering in there,' said Ruby, joining them. 'They'd probably have been all right had the debris from the damaged offices not fallen down into it.'

All Nancy could do was shake her head in despair.

Even as they spoke, railway staff were beginning the task of clearance, digging with their bare hands to get the trapped people out. By the time the official rescue teams and first-aid parties arrived, people had made inroads into the rubble, while Nancy and her friends made themselves busy comforting the injured while they waited for first-aid treatment.

'Old Perce is really getting stuck in over there,' remarked Polly when they met up again later, glancing towards the supervisor, who was on his knees helping to move the debris, right at the centre of things. 'I didn't realise the old bugger had it in him.'

Nancy looked across. 'He was the first out of the shelter to see what he could do, too. So maybe he's not all bad, after all.'

'Perhaps not.'

Percy was in an extremely dangerous position, so close to what was left of the damaged offices, Nancy observed. The unstable ruins looked about to collapse at any moment. She was about to turn away to go back to the queue at the emergency canteen to get tea for the distressed and injured when she spotted a huge metal girder, suspended almost directly above where Percy was working. It was swaying and looked about to fall at any moment, unnoticed by the supervisor, who had his head down while he moved broken bricks and other debris.

Acting on instinct, Nancy dashed across and threw herself forward, pushing him to safety just seconds before the girder fell. She landed on her stomach only a matter of inches from where it hit the ground. Shaken to the core, she scrambled to her feet. Percy did the same and they stared at each other in silence. Nancy was trembling. He was as white as a sheet. They both knew she could have lost her life, while saving his.

'You all right?' His voice was quivering.

'Yeah, I think so. Just a bit shaken up.'

'Thanks,' he said unsteadily.

'It's all right.'

'It was very brave of you, Miss Sparrow,' he muttered, still looking unnerved. 'Very brave indeed. A split second later and I wouldn't have been here to tell the tale.'

'Anyone would have done the same.'

'I'm not so sure about that, but I'm very grateful to you anyway, Miss Sparrow.'

Just then, Nancy experienced something she'd thought she never would – a brief moment of affinity with Percy as they stood there in a state of shock, looking at each other. Their positions in the company had been stripped away by the gravity of the situation, and they were just two people who'd survived a near miss. 'But now I must get on.'

'Me too.'

As he went back to work on his hands and knees, she turned and hurried back to Polly and Ruby who'd seen the whole thing.

'Blimey, Nance, you played a blinder there,' Polly praised her. 'Old Perce was nearly no more. That took a bit of guts on your part. Well done, kid.'

'That goes for me too,' added Ruby.

'He's been a bit of a hero himself tonight,' Nancy said, modestly moving on.

'Yeah, credit where it's due to the old devil. He turned up trumps.'

As Nancy hurried over to do what she could for a woman who was sitting on a suitcase sobbing her heart out, she had a feeling that things would be better between herself and Percy Wellington in the future.

'Phew! What a night,' said Polly when they were finally in the cloakroom preparing to go home. 'I'll be bloomin' glad to get out of here.'

'Me too.'

'We don't want too many like that.'

'I heard someone say that eighteen people were killed here tonight,' mentioned Nancy in sombre mood, washing her hands and face at the basin to remove the grime. 'Some of them were in the waiting room.'

'It turns your stomach to think of it, dunnit?' nodded Polly.

'Six of them were station staff, too,' put in the unsociable Ruby unexpectedly.

103

'God knows how many injuries there were, all told,' said Nancy, drying her face on the almost threadbare roller-towel. 'There were some terrible cases. One poor woman lost a foot. I've never seen so much blood.'

'Plenty of that's been spilled tonight,' Polly agreed.

'Oh, well, let's go home and get some kip before it's time to come back on duty.' Nancy ran a comb through her dusty hair, her eyes sore and itchy with grit and tiredness, and put her coat on over her uniform. 'You ready then, Poll?'

'Yep.'

'See you tomorrow, Ruby.' Nancy had given up inviting her to join her for the journey.

'See you.'

The two women left.

'I hope to God the Tubes are running,' remarked Nancy. 'I don't fancy walking to Ealing Broadway to collect my bike after the night we've had.'

'You can stay at my place if you like,' invited Polly, who lived within walking distance of the station. 'If it's still there, that is. None of us can be sure of that these days.'

'Which is why I must go home to see if the family are all right, and the house still standing,' Nancy told her. 'But thanks for offering. If there are no trains, I'll try the buses. I'll get home somehow.'

They reached the point where they went their separate ways and Nancy headed for the underground. She felt someone tap her on the shoulder.

'Ruby,' she said, turning.

'Mind if I tag along?'

'Course not,' smiled Nancy, with no bad feeling towards her for her previous attitude, having just had a stark reminder of how short life really could be. 'I'll be glad of the company.'

'Me too.'

'That's unusual for you,' remarked Nancy amiably. 'You're usually so self-contained.'

'Yeah, well, it's been a bit of an unusual kind of a night, hasn't it?'

'To say the very least.'

'I was frightened out of my wits,' admitted Ruby.

'I think everybody was,' said Nancy. 'You'd have to be a bit thick not to be. We all live with constant fear nowadays, even if we don't show it.'

'I was sorry to hear about your dad, by the way,' mentioned Ruby.

'Thanks.'

'It must be terrible for you all.'

'Awful. But Mum's the worst hit, naturally. They'd been married a long time. She's pregnant too.'

'Oh dear. I hope she'll be all right.'

'I'm sure she will be. She's a tough lady, my mum. A natural survivor.'

Warmed by Ruby's concern and change in attitude, Nancy linked arms with her in a friendly manner as they walked on. They were both too tired to say much, but the silence was a companionable one.

For the third time that night, Nancy felt as though she had been through some sort of a watershed. She'd seen another side to Percy Wellington; a side that showed he had courage and compassion, as he faced danger with no thought of his own safety. Her own strength of character had also been tested. And now Ruby was beginning to thaw out. It might be only a temporary thing, but it was a start. About the only good thing to come out of this war was that it brought out the best in people.

'What a smashing film,' said Lily, emerging from the cinema into the moonlit night, a month later.

'Yeah, it was good,' agreed Nancy. 'I thoroughly enjoyed it.'

'You couldn't help laughing, even though it was a bit daft in places.'

'I thought it was a scream,' smiled Gladys.

'You're glad I twisted your arm about coming now, then, Mum?' suggested Nancy in a light tone.

'I am, love. I really am. It gets morbid sitting at home, wondering if the siren will go, and if the twinges I've been having lately are going to develop into anything.'

'Nothing like a good film to give you a lift,' put in Gladys. 'Especially a comedy like that. They say laughter is the best medicine, and that film was worth a good few bottles of doctors' tonic.'

Nancy had decided that her mother needed to be 'taken out of herself'. She was missing the stimulation and company of going out to work, and it was giving her more time to dwell on the bad news about Dad last month, the fact that Micky was now a soldier, and the youngest family member being away from home. So, noticing that *Road to Singapore* with Bob Hope, Bing Crosby and Dorothy Lamour was on locally, and having a Saturday night off, she'd got to work on her mother, who seemed to think that any form of pleasure was disrespectful to her late husband. Mourning probably was more strictly adhered to in normal times but – as far as Nancy could see – these days it was perfectly acceptable to carry on as before, even if your heart was breaking.

'It's a wonder I managed to squeeze into the seat,' chuckled Lily. 'I didn't think there could be a cinema seat big enough for someone of my size.'

The other two giggled at this.

'It's a pity Jean didn't come with us,' remarked Gladys. 'She would have enjoyed it.'

'The cinema is a bit too tame for Jean on a Saturday night,' Nancy replied affectionately. 'She's out dancing, looking for a replacement for her Polish boyfriend, I expect.'

'He didn't last long, did he?' said her gran.

'Hardly any time at all,' agreed Nancy. 'She only saw him a couple of times, I think.'

'That girl is either fickle or very fussy,' said Gladys. 'I'm not sure which.'

'I think she's just looking for that special someone and having fun along the way,' said Nancy.

'She's staying at a friend's place tonight, someone who lives near the dance hall,' mentioned Lily. 'So at least she won't have to worry about getting home if there's a raid. That's one less thing for me to worry about.'

They walked along the main road from Ealing Broadway in the spring night, the moon's pearly glow spreading over everything and making it easier to see in the blackout. Taking it slowly, with consideration for Lily's extra weight, they chatted companionably.

'I bet you'll be pleased to see Micky, won't you, Mum?' said Nancy. They'd had a letter from him this morning to say that he'd got a forty-eight-hour pass next weekend.

'Not half.'

'Me too,' said Nancy. 'I'm really excited.'

'He seems to be getting on all right, from what he says in his letters,' said Gladys.

'Even if he wasn't, he'd never admit it,' opined Lily. 'He couldn't wait to get into uniform and everyone knew it. If it's tougher than he imagined, he'll keep it to himself.'

'Everyone says the training is terrible,' added Nancy.

'All the more reason for me to make a fuss of him while he's home.'

'I can't wait to see him in uniform,' said Nancy. 'I bet he'll look handsome.'

'I'll be as proud as punch,' said Lily. 'Food shortage or not, we'll make a special occasion of it in true Sparrow fashion. I'll ask Wilf if he can get hold of some booze to welcome him home.'

'We'll have a sing-song down the pub too,' said Nancy with enthusiasm.

The conversation turned back to the film, and they were recalling their favourite parts, roaring with laughter, when a familiar chilling sound filled the air.

'Oh no, not again,' groaned Nancy. 'We might have known they would use the moon to their advantage.'

Instinctively, they quickened their pace, Nancy and Gladys holding Lily's arms to help her along. But they still had quite a way to go when the raid got underway, bangs and crashes erupting all around them, an orange halo rising above the rooftops.

'This one's a bit too near for my liking,' said Gladys.

'We'll be all right, Gran,' encouraged Nancy, making a joke of it. 'Only the good die young, remember.'

'Oh!' gasped Lily shakily, suddenly halting in her step. 'Oh, my Lord. That's torn it.'

'Don't worry, Mum,' soothed Nancy. 'We'll be home soon and we'll be all right once we're in the Anderson.'

'The air raid is only one of my problems,' her mother explained nervously, looking down. 'My waters have broken and I'm soaked from the waist down. How's that for bad timing?'

'Ooh, blimey,' said Gladys.

'Seems like I'll be giving birth in the air-raid shelter.'

'You won't be the first.' Nancy knew she must stay strong and positive for her mother's sake, even though she felt panicky inside. 'Anyway, the all clear will probably have gone by the time it actually happens.'

'You lot were all quick, so I wouldn't bank on it,' warned Lily.

'As soon as we get home I'll go and get the midwife,' said Nancy.

Nancy climbed back into the candlelit shelter with some worrying news.

'Jessie's out delivering another baby,' she said breathlessly, having run through the streets with bombs raining down all around her. 'I left a message for her to come as soon as she can. They don't think she'll be too long.'

'We can't expect her to come out while there's a raid on,' mumbled Lily, who was hunched up on the bunk, holding her stomach, obviously in a great deal of discomfort. 'Midwife or not, she has to look after herself. She has a family of her own to worry about, remember.'

'She's out on a job now, so she must be carrying on regardless,' Gladys pointed out. 'It'll take more than an air raid to stop her doing her work, if I know Jessie. She's delivered all your babies and she won't want to miss out on this one. As far as I know, she's never let anyone down yet.'

'Not in peacetime, no, but it's dangerous out there tonight, Mum,' Lily returned, breathless with the pain.

'They seemed to think she'd come,' Nancy put in.

'Ooh! Bloody hell!' yelled Lily. 'This childbirth lark is worse than I remember.'

'It's a long time since you last did it, love,' her mother reminded her. 'You've forgotten, that's all.'

'I'm too old to be doing it at all.' She sounded tortured, even though she was hanging on to her sense of humour. 'And if anyone suggests that I should have thought of that before, I shall crown 'em.'

'We wouldn't dare,' grinned Gladys.

The labour went on and on; hour upon hour of agony, interspersed with periods of sweating and vomiting. Nancy had to constantly remind herself that childbirth was the most natural thing in the world, because she could hardly bear to see her mother suffering in such a way, and could almost feel her pain.

'The contractions are coming closer together now,' said Gladys. 'So you shouldn't be too much longer.'

'Take my hand, Mum,' offered Nancy.

Clutching her daughter's hand so hard it felt to Nancy as though she would crush the bones to dust, Lily lay back and let out a blood-curdling scream, while Gladys mopped her brow with a cold flannel.

When the contraction finally died away, Lily said weakly, 'Why is it taking so long? I usually shell 'em like peas. It doesn't feel right this time.'

A violent explosion shook the ground so hard everything rattled and various items fell off the shelf. 'I doubt if Jessie will come, you know,' groaned Lily. 'She could get herself killed if she tried to get through while this lot is going on.'

'If she can't make it, we'll have to deliver the baby ourselves,' said Gladys, sounding positive.

'Course we will,' supported Nancy, stroking her mother's sweat-soaked hair back from her brow with a cool cloth. 'It won't be the first baby to come into the world without a professional in attendance, especially these days, with everything being out of the norm. Someone had a baby in the station waiting room the other week. Another gave birth on the train.'

'All right, Nancy, I don't need convincing. I trust you to look after me.'

Still it went on. There seemed no end to it and Lily was

exhausted. She stopped making jokes, just begged for the pain to end, and seemed semi-conscious for part of the time.

'This doesn't seem right to me, Gran,' said Nancy worriedly when her mother seemed to have drifted off.

Gladys looked anxious too. 'She does seem to be having a very bad labour,' she said.

'I'm going to the phone box to call an ambulance,' Nancy decided, refusing to allow thoughts of the past to intrude. 'I know the hospitals will be busy with bomb victims, but Mum needs help too.'

As Nancy went to climb out of the shelter, someone was on the way in.

'Thank God for that,' Nancy greeted her.

'Sorry it's taken me so long,' puffed Jessie, a soft-eyed woman of middle years, her face streaked with black smoke dust, her brown hair all over the place. 'It's ruddy chaos out there. Fires everywhere, roads closed. I narrowly missed taking a tumble off my bike too. There was a damned great crater in the road. I spotted it just in time.'

'We wondered if you'd come, with things being so bad,' said Nancy. 'It's very good of you.'

'I work in essential services, dear. It's my job to be here,' Jessie assured her. 'Babies don't stop being born just because there's an air raid on. It's my duty to see them safely into the world.'

'I was just going to ring for an ambulance,' Nancy explained. 'Mum's in a bad way.'

'If you haven't seen a birth before, it seems worse than it actually is. People do look rough when they're in labour.

Let's have a look.' She went over to Lily, who was puffing and groaning. 'Hello, Mrs Sparrow, dear. Here we are again, with number five to add to your lovely family. Let's have a little peep at you now.'

She examined Lily's stomach and took her blood pressure, seeming thoughtful.

'As she's having a bit of a struggle, I think it might be a good idea to call an ambulance after all. Given that she's getting on a bit in years in terms of childbirth.' As Nancy's eyes widened with fear and Gladys's hand flew to her throat, she added, 'Just as a precaution.'

Tearing down the street to the phone box on the main road, sheets of flame lighting the sky, a shop on fire further along, bells ringing against the sound of aircraft and guns, Nancy felt surprisingly calm about the close proximity of the explosions and the fact that she might be killed at any moment. Her mind was focused entirely on her mother.

Reaching the phone box, she pushed open the door and dialled 999.

She could hear her mother's screams as she approached the shelter.

'You're doing very well, Mrs Sparrow,' Jessie was saying as Nancy climbed in. 'Come on, now, one more push.'

'I can't. I don't have the strength.' She was lying on the bunk with her legs wide open and knees bent. 'I can't do this any more. I can't.'

'Yes, you can, love,' encouraged Gladys from the opposite bunk. 'You're almost there.'

Jessie moved away so that Nancy could get close to her mother.

'You're doing well, Mum,' she told her, taking Lily's hand. 'I know it must be terrible, what you're going through, but Jessie says you haven't got long to go now.'

Accompanied by a deep-throated scream, Lily gave one almighty push.

'Oh, Mum! Oh my God!' cried Nancy excitedly. 'I can see the head. The head's there.'

Lily yelled as she pushed and strained.

'That's the stuff, Mrs Sparrow, dear. You're doing fine,' praised Jessie warmly.

As her mother gave that one last shove, Nancy witnessed something so amazing she wept with the joy of it. A tiny blood-soaked person slipped out and lay between the exhausted Lily's legs.

The nurse cut the cord, lifted the baby and rubbed the top of its back, so that it emitted a lusty cry, then laid it in Lily's arms.

'You've a lovely little girl, Mrs Sparrow,' she told her, pressing Lily's stomach to help release the placenta into a bowl. 'Another beautiful daughter.'

Lily seemed to be too weak to notice.

'Water and towels, please,' ordered the midwife.

Nancy handed her both. Everything had been brought down here ready when they'd got back from the cinema, and Nancy had gone up to the house for hot water when the birth seemed imminent.

'I shall call her Evie, after my grandmother.' Lily's voice

was barely a whisper. She looked very ill indeed. Her face was grey and soaked with sweat. The sheet was covered in blood.

'Hello, little girl,' said Nancy, leaning close to the tiny head. 'I'm Nancy, your big sister. Welcome to the family.'

'And I'm your gran,' added Gladys. 'Welcome to the world, little one.'

Witnessing this little piece of perfection make her entrance had moved Nancy and made her want to cry for what might have been long ago. She was overwhelmed with love for the new arrival.

But Lily still seemed too distressed to pay much attention.

'Mum,' said Nancy. 'Mum, what is it?' She turned to Jessie. 'What's the matter with her?'

'Your mother is bleeding heavily, losing far more blood than is normal. We need more towels.' She felt Lily's pulse and took her blood pressure. 'Her blood pressure has dropped dramatically, and her pulse is thready. We need to get her to hospital right away, but I'll do what I can to stem the flow of blood until then. I'll try padding her with towels until we can get a doctor to see her.'

Lily opened her eyes. 'Nancy. Mum,' she said, her voice barely recognisable in its feebleness. 'Don't go away. I need to talk to you.'

'We're not going anywhere.'

'I want you to promise me something.'

'Anything,' said Nancy.

'There's nothing you need to fret about at this moment,'

115

said Gladys. 'Whatever it is, it can wait. You need to rest now.'

But there was no stopping her. 'I want you to make sure that Arthur is named as the father on Evie's birth certificate.' Her voice was so faint it was barely audible. The towels Jessie was using as padding were turning red. 'We have to protect her and give her a proper place in society. Arthur is dead so he can't be upset by it. I want her brought up as a Sparrow.'

'Of course,' agreed Nancy. 'We'd all just assumed she would be anyway. But you'll see to all that side of it when you're back on your feet.'

'Just Evie as it is, not Evelyn shortened or anything; just Evie. My grandmother was big Evie. My new daughter will be little Evie,' she went on, her lips almost as pale as her face.

'All right, Mum,' soothed Nancy, 'but you'll be registering her yourself once you're up and about again.'

'She's to be brought up as a Sparrow,' repeated Lily, as though Nancy hadn't spoken. 'Promise me you'll bring her up as one of the family.' She fell silent, as though trying to summon the strength to speak. 'It's important to me that you give me your word.'

'Please don't talk like this, Mum,' Nancy entreated. 'You'll be there to make sure it's done.'

'Promise me . . . please.'

'We promise,' said Gladys, who was kneeling by the bunk, holding her daughter's hand while Jessie struggled to stop the flow of blood.

'It means so much to me,' Lily said weakly, her strength

fading with every word. 'Look after each other. Tell the others I love them.' Her head rolled to one side.

'Mum!' cried Nancy. 'Mum, come on. You're really scaring me.'

'Lily,' said Gladys. 'Come on, now, ducks. Don't mess about.'

Nancy turned to Jessie. 'What's happening to her?' she asked, her voice shrill with fear.

'Where's that bloomin' ambulance?' tutted Jessie, wrapping the baby in a towel and handing her to Nancy, while she felt her mother's pulse again.

Nancy had never been so frightened.

'I'm going to ring nine-nine-nine again.' She handed the baby to her grandmother and started to climb up out of the shelter just as an ambulance bell sounded close by. 'Thank goodness for that. It's here at last. I'll go and make sure they know where we are.'

'Nancy,' Jessie called out suddenly.

'Yes?' she replied, turning.

'They're too late, dear, I'm afraid,' she said sadly. 'Your mother's gone.'

'Oh no . . . please God no.' Nancy couldn't believe what she was hearing. 'She was perfectly all right before she went into labour,' she said, in an almost whispered shriek. 'She's only had a baby, not an illness or an operation. Tell her, Gran, will you? Tell her she's got it wrong.'

But her grandmother couldn't speak. She was clutching little Evie as though frozen to the spot.

With infinite gentleness, Jessie closed Lily's eyes and took the baby from Gladys. 'Now we have to get you fixed up, baby Sparrow, before we do anything else.' Looking from Gladys to Nancy, she added with tears in her eyes, 'I really am so very sorry. There was nothing I could do.'

Nancy so wanted to be brave, but she could feel her strength draining away. She stifled a cry that was welling up inside her as she kneeled by her mother's bloodstained body, almost choking with uncontrollable weeping. Then, becoming aware of her grandmother's grief, she stood up and put her arms around her, holding her as she sobbed, and this was how the ambulance men found them.

Chapter Five

The Devonshire countryside was gloriously verdant and fragrant with May blossom as Nancy made her way to the farm that Saturday afternoon. The silence was unfamiliar to an urbanite like her. All she could hear was the soft thud of her own footsteps on the earthy ground, the twitter of the birds and the rustle of leaves moving lightly in the breeze. It was so peaceful here, in direct contrast to the noisy throb of town life that she was used to. The sun was pleasantly warm and the air fresh and clean – the complete opposite to the urban blight in London, where the atmosphere was polluted with brick dust and the lingering smell of bomb smoke.

But Nancy was far too dejected and preoccupied with her thoughts to fully appreciate the beauty and salubrity of her surroundings. The last couple of weeks had been hardly bearable, and she was no newcomer to trauma.

According to all reports, the night of her mother's death had been the worst of the war, with the heaviest air raids on the capital so far, killing 1400 people, seriously injuring thousands more and leaving many homeless. Every mainline railway terminus had been hit and many important buildings damaged, including Westminster Abbey and the debating chamber of the House of Commons. Large numbers of private houses, factories and hospitals had been destroyed or damaged. It was no wonder the ambulance had taken such a long time to reach her mother.

People had wept in the streets at so much destruction, but knowing the terrible extent of the suffering all around her didn't lessen the intensity of Nancy's own personal grief over the loss of her mother. It was as though all the warmth and light had gone out of her life. Nothing could ever be the same without Mum. How could it be? She'd been comforter, mentor and friend; she'd lifted them up and carried them through; had been the very heartbeat of the Sparrow family. The only positive thing in Nancy's life at the moment was the legacy her mother had left them – little Evie.

There had been no time to wallow in self-pity in the immediate aftermath of that terrible night. As the eldest child, Nancy had considered it her duty to keep a grip for the sake of the others, even though her pain was hardly bearable. Micky had been surprisingly brave and practical during his compassionate leave, helping with the funeral arrangements and the other grim formalities of death. Jean had gone to pieces and been no use to anyone, and Uncle Wilf had been too distressed to maintain his usual manly persona and had done the unthinkable – he'd cried in front of everybody. Even the family's beloved cat, Smudge, had seemed lost, and had padded about the house for days looking for Lily, emitting a poignant, deep-throated cry.

Gran's salvation had undoubtedly been little Evie. Caring for the baby had given her something to occupy her mind and seemed to ease the pain a little. Lily's dying wish regarding Evie's birth certificate had been taken care of, and it was mutually agreed that the child would be a joint family responsibility, each member chipping in something from their pay-packet towards her keep, with Micky arranging to have a small amount sent home from his army pay. Gran didn't have any spare cash, so her contribution came in the form of childcare for the majority of the time, since none of the others were in a position to do it.

They decided it would be too much for Gran to have the baby overnight as well as during the day, so Evie slept at the house and Nancy and Jean took care of her between them. Predictably, Jean's contribution was extremely limited and didn't involve getting up in the night, changing nappies or doing anything that would interfere with her social life. Going out dancing was her way of coping with her grief, and everyone accepted that and left her alone.

Neighbours had been kind and sympathetic, though many of them had losses of their own to cope with, including sons killed in action and relatives bombed in their homes. A huge number of people were bereaved and it created something of a bond between them, based on mutual grief.

An unexpected visitor had particularly warmed Nancy's heart. Ruby had called at the house to offer her condolences after work the day before the funeral, having heard what had happened through the station grapevine.

She'd been enchanted with little Evie at once; so much so that she'd taken her for a walk in her pram because Nancy and Gladys couldn't get her to sleep and were struggling to make a spread for the wake the next day with what little ingredients they could conjure up. When Ruby returned, Evie was sleeping soundly.

As Nancy became better acquainted with Ruby, she found her personality to be curiously at odds with itself. Although she was friendlier now towards Nancy, and displayed the tender side of her nature in the way she behaved towards the baby, she was still uncommunicative at times, and could be quite snappy with the other women on the team at work.

She made an absolute point of keeping her distance, but at the same time seemed to be reaching out for friendship. It was strange. She never mentioned her private life and didn't welcome enquiries on the subject. About the only thing Nancy knew about her was that she still lived at home. But for all that she wasn't an easy person to get along with, Nancy liked her, and suspected that there was more to her than met the eye.

Mercifully, there had been no raids since that last violent night, so people were getting some sleep again, though Nancy had barely closed her eyes since her mother's death. When she did finally doze off, she had to go through the agony of waking up and remembering all over again.

Micky was now back at camp, Jean and Nancy had returned to work, and Nancy's purpose here in Devon this weekend was to break the shocking news to her young brother that both his parents were dead. The poor lad. He was going to be devastated. But he had to be told; it couldn't be left until he came home. Not now that both Dad and Mum had gone. He had a right to know. Nancy took heart in the knowledge that he had good and kind people to look after him when she had returned to London.

It had been a family decision not to have Leslie home for the funeral. Apart from the horrors of wartime travel, it was still considered dangerous to have children in London because nobody knew when the raids would resume, and in any case, it had been mutually agreed that the funeral would be too harrowing for the boy.

Nancy had written to tell him that she was coming, but had carefully omitted to mention the reason why. It would be too cruel for him to receive such news without a member of the family with him.

As she entered the farmyard and saw him coming towards her, her stomach tightened and she braced herself for what had to be done.

'So you're enjoying country life then, Les?' she said as they sat on a bench on the village green, in the absence of anywhere else where they could go to talk.

'Yeah.'

'You'll miss all this lovely countryside when you come home, won't you?'

'I s'pose.'

'It's so lucky that Mr and Mrs Farley are such lovely people.' Indeed, they had given her the warmest of welcomes and spoken highly of Leslie. They seemed to be very fond

123

of the boy and she'd been comforted by this. 'Mum told us that they were nice and I agree with her. You all get on really well by the sound of it.'

'They're all right.'

'Do you ever get to watch Mr Farley milk the cows?'

He did a lot more than just watch, but he daren't tell her that. 'Sometimes,' he said.

'Is it fun?'

'Mm.'

Had Nancy not known it was impossible, she'd have sworn he had already been given the news she had yet to break to him. He looked so dreadfully sad, even though he was doing his best to hide it. He seemed healthy enough – his skin was tanned from the fresh air and he was shining with cleanliness – but he had used to be such a bright-eyed, cheerful little boy with plenty to say for himself. Now his dark eyes were lacklustre, and he'd become distinctly taciturn. Worryingly, too, he seemed to have developed the nervous habit of blinking his eyes in quick succession for sustained periods.

'Is everything all right, Les?'

'Yeah.'

'Made any friends at school?'

'A few.'

'Good. It's always nice to have some pals to knock around with, isn't it?'

'Mm.'

She realised that she was fudging the issue; she should have come right out and told him the purpose of her visit when they'd first left the farm and he'd asked where his mother was and why Nancy had come in her place. Instead, she'd mumbled something about Mum not being able to make it this time. He'd seemed so strange, so quiet and withdrawn, she couldn't bring herself to inflict the pain on him.

'Are you sure you're all right, Les?' she asked again.

His gaze slipped away from hers. 'I've just said so, haven't I?' he snapped.

'If there's nothing wrong, why are you being so snappy and cold with me?'

'I'm not.'

'Is someone being mean to you at school?'

'No.'

'And you can keep up with your schoolwork?'

He bristled at the implication. 'Do you think I'm a thick-head or somethin'?'

She put her hand on his arm. 'No. I'm just trying to find out what's the matter with you.'

He gave a careless shrug. 'I dunno what you're talking about.'

'Mr and Mrs Farley are nice, so it can't be that.' She hesitated briefly, looking at him. 'So what's bothering you, Leslie?' she persisted. 'Tell me, please.'

His eyelids moved rapidly in blinking mode. 'Nothin'. How many more times do you want telling? Why don't you just go home and stay there, instead of coming down here and making trouble for me?' he said dully.

'Trouble? What do you mean?'

'Stop asking all these bloomin' questions, will yer?' He pushed his fingers through his short dark hair in an agitated manner. 'You're really getting on my nerves.'

'I won't stop until I get some answers. We are not leaving here until you tell me what it is. I'll wait all afternoon if I have to.'

He got up and walked away, shoulders down, hands sunk deep into his pockets. She was after him like a shot, grabbing him by the arm.

'Get off me!'

'Leslie, this is me, Nancy, your big sister. I only want to help you.'

He turned to her, his eyes suddenly hot with temper. 'Why are you pretending to care all of a sudden?' He was simmering with umbrage, his cheeks brightly flushed.

'I'm not pretending. Of course I care.'

'No you don't. If anyone at home cared, I wouldn't be here.' His voice was quivering on the verge of tears.

'That isn't true. You were sent away for your own safety, not because we didn't care. You know that.'

'Maybe I do,' he admitted grudgingly. 'But it doesn't feel like that to me. It's all right for you, you can go home. I can't. I've got to stay here, so just go back to London and leave me alone, will yer?'

He went to walk away from her, but she fell into step beside him and put her arm around him.

It was so long since he'd had any sort of affection, it was too much. The brave front just fell away and his body heaved with sobs. 'Get off me,' he choked, wriggling away, wiping

126

his eyes with the back of his hand. 'The village boys might see and think I'm soft.'

She moved back slightly and gave him a handkerchief. 'Let's take a walk, where there's no one about, and you can tell me what's bothering you.'

'It'll only make it worse.'

'I won't let it. I promise.'

He could hold back no longer. All the misery of the past long months, the loneliness, the weariness resulting from a man's work on a boy's shoulders, the terror of the Farleys' punishments and the pain of their constant hostility, had finally taken their toll, and he sobbed in his sister's arms, all fear of being seen forgotten in the relief of letting go. When he was feeling calmer, they walked into deep countryside and he told her what had been happening.

'Please don't tell them I've told you,' he begged her, his mouth parched with fear. 'They'll lock me up in the coal shed, and I really hate that.'

'No, they won't.'

'They will. Honestly, Nance. They'll swear blind to you that they won't, but as soon as you've gone home, I'll really cop it.'

She halted in her step and turned to him, placing her hands on his shoulders. 'No, Leslie. They won't do that to you, or anything else, ever again, I can promise you that, because you're coming home with me.'

He looked at her, disbelieving at first, then a cautious gleam of hope shone in his eyes. 'What really home? Back to London, you mean? Not just to another billet?'

'No, not another billet. You need to be with your family after what you've been through.'

The relief made him cry again, and Nancy wept too, for all he'd had to endure without any support from anyone. 'Come on, let's go back to the farm and get your things.'

He looked terrified. 'What about the Farleys?' he asked.

'I'll take care of them,' she assured him. 'You need never worry about them again.'

'We won't be staying for tea,' Nancy told Mr and Mrs Farley in the big farmhouse kitchen where Mrs Farley had laid the table with homemade bread and cake.

'Oh? Why is that, then?' she asked.

'Because I'm taking my brother home and the sooner we're out of here the better.' Leslie was standing beside her, pale with fright. 'Go and pack your things, love.'

'What are you goin' on about?' demanded Mrs Farley as soon as the door had closed behind him.

'It's over,' Nancy informed the couple. 'Your free child labour ends here, so you can drop the act. I shall see to it that you're never allowed to look after another child.'

Mrs Farley stood with her back to the wide black cooking range, her huge arms folded. Her husband was sitting at the table. 'What's that young heathen been saying?' she asked.

'Oh, so he's a heathen now, is he?' Nancy came back at her. 'You couldn't stop singing his praises to me when I first arrived, when you were trying to convince me how wonderfully well you've been looking after him. He's told me everything. All the dreadful things you've done to him. You're wicked and cruel, the pair of you.'

'We've never laid a finger on him.'

'You're far too clever for that. You wouldn't mark him in case someone spotted it. One of the teachers at school, since you never let him go anywhere else.'

'Well, I've never heard the—' began Mrs Farley.

'Don't waste your breath denying it, because I know what my brother was like before he came here, and I've seen what a nervous wreck he is now,' Nancy cut in. 'Somehow you managed to fool my mother into believing that you were doing a good job. I think you must have piled on the pressure since she was last here, because if she'd seen him as he is now, she'd have had him out of here like a shot.'

The other woman's mouth was turned down at the corners as she stared at Nancy with contempt. 'Why shouldn't us farmers make use of these kids when they come into our homes, knowing nothing of country life? Discipline is what they need.'

'Discipline is one thing, cruelty quite another,' returned Nancy.

'I was working a darned sight harder than he's had to when I was younger than him,' put in Mr Farley, 'on my father's farm.'

'It's how we do things in the country,' added his wife.

'No. It's how *you* do things, because you're evil-minded, greedy and want something for nothing.'

'Nobody wants the evacuees,' Mrs Farley stated categorically, dropping all pretence. 'They're nothing but trouble, the lot o' them.'

'You didn't do too bad out of our Leslie, though, did you?' Nancy reminded her. 'A free farmhand and an allowance for having him.'

Leslie came back into the room, with his gas-mask case slung over his shoulder, and carrying only a small travel bag because evacuees were instructed to travel light.

'Come on, love, let's get you away from these monsters.' His sister ushered him towards the door, then turned and added as a parting shot, 'You haven't heard the last of this.'

Leaving the couple staring after them in shocked silence, she took her brother's hand and departed.

'Cor, you really told 'em, Nance,' praised Leslie, full of admiration as they walked through the farm gates to the freedom he had longed for.

'Someone else will be telling them, too,' she told him. 'I'm going to make an official complaint when we get back to London. Make sure those two aren't allowed to have any more children billeted with them.'

'I can't believe I'm out of there.' His voice sounded lighter already, much more like that of the boy she remembered. 'It feels so lovely.'

'For me too, kid,' said Nancy. 'When I think of what's been happening to you down here, while at home we thought you were happy and enjoying yourself, it turns my stomach.'

'I'm really coming home for good, aren't I?' He still needed reassurance.

'Yep, air raids or not, you're really coming home, and staying there,' she assured him. 'After what you've been through, it's the only place for you.'

'Smashing.'

'There's only one snag, though,' she said jokingly. 'You'll have to share a bed with me tonight at the boarding house, because they're fully booked and our train doesn't go until tomorrow morning.'

'I don't care where I sleep, as long as it isn't at that rotten farm,' he said.

'That's what I thought you'd say.'

'I can't wait to see Mum and everyone.' His voice rose with excitement. 'Micky won't be there, though, will he, now that he's in the army.'

'No, he won't be there, so you'll have to wait until he comes home on leave to see him.' Her heart ached with what she could put off no longer. After all her little brother had already endured, she was about to inflict more suffering on him.

'The thing is, Les,' she began, hardly able to utter the words. 'There's something I have to tell you, and you're going to have to be very, very brave . . .'

There was a corner of a small park in Ealing that had a special place in Nancy's heart, and whenever she was upset or worried she found herself drawn to her own little oasis.

One Sunday afternoon a few weeks later, when she was out walking with Evie in her pram, she wandered over there and sat down on a bench under a tree. The war had left its mark on the landscape here, as in most other public parks. The well-trodden grass had been turned into trenches and allotments for vegetable-growing, the park railings had fallen

131

victim to the government's scrap-metal collection campaign and gone into the melting pot to be made into aeroplanes, and autumn seemed to have come early for some of the trees that had been stripped bare of their foliage by the bomb blasts, their leaves rotting on the ground.

But sitting here in the sunshine as Evie slept in her pram beneath the tasselled canopy, Nancy was transported back to another summer, long ago. Its sweet essence washed over her, soothing and comforting her; she could hear the laughter, smell the lilac in the early evening, feel the excitement of the back row of the cinema opposite, and remember the overwhelming feelings she had experienced then. The happiness had been ecstatic, the sadness intense. She'd been fifteen years old and in love. But she knew she could never go back. That chapter of her life was over.

Yet this place gave her inner strength. When the dark times edged in, she chased them out and let the joyous recollections calm her and give her the courage to face the problems of the present.

She thought of poor Leslie and how stricken with grief he'd been on hearing about the death of his parents, particularly his mother. He'd cried himself to sleep in her arms that night at the boarding house. But at least now he was home, and had the support of his family on hand. Bringing him back to London had been an impulsive decision on her part, but she knew it was the right one.

Something that had helped him enormously was the return from the country of some of the other children in the neighbourhood. People had risked bringing them home as there was currently a lull in the bombing, so he had pals to play with and had returned to his old school.

He hadn't quite lost the blinking habit inflicted on him by the Farleys' imprisonment of him in the coal shed, and he still cried for his mother when he thought no one could hear. There was no way of knowing how deeply the bad evacuation had affected him. Maybe he was young enough to put it behind him with no later repercussions. Kids were said to be very resilient.

Nancy's own grief for her mother was still all-consuming. It felt as though the heart had been plucked from the family. But somehow they had to carry on, take good care of Evie and do their best to give her the happy childhood she would have had if Mum was still around.

Before her mother's death, Nancy's sense of adventure had often been aroused by the persuasive recruitment posters for the ATS. Now she knew she must put all thoughts of going into the services out of her mind, because her duty lay at home.

Meanwhile, there was a job that must be done which Nancy hadn't yet been able to face. The surprise announcement on the wireless that new clothes were now rationed, and that people must use their margarine coupons to buy them until special ration cards had been printed, was just the incentive she needed to get on and do it.

Evie began to emit the little grunting noises which usually developed into full-blown shrieks.

'Come on then, little one,' Nancy cooed. 'Let's take you home and give you a bottle.'

The motion of the pram quietened the baby and by the time Nancy had wheeled her across the park and on to the road, she was fast asleep.

'Nancy,' came Jean's strident tones from downstairs, later that same afternoon. 'The baby's crying.'

Nancy went to the door of her mother's bedroom and called down. 'She can't need feeding because I've just given her a bottle.'

'Why is she yelling then?'

'Have you checked her nappy?'

'Ugh, no. I'm not doing that.'

'You'll have to, because I'm busy.'

'Doing what?'

'Getting Mum's clothes ready to give to the Women's Voluntary Service.'

'Shall I take Evie along to Gran's then, if you can't come down and see to her?'

'No, certainly not! On a Sunday afternoon Gran deserves a rest and we make sure she isn't disturbed,' Nancy reminded her. 'You know the system.'

'You'll have to come down and see to her, then. I can't change her nappy. You know it makes me queasy.'

'Tie a handkerchief over your nose if it upsets you,' Nancy suggested.

'I still won't be able to deal with it. I can't bear anything like that.'

Nancy sighed heavily. Sorting through her mother's clothes was distressing enough without having to stop before

134

she'd properly begun. Besides, Jean must get used to handling Evie. She needed to gain confidence.

'She's a little baby who is reliant on us for everything, including keeping her clean and comfortable, so get on and change her nappy,' she called down. 'You're an adult, for heaven's sake. It's a perfectly natural thing.'

'Why do you have to do Mum's clothes now?'

'Because clothes rationing has started and there are people at the rest centres who are desperate for clothing because they've been bombed out and lost all their own things. Mum would want us to make good use of her clothes in these hard times.'

'Yeah, I s'pose so.'

'If you really can't find out what's the matter with Evie, I'll come down and see to her, but try the nappy first.'

All was silent downstairs. Then, 'Oh, it's all right. She hasn't filled her nappy. I've picked her up and she smells sweet. I think she just wants a cuddle.'

'I'm sure that isn't beyond you.'

'I think I might be able to manage that, but you'll have to come down if she won't stop. I can't cope with that screaming she does when she goes all red in the face.'

'All right,' agreed Nancy. 'I'll come down if you can't pacify her.'

Nancy went back into the bedroom and closed the door. One by one she took the clothes out of the ancient mahogany wardrobe, removed them from the hangers and laid them on the bed. That did it. The sight of the empty wardrobe was too much to bear. It seemed to be a ghastly symbol of the

135

emptiness her mother had left in all their lives, and she sat on the edge of the bed and wept.

Eventually managing to calm herself, she wiped her eyes, blew her nose and forced herself to continue, realising that she hadn't checked the pockets. It wouldn't be fair to leave the job of clearing out old bus tickets and sweet wrappers to the WVS. They had more than enough to do in their charitable works.

As it turned out, it was fortunate that she did check, because there was an envelope in the pocket of Mum's maroon winter coat, which was on the top of the pile. Probably a letter from Leslie, Nancy thought absently. Opening it, she stared, reeling from the contents. It was more of a note than a letter, but passionate nonetheless.

'My darling Lily,' it began. 'There are no words to describe how much you mean to me. You light up my life and I love you so much. You're everything to me.'

Shaken to the core, Nancy tried to gather her scrambled thoughts. It must be from Evie's father. Her mother had said he used to write her little love notes. With her heart banging against her ribs, Nancy moved her gaze down to the bottom of the letter, which was signed, 'Your ever-loving Blue.'

Blue? What sort of an idiot called themselves that? she asked herself, instinctively hostile towards the man who had cost her mother her life. She supposed it must have been a pet name between them. Whoever he was, it gave her a very strange feeling to be reminded in black and white of the fact that her mother had had a lover.

The door opened and Leslie stood in the doorway.

'What's for tea, Nance?' he enquired.

'Whatever I can find in the larder,' she told him, trying to sound normal. 'Probably bread and dripping or something like that. There's some fresh dripping from the meat we had at dinner-time in the bowl. And Gran will probably bring one of her wartime specials over – an eggless sponge cake.'

'Can I have a bit of bread while I'm waiting?' he asked. 'I'm starving.'

'As long as you go easy on it,' she told him. 'And be careful with the bread knife.'

'What's that you're holding?' he wanted to know. 'Is it a letter from Micky?'

'No, I'm afraid not. It's just an old shopping list I found in Mum's coat pocket,' she fibbed, wanting to spare his feelings. She put the letter safely out of sight in her blouse pocket. 'I'll throw all the rubbish away together when I come downstairs.'

'All right. I'm going out in the street to play when I've had a bit of bread.'

'OK. But don't go away.'

'You sound just like Mum,' he said wistfully. 'She always used to say that.'

'I must be doing something right then, mustn't I?' she smiled. 'Off you go, then.'

As soon as the door closed behind him, she took the letter out and reread it, her hands trembling slightly. She knew somehow that she would neither throw it away nor tell anyone about it. Mum had taken the identity of Evie's father to the grave with her, and this letter contained nothing to change that. A pet name could belong to anyone. There was no point in upsetting the others by showing them this.

She ought to tear it up or burn it, of course. But some little part of her felt that it didn't seem right to destroy something that must have meant a lot to Mum for her to have taken the risk of keeping it.

Taking the letter into the bedroom next door, Nancy carefully placed it at the back of her own personal drawer in the dressing table she shared with Jean, concealed beneath her underwear. It would be safe from prying eyes there. Her underwear drawer was about the only area of privacy she had in this house.

Chapter Six

It was seven-thirty a.m. and Nancy had already been on duty for over an hour. She was busy with a broom and duster in one of the waiting rooms, having already met some early trains and dealt with passenger luggage, parcels and packages of fish. She was polishing the big wooden table and tidying the magazines when Ruby came in.

'I've come with a message from Percy,' she announced.

'Let me guess,' said Nancy waggishly. 'He's given us all the day off and is paying for us to go to the pictures.'

'Some hopes,' grinned Ruby. 'It's instructions, as usual. He wants us over at the goods depot immediately we've finished meeting the next train, which is ahead of schedule and will be here in a few minutes. Strict instructions from the big man himself to get over there sharpish. No hanging about.'

'What's all the rush?' wondered Nancy.

'Broccoli.'

'Ah, enough said.' Nancy nodded knowingly. 'But if the train is due at any minute I'll have to get my skates on here. I still haven't swept up or given the windows the once-over.'

'I'll do the floor while you get on with the windows, if you like,' offered Ruby, already grabbing the broom.

'Thanks, you're a pal.'

Leaving the waiting room shipshape a few minutes later, they went out on to the platform – where the train was just coming in – and began their duties by walking alongside the train calling out the name of the station, loudly and repeatedly so that no arriving passenger could possibly be in any doubt as to their whereabouts. They greeted the alighting masses politely, and assisted as many as possible to the exit with their luggage, whereupon they were buffeted by a stream of enquiries from the incoming crowd as to train times, platforms to go to and a host of other questions. A distressed woman who'd left something on a departed train was pacified by Nancy, who set the lengthy procedure in motion to organise a search. Finally the two porters hurried over to the goods sheds where there was crate upon crate of the Great Western's best known special goods traffic: broccoli.

The vegetable came from Cornwall to the capital in special high-speed trains, allowing Londoners to obtain fresh produce quickly. An army of porters – a high proportion of them women, the rest mature men – were busy sorting it and loading it on to hand-held two-wheeled trolleys and pushing it out to the waiting trucks and carts for distribution. Nancy and Ruby didn't waste any time in joining the ranks and getting busy.

With the broccoli safely on its way, there were sacks of cabbages and potatoes to be dealt with. Immediately the job was finished, Nancy and Ruby were needed back on platform duty with barely a chance to take a breath.

Around mid-morning, Percy came over and said unexpectedly, 'You two had better take a tea break now. I reckon you've earned a breather.' He gave them a hard look and wagged his finger. 'Ten minutes, mind. Don't go taking liberties.'

'As if we'd do a thing like that,' grinned Nancy.

'Enough of your cheek, Miss Sparrow.' His manner was as bossy as ever, but contained a hint of cordiality.

'He's in a good mood today,' observed Ruby on the way to the staff canteen. 'He's almost human sometimes lately. I wonder why.'

'Possibly because he's had to accept the fact that times have changed and women are a part of the team, now that we outnumber the men,' suggested Nancy. 'It's probably a question of if you can't beat 'em, join 'em.'

'Or it could be that he's less horrible to you since you saved his life, and anyone who happens to be working with you gets the same treatment.'

'You'd better stick with me then, kid. Just in case that is the reason,' laughed Nancy.

Whilst Percy still found it necessary to make his authority known on every possible occasion, Nancy had noticed a definite lessening of his megalomania since his brush with mortality. So some good had come of it.

When they were finally settled at a table in the canteen with a mug of tea each, Ruby emitted a grateful sigh. 'Ooh, isn't it a treat to get off your feet for a bit?' she said. 'I'm shattered already, and feel as if I need to go home to bed.'

141

'Fat chance of that. You've a long way to go until the end of the shift.'

'Don't remind me,' she said, yawning.

'You'll probably liven up after a break,' suggested Nancy, rather absently because she had other things on her mind. 'It usually does the trick.'

'I hope so or I'll be falling asleep on the platform.'

'Mm.'

'Is everything all right with you?' enquired Ruby. 'You seem a bit preoccupied.'

'I am, as it happens.' She made a face. 'My brother's going back off leave on Sunday. He's been home on embarkation leave, and is going overseas when he goes back.'

'Oh dear, the poor thing.'

'Ooh, don't let him hear you say that,' said Nancy. 'He looks on it as a big adventure.'

'He's in for a shock then, from what I've heard.'

'He knows it'll be tough, but he's still dead keen,' Nancy told her. 'You know what some men are like about proving themselves and doing their bit for their country. He's dying to show what he's made of, and full of patriotism and talk about fighting for freedom.'

'Where will he be going?'

'He doesn't know yet. He thinks he probably won't find out until he's actually on the way. Everything is so hush-hush in the military.'

'It has to be, I suppose,' remarked Ruby. 'They wouldn't want the enemy to find out the movements of our troops in advance, would they?'

'True enough. Anyway, we're having a bit of a knees-up at our local pub on Saturday night,' she mentioned chattily. 'To give him a good send-off.'

'A party for him to remember, eh?'

'That's the plan. It'll be a long time before he gets any more home leave.'

'That's for sure.'

'I hate the thought of him being out there fighting,' confessed Nancy, her brow creasing into a frown. 'I'll just have to toughen up after he's gone. Meanwhile, I'm going to make sure he lets his hair down on Saturday night.' She was determinedly cheery. 'It won't be anything posh, just a few drinks with family and friends. With everyone together, there's bound to be plenty of laughs to send him on his way.'

'What about Evie and Leslie?' Ruby enquired, by way of conversation. 'Are you having someone in to sit with them?'

'No, we'll do it between us.'

'It's a shame you can't all be at the pub together.'

'Mm. Still, as long as we all get there at some point to wish Micky well, that's the main thing.' Nancy cradled her mug in her hands and looked at Ruby over the rim. 'I expect they'll get me on the piano. They usually do at these things.'

Ruby seemed to be mulling something over. 'Why don't I come and sit with the children so that you can all go together?' she blurted out.

Nancy looked at her. 'I can't ask you to do that.'

'You're not asking. I'm offering.'

'It's very nice of you, but . . .'

'I could cycle over to your place. I've got some batteries

143

for my lights.' She was full of it but stopped suddenly and made a face. 'But hark at me, organising everything when you might prefer that I didn't do the babysitting. I realise that Evie is still quite little to be left with a stranger.'

Remembering how caring and competent she'd been with Evie on a previous occasion, Nancy said, 'You're not a stranger. I didn't hesitate because I don't trust you with her; it's just that it seems a bit of an imposition.'

'Not at all. I wouldn't have offered if I didn't want to do it. You know me well enough to know that.'

'I do, yeah.' She gave a wry grin. 'But if you're sure . . .'

'I am, so that's settled then.' She was obviously delighted. 'Shall I get there about eight o'clock?'

'Perfect.' Nancy noticed something out of the corner of her eye. 'Uh oh. Percy's just poked his head around the door, so we'd better get back on duty. I don't think the improvement in his attitude runs to extended tea breaks.'

'I don't think anything would make him agree to that,' smiled Ruby. 'Not even if you saved his life three times over.'

Later in the day, Nancy casually mentioned the babysitting arrangement to Polly.

'You're getting very pally with Ruby, aren't you?' was Polly's response.

'She does seem to be a bit more sociable lately,' replied Nancy.

'Only with you. She's still stand-offish with the rest of us,' Polly pointed out.

'It's funny, that.'

'Downright rude, I call it. She's a moody cow. I don't know how you put up with her.' Polly had tried to ignore Ruby's rudeness but it had finally proved too much.

'I don't have any trouble with her now,' explained Nancy. 'She's still not all that easy to talk to, though. Doesn't open up much. But she's all right at heart.'

'She'd better be, as you're going to trust her with your little sister on Saturday night.'

'Evie will be fine with Ruby.'

'You sound very sure.'

'I am. I wouldn't let her do it if I wasn't.'

Nancy didn't know Ruby all that well, but she did know she was right about that. For some reason, Ruby had really taken to Evie, and Nancy was grateful for all the help she could get.

As the beer shortage worsened, the Rook and Raven sometimes had an advantage over the other pubs in the area. Wilf's dodgy contacts meant he could occasionally get hold of booze through the back door, and always made a special effort to do so when they had a particular event on at the pub. Word soon got round among the punters if a pub had stock, and when it did they came from further afield.

So, what with all the extra locals who'd come to wish Micky a cheery farewell, and thirsty strangers from other parts of the borough, the saloon bar of the Rook and Raven was bulging at the seams on Saturday night.

Jean had even forgone her Saturday night at the Palais in favour of the celebration, and the family were all sitting together in a group with some friends and neighbours and a couple of Micky's local mates who happened to be home on leave too. The evening was well underway and everyone was feeling merry. Micky was full of fun and laughter, seemingly undaunted by the 'adventure' that lay ahead of him.

'I hope you realise that I've missed a night's dancing for my kid brother,' Jean said to him in fun. For all her self-centred nature, she was actually very fond of Micky. 'I could have met the man of my dreams tonight.'

'You might yet,' he suggested.

She rolled her eyes and tutted. 'What? In here, with the family cramping my style? Don't make me laugh.'

'You never know,' encouraged her grandmother. 'You find love where you least expect it. Isn't that what they say?'

'Some idiots might say it, but they're talking a load of rubbish,' was her answer to that. 'If it was as easy as that, they wouldn't have invented dance halls, would they?' She cast her eye around the room. 'Anyway, the men in here who are anywhere near my generation I've known all my life and couldn't fancy if you paid me, and all the others are on their last legs.'

'Bloomin' cheek,' admonished Uncle Wilf.

'Oh, you know I didn't mean you, Unc,' said Jean, grinning at him. 'I meant . . .'

'I know what you meant and I'll let you off this time.' He was too used to her lack of tact to be offended.

'The Palais is the place to meet eligible men,' she went on.

'I've saved some bloke from your clutches tonight, then,'

grinned Micky. 'If it hadn't been for me you'd have been there on the prowl for someone to get your hooks into. So I've done my bit for my fellow men.'

'Oi! Don't get saucy just because you're going away,' she admonished, slapping him lightly.

Wilf went over to the bar and managed to achieve silence by means of the last-orders bell. 'Listen up, everyone,' he shouted. 'I know a lot of you are here to wish young Micky well overseas, so can I ask you to raise your glasses to him?'

Up went the glasses against a background of rousing cheers and goodwill messages.

'I think it's about time we had some music,' Wilf continued when the noise had finally subsided. 'So will you do the honours, Nancy?'

'Course I will,' she said, and made her way over to the piano.

As she settled down to play, Wilf went back to join the family. The landlord allowed him leeway when there was a family party in. Wilf more than earned his wages here, and was a very useful man to know.

As Nancy began her repertoire with 'We'll Meet Again' and the singing began, two soldiers came into the pub – one with his arm strapped up and in a sling – and went to the bar.

'Any chance of a drink?' the wounded soldier asked the landlord, producing a pint pot, since glasses were in such short supply you often couldn't get served unless you brought your own. 'Or do you only serve regulars?'

'I'm happy to serve you any time, mate.' Soldiers were

welcomed everywhere, especially wounded ones. 'What will you have?'

'Bitter if you've got it, please.'

'Coming up.' He winked. 'I might even be able to find a drop of Scotch for a couple of lads in uniform.'

'Bitter will be fine for us,' said the soldier, getting some money out of his pocket with his free hand and putting it on the counter. 'Save the whisky for your regulars.'

The landlord served them and went to attend to someone else.

'Not a bad little pub this, Bobby,' said the other soldier, whose name was Frank. 'It was worth making the effort to come.'

'When there's a sign saying, "No beer," on the door of your own local you have to use your savvy and try somewhere else, don't you?' said Bobby Collins, his dark eyes smiling. 'We'd die of thirst otherwise.'

'And I couldn't let that happen, seeing as you took the trouble to come over to see me.'

'No trouble, mate. I fancied a spot of company and heard you were home on leave, so hopped on the bus from Acton.'

'Glad you're still in the land of the living,' said Frank. 'I heard you were wounded.'

'It'll take more than a Jerry bullet in the shoulder to finish me off.'

'How long do you think you'll be on sick leave?'

'I'm not sure. I've already been home for a few weeks since being discharged from the military hospital,' Bobby explained.

'Very nice too.'

'The bullet did quite a lot of internal damage, apparently,' he went on. 'That's why they kept me in hospital so long, and why I haven't been signed off yet. But I'm on the mend now, that's the main thing.'

'Jammy bugger,' joked Frank, who was an old pal of Bobby's from Acton, now married and living in rooms with his wife in West Ealing, when he wasn't away in the army. 'A couple of months with your feet up; I could do with some of that.'

'You call *me* jammy! What about you?' Bobby returned laughingly. 'A cushy job in the stores down at Catterick. I wouldn't mind some of that.' They both knew he was only joshing, because Frank had been wounded at Dunkirk, and had had a home posting ever since.

'Come off it,' chortled Frank. 'Pen-pushing would drive you barmy. You're the sort of bloke who likes to be where the action is.'

'That's true, but Catterick's a lot more comfortable than the desert.'

'With a bit of luck they'll give you a home posting for a while when you go back,' suggested Frank.

'Maybe, we'll see.'

They lapsed into a comfortable silence, drinking their beer and listening to the music.

'Cor, take a look at the redhead on the joanna,' enthused Frank, peering through the crowd. 'I wouldn't mind coming up against her in combat, would you?'

Bobby shifted his position so that he could see through

the gap in the crowd and took a good look . . . and looked and looked some more. He couldn't believe his eyes. The woman looked just like a girl he'd once known. Or was it just wishful thinking because he'd wondered so often about her and what she would be like now? This was her neck of the woods, or had been when he'd known her, so it was possible. But it was a long time ago. She'd been just a kid when he'd last seen her.

If it was her, that pretty slip of a girl who had captured his heart and subsequently broken it had grown into a beautiful woman. He couldn't take his eyes off her, and was hoping she would turn so that he could see her full face. Only her profile was in view but then suddenly he knew that it *was* her. It was all there in the lovely hair and the way she held her head.

'What's up, mate?' asked Frank. 'You look as though you've seen a ghost.'

'I feel as though I have . . . in a manner of speaking,' he muttered absently.

'It isn't like you to be lost for words when you see a nice bit o' skirt,' remarked Frank jokingly. 'You'd better watch yourself, mate. Once you stop enthusing over women, you could easily lose the will to live.'

'Oh, give it a rest,' said Bobby irritably.

'Ooer. What's rattled your cage?' Frank wanted to know.

'Nothing,' fibbed Bobby. 'Nothing at all.'

Over at the piano, Nancy – who was looking stunning this evening, having managed to tease some lipstick out of an almost empty Max Factor tube, and found a few drops of Drene shampoo with which to wash her hair – was enjoying herself enormously. When she was playing the piano and singing she could forget the awful things that had happened and the fact that her brother was going away to face unimaginable danger. The sound of the singing uplifted her and she hoped the memory of it would do the same for Micky when he was in a foreign field somewhere. Meanwhile, she had to go to the ladies, so would have a break at the end of this number.

Making her excuses and saying she'd be back in a minute, she slipped off the stool and headed across the pub.

'Hello, Nancy,' said a man's voice.

Looking up, she found herself staring into the eyes that had filled her thoughts and dreams as a young girl. She studied the once-familiar face, the square jawline, the firm, well-shaped mouth and the neck thickened into manhood since she'd last seen him. His appearance had changed completely, but she could still see something of the boy she'd known. It was all there in his brilliant dark eyes.

'Hello, Bobby,' she mouthed, her voice ragged with shock.

'It really is you, isn't it?' he said. Even his voice sounded different. It had been light and youthful when she'd known him. Now it was deep and gravelly.

'Yes, Bobby, it really is me,' she said through dry lips. Her insides were all of a tremble.

'You've changed so much I wasn't sure at first.'

'Same here,' she said, studying his face. 'We've both done a lot of growing up.'

151

'So . . . how have you been?'

'Fine.' She looked towards his sling. 'The same can't be said for you, though.'

'A bit of a skirmish out in the desert,' he explained, 'but I'm getting better now.'

'I'm glad to hear it.' She struggled to sound normal but it wasn't easy. 'So, what brings you to these parts?'

He grinned in the saucy way she remembered so well. 'Beer is the short answer to that,' he told her. 'I'm visiting a mate in the area. His local pub is dry and we heard that this one had something to sell.'

'That's Uncle Wilf's doing,' Nancy explained. 'He can sometimes get stuff, no questions asked.'

'Good old Uncle Wilf, I say.'

'Are you still living in Acton?' she asked.

Bobby nodded. 'I'm staying with Mum at the moment, though,' he explained. 'My flat was bombed and as I'm away most of the time it isn't worth looking for somewhere else until after the war.'

'I doubt you'd find anything, anyway.'

'Exactly. Anyway, it's company for Mum when I'm on leave, now that she's on her own,' he went on. 'Dad died recently. I help her with the business when I'm home, too. She needs me now that Dad isn't around.'

'Sorry to hear about your father,' she said. 'I know how it feels. I lost both my parents.'

'That's tough.'

'Yes. We were all gutted. I don't think we'll ever stop missing Mum in particular.'

'I know what you mean.'

Tension drew tight between them. They were strangers now. How could it be otherwise when they were totally different people? The adolescents they had been when they'd last set eyes on each other had gone and been replaced by full-grown adults. Nancy was imbued with a plethora of emotions: guilt aplenty, pain and sadness, but there was also a great sense of joy and excitement at seeing him again.

'Will you be going back overseas?'

'Eventually, I'm sure to, I should think, though they'll probably give me a home posting for a while.'

'That'll please your mum.' She was rapidly running out of small talk and her legs were shaking. Escape was vital. 'Well, I must go now or they'll be shouting for me to get back to the piano,' she said, forcing a casual tone. 'I'm just on my way to powder my nose.'

He nodded.

'I hope your wound gets better soon and good luck when you go back on duty.'

'Thanks.'

'Ta-ta then.'

'Ta-ta, Nancy.'

In the ladies' cloakroom, Nancy felt so weak from the encounter, she had to hold on to the sink. It was such a shock, seeing Bobby again after all these years.

'You all right, love?' asked a woman who was washing her hands.

'Yeah, I'll be all right in a minute, thanks.'

Nancy took some deep breaths in an effort to calm herself, mulling over the conversation with Bobby and recalling that he hadn't mentioned the one thing that must have been uppermost in his mind. She'd hurt him badly, and fate had dealt her a double blow, so they'd both had their share of suffering. Perhaps he'd left it unsaid because it had lost all importance with the passing of time. After all, he had been just a boy, and would have other things on his mind now. But from the way he'd spoken about living with his mother, Nancy had got the impression that he wasn't married.

She must put him out of her mind. She knew she couldn't go back; it was all too painful. Up until now she'd been able to remember the good times and blot out the bad. But seeing Bobby again had brought the whole thing back.

When she went back into the bar there was no sign of him, and that stabbed at her heart too. Taking a deep breath, she held her head up and went back to the piano.

'I don't understand why we've had to come out of a pub that has beer, before closing time,' said Frank to Bobby when they were outside. 'Where are we going now? You got another well-stocked hostelry in mind?'

'No. I think I'll call it a night if you don't mind, mate,' he told him.

'Surely you're not going home at this early hour?'

'That's right.'

'Are you not feeling too good?' asked Frank. 'Is your wound playing you up?'

'No, no. Nothing like that.' He shrugged. 'I'm just not in

the mood for a long boozing session so I think I'll walk down to the bus stop and get the bus back to Acton.'

'It's that redhead, innit?' speculated Frank. 'I saw you chatting her up when I was on my way back from the gents.' He laughed. 'She turned you down, didn't she? That's why you want to get away, because you don't like rejection.'

'It wasn't like that . . .'

'Blimey, Bobby, you don't usually have any trouble getting women,' joshed his pal. 'You must be losing the magic Collins touch.'

'She's just someone I knew a long time ago,' he explained. 'I wasn't trying it on.'

'Yeah, yeah. We all say that when they turn us down,' guffawed Frank, who was a bit of a flirt even though he was happily married. 'I think I'll go back in there and have a go at her myself. See if I can do any better.'

Bobby turned to him and, with his good arm, grabbed hold of him. 'You stay away from her, do you hear,' he commanded, putting his face close to Frank's. 'She's not the sort for a bit of fun in a back alley. She's a decent girl. So leave her alone.'

'All right, all right,' protested Frank. 'There's no need to blow your top. I was only kidding.'

'You'd better have been, too,' Bobby warned gravely.

'You're in early, son,' observed Mabel Collins, looking up from the paperwork she was doing at the table as Bobby walked into the living room.

'Yeah, I fancied an early night.'

155

'Well, well, that isn't like you, wounded or not.' His mother was a woman of diminutive proportions, with small, sharp features and shrewd dark eyes, the hair that had once been black now heavily streaked with grey and taken back off her face. 'You're usually the life and soul of the party and the last one to leave.'

'I wasn't in the mood tonight.' He squinted at her with concern. 'You shouldn't be working at this time of night, Ma. It isn't good for you.'

'You know me, I like to keep everything up to date,' she reminded him. 'And we're so busy lately I never seem to get the chance to do it during the day. The war has given employment and money to the people, it's true, but there are still plenty struggling to manage. Women losing their husbands and trying to bring their kids up on their own on a pittance. Soldiers' wives trying to manage on the little they're paid. It's a good job there are people like us around. At least they can get something to tide them over.'

'There'll always be people who need pawnshops, Ma, whatever the state of the economy.' He went over and put his hand on her shoulder. 'But stop changing the subject. Go and sit down. I'll deal with the rest of the paperwork tomorrow.'

'You're not supposed to be working when you're on the sick list.'

'It's only my left hand that's out of use, remember,' he stressed. 'I'm not completely useless.'

'Far from it,' she was swift to point out, 'but you are on sick leave and supposed to be taking it easy. You must give your wounds time to heal properly. There's a lot of damage inside, remember.'

'I've done enough sitting about lately to last me a lifetime,' he told her. 'I like to be involved in things, you know that, whether it's being in the army or working downstairs in the shop.'

'Yeah, I know, son, but I've almost finished here. Another few minutes is all I need. So let me get on and do it without nagging me, will you?'

'All right. Fair enough.'

He put his cap on the sideboard and eased himself into an armchair — somewhat awkwardly — with his free hand. The Victorian-built pawnshop was in Acton High Street and had been in the Collins family for generations. Bobby had grown up in this flat above the shop, which was on two floors and had high ceilings, sash windows and a yard at the back. The smallest bedroom upstairs was used for the storage of pawns overnight to protect them from burglary while the family slept. The Collinses took their responsibilities very seriously, were scrupulously fair and totally discreet. Pawnbroking was the only employment Bobby knew apart from being a soldier.

'Fancy a cup o' cocoa?' his mother asked a few minutes later as she cleared the paperwork away.

No reply.

'Bobby . . .'

'Sorry, Ma. Were you saying something?'

'What is the matter with you tonight?' she asked, tutting. 'You come home early looking as though you're about to face a firing squad tomorrow, and are sitting there miles away. Are you not feeling too good?'

'I'm fine.'

'It must be woman trouble, then.'

'No, no. Nothing like that. There's nothing wrong with me, really.'

'It's time you had a wife . . .'

'Oh no, not that again, Ma.'

'You're twenty-five, Bobby,' she persisted. 'You need a good woman to look out for you. It isn't as if you've had any shortage of girlfriends.'

'None that I wanted to marry. I've never met anyone I've felt that strongly about.'

'If you're looking for perfection you won't find it, you know,' she warned. 'Because it just isn't there.'

'You know I'm not like that.'

'Yeah, I do,' she admitted, because her son took everyone at face value. His easy charm and natural wit made him a popular man wherever he went. 'I'm just being a mum. I want the best for you. I want you to have someone who really cares for you and isn't just after your share in the business. Besides, who else is going to provide me with grand-children?'

There was a brief pause before he said lightly, 'All in good time, Ma. Everything comes to those who wait.'

'I hope I don't have to wait too long.'

'What's the point in people getting married while this war is on? Couples can't be together with the men being away.'

'Plenty of people think there's every point,' she came back at him. 'Weddings have shot up since the war, apparently. I suppose they want to tie the knot while they can, just in case anything happens and they don't get the chance.'

'If you say so,' Bobby said patiently.

'Of course, they can't have all the trimmings these days,' she went on, undeterred by his lack of interest in the subject. 'No fancy wedding dresses. And iced cakes are banned, so people have to borrow a cardboard wedding cake cover from a baker's shop for the photographs. But it still doesn't put them off.'

'Well, I'm not about to join them, so you won't have to save your clothing coupons for a new outfit.' He grinned at her. 'Besides, what would you do without me around the place?'

'I manage while you're away in the army,' she reminded him in a jovial tone. 'You'll be moving into your own place again after the war anyway. Be nice for you to have someone to share it with.'

'Stop your nagging and come and sit down,' he reproached affectionately.

'I'll make the cocoa first.'

As his mother disappeared into the kitchen, Bobby's thoughts drifted back to the meeting with Nancy, and he reflected on the fact that she still had the gentle, expressive eyes he remembered so well. They used to change from corn-flower blue to pools of sunshine when she was excited or especially happy. It was an odd feeling to see someone you'd been very close to after so many years, especially when that

159

person had changed so much physically that she was only recognisable by a few noticeable features. She'd been lovely as a girl; she was even more beautiful as a woman.

He was shocked to find himself so deeply affected by the meeting. It had, after all, been a long time ago. He thought about the questions that had been left unasked by him and wondered why. Probably because the meeting had been so unexpected and brief that he hadn't had the chance to gather his wits. Or could it have been because he'd known that pain lay along that route?

It was a crazy idea, but he wanted to see her again; knew he *had* to see her again even after everything that had happened. The meeting hadn't been too short for him to observe that she wasn't wearing a wedding ring. There were things he *had* to know.

An inner voice warned him, 'Don't go down that road, leave it in the past where it belongs. Put Nancy Sparrow out of your mind.' It didn't seem so easy now that he'd seen her, though. Not easy at all.

Jean was in a chatty mood when she and Nancy finally got to bed that night.

'Quite a good night, wasn't it?' she remarked.

'I enjoyed it. Glad to hear that you did too. Was it worth missing the Palais for?'

'Ooh, I wouldn't go so far as to say that,' she said with a smile in her voice. 'But I'm glad I was there, because Micky is my brother and he's going away to the war. You have to put yourself out sometimes, don't you?'

There was hope for Jean yet, thought Nancy, but said, 'He had a good time, that's the main thing.' She yawned. 'Anyway, I think I'll go to sleep now.'

'Oh and by the way,' said her relentless sister, 'I meant to ask you earlier. Who was that absolutely gorgeous soldier you were talking to?'

'Just someone I used to know,' she said with feigned indifference. Jean wouldn't recognise him as a man. She'd been just a little girl when the boy Bobby had been around.

'Looked to me as though you were well in with him,' Jean went on. 'He seemed very smitten.'

'Don't be so ridiculous.'

'Ridiculous nothing,' she persisted. 'He couldn't take his eyes off you.'

'You and your imagination.'

'I wasn't imagining things,' she said. 'So spill the beans.'

'There are none to spill.'

'Did he ask you out?'

'No, he didn't. It isn't that sort of thing. I've just told you, he's just someone I used to know.'

'Married, is he?'

'Not that I know of.'

'How could you have missed out on a chance like that, then?' She just wouldn't give up.

'For goodness sake stop rabbiting and go to sleep,' snapped Nancy.

'Ooer, the handsome soldier must really have got under your skin.'

Honestly, there was never so much as a grain of privacy

in this damned house, thought Nancy crossly, turning over and pulling the covers over her head.

'I'm going to sleep now, so will you please stop yattering,' she said.

'All right then, you old miseryguts. G'night.'

'G'night.'

Nancy lay awake listening to her sister gently snoring, and thinking about the meeting with Bobby. It was amazing the effect seeing him had had on her, considering that the whole episode had been so long ago. She felt different, sort of warm, alive, excited and full of hope. Just like when they'd been together. She *so* wanted to see him again, to be with him as before.

Then she remembered the pain and knew she never could be. It hurt too much. And while he was around it would never go away. With tears in her eyes, she resolved to put him out of her mind. It was almost dawn before she finally drifted off to sleep.

She was preparing the Sunday lunch the next day when she was thrown into turmoil once again. She answered a knock at the door to see Bobby standing there. Telling her grandmother she had to go out for a short time, she slipped out into the sunlit street and suggested they head for the park.

'I had to come,' he said as they sat down on the bench.

'Why?'

'Because there are things I need to know.'

She turned to him. All these years she'd tried to blot out the howling echoes of the past because it was too painful. But he had a right to know. So she must face up to it and tell him, then finally put it behind her.

'I lost the baby,' she informed him, swallowing hard on a lump in her throat, 'when I was seven months pregnant.'

'Oh, Nancy. I'm so sorry,' he said with genuine sorrow. 'All these years I've thought so much about it, wondering if it was a boy or girl, hoping he or she had gone to good people.'

'It was a little girl.' She just about managed not to break down.

'It must have been awful for you.'

'The worst time of my life,' she forced herself to go on. 'If our daughter had lived, I wouldn't have given her up for adoption as Mum and Dad had arranged. When I lost her, I knew I could never have gone through with it. I couldn't have let my own child go.' She gave a helpless little shrug, still managing to stay in control. 'Still, it's irrelevant now.'

He was quiet, looking solemn. 'Why did you shut me out?' he asked eventually. 'Why did you tell me you didn't love me any more and never wanted to see me again? I know your dad was putting pressure on you, but you could have stood up to him a bit more. You didn't have to cut me out of your life altogether. I told you I'd stand by you when you found out you were pregnant. Surely you trusted me to look after you?'

She fixed her eyes on her feet, her hands clasped tightly together on her lap as her heart ached at the memories.

'Before I got packed off to an aunt in Essex, where I was to stay until after the baby was born and taken for adoption, Dad told me that if I didn't finish with you in such a way that you would never try to contact me again, he would go to the police and have you done for underage sex with a fifteen-year-old girl. I couldn't let that happen. I had to protect you.'

'That was a wicked thing for him to do.'

'He thought he was doing the right thing for me, to save me from wrecking my life, as he saw it. I think Mum would have let me keep the baby, even though it would have brought shame on me and the family. But Dad just happened to be between ships and all hell was let loose.'

'You're telling me. He gave me a rollicking every time I came to the house trying to see you.' Bobby leaned forward, looking into space. 'But I would have coped with whatever charges he made against me. I'd rather that than be pushed out of your life the way I was.'

'What sort of person would I have been if I'd allowed your name to be dragged through the mud?'

'I'd have got through it.'

'It's easy to say that now, but you don't know how you would have felt.'

'It's impossible to know for sure, but I do remember wanting us to be together, no matter how tough it got. I was sixteen, already working in the family business and earning. We'd have got by.'

'It's all supposition, Bobby. Neither of us can know what we'd have been like together if our baby had lived.'

'We weren't given the chance to show what we were made of,' he said gravely.

'It's only natural my dad would want to protect his daughter from disgrace,' she said. 'Maybe I should have tried to find another way. But I was fifteen. Just a kid without any power.'

'Yeah, I know,' he sighed, leaning back with his arms spread along the top of the bench. 'Such times we had together, Nancy. We must have spent hours on this seat talking.'

'You always needed a sit-down after cycling down here from Acton,' she recalled.

'I must have had leg muscles of iron with all the cycling I did to see you.'

She smiled, looking back on it. She'd first met Bobby when his youth club at Acton had merged for the evening with the Ealing youth club she went to. He'd had a swagger about him even then and all her friends had fancied him. But he'd only had eyes for her, and she for him. They'd lived for each other that summer.

'We were so close back then,' she said.

'Besotted.'

'What a couple of daft kids we were,' she said. 'We're all grown up now; different people.'

'I wouldn't say that.'

She looked at him and saw something in his eyes that both thrilled and frightened her. Then all the sadness of the memories she'd just had to relive swept over her and her face crumpled.

'That's it, let it all out,' he said, putting a comforting arm around her while she sobbed. 'I'm sorry I wasn't there to help you through it.'

'It wasn't your fault.'

'Maybe I can make up for it now.'

'No, Bobby,' she said thickly. 'We can't go back. It's just too painful.'

'But I can't let you go again, Nancy.'

She pulled away and stood up. 'There's no future for us, Bobby,' she said, her eyes swollen from crying. 'What we had has gone. All that's left are sad memories. You've seen what it does to me when it's dragged up again, and while you're around the pain will never go away. Now that you know what happened, we can both put it behind us. We have to get on with our lives.'

'Oh, Nancy.'

'Please, Bobby. If you care for me at all, just leave me alone.'

He was very downcast. 'All right, Nancy,' he agreed with reluctance. 'I don't want to hurt you, so I won't try to see you again.'

Walking away from him was one of the hardest things she'd ever had to do. But she forced herself on, tears streaming down her cheeks.

Forcing himself not to go after her, Bobby stayed where he was on the bench, mulling things over. Hearing of the death of his child had hit him hard. It hurt him to think of Nancy suffering the loss on her own, too. Time had not changed his feelings for her. In fact, they were stronger than ever.

But he had to respect her wishes. He'd seen what the memories did to her, so he must do what she asked and leave her to get on with her life. As he walked to the bus stop, thinking about what might have been, he felt his heart was breaking all over again.

Chapter Seven

'I've got the most terrific news,' announced Jean one Sunday morning in March the following year, 1942. 'It's *so exciting*.'

'The most exciting news around here at the moment is that you've managed to drag yourself out of bed at last, just as Gran and I are serving out the dinner,' admonished Nancy, who was in the kitchen straining the greens over the sink while Gladys stirred the gravy.

'Oh, come off it, Nance. It's Sunday, so I'm entitled to a bit of a lie-in,' she protested, dressed in her old red woollen dressing-gown, her dark hair in curlers.

'A *bit* of a lie-in! That was more like a coma,' chortled her sister.

'You don't half exaggerate.'

'So, what's this exciting news, then?' asked Nancy.

'The Americans are in London and up the Palais,' she informed them with jubilation. 'We saw some of them there last night.'

'And you obviously liked what you saw.'

'Phew! I'll say I did. They're gorgeous,' she trilled. 'I've never seen fellas like them before in my life. Talk about good-looking. They're out of this world.'

'And you accuse *me* of exaggerating!'

'I'm not exaggerating about this, honest. You wait till you see them.'

'They're only human beings, Jean,' Nancy pointed out. 'They can't be that much different to other men.'

'The ones I saw were,' she stated categorically. 'They're so smart, too, in their beautiful uniforms. They look like film stars.' She picked up one of the roast potatoes that were sitting around a tiny piece of beef in the meat dish just removed from the oven, and ate it with her fingers, blowing on it to cool it down. 'Oh, and you should see them do the jitterbug. They're brilliant. Talk about light on their feet.'

'You've been watching too many American films, that's your trouble,' warned her grandmother.

'So what if I have?' Jean said lightly. 'America is a magic place, clean and bright with picket fences and plenty to eat. It isn't dark and gloomy like here.'

'It's only bright and pretty in the films. I don't suppose it's really like that,' Gladys pointed out. 'Not all of it, anyway.'

'I know what she means, though, Gran,' put in Nancy. 'I love watching American films, with all those lovely clothes and pretty houses.'

'Films are one thing, real life quite another,' reminded their down-to-earth grandmother.

And didn't Nancy know it. Real life was wanting to see

Bobby so much that it hurt, and feeling sad because he'd kept his word and not contacted her. Real life was an aching heart every time she thought about him. She was getting on with her life and trying not to think about him but, somehow, he was always there.

Now she said, 'Exactly, and I'm not about to go overboard about the GIs like this one.' She turned to Jean. 'So, how many of these amazing creatures did you dance with?'

'Er . . . none, actually.'

'Well, well. You must be slipping.'

Jean looked miffed at the suggestion. 'No, not at all,' she denied. 'There were only a few of them there and all the girls were after them. I didn't get close enough to show myself off properly.'

'Better luck next time,' said Nancy.

'I will have, don't worry.' She drew in her breath to emphasise her enthusiasm. 'They've got loads of money to splash around, apparently, because they get really good pay. And they're ever so friendly. I want one. Ooh, not half.'

'You watch yourself, my girl,' advised Gladys. 'That sort of attitude could get you into trouble.'

'Don't worry, Gran. There's too much competition for them for me to get a chance to misbehave at the moment.' She paused thoughtfully. 'But I've heard that there are more of them coming over to this country.'

'The place will be swarming with them soon enough,' said Gladys.

'The more the better, I say,' enthused the incorrigible Jean. 'They've got what it takes as far as I'm concerned, not to

171

mention the nylons, lipstick, perfume and chocolate you get if you go out with one.'

'You'll get yourself a bad name,' said Gladys. 'Nice girls don't go out with Americans.'

'This nice girl will if she gets half the chance.'

'They're only after one thing; everyone knows that,' said her grandmother. 'They're young and away from home and have girls queuing up to go out with them. What else can you expect?'

'Don't worry, Gran, I won't bring any trouble home.' She wouldn't be deterred. 'I'm really glad they're over here to brighten things up.'

'I am, too, as it happens,' said Nancy.

'Not you as well,' tutted Gladys. 'I thought you had more sense than to have your head turned by a fancy uniform and a bit of extra dosh.'

'I have,' she confirmed. 'I'm glad they're here because it's such a comfort to know that we have such a powerful country behind us in the war.'

'I don't think anyone will argue with you about that,' Gladys admitted. 'As long as everyone remembers that our boys are doing a good job too.'

The decision last December of the United States to come into the war, following the devastation wrought on Pearl Harbour by the Japanese, had boosted British morale in general. The national spirit had never been broken, not even during the worst days of the Blitz, but American involvement had definitely given people a new sense of optimism. There was a feeling now that the news from abroad might begin to improve. It had been grim lately, with the fall of Singapore last month and hundreds of thousands of British soldiers being taken prisoner.

Leslie appeared in the doorway, looking worried. 'Someone had better come quick. Evie's trying to cuddle the cat and he doesn't like it at all,' he announced. 'He's hissing and spitting at her.'

'Oh Leslie, you're supposed to be watching her while we put the dinner out,' rebuked Nancy, hurriedly setting down the colander on the wooden draining board and wiping her hands on a tea towel. 'That moggy is really going to go for her one of these days.'

'I only looked away for a second and she went crawling after him.'

Nancy left what she was doing and rushed into the other room, where Evie was sitting on the rug by the fireguard, staring at Smudge who had his back arched and his tail standing on end. As soon as he saw Nancy he took cover behind the sofa. Nancy scooped her little half-sister up into her arms.

'What are we going to do with you, eh? You're a real pain now that you can get around. Nothing's safe from you.' She lifted her in the air whereupon she erupted into chuckles. 'But we all love you to bits and you know it, you little horror.'

Indeed, Evie at ten months old was totally adorable. The image of her mother, with blue eyes and light ginger hair, she was bright, alert and a source of joy to the whole family.

'Hello, Pickle,' said Jean, making a face that made Evie

173

laugh even more. 'What have you been up to this time, eh? More mischief, I suppose.'

Nancy handed her to Jean and made a request. 'Can you put her in her high chair while I go and finish helping Gran in the kitchen?'

'Come on, Little Miss Trouble.' Jean was much more competent with Evie now that she was bigger and more responsive. 'It's time for your din-dins.'

During the meal there was a news bulletin on the wireless that mentioned German bombing in Malta and other foreign parts.

'Poor devils,' said Nancy, feeding Evie her mashed-up food.

'At least the Germans aren't giving us such a bad time here, for the moment, anyway,' said Jean, who was now dressed in a red jumper and skirt, her thick hair out of curlers and falling to her shoulders in curls.

The others nodded in agreement.

Indeed, since the end of the Blitz last May, there had been much less enemy activity over London. Rumours abounded, and there was talk of Hitler planning something big, as well as speculation about secret weapons. Londoners guessed they hadn't seen the last of the air raids, but enjoyed the quiet nights while they could.

'Good girl, Evie,' praised Nancy as the baby finished her food. 'You're such a little sweetheart.'

'She takes after her sweet-natured sister, Jean, don't you, darlin'?' said Jean in a baby voice. 'Pity you've inherited your mum's ginger hair.'

'She's got her mother's sweet nature as well as her pretty colouring.' Gladys looked at the clock on the mantelpiece. 'We're late with dinner today. I shall miss *The Brains Trust* if we don't get a move on.'

'You and your Professor Joad.' Jean was referring to the most well-known character in a popular radio programme in which a panel of academics answered questions on various topics and discussed them. 'You'll get to be an egghead if you listen to that too often.'

'Just because I'm not an educated woman it doesn't mean I don't have the brains to enjoy an intelligent programme. You're never too old to learn.'

'It's the first serious programme to attract a mass audience,' Nancy put in. 'I read about it in the paper. Some people I know at work tune in to it.'

'The strain of the air raids must have sent them soft in the head,' giggled Jean.

'It wouldn't do you any harm to listen to it,' suggested Gladys.

'The only question I want answering is when am I going to meet the Yank of my dreams who'll give me a taste of the good life,' she laughed.

'Talk about materialistic,' disapproved Nancy. 'You could win prizes for it.'

'Life is short. You have to get what you can out of it while you're still around to do so.'

'I'll go and get the rice pudding out of the oven if you've all finished your dinner,' was Gladys's way of changing the subject before things got too heated.

175

'I'll clear the dinner plates,' offered Nancy, rising. 'Keep Evie amused, will you please, Jean?'

She nodded.

Gladys had just sat down and was about to serve out the rice pudding when there was an unexpected noise in the hall – the sound of the front door opening and closing. Someone had come in.

'Who's that?' Nancy was somewhat wary because neighbours always knocked, even though the key was on a string behind the letterbox, and Uncle Wilf used the back door.

No reply, just the sound of footsteps plodding up the hall. They all stared at the door, waiting. It opened and an emaciated man with a deeply tanned, weather-beaten face appeared in the doorway.

There was a stunned silence.

'Well, aren't you going to say hello to your old dad?'

'This is a fine sort of a homecoming, isn't it?' he said a few moments later, when they were all still gaping at him in silence.

'It's so good to see you, Dad,' Nancy managed at last, going over to him and hugging him in rather a restrained way, since he'd never been demonstrative towards his children so she felt awkward. 'Welcome home.'

'Yeah,' added Jean, standing back.

'Hello, Dad,' said Leslie, staying close to Jean.

'That's more like it.' He was smiling, but sounded very weak and breathless.

'You nearly gave us all a heart attack.' Gladys recovered

sufficiently to throw her arms around him and smack a kiss on his cheek. 'We thought you were dead.' She drew back and studied him closely. 'By God, Arthur, you look as though you almost are. You've altered so much it's a wonder we recognised you. Sit down before you fall down.'

'I've lost a bit of weight, that's all,' he said, easing himself into an armchair.

'You look terrible,' Gladys blurted out.

'I haven't been too good, as it happens.' He pointed to his chest. 'Damaged my lungs.'

'What's been happening to you, Dad?' asked Nancy. 'We had official notification that you were lost at sea.'

'I was . . . in a manner of speaking,' he puffed. 'It's a long story.'

'Let's get you something to eat and drink and you can tell us all about it,' suggested Gladys.

Arthur looked at his two younger children. 'I won't bite, you know,' he said.

Jean went over and gave him a dutiful hug, followed by Leslie, who rather uncertainly shook his hand.

'You've grown a bit since I last saw you, boy.'

Leslie nodded shyly.

There was a sudden interruption as Evie decided it was time she had some attention and began banging her spoon on the tray of her high chair.

'Who's this? A new addition to the family?' The question was a rhetorical one. 'Cor, you're a proper little smasher, aren't you, sweetheart?'

Evie sucked her spoon, sizing him up.

He looked at Nancy. 'So, you've made me a grandad at last then,' he presumed.

'Er . . . no, not exactly,' she said, fiddling with a stray lock of hair nervously.

'Ah, so the baby's yours then, Jean?' he said. 'You beat your big sister to it.'

No one knew what to say.

'Well, don't be coy, Jean,' he coaxed. 'You're a grown woman. You're entitled to get married and have babies. Your bloke couldn't ask my permission if I wasn't here, could he? So I'm not going to give you earache about that.'

The silence was suffocating.

'What's up with you all?' He looked from Nancy to Jean in an enquiring manner. 'I hope it's all above board and you've got yourself properly hitched, whichever one of you it is.' He looked around the table. 'But first things first. Where's your mother? Upstairs?'

They didn't know how to tell him.

'No, Dad,' said Nancy at last through dry lips, her cheeks flaming. 'She isn't upstairs.'

'Just popped out to a neighbour's on some errand of mercy then, I suppose,' he speculated. 'Always was one to do a good turn, my Lily.'

Nancy and Gladys exchanged a look.

'Could you take Evie to your place for a little while, Gran, while I talk to Dad?' She moved her gaze to Jean. 'You and Leslie might as well go, too.'

Jean didn't need any second bidding. Such a difficult family situation was an anathema to her.

Leslie took a more practical view. 'But I haven't had my pudding,' he reminded them.

'You can have it at my place,' said Gladys, quickly taking Evie out of her chair. 'Bring the dish, will you please, Jean.'

'What's all this about?' Arthur enquired of Nancy as the others left with frantic haste. 'Why have they scarpered like that?'

'Because there's something you have to know, and I seem to have landed myself with the job of telling you,' she burst out. 'But . . . er, I'll make you a cup of tea first.'

'Forget the tea,' he demanded, frowning at her, his voice rising with anxiety. 'Just get on with whatever it is you have to say. Judging by the way you're all carrying on, it isn't good news.'

'So who's the father, then?' came the shocked enquiry when Arthur had recovered sufficiently to speak after the double blow that Nancy had just dealt him.

'We don't know,' she replied, feeling terrible. 'Mum wouldn't tell us.'

'Don't take me for a fool, Nancy,' he reproached. 'She must have told you.'

Nancy shook her head. Too tense to sit down, she was standing up near his armchair.

'You must know who he is,' her father persisted. 'You'd have seen him about the house if he'd got his feet that well under the table.'

'He never came here, Dad,' she explained. 'I know it might

be hard to believe, but we didn't even know she was seeing someone.'

'Come on, love. Don't mess me about. I might not be in the best of health, but I've still got my wits about me.'

'I'm telling the truth, Dad. When she went out of an evening we thought she was with her mates from work. We were all as flabbergasted as you are when she told us she was pregnant, and we begged her to tell us who the father was.' She looked into his thin, wrinkled face, observing the sunken cheeks and the pain in his dark eyes. His hair was thinner than she remembered, too. 'But she said that it was nobody we knew and that he was dead anyway so there was no point in naming him. He was married, apparently, that's why. She ended the affair as soon as she found out.'

'Gawd Almighty! What a thing to come home to, eh?' He was very shaky. 'My wife's dead and she died giving birth to some other bloke's bastard.'

'Don't call Evie that, Dad,' Nancy asked, her voice rising. 'I know you must be devastated, understandably so, but Evie is just an innocent victim.'

'If it wasn't for her your mother would still be alive today.'

'You can't blame Evie.'

'I don't. I blame your mother. If she'd not behaved like a tart, she'd be here now and we wouldn't be having this conversation. But that doesn't mean I have to think kindly of the child, innocent victim or not.' His face seemed to crumple and his eyes brimmed with tears. 'How could your mother do a thing like that? How could she?'

'I think she was lonely when you were away, Dad.' Nancy

tried to soften the blow. 'It wasn't that she didn't love you. She told me that she did, and I believed her.'

'She was too used to my being away to be lonely.' He looked hurt and bewildered. 'I was away at sea for most of our married life. She'd never known anything else.'

'I suppose it was easier for her before the war,' Nancy suggested, her hands tightly clasped in front of her. 'But things have been very hard for us here, especially during the Blitz. With bombs falling and everyone expecting a German invasion any day. Well ... people found comfort where they could.'

'Don't make excuses for her.'

'I'm just trying to make you realise how difficult it's been here in London, and why, perhaps, Mum behaved as she did.'

The stark reality of his bereavement was really beginning to hit home and his face was creased with pain. 'You talk about having it hard,' he said, his voice tight and cold. 'Do you think it's been a picnic for me?'

'Of course not.'

'Lost at sea,' he went on, his lean face working with anguish. 'I'll say I was lost at sea. I was in the water for days with my lungs giving me hell.'

'Oh Dad, how terrible. What happened?'

'When the ship was bombed I was hit in the chest by flying shrapnel which got into my lungs. The blast must have thrown me overboard, because the next thing I knew I was in the water. I thought I was a gonner, but my luck was in because I found some wreckage and managed to climb on to it. I'm beginning to think it would have been better if I'd gone down with the ship.'

'Please don't talk like that.'

'Well, after what I've just heard . . .'

'I know it must be terrible for you. Anyway,' she said, swiftly moving on before he drowned in self-pity, 'what happened after that? Did another ship pick you up?'

'No, I was eventually washed ashore on the coast of Australia, half dead from starvation and in agony from my wound. I was laid up for months in a hospital after an operation to remove the shrapnel. They got it out but the damage it did to my lungs is something I'll have to live with for the rest of my life.'

'Oh Dad, I'm so sorry.' She could have wept for him and moved forward to touch his hand.

'The staff at the hospital were marvellous,' he continued. 'I was looked after by nuns. A wonderful bunch of women.' He paused, looking sad. 'Maybe it would have been kinder if they'd left me to die, as things have turned out.'

'Dad, stop it, please,' she begged him. 'We've lost our mum and we thought we'd lost you too. I know you must be feeling wretched, but we're still your family, whatever Mum did. That sort of talk is hurtful to us.'

'I suppose so,' he sighed. 'Sorry, love.'

'Why did it take you so long to get home?' she wondered. 'It's been a year since we had that telegram from the shipping company.'

'As I've just said, I was in hospital for a long time and when I was finally discharged I couldn't get a ship,' he explained. 'I wasn't fit enough for work at sea so I wasn't much use to anyone, though I did what I could around the seamen's hostel to pay for my keep there.'

'So, how did you eventually get back?'

'The captain of a small ship took pity on me in the end,' he explained. 'I managed to convince him that I could work. By the time he realised that I couldn't do much more than a few light duties, we were on our way. Luckily for me, he didn't put me off at any of our ports of call on the way. He was a good bloke.'

'Did you never think to write to us, Dad?' Nancy asked. 'A note would have done. Just to let us know that you were alive.'

'I've never written a letter in my life, you know that,' he reminded her. 'Your mother and I had an understanding about it. She saw me when I turned up and didn't expect to hear from me in between. It was the way it always was between us and it worked.'

'Surely in wartime, with merchant seamen losing their lives every day, you could have made an exception,' said Nancy in mild admonition. 'It would have saved us a whole lot of worry and pain.'

'How was I to know you'd been told I was dead?'

'You must have guessed that the shipping company would presume that and notify us.'

'I was too busy trying to survive to give that side of it much thought, I suppose,' he admitted. 'It was wrong of me, I can see that now, and I'm sorry. It's just the way I am, and the only thing on my mind at the time was how I was going to get home. So give us a break and stop going on about it.'

'All right.' He'd always been such a strong, robust man, with broad shoulders, ruddy cheeks and a wide grin. Even though he'd never been a family man who'd involved himself with his children, it still broke Nancy's heart to see this sad shadow of the person he'd once been. He looked absolutely ghastly and had aged considerably. 'Anyway, despite every-thing, you're here now and that's the important thing.'

'Getting back home was all I lived for and thought about when I was in Australia.' He shook his head, sighing. 'Little did I know what I was going to come home to.' He leaned his elbows on his knees and put his head in his hands. 'I still can't believe what's happened.'

'It is hard to take in, I know,' she sympathised. 'I don't think I'll ever get used to it.'

He lapsed into silence for a while, then raised his head and asked, 'What's the kid doing here, anyway?'

'She lives here,' Nancy replied, worried by his tone.

'Why would she do that?' he demanded. 'She's got nothing to do with us.'

'She's our sister and Gran's granddaughter,' Nancy reminded him.

'But she's nothing to do with me, is she?' he stated harshly. 'Nothing whatsoever.'

'Well, technically, I suppose that's true.'

'There are no two ways about it.'

'She is the child of the woman you loved, though,' his daughter suggested hopefully.

184

'Turn the knife, why don't you?' he grunted.

'Sorry, I didn't mean . . . I was just—'

'I want nothing to do with her at all,' he cut in. '*Nothing!* Is that clear?'

There was nothing else for Nancy to do now but tell him the whole truth. She took a deep breath, bracing herself. 'Gran and I were with Mum when she died and she made us promise to bring little Evie up as one of the Sparrow family.' She moistened her dry lips with her tongue, dreading her next words, but knowing she had to say them. 'She asked us to name you as the father on the birth certificate.'

He stared at her in silence while it registered fully. His eyes were black with rage. '*How dare she do that? How dare she?* That's nothing short of fraud.'

'It isn't the first time that sort of thing has been done and I'm sure it won't be the last.' She could hear the lame ring to her words, and could understand his being upset.

'And that's supposed to make me feel better, is it?'

'No, of course not. I'm just trying to explain why Mum did it. She wanted to protect Evie. The child's father was dead, so who else would look after her but her siblings and her grandmother? Surely you wouldn't want to see her going into care?'

'I don't care what happens to her as long as she's out of my sight and my house,' he declared. 'I don't want to have to set eyes on that child *ever again.*'

'Please let her stay, Dad. It's what Mum wanted and what we want. This is her home.'

'Not any more, it isn't,' he pronounced. 'I won't have her in this house. Is that clear?'

'She's such a dear little girl and none of this is her fault.' Nancy was pleading with him now.

'She's your mother's bastard and a reminder of how my wife betrayed me.' He was adamant. 'So, for pity's sake, show some respect for my feelings and make sure I never have to see her again.'

'I can't promise to do that, Dad,' she told him frankly. 'She's my sister. I love her and I'll always be there for her. I'll never desert her. Never, ever! You must be able to understand that.'

'If that's the way you feel, you'd better take her and sling your hook because she isn't staying here. Take the others with you if they can't live without her.'

'What!'

'You heard.'

'You're throwing us out?'

'If you want to bring the child up, you're not doing it here, so that's what it amounts to.'

'And how exactly are we supposed to find somewhere to live when London is already overflowing with people who have lost their homes in the bombing?' she wanted to know.

'That's your problem, Nancy,' he replied, surprising her with his heartlessness. It was a side of his nature she'd never seen before. 'You want to bring her up, go ahead and do so. But you're not doing it in my house.'

'But Dad, she's just a little girl with a right to live,' she pointed out. 'She's no trouble, honestly. She sleeps through the night now. She's a very contented baby.'

'I don't care if she's the most well-behaved child in the whole of the British Isles, she's not staying here.' He gave Nancy a hard look. 'I mean it and that's my last word on the subject. I don't care what happens to her, but she is not staying here and that's that.'

'It's an understandable reaction, I suppose,' said Gladys, looking worried. 'The poor man has come home to find that his wife has died giving birth to another man's child. It must have been one hell of a shock for him, especially in his poor state of health. We can hardly expect him to welcome little Evie with open arms, can we?'

'No, of course not,' said Nancy. 'But I certainly didn't expect him to turn her out into the street and us along with her. I didn't think he could be that cruel.'

'Your dad isn't a cruel man,' Gladys told her. They were in her living room. Leslie had had his rice pudding and gone out to play, having been told that his father's reaction to Evie was a grown-up matter and nothing for him to worry his head about. Evie was having a nap in the bedroom. 'But he's been through a lot and this on top of everything else is bound to have an effect on the way he behaves.'

'I understand all that and I don't want to hurt Dad, but I'm not turning my back on Evie. I can't.' Nancy looked at Jean. 'How about you?'

'Course not.' She sounded much less certain about it than her sister. 'But it's going to be so difficult. I mean, where will we live? We'll never find anywhere around here. And it's hard enough to manage on our money as it is without having to pay more in rent.'

'You won't need to,' proclaimed Gladys. 'Evie moves in here with me and you kids stay where you are with your dad. Problem solved.'

'But . . . it's a lot for you, Gran, having Evie all the time,' Nancy pointed out.

'We'll have to see how it goes of course. But I have her during the day anyway and for longer when you're working late or going out.'

'It'll still be hard work for you.'

'The two of you can come in here to give me a break whenever you can,' she suggested. 'Your father can't object to that, since Evie won't be in his house.'

'I suppose it might work,' said Nancy, thinking it over.

'You can't move out of your dad's place, anyway,' Gladys went on thoughtfully. 'He'd sooner die than admit it, but he's going to need you there to see that he's all right. He's in a low state, both physically and mentally. Left alone he might let himself go, not eat properly and so on. Anyway, there's Leslie to be considered. Someone's got to look after him, haven't they?'

'Mm, there is that,' agreed Nancy. 'Well, if you're sure you don't mind, Gran, it does seem to be the only solution. We'll do everything we can to help, won't we, Jean?'

Considering the matter from her own perspective, as usual, Jean thought it was an excellent idea. As much as she loved Evie, she didn't enjoy the chores that came with her, changing her nappy, bathing her and so on, especially when she wanted to get ready to go out and Nancy was on late shift so wasn't there to be persuaded to take Jean's turn. With Evie living at Gran's place there would be much less of that and Jean could still see the baby whenever she wanted. It was the perfect solution. 'Oh yeah, we'll do our bit, Gran,' she said buoyantly. 'Then, when Dad goes back to sea, we can go back to normal.'

Gladys shook her head sagely. 'He probably hasn't even admitted it to himself yet, but I think your dad's sea-going days are over.'

'A railway porter! What sort of a job is that for a woman? Lugging heavy luggage about all day,' said Arthur to his brother-in-law Wilf.

'Needs must when the devil drives,' replied Wilf, leaning on the bar of the Rook and Raven and sipping his beer slowly to make it last. It was his night off and he was keeping Arthur company. 'The men are away so women have to do their work to keep the country running. We all have to do what we can in wartime, and the women are certainly doing their bit.'

'The doctor still hasn't signed me off,' said Arthur, who had now been home for a month and was sensitive about not being in employment. 'Or I'd be out there doing my bit to help.'

'I know that, Arthur.'

'The doctor reckons I won't ever be fit enough to go back to sea, though.'

189

'I can't say I'm surprised, with your injuries,' Wilf told him. 'Still, it's time you had some home comforts, what few of them there are around at the moment, with everything being so short.'

'A spot of leave is all right, but I don't want to be at home permanently,' Arthur told him. 'The sea is in my blood.'

'You'll just have to settle for something else.'

Arthur sighed. 'What a life, eh! Everything I valued has gone. My wife, and now my livelihood.'

'You'll get a job when you're fit enough,' encouraged Wilf. 'People are urgently needed for all sorts of occupations.'

Arthur stared moodily into space.

'Lily was very cut up about what happened, you know,' said Wilf.

'I expect she was when she found out that she was up the duff, especially at her age.'

'About being unfaithful to you, I mean,' he corrected. 'She was very ashamed.'

'She shouldn't have done the deed, then.'

'It's the war, mate.' Wilf tried to make him understand. 'Lily wouldn't have done something like that under normal circumstances. I was stunned when I heard about it. I had a right go at her. But she was my sister when all is said and done, so I stood by her. You don't turn your back on one of your own, do you?'

'My kids have done that to me, all except my Micky.'

'No, they haven't,' Wilf disagreed. 'They would never do that.'

'How come they're always down at their gran's with that nipper of Lily's, then, when they know how I feel about it?'

'Evie's their sister. It's natural they want to see her. Anyway, Nancy promised her mother she'd look out for her. You told them to get the child out of your house and they have done. It doesn't affect their feelings for you.'

'If they were loyal to me they'd want nothing to do with her,' Arthur said.

'You can't expect those kids to turn away from their little sister. That's just selfish.'

'And Lily wasn't being selfish when she found herself a fancy man . . .'

'So Lily was weak for once in her life,' said Wilf. 'That isn't your kids' fault and they shouldn't be made to pay for their mother's mistake.'

'Family life, eh?' sighed Arthur. 'I'm not cut out for it, not for any length of time, anyway. I'm certainly not used to it without Lily. I feel out of place in my own home.'

'You need to find some common ground with your children.' Wilf stared into his glass meditatively. 'Look, mate, what's done is done and nothing can change it. I can understand you're feeling bitter, but Evie exists and there's nothing you can do about that, either. If you can't beat 'em, join 'em, I say. Make an effort to get to know her and it'll bring you closer to your own kids. I know I'm biased because she's my niece, but she really is a joy to have around.'

Arthur looked grim. 'That's exactly my problem,' he said. 'She's your niece, Gladys's grandchild, and my children's sister.'

His voice rose. 'I'm the only one around here who has no blood tie with her.'

'It isn't that I'm not sympathetic, mate.' Wilf was doing his best to help. 'Any man would be gutted to come home to find what you did. But it happened and you've got to get used to it and get on with your life.' He paused, looking at him. 'The truth is, you're getting to be a right miserable git. You're always moaning. You'll end up having no mates at all if you don't cheer up.'

'Why do you bother with me then, if I'm such a pain in the arse?' asked Arthur.

'Because you're my brother-in-law . . .'

'We're not related now that Lily's gone, so you needn't feel obliged.'

'I was going to say that we've always been good mates as well as brothers-in-law.'

'Oh, right . . . sorry,' Arthur muttered.

'I should think so, too. Now finish that drop of beer in your glass and I'll see if I can get you another.' He threw him a look, his mouth turning up at the corners. 'But only on the condition that you promise not to bend my ear any more tonight about how badly life has treated you.'

'All right.' Arthur nodded miserably.

'A pint coming up, then,' grinned Wilf. 'With a bit o' luck.'

Chapter Eight

The National Wheatmeal Loaf was not greeted with enthusiasm by the public.

'Disgusting,' was Polly's considered opinion when she and her workmates were discussing the subject during their dinner break. 'It isn't even proper brown bread. It's mucky beige bordering on a dirty grey.'

'Foul,' added one of the others.

'Filthy stuff,' opined another, sipping her tea then drawing on a cigarette. 'It's so flippin' coarse you can hardly swallow it, and talk about indigestible. Ugh! I could still feel it when I went to bed last night after a sandwich at six o'clock.'

'I suppose we'll get used to it eventually, as there's no other bread on sale,' suggested Nancy.

'We'll have to, won't we? But Gawd knows what the Minister of Food will think of next,' tutted Polly. 'Dried eggs are bad enough, and margarine instead of butter, but taking white bread out of the shops and replacing it with this horrible dark stuff shows a definite sadistic streak.'

'It's been done to save grain imports and shipping space, so it's in a good cause,' came Nancy's cheery reminder.' And the politicians have to eat it as well, remember.'

'There is that, I suppose,' she conceded. 'It's just that everything we like is being taken away. There'll be nothing left to give us pleasure soon.'

'As long as they don't ban how's yer father,' grinned one of the group.

'They'd ban that if they thought it would help the war effort,' said someone else. 'But there's more of it about than ever according to the *Woman's Own*. Some women are getting up to all sorts of mischief while their nearest and dearest is away fighting the war, apparently.'

'That's not right, is it?' Polly was fiercely disapproving. 'Not while your old man's fighting for his country. I'm no prude, but I draw the line at that.'

'We're all only human,' said Nancy, with her mother in mind. 'People get lonely and drift into things.'

'Well, the advice from the *Woman's Own* to those of us who are tempted is "no, no, a thousand times no",' the magazine reader laughingly informed them. 'So hang on tight to your drawers, girls.'

'I'm not likely to get the chance to do anything else,' said a large and jolly mother of three teenagers. 'But I don't know if I could promise to say no if I had an offer from one of those gorgeous Yanks.'

Everyone knew she was just joshing and there were shrieks of laughter. This job had brought even the most inhibited of women out of their shells to some degree. When the merriment finally subsided, there was a dramatic change of mood due to Polly saying something unexpected.

'I'm really going to miss you lot,' she said.

'Miss us? Why?' asked Nancy.

'I'm leaving,' she informed them, sounding pleased. 'I've been accepted for the ATS.'

There was a general gasp of surprise, then they all wanted to know the why and wherefore.

'I decided to be a bit adventurous,' was her candid reply. 'Well, my husband's away, so there's nothing much to keep me at home, so I thought I might as well take the opportunity of a change of scenery at the government's expense. May as well try and get something positive out of this war.'

'It isn't as glamorous as they make it look in the recruiting posters,' warned someone.

'I'm not daft, I know that. I've heard all the horror stories, but I still want to do it,' she told them. 'It'll be interesting to try a different way of life. I might learn something new.'

'Are you allowed to leave this job just like that?' wondered Ruby.

'As long as you're going into another form of war work, yeah,' she replied. 'Why? Are you thinking of joining?'

'Oh no, I just asked out of interest. I wouldn't want to leave my mother on her own as there's only the two of us,' Ruby replied, being unusually forthcoming.

'I wasn't given a choice when I volunteered for war work,' Nancy mentioned. 'Porters were needed here so that's where they sent me.'

'Me too. But going out to work has become compulsory for women since then, so there are more of us to do the jobs,' Polly pointed out. 'Maybe that has something to do with it. Anyway, I didn't have any trouble in making the move. If any of you fancy it, you could follow in my foot-steps.'

'No fear,' said one woman adamantly. 'I've heard it's all cooking and scrubbing.'

'Yeah, I heard that too, but I've been assured that there are opportunities for more interesting jobs,' Polly told her. 'I'm hoping to become an army driver.'

'I can see that there might be advantages, but I wouldn't want to leave home,' said someone else.

'I don't fancy the idea of the discipline twenty-four hours a day,' said another woman. 'At least we can leave old Perce and his cronies behind when we go off duty.'

'Stop trying to put her off, you lot,' admonished Nancy. 'It'll be a very good experience for her, and from what I've heard there's fun to be had as well as hard work.'

As a clamour of opinions erupted, Nancy drifted into her own thoughts. Up until the time of her mother's death, she herself had been tempted to try for the services, but the idea had had to be abandoned as she was needed at home because of Evie. Now there was Dad to consider as well . . .

He wasn't quite as physically frail now, but he was still at a very low ebb mentally. His presence in the house without Mum around as a kind of intermediary had made Nancy realise just how little she and her siblings actually knew their father. He'd never been the pipe and slippers type. Even when he was on leave between ships, he'd never been at home much, had always spent a lot of time in the pub playing darts or dominoes. Now he was around all the time, only occasionally agreeing to go out for a drink after relentless persuasion from Uncle Wilf.

His damaged lungs meant that he wasn't legally obliged to find employment and was entitled to a small disablement benefit. Nancy sometimes wondered if it might have been better for his general well-being had he been forced to take on some sort of light work, as it had now been confirmed that his sea-going days were over.

Without the discipline of a daily purpose, he had far too much time to brood on what had happened and his bitterness grew and festered. Even apart from the need of an income, some sort of an outside interest was vital to stop him sitting at home all day feeling sorry for himself. So – as inviting as it was to follow Polly into the ATS – Nancy simply couldn't do it.

But now, she was recalled to the present by a familiar booming voice.

'Oi, you lot. What's all this, then? You're supposed to be having a dinner break, not a ruddy afternoon off,' shouted Percy. 'So let's be having you, back on duty. Chop-chop.'

'That's one thing I won't miss,' Polly whispered to Nancy as they headed back to the platform. 'Him shouting his mouth off all day long.'

'Us girls won't half miss you, though,' Nancy told her with sincerity. 'It won't be the same here without you.'

'Aah, that's nice,' responded Polly warmly. 'I'll miss you like mad, too.'

It was true what people said, thought Nancy. Friendships were more easily made and closer in wartime.

There was no sign of a bus on the Uxbridge Road at West Ealing so Bobby Collins started walking home, with the idea of catching one further along the route, if there were any about. The service was unreliable to the point of non-existence some nights. Still, he didn't really mind the walk. It was a pleasant summer's evening and the bright moon meant visibility wasn't too bad, especially if he stayed close to the kerb. Maybe the exercise would soothe his shattered nerves after the dreadful shock he'd just had.

He hadn't even known that Frank had gone back on active service. As far as Bobby knew, his pal was going to be at Catterick for the rest of the war. Bobby himself was back with his regiment in Aldershot after his sick leave last year. But instead of being sent back into battle, he'd been given the job of teaching recruits how to use arms. It was better than working in the stores all day, but he'd rather be doing what he'd been trained for as a soldier. At least then he would feel as if he was making a difference.

Currently home on a forty-eight-hour pass, he'd decided to go down to Ealing on the off-chance of Frank being home on leave. His wife had been holding the baby when she'd answered the door. She'd invited Bobby in, in the usual way, had said she appreciated him calling. It then began to transpire that she'd assumed Bobby had heard through the grapevine of her husband's demise and had come to offer his condolences. Frank had been killed in action in the Middle East several weeks ago.

Bobby had felt it like a bullet in his chest and been unable to hide it. Frank's widow had offered him tea and sympathy. *She'd* offered *him* sympathy! He was ashamed to remember that he'd sat on her sofa in shock, shakily smoking a cigarette and drinking tea as she told him – with tears in her eyes – that she and the kids were managing.

Ostensibly, he'd pulled himself together, had offered her his heartfelt sympathy and told her to let him know if there was anything he could do at any time. He'd left as soon as it was possible without causing offence. Outside in the street, he'd thrown up in the gutter.

Maybe death shouldn't faze him, having seen so many army mates die in battle. But it never got any easier, and was especially hard when it was an old friend like Frank whom he'd known all his life.

Now, with his head down and his hands in his trouser pockets, he walked on. Stopping to light a cigarette, he realised that he was outside the park, currently bathed in moonlight. The railings had gone and he found himself wandering in.

Sitting there in the cool of the evening, he drifted back to happier times. The world had changed since this place had been at the centre of his life. There had been hardship, unemployment and poverty aplenty then. But not the grotesque horrors of today. Not mass slaughter of young men in their prime, and civilians struck down in their homes. He'd been just a lad finding his way and life had been a thing of adventure and discovery. Those had been his halcyon days.

Tonight the park was washed with a luminous glow from the moon. Back then, everything had been tinged with sunlight whatever the weather. He recalled glorious days and feelings so intense he could still remember the dragging sensation in the pit of his stomach when it had all come to an end.

He leaned back, drawing hard on his cigarette and exhaling the smoke slowly. His memories were so sharp and clearly defined he could feel them all over again, the images so real and bright he could almost reach out and touch them. Recalled to the present, he took himself in hand. He was a young man, far too young to be hankering for times gone by.

In the distance he could hear the muffled sound of a man singing, then the roar of applause. Someone's having a good time, he thought, getting up, grinding out his cigarette under his shoe and heading back towards the main road. Good luck to them. Let them enjoy themselves before it was too late.

It was too late for poor Frank. His pal's death had made Bobby even keener to return to active duty; he wanted to fight back for Frank and all the others who had lost their lives to the Germans.

Reaching the main road, he continued on his journey home, deep in thought and unable to stop himself drifting back to the past.

Unbeknown to him, the sounds of jollity were coming from a community hall in a nearby sidestreet where there was a concert in progress to raise money for war orphans. Providing the music for the evening, at the piano, was the person who filled his thoughts – Nancy Sparrow.

Evie had been a joy to Nancy since the moment she was born. As a toddler she was even more loveable, and a source of constant entertainment for everyone who was close to her. With her bright ginger curls and saucer eyes of cornflower blue, she trotted about bursting with life and observing every little thing, from the smallest leaf on the privet hedge to the tiniest stone on the ground. Nancy, her grandmother, Uncle Wilf and her other siblings all doted on her.

But as wonderful as her mobility was, it did cause one problem to which Nancy could see only one solution.

'I know you won't allow Evie to come in the house, Dad,' she began one evening when Jean was out and Leslie in bed, 'but would you let her play in our back garden for a little while, every now and again?'

'You know the answer to that,' he replied grumpily.

'But we need somewhere for her to play now that she's running around. She needs to be out in the fresh air,' Nancy explained. 'Gran doesn't have a garden, but we do, so the obvious thing is for her to use it.'

'She's not to come anywhere near the property.' He was adamant. 'Your gran will have to take her to the park.'

'She does, as often as she can, and so do I when I'm around, but it isn't enough.'

'You knew she wouldn't stay a baby for ever when you took her on.' He was completely uncompromising.

'I know that, but we've had to deal with things as they've come along.'

'And that's what you'll have to do now, because I am not having that . . .' he paused, clearly having trouble controlling himself, '*child* in this house.'

'She won't be in the house. She'll be outside in the garden,' his daughter reminded him. 'We'll take her down to Gran's if she needs to go inside for any reason, so you won't even know she's here.'

'If I let her in the garden she'll be in the house before I've had a chance to turn round.'

'I'll make sure she doesn't come in,' Nancy assured him. 'I promise. And it wouldn't be all that often. All I'm asking is for her to be allowed in the garden for an hour or so when it's sunny and warm.'

'No. So stop going on about it.'

Nancy didn't give up that easily. 'She's a little girl, not a contagious disease. What harm can it do?'

'It can upset me,' he barked, scowling at her. 'Whatever happened to respect for your parents? Just remember that I am still your father even though you're grown up.'

'I know how hurt you are about what happened, Dad. But I can't believe that my father is the sort of person who would refuse an orphaned child something that would give her a great deal of pleasure at no cost to himself.'

'Maybe I'm not normally that sort of person, but these aren't normal circumstances.'

'But the poor mite doesn't have a mum or dad. She doesn't have anyone except us.'

202

'So take her to an orphanage if you can't manage her,' was his harsh suggestion.

'We *can* manage, and while Evie has relatives who love her she'll not be bundled off to any orphanage,' she told him heatedly. 'All we are trying to do is give her the best out of life that we can. I'm not asking you to do anything for her. You won't have to lift a finger.' She couldn't let it go. 'You don't even have to look at her if it offends you.'

'The answer is still no.'

'Right. I see.' She was furious now, eyes blazing, mouth set grimly. 'As you're too busy wallowing in self-pity to let so much as a chink of light into your life, I'll have to find somewhere else for her to play.'

'Self-pity? Me?'

'Yes, you.' The words came tumbling out as if of their own volition. She was too upset on Evie's behalf to control them. 'You're so eaten up with your own problems, you seem to have forgotten that there are other people in this world who need consideration.'

Cheeks flaming and on the verge of tears, she fled from the room. Upstairs in the bedroom, she sat on the edge of her bed, smarting from the memory of what she'd said and the hurt and bewildered look she'd put on his face. So what if her comments had been justified? He was her dad and he'd been through a lot. The fabric of his life had been destroyed. He'd lost his wife and his trust in her, his liveli-hood and almost his life. The man's heart was broken. It was too much to expect him to accept Evie. She could see his point. Nancy adored Evie and would never, *ever* desert her, but she loved her father too. She would just have to solve the problem some other way.

Full of remorse, she tore downstairs and almost collided with him at the bottom as he made his way up. 'I'm sorry, Dad,' she said humbly. 'I shouldn't have said those things. It was disrespectful and unkind.'

'I won't argue with you about that,' he said gruffly. 'You should show some respect, speaking to me as though I'm something the cat dragged in, then rushing off like that.'

'Sorry,' she said again.

'You've worn me down and I was on my way up to tell you that she can play in the garden.' He looked at her sternly. 'But only the garden mind; she doesn't put a foot in this house. Do you understand?'

'Yes, Dad.'

'And don't expect me to take any notice of her, because I won't,' he added. 'I want nothing to do with her at all. So keep her well away from me.'

She gave him a wary smile, her eyes shining with tears. 'Thanks, Dad.' Her instinct was to hug him, but she knew it would only embarrass him.

'I'm only agreeing to get you off my back,' he warned her gravely. 'So don't start thinking I've gone soft. I'm going to listen to the wireless now.'

'Why don't you go down the local for an hour or so?' she suggested, following him. 'It'll do you good to get out of the house for a break.'

'I don't fancy it.'

'I'll treat you if you're short,' Nancy offered. 'I've done a lot of overtime this week so I can afford it.'

'Thanks for offering, but no.' He was very definite. 'The nine o'clock news will be on in a minute and I'd appreciate being able to listen to it in peace.'

'Would you like me to make you a cup of cocoa, then?'

'Yes, please.'

Her dad and cocoa in the armchair at nine o'clock in the evening was still not a combination that seemed natural, even though he'd been indoors almost every night since he'd arrived home four months ago. Day after day he sat in his chair. About the only thing he roused himself for was to let the cat in and out.

Part of her wanted to shake him, the other part wanted to put her arms around him and hold him close, something she knew he wouldn't feel easy with. She sighed heavily as she watered down the milk for his cocoa.

Arthur sat in his armchair listening to the nine o'clock news and drifting in and out of his thoughts. Nancy had gone down the road to see her gran so he was alone. The news bulletin was full of gloom. Twenty-three merchant ships and one rescue ship had been sunk in the Arctic Ocean. They'd been part of a convoy of thirty-six on their way to Russia with an urgent cargo of tanks, aircraft and vehicles. All those lives lost heroically and he was sitting here in his armchair in comfort, drinking cocoa and feeling sorry for himself.

But knowing he should count his blessings did nothing to lift the black depression that consumed him so completely

it drained him of spirit. How could he take up Nancy's suggestion and go down the pub when he wasn't doing his bit for
the war effort and so didn't deserve to go out for pleasure?
Besides which, there was hardly anything left out of his benefit
after he'd made his meagre contribution to the household
expenses. Nancy had said he need only pay a bit towards his
food as he wasn't working, and she and Jean would make up
the rest. Nancy was a diamond girl. On top of everything
else she had to contend with, she regularly offered to pay for
him to go out for a drink. He never took her up on it; he
might not be much of a father, but he wasn't going to sink
so low as to sponge off his daughters. They were already
burdened with Lily's wretched sprog, and he wasn't able to
fully support young Leslie so that fell to them too.

Reaching out to the coffee table for his cigarettes and
realising almost immediately that they weren't there, because
he couldn't smoke in his state of health, it occurred to him
that he should be used to it after all this time. But old habits
died hard. It was just as well he couldn't smoke, since he
wouldn't be able to afford cigarettes now anyway.

Family life wasn't something he was used to in large doses,
and he wasn't at all comfortable with it; he felt constrained,
an outsider. He was more at home with the rough discipline
of life at sea, and the bawdy company of other men. The
worst thing of all was the guilt; guilt because, although he
was breathless and weak, in his heart of hearts, he knew he
was physically fit enough to do some sort of light work. But
what? He hadn't done a job on dry land since he was a lad,
and had no skills he could put to use outside of a ship.

His options were limited by health problems. Factory work would kill him, and his body simply wouldn't stand up to anything too demanding. But there must be something out there he was capable of. So why didn't he at least make some effort towards making enquiries?

Fear of failure, that was the truth of it, and since there was no pressure from the authorities for him to work, because he was officially unfit, he just sat here day after day, sinking deeper into a trough of despair. He'd faced danger at sea without any lack of bottle. Even before the war it had been a hazardous occupation, being so vulnerable to gales and storms on the high seas, and since the outbreak of war he'd been bombed, almost burnt to death and spent days in the water with little hope of rescue. He'd got through all of that, yet he was terrified to go out and find work. He felt weak with incompetence, had lost all his confidence along with his robust health and his wife.

His actual grief for Lily was by far outweighed by bitterness in the knowledge that he had lost her before she'd died. If she'd loved him enough to stay faithful to him, she'd have been alive today. She'd have been by his side through all of this, and he would have been strong with her to support him.

He and Lily had never had much of a family life together. But the arrangement had seemed to work and his love for her had never faltered. Away at sea, he felt self-assured and didn't need the support of anyone. At home, he was lost and alone without Lily.

How could he expect his children to understand how

he felt about Lily's child? She was their sweet baby sister and he was simply someone to whom they'd never been close and was now suddenly under their feet the whole time. They were young and full of life; in their eyes he was just their dad. They would probably be shocked to know that just the mention of the child's name conjured up vivid images of the circumstances of her conception. That was why he could hardly bear to think about her, let alone look at her.

And yes, Nancy was right, the child was just an innocent victim, but he still couldn't bear to have her near him. She caused too much pain, too much suffering. She wasn't a child to him, but a dark reminder of her mother, a woman he now believed he had never really known at all. So he would make sure he didn't even go near the window when the blasted infant was playing in the garden.

It was Saturday afternoon and Bobby Collins was looking after the shop while his mother had a break. He took a necklace from an elderly woman on the other side of the counter and examined it carefully.

'Three quid,' he offered.

'That's twenty-four-carat gold, mate,' she told him in a tone of admonition. 'Three quid is an insult to my intelligence.'

'I'll make it four, then.'

'Don't make me laugh,' she said. 'That's a valuable piece of stuff.'

'Four's a fair price.'

'Have a good look at it, go on,' she urged. 'As you don't believe me about its value.'

'I do believe you and I have had a good look.'

'You ought to get yourself some specs then, if the best you can offer me is four quid.'

'There's nothing wrong with my eyesight, Dotty, and four quid is my final offer.'

'Oh, go on then,' she said, as though they hadn't been through this same ritual before, when in actual fact, this necklace had been in and out of this pawnshop almost as many times as he had. But there was a certain etiquette to be upheld towards the customers in the pawnbroking trade. People deserved respect and Bobby always made sure he gave it to them. Dotty liked to pretend the necklace was making its first trip to the shop, so he pleased her by playing along.

He got her to sign the credit form, wrote out the pawn ticket and put the necklace on the counter, ready to add to the multitude of artefacts behind him that had been left as pledges. There were bikes, blankets, watches, clocks, jewellery and even a few wireless sets.

'There you are, my dear,' he said, handing her the money and the pawn ticket.

'Ta very much.' With the transaction complete, she was now ready to exchange a few sociable words. 'You home on leave, are you, son?'

'Just a weekend pass.'

'Not long enough, I bet.'

'No. It flies past.' He paused. 'Still, it's better than not getting home at all.'

'Mm.' She went to the door, opened it, looked both ways and came back inside. He guessed she'd spotted someone she knew and didn't want to be seen leaving here. Despite the fact that it was a summer's day, she was wearing a dark coat and a headscarf. 'Is your mum keeping well?' she asked, just passing time until the coast was clear.

'She's fine, just having a bit of a rest at the moment.'

'You're a good boy to your mum, Bobby,' she approved. 'It'll be a blessing when you're home for good and can help her with the business all the time.'

'That time can't come quick enough for me.'

'Bloody Hitler,' the old woman mumbled. 'He'd know all about it if I got hold of him.'

'I wouldn't want to be in his shoes if you did,' Bobby grinned.

She went to the door again, looked each way and said, 'Ta-ta,' and left quickly.

Watching the small, bent woman scurrying past the window, he smiled affectionately. Dotty was a well-known local figure, a mother of eight with umpteen grandchildren whom she liked to indulge, which – he guessed – was why she found herself short of cash and had to pawn her neck-lace on a regular basis. But it wasn't his place to judge or even wonder why.

The shop door opened and a much younger woman came in. Tall and slim and in her mid-twenties, war widow Irene Brown was extremely attractive, with a good figure, lustrous brown hair worn in a pageboy and warm, hazel-coloured eyes.

'Hello, Irene,' he greeted her with a warm smile.

'Wotcha, Bobby.' She walked over to the counter and leaned on it, looking up at him and smiling. 'I was just passing, so thought I'd call in to confirm our date for tonight. You didn't say what time in your letter.'

'That depends on whether you fancy the pictures or the Palais.'

'The pictures would be nice.'

'I'll call for you about seven, then.'

He'd been seeing Irene for the past few weeks, but had known her by sight for ages because she worked as a counterhand in the grocery shop in this parade. They'd got talking one day when he'd called in to the nearby café for a cup of tea, and she'd been in there. Her husband had been killed at Dunkirk so she was on her own, and made no secret of the fact that she fancied Bobby. He'd been a bit down, having just heard about Frank's death, so was susceptible to her admiration and had asked her out. Having a home posting meant that he quite often managed to fiddle a forty-eight- or a twenty-four-hour pass.

He was attracted to Irene physically, but that was as far as it went. There was only one woman for him but, having resigned himself to the fact that he could never have Nancy, it made sense to go out with someone else in the hope that it might help him to forget. Irene was lively, sexy and all over him. What man wouldn't be flattered?

'Afternoon, Irene,' greeted his mother, appearing at the door at the back of the shop.

'Wotcha, Mrs Collins,' the younger woman replied. 'How are you?'

211

'Bearing up.' Her manner was polite but cool. 'I'm enjoying these quiet nights we're having lately.'

'Aren't we all?' Irene responded. 'I don't suppose we've heard the last of Jerry. They'll be back with their bombs when they're ready. But let's enjoy the lack of air raids while we can.'

Mabel nodded.

'Anyway, I'd better get off and leave you two to your work,' said Irene. 'See you later, Bobby.'

'Nice woman, eh, Ma?' he remarked as the door closed behind her.

His mother shrugged.

'What's that supposed to mean?'

'It means that you need to be careful,' she said. 'Don't get too carried away.'

'Oh yeah, and why is that?'

'I think she might be after you for the wrong reasons,' she replied. 'You're a good catch for someone with an eye to the main chance. I don't suppose she earns much in that shop.'

'Irene isn't out for what she can get,' he said sternly.

'You can't be sure of that, son. There are plenty of young war widows about and some of them will be looking for a husband as a means of support,' she lectured. 'You're part of a solid business and the answer to a prayer for some women.'

'You're always on at me to find someone to settle down with.'

'Not someone like Irene who's only after what she can get out of you.'

212

'I'm not completely stupid. I'd know if I was being taken for a ride,' he said. 'Anyway, there's nothing serious between us.'

'There will be if she has her way.'

'I'm quite capable of knowing the wheat from the chaff, you know.'

'When it comes to business, you're as sharp as your dad used to be. But, like all men, you're influenced by a pretty face,' his mother lectured.

'You don't reckon I could get someone who'd want me for myself then,' he teased her.

'Leave off, you can take your pick.'

'I'm not thinking in terms of marriage, to Irene or anyone else, so you've no need to worry.'

'Just be careful, that's all I'm saying.'

He turned to her, grinning. 'I'm a big boy now, Ma; old enough to look after myself and choose my own women.' He tapped his nose with his forefinger. 'So keep that out.'

She rolled her eyes. 'Honestly, is that any way to talk to your old mother?'

'When she starts trying to organise my love life, yep, it certainly is.'

The arrival of a customer brought the conversation to an end. There was never any bad feeling between Bobby and his mother. They had always been able to speak openly to each other and he valued their easy-going relationship enormously.

'You're nearest, Jean. Be a dear and get her out of harm's way, will you?' requested Nancy, referring to Evie, who was about to start investigating the loose coal around the delap-idated coal bunker. 'Everything goes in her mouth and that will too if she gets half the chance.'

'We can't have you eating coal, can we, tiddler?' said Jean, getting up from a kitchen chair in the back garden where she had been sitting with her skirt pushed up above her knees and her face poised towards the sun. She picked Evie up and moved her to the other side of the garden. 'Coal won't make you grow into a big strong girl. Besides, we'll need every little bit for the fire when the cold weather comes.'

'You can say that again,' added Nancy, who was perched on the back doorstep. 'They say fuel is going to be shorter than ever this winter.'

Evie tottered towards the coal again and was scooped up by Jean to screams of protest.

'Where's your dolly, Evie?' said Nancy, going over and holding out a rag doll her grandmother had made for her. 'Come and see Dolly. Come on, darlin'.'

She toddled over and was pacified as Nancy put the doll in the secondhand dolls' pram they'd managed to get for her. Jean went back to her kitchen chair and sat facing the sun.

It was a glorious Sunday afternoon in September, the low sun filtering from a hazy blue sky. The three Sparrow sisters were on their own in the garden – Leslie was playing in the street with his friends and their father was indoors. Gran was at home, having her usual Evie-free Sunday afternoon. Nancy always made absolutely certain of that when she wasn't on duty. As beautiful as Evie was, she was a real handful at this

214

age. On the go every waking moment, she was into everything.

Right now, Nancy needed to answer a call of nature. 'Keep an eye on her for a minute, will you please, Jean?' she requested. 'I've got to pop indoors.'

'Yeah.' Jean didn't even open her eyes.

'You can't do it with your eyes shut,' Nancy pointed out.

Her sister sighed impatiently. 'She's all right, playing there. I don't need to watch her every single second. I'm trying to get some colour on my face so that I won't need to use rouge.'

'You do need to watch her, so sit up with your eyes open while I'm gone. Shan't be a minute.'

'Oh, all right,' conceded Jean, sitting up and looking in Evie's direction.

As soon as her sister was safely out of sight, Jean leaned back and thrust her face towards the sun again, her eyes closed against the glare, Evie forgotten. She'd been using her lipstick on her cheeks because she couldn't get hold of any rouge and now the lipstick had almost run out. Another hour of this and she shouldn't need any false colour on her cheeks for a good few days, which would lengthen the life of her last bit of lipstick nicely. Besides, it felt good to have the warm sun on her face.

Arthur was sitting in his armchair, reading the paper and dozing. He could hear his daughters talking in the garden, but not what they were saying because he'd closed the French windows when that damned kid's voice had drifted in to him just now.

Sunlight beamed through the net curtains, making square patterns on the wall and depressing him even more, for some reason. After living so close to the elements at sea, the weather was irrelevant to him now. The indoor life made him feel so utterly lethargic. He never seemed to have any energy lately. The newspaper dropped from his grasp and his head nodded on to his chest as he drifted off to sleep.

He came to with a start as something touched his knee. His eyes snapped open and he found himself under scrutiny from two enormous blue eyes. Oddly tongue-tied, he stared back at Evie, the likeness to her mother twisting his heart. He hadn't seen her this close before, had always avoided it. Now he couldn't seem to look away. They observed each other in silence.

Then she put her arms out for him to pick her up. It stirred something deep inside him which he didn't understand and was quite unprepared for. To his amazement, he realised that he was trembling. Instinctively, he mentally fled from her. He didn't want to look at her or think about her or analyse his feelings. He wanted to feel nothing.

Moving her out of his way, he leapt up, marched to the kitchen door and shouted at the top of his voice, 'Nancy! Jean! One of you come and get this child – this minute.'

At which point Evie's huge blue moons filled with tears and she started to cry.

When Nancy came into the room, Evie was standing by

Arthur's chair sobbing her heart out and he was by the door looking terrified. Jean followed her sister in.

'Ah, what is it, darlin'?' Nancy picked her up and cuddled her protectively. 'Honestly, Dad. What have you done to her? The poor little thing.'

'I haven't done anything.'

'Something's upset her,' declared Nancy. 'She wouldn't be crying for nothing.'

'She was by my chair,' he roared with savage disapproval. 'I was having a snooze and she woke me up. Frightened the life out of me.'

'How can a dear little thing like Evie frighten anyone?' asked Nancy.

'Yeah,' supported Jean.

'I mean she startled me,' he corrected. 'I think she wanted me to pick her up or something.'

'Sorry, Dad, but she was only being friendly,' said Nancy.

'Course she was.' Besides loving Evie and wanting to protect her, Jean was keen to get back into Nancy's favour, since she was responsible for this altercation. 'All she wanted was a bit of attention. It wouldn't have hurt you to pick her up, instead of upsetting her.'

'You gave me your word that she would stay in the garden. We had a deal, remember,' their father growled.

'I know and I'm sorry,' Nancy apologised again. 'Jean was supposed to be watching her.'

'I *was* watching her.'

'Oh yeah. With closed eyes while you were sunbathing.'

'No . . .'

'How did she come to wander indoors then, if you were supervising her?' rebuked Nancy.

'For about one second I took my eyes off her, that's all,' lied Jean.

'Honestly, am I the only person in this house capable of looking after a small child?' asked Nancy. 'Come on, darlin'.' She wiped Evie's eyes and held her close. 'Let's go and find your dolly again. It'll soon be time to take you home to your gran's.'

With that, Arthur's daughters swept out, leaving him feeling like the devil himself. It really wasn't fair that he should be made to feel like a villain when he was the injured party in all this. Well, at least the incident had done one thing for him. It had forced him into a decision. He wasn't prepared to stay in this house from morning to night at the mercy of women and children any longer.

Even when his daughters were out at work, he felt vulnerable to them, as though they were in charge. If he was out for at least part of the day, and paying his way properly, he might begin to have a say in things around here again.

First thing in the morning, he would go to the labour exchange and ask them if they had any work that an unfit middle-aged ex-sailor could do. He'd sooner sweep the streets than spend another day sitting around the house.

Chapter Nine

As it happened, the labour exchange had employment to offer Arthur that was rather more to his liking than street-sweeping.

'Are you sure it won't be too much for you, Dad?' asked Nancy the next day when he announced his news over their evening meal. 'I mean, you're not a hundred percent fit and you'll be out in all weathers and working odd hours with this job. You don't have to go out to work, you know.'

'I think we all know that I do,' he wisely pointed out. 'For the sake of my own sanity, as much as anything else.'

In all honesty, Nancy couldn't argue with him about that. 'You'll just have to see how you get on then, and make sure you don't overdo it.'

'Going out collecting insurance premiums isn't going to do me any harm,' he said. 'It'll be better than being in a factory all day. I know I couldn't cope with that. At least I'll be out and about in the fresh air, with no one breathing down my neck. As long as I do the round every week and collect the money, it's up to me when I do it. And after the weather conditions I was used to at sea, a bit of frost or rain won't hurt me.'

'You'll need a bike,' Nancy suggested. 'I'd offer to lend you mine, but I use it most days.'

'You can borrow mine, Dad,' offered Leslie. 'Though it might not be big enough for you.'

'Thanks son, but I've got that all sorted. I called round to see Wilf and he reckons he can get hold of a secondhand one for me sharpish,' he explained. 'If anyone can find one, your uncle will.'

'You, an insurance man, Dad.' Jean found it hilarious. 'Isn't it a scream?'

'Is it? I can't see anything funny about it.'

'She means funny in that it's different to what you've done before, I think, Dad,' Nancy said, throwing her sister a warning look.

'Yeah, that's right,' Jean confirmed, ignoring Nancy's admonitory stare. 'It just seems a bit dull and drippy for an old salt like you. I mean, after your going away to all those exotic, faraway places and coming back all suntanned, I just can't imagine you cycling around the London streets in a mac, with your black book and bicycle clips on.'

'Take no notice of her, Dad,' Nancy intervened. 'It's a very respectable job.'

'It'll take some getting used to, and I don't even know if I'll be any good at it. But I've got to grit my teeth and get out there and do my best.' He gave a resigned sigh. 'I suppose we all have to adapt to change as we go through life.'

'That's the spirit, Dad,' praised Nancy.

'I know it's taken me long enough to get off my arse and do something, but I got there in the end.'

There was a new confidence and geniality about him, now that he'd taken that first positive step of finding a job, Nancy observed with a feeling of exquisite relief. It would be wonderful if the improvement in his mood were to stretch to his attitude towards little Evie, too. But that was a far more complicated matter altogether.

The winter of 1942 began on a gloomy note, with the fuel shortage meaning a cold and empty fireplace. People were urged not to light their fires until November, so coats, scarves and gloves became normal indoor wear.

There was little comfort – when shivering by a cheerless hearth – in reading in the papers that the coldest places in London were government offices where the civil servants' hands were so numb with cold they could barely handle the papers they were working on.

Nancy thought there could be no sweeter moment than when they finally lit their first fire of the winter. The family pulled their chairs right up close and huddled around it, warming their hands and thrusting their feet towards the red coals almost to scorching point. The glorious warmth seemed to melt Nancy's frozen bones. Even the fact that the heat made her chilblains throb didn't spoil the pleasure.

As an escape from the bleakness of yet another wartime winter, Nancy and Ruby joined the crowds pouring into the cinemas to see Noel Coward's *In Which We Serve*, the life story of a destroyer, which proved to be well worth the long, cold wait in the queue.

Much to everyone's relief, the expected resumption of the air raids over London didn't materialise, and there was good news from abroad of the allied landing in North Africa. In November Mr Churchill gave a cautiously optimistic speech, though warning of hardships still to come for the people of Britain. 'This is not the end. It is not even the beginning of the end, but it is, perhaps, the end of the beginning.'

Whilst realising that the war was far from over, Nancy was encouraged by the current climate of hope which had put a spring back in people's steps. The Sparrow family had a special reason to be cheerful, too, when Arthur appeared to enjoy his new job and was noticeably less bad-tempered. He went off on his round complaining neither about the weather nor the evening work.

Unfortunately, there was no sign of a change of heart regarding Evie, but Nancy put her foot down about the Christmas arrangements. She told her father that she wasn't prepared to stand by and allow her grandmother to spend the festive season apart from the rest of the family just because little Evie wasn't allowed into the Sparrow home. 'If you won't allow Evie to come here on Christmas Day, we'll all go to Gran's and you'll have to stay here on your own,' she threatened. 'And don't expect Uncle Wilf to come and keep you company, because he'll want to be with the family.'

Finally, he grudgingly agreed for her to come, muttering, 'As long as no one expects me to take any notice of her.'

With persistence, ingenuity and downright determination,

the Sparrows made Christmas Day a success. In the preceding weeks, Nancy spent a large chunk of her off-duty time queuing for anything that could be given as a gift or used as festive fare, while Gladys created a Christmas pudding with grated apples, chopped prunes and dried elderberries to replace the traditional, unavailable dried fruit.

They were especially frugal with the coal, so that they could have a fire all day on Christmas Day. Gladys knitted dolls' clothes for Evie and Nancy made her a teddy bear out of an old coat. Even though their Christmas dinner was only mutton and two veg, they managed to have a good time.

They listened to the wireless, sang songs and played games with Evie. Later – when she was asleep – they had a few games of cards, adding spice by playing for loose change. It was lovely, though Mum's absence was particularly poignant for them all at this time of the year. They all raised their glasses to dear Micky too, still out at the front somewhere. Arthur's studious indifference towards Evie passed without comment, though obviously everyone noticed it. And for all his overt contempt towards her, the little girl seemed devoted to him and pursued him relentlessly, following him around but seeming, somehow, to accept that she would be ignored.

It broke Nancy's heart to see it and she never gave up hoping that one day he might be able to see her as a sweet child, instead of merely the manifestation of his wife's betrayal. But there was no sign of it as the year ended.

'Do you fancy coming up the Palais with me on Saturday night, Nance?' asked Jean one day in the new year. 'I've got no one to go with. All my mates are busy doing other things this week.'

'Here we go again,' responded Nancy. 'You always try and drag me out when you can't find anyone else.'

'Well, sisters are supposed to do things for each other, aren't they, Gran?'

'There's no law about it, but it's nice if they do,' replied Gladys. 'And Nancy does plenty of things for you.'

'Oh well, I'm sure I must have done things for you at some time or other,' Jean said to Nancy, cheerily brushing the issue aside. 'Anyway, it goes without saying that I'm doing *you* a favour in asking you to come out dancing with me.'

'Oh no! Not the "let's try and get poor old Nancy hitched" thing again, please.'

'It could happen. The Palais is well known for bringing couples together.'

'How come you're still single then, when you spend half your life there?'

'Give me time. I'm still working on it, which is why I want you to come with me on Saturday night. I don't want to go on my own and I can't afford to miss it.'

'Why don't you go with her, Nancy?' Gladys decided to enter into it. 'It might be a bit of fun, two sisters going out together. It would be nice.'

'Oh no, not you as well,' groaned Nancy. 'Don't say you're getting panicky about my not having a man.'

Her grandmother put her head to one side and grinned. 'Well . . . you're not getting any younger.'

'Past it and desperate at twenty-six. So that's what you think, is it?'

'Just kidding, dear.'

'Anyway, are you coming on Saturday or not, Nance?' Jean was getting impatient.

'Go on, Nancy, be a devil,' encouraged Gladys. 'A spot of jitterbugging will do you the world of good. I wish I was young enough to come with you.'

'I'll look after Evie and you go with Jean then, Gran,' smiled Nancy.

'If I was your age, there would be no stopping me, and that's a fact,' she told them. 'If you go with Jean, I can look forward to hearing all about it afterwards. So why not give your old gran a treat?'

Nancy pondered.

'All right then, I'll come, Jean, but only because of the dancing and the music,' she made clear. 'I am not going there to find a man and if you so much as mention it again, you'll be going on your own.'

In the late morning of the next day, Gladys was putting a milk bottle on the step when Arthur went by on his bike, heading homewards.

'Morning, Arthur.'

'Wotcha, Gladys,' he said, stopping and turning to look at her. 'You all right, love?'

'Not so bad, thanks,' she said, going out on to the street. 'Been out on your round?'

He nodded. 'I'll have to go out again tonight to see the

225

ones who are out during the day. Still, I don't mind. It gets me out from under the kids' feet.'

'Got time for a cup of something hot?' she asked, shivering and hugging herself against the penetrating cold. 'You look as though you could do with one.'

He didn't reply.

'Evie's having her nap, if that's what you're worrying about,' she said. 'So you won't have to see her.'

Another long pause. 'Well—'

'For Godsake man, come in before we both freeze to death out here,' she cut in. 'I have to keep a bit of a fire going for the baby so you might as well come in and have a warm. I don't suppose you have a fire going all day in your place.'

'Not with the coal situation as it is.'

'Come on, then.'

He wheeled his bike up to her door and leaned it against the wall.

'I don't see much of you these days,' she mentioned as they sat down in her living room with a mug of weak tea each.

'Inevitable now, I suppose . . .'

'With my place being out of bounds, you mean?'

'Exactly.'

'Don't you think you're taking the whole thing too far now, Arthur?' she suggested, seizing the opportunity to broach the subject. 'It's making it very awkward for all of us. I miss coming in and out of your place. And I know the kids aren't happy with the situation.' She paused for a moment. 'Lily never stopped loving you, you know. These are crazy times we're living in, and that was doubly true back then in the

Blitz with bombs dropping and no one knowing if they'd live to see another day. People weren't thinking straight. She used to get very lonely.'

'That's no excuse. She had the kids. She had you.'

'That isn't always enough,' Gladys pointed out. 'Besides which, the older children are all grown up and Leslie was away in the country. This man, whoever he was, obviously came into her life at a time when she was particularly susceptible. These things happen in wartime.'

'You can't blame the war for everything.'

'Look Arthur, Lily went off the rails, but she paid the price and lost her life because of it. She isn't ever coming back, so all this anger you're clinging on to is just a waste of energy. *It's done. It's over.*' Her eyes were hot with tears and she bit them back. 'The one you're hurting most of all is yourself. So let it go. For pity's sake.' She swallowed hard and wiped her eyes. 'Sorry about all the emotion, but I still miss her so very much.'

He reached over and put his hand over hers. 'I know it must be hard for you.'

'It's hard for you too.'

'Yeah. But it's different for me . . . because of what she did. I don't know which hurts most, her death or her betrayal.'

'No matter how much she's hurt you, she left a precious gift, a beautiful child who didn't ask to be born,' said Gladys. 'Lily knew she was dying and she trusted me and the family to do our best for her.'

'None of it had anything to do with me, though.'

'All right, so technically Evie is nothing to do with you.

227

But she is in as much as your children adore her and want to be with her.'

'I'm not stopping them.'

'You're making it damned difficult for them, though. Even an insensitive bugger like you can't really believe that your attitude doesn't make it hard for them,' she told him. 'They want to have Evie in their lives without feeling guilty about it, because they know that they are hurting you by being with her. Why can't you find it in your heart to let them have that? She's their little sister for Godsake.'

'You're asking too much of me,' he said grimly. 'Why can no one see this thing from my point of view?'

'I *can* see it from your point of view. I do have a brain in my head and I know that you've been terribly hurt. You have every right to be angry, but not for the rest of your life, man. You can't feed on that same anger for ever, letting it make you bitter and twisted.'

'Look, I just can't bear to have that child anywhere near me,' he explained. 'I realise that this might seem heartless, but I can't help the way I feel.'

She sighed. 'You and me used to get on so well when Lily was alive. We were never the stuff mother-in-law jokes are made of. We were more like mates.'

'We still are.'

She shook her head. 'You've driven a wedge between us with all this resentment. It's splitting the family up.'

'It isn't me who's doing that,' he insisted. 'You and the girls wanted to take the kid on, regardless of my feelings.'

'At the time, we thought you were dead.'

228

'You'd have taken her on anyway.'

'Yes, I would. I promised my daughter I would and I've never regretted it for a moment,' she told him without hesitation. 'Evie has brought such joy into my life, I wouldn't be without her for the world.'

'You would feel like that, wouldn't you?' he pointed out. 'Since she's your granddaughter.'

'Blood ties aren't the only aspect of love. I think I'd love her whoever she belonged to because she's such a dear child. Where she came from doesn't matter to me. It's who she is as a person that's important, not what her mother did – a woman she never even knew.'

'I know all that in here,' he said, touching his head and, pointing to his heart, added, 'But here says something quite different.' He finished his tea and stood up. 'Anyway, it's time I went.'

She saw him to the door and watched him as he wheeled his bike homewards since it wasn't far enough to cycle. Just a few doors down the street from each other and worlds apart, she thought, separated by the sins of the past, someone else's sins at that. He'd aged dreadfully. He used to be such a strong, upright man. Now he had a noticeable stoop and did everything more slowly because he suffered from shortness of breath if he hurried too much. He was a very sad figure now, quite different to the jolly character who used to come home from foreign parts full of entertaining stories.

There were tears in her eyes as she closed the door, and they weren't all tears for her beloved Lily . . .

*   *   *

It was Saturday night and Nancy was having a wonderful time, jiving, jitterbugging and waltzing the night away to the music of Lou Preager and his band at the Hammersmith Palais. It was crowded, smoky and noisy, but there was almost a party atmosphere, with the colourful decor, bright lights and friendliness, the women defying wartime shortages of clothes and make-up by managing somehow to look smart and pretty, the servicemen of many nationalities handsome in uniform. It was the perfect antidote to the harsh, dark streets outside. Nancy had had no shortage of partners, so her fears of being a wallflower had proved to be unfounded.

'I hope that gorgeous Yank asks me to dance again,' said Jean anxiously, as they stood among the throngs of people around the dance floor, waiting for the next dance to start. The air was heavy with cigarette smoke and some lucky woman must have tracked down a wartime rarity because Nancy detected a hint of Evening in Paris perfume wafting from somewhere, a sweet reminder of more plentiful times. 'Nance, he's looking over. I think he fancies me. I do hope so.'

'Which one is it?'

'The one I danced with just now.' As Nancy peered through the crowds, she received a dig in the ribs. 'Don't let him see you looking. I don't want him to think I'm too keen.'

'I'm not sure which one you're talking about.'

'The really good-looking one standing next to the pillar. Oh, isn't he just the most stunning man you've ever seen in your life?' she swooned.

Nancy was puzzled, because she could see no one of that description. 'I think I must be looking in the wrong place,' she remarked.

'The tall hunky one with the brown hair; he's with that blond bloke.'

'Oh, *that's* the one.' She had been looking in the right place after all.

'He's looking this way. Quick, look away,' Jean said in an excited whisper. 'He's going to ask me. He is, he is. Please God, let him ask me.'

The saying 'beauty is in the eye of the beholder' was never more true than in the case of the man of Jean's dreams, Nancy thought, as he came over and asked her sister to dance. He had the wholesome, well-nourished glow that seemed to be common to all American servicemen, with their smart uniforms, healthy complexions and confident manner. But handsome he was *not*. He towered above Jean and had a strong, muscular look about him, but even his mother wouldn't call him good-looking. A long, bumpy nose rose unevenly beneath small, deep-set eyes and his ears seemed to be trying to escape from the rest of him.

But Jean obviously saw something that wasn't apparent to Nancy and sailed off with him on to the dance floor in a state of near ecstasy. Nancy was so busy watching and wondering what her sister saw in him as they launched into the dance, she was startled when she turned to see a chap in RAF uniform looking at her with a grin.

'Would you like to dance?' he asked politely, treating her to a melting smile.

231

Now this man was undeniably handsome, with dark wavy hair and deep velvet eyes under thick, well-shaped brows. He was tall and slim with perfect facial features and the most wonderful set of white teeth. He was the nearest thing to a film star she'd ever been close to.

'Well . . . would you?' he asked her again, looking a little uncertain.

'I'm so sorry, I was miles away, but yes I would, yes please,' she said.

As he led her on to the floor, she noticed that he had wings on the front of his uniform, indicating he was a pilot, and was even more impressed. To add to his growing appeal, he was a master of the jitterbug and twisted her around with as much expertise as any American, to the catchy tune of 'Chattanooga Choo Choo'. Fortunately, Nancy had had some tuition from Jean at home before they came and had also jitterbugged with other partners earlier, so didn't make too many embarrassing mistakes.

'How did you learn to dance like that?' she enquired when the music ended and he escorted her back to her place.

'Plenty of practice away from the dance hall. It pays us British boys to learn fast,' he grinned. 'We can't let the Yanks steal all the limelight.'

'That's the spirit.'

This time it was Nancy's turn to wonder about her partner for the next dance. 'That airman I danced with is very good-looking, don't you think?' she asked Jean.

Her sister looked over after Nancy had surreptitiously

232

pointed him out. 'He's all right, I suppose,' she said, but she really only had eyes for the jug-eared American.

The airman did ask Nancy for the next dance, and all the others after that. His name was Pete, he was twenty-eight and currently stationed at Northolt. It was obvious to Nancy as soon as he opened his mouth that his background was different to hers. Those cultured vowels didn't come from growing up in a backstreet like Sycamore Road. He wasn't upper class, but was definitely more refined than the people she was used to mixing with. He seemed very taken with her and she found it rather flattering.

During the last waltz he held her close, but explained that he couldn't ask to see her home because he had to be back at camp by midnight.

'That's all right,' she assured him. 'I shall have to go home with my sister anyway, as we came together.'

He asked if he could see her again the following Saturday and they arranged to meet outside the Palais. 'Dazzled' was the only way to describe her feelings for him, mainly because he was totally different to anyone she'd ever been out with before. Perhaps a date with him might help her to stop hankering for the past and her first love, she thought, and was mulling it over all the way home on the train – *on her own*. Jean had gone off with Mr Wonderful from the USA without a thought for her sister.

Nancy was in bed when Jean finally came in, full of her new man, whose name was Ed.

'I've got a date with him for Friday night,' she squeaked excitedly. 'Guess where he's taking me.'

'The Palais?'

'No. Better than that. Much better.' Her voice was vibrant. 'He's taking me to a dance at Rainbow Corner, that American forces club in Piccadilly.'

'You've struck lucky then, kid.'

'I'll say I have. He seems dead keen, too.'

'Good.'

'It's better than good, Nance, it's bloomin' marvellous.'

'And does he meet with your criteria as regards a ranch and a rich daddy back home?'

'Dunno.'

'You mean you're seeing him again and you didn't find out if it would be materially worth your while?'

'That's right,' she said absently. 'I just didn't seem to get around to it.'

'That isn't like you.'

'It didn't seem to matter somehow,' Jean said dreamily. 'He's so gorgeous I'd go out with him whatever his background.'

'You must be smitten.'

'Totally. And you'll never guess what,' she went on excitedly. 'He's in the American Military Police, stationed at their headquarters in Piccadilly, which is highly convenient. Me going out with an MP, though, Nance. Snowdrops, they call 'em, because of their white helmets. Talk about charisma. Just the thought of being with a man with all that strength and authority sends shivers down my spine.'

234

'You're a case, you really are.' This was one of the rare occasions when Nancy found her sister's pleasure-seeking outlook on life amusing.

Coming down from the stars sufficiently to think of something else for a moment, Jean looked towards her sister, who had the eiderdown pulled right up to her eyes because of the sub-zero temperature in the bedroom.

'What about you?' she asked. 'How did you get on with that airman?'

Nancy told her.

'Meeting him *outside* the Palais, eh?' approved Jean. 'I'm impressed. Some British servicemen make a point of meeting a girl inside so that they don't have to pay for her ticket.'

'Don't criticise our own just because you're Yank mad,' admonished Nancy. 'Our boys don't get paid nearly as much as the American forces, so they can't afford to splash their money around.'

'Yeah, yeah, I know.' She started getting undressed, shivering, groaning and pulling her striped winceyette pyjamas on quickly. 'Cor, blimey. It's cold enough to freeze your tits off in here.'

'You're telling me. The sheets were like solid ice when I got in and I've only just got warm so don't let all the cold air in when you get in.'

'As if I would,' she said, turning the light off and climbing into bed, letting in an almighty draught as she did so.

'You did that on purpose,' accused Nancy.

'I can't get in without lifting up the covers, can I?' she pointed out.

'I'll be glad when you get married and leave home so I can have the bed to myself.'

'It can't come quick enough for me either,' Jean retaliated. 'But maybe you'll be the first to go, now that I've got you out there meeting men.'

'Give over and go to sleep,' said Nancy.

'So you can lie there dreaming of your Brylcreem boy?' she teased.

Without replying, Nancy turned over on to her side, with her back to her sister.

'Now who's letting all the cold air in?' objected Jean, pulling the covers back to her side.

On Friday night Jean was transported from the heart of London into another world, simply by walking through a door in Piccadilly into Rainbow Corner. A multitude of American accents was all around her and the air was fragrant with the aroma of roast pork, apple pie and Camel cigarettes.

They were strict here about who the US servicemen brought into the club and Ed had apparently had to apply in advance for approval to bring Jean in as his guest. Once her details had been checked at reception, Ed helped her off with her coat and handed it over to the attendant, impressing Jean even more with his good manners. Then he led her along a corridor towards the sound of an up-beat dance-band playing 'Don't Sit Under the Apple Tree'. They passed several other doors, some of which were open to reveal pool tables, a writing room, arts and crafts facilities, dining rooms, even a place where the troops could get their hair cut American style, their socks darned and their shoes shined. There were pinball machines and juke boxes. All the rooms were full of GIs enjoying themselves.

'Impressed, huh?' said Ed, as Jean stared goggle-eyed at everything.

'I've never seen anything like it in my life, let alone in wartime,' she replied.

'We're very well looked after,' he said in his deep, drawling voice. 'As long as US troops are fighting the war in Europe, this place will be open to us twenty-four hours a day.'

'How marvellous.'

'It sure is. We can get most things from home here. It's all shipped over. They don't serve liquor, though. Wanna make sure we behave while we're in here, I guess.'

'It's . . . just amazing.'

'Sure glad you like it,' he said proudly. 'Shall we head for the dance floor now?'

There wasn't much floor to be seen in the dance hall, which was a moving, jumping mass of people. There wasn't sufficient space for jitterbugging, but people were doing it anyway. Men and women stood on benches, watching the dancers twirl and leap under the arc lights. In the corner there were silver machines making doughnuts rolled in powdered sugar. Jean was mesmerised by the whole thing. Her pre-conceived ideas about America, it seemed, were true.

She and Ed joined the dancers on the floor and in the interval he took her to the snack bar in the basement and bought her coffee and doughnuts. There were people devouring food and drink the like of which Jean had never seen before: waffles, hamburgers, hash browns, bottles of Coca-Cola. Having a sweet tooth that had been starved since the beginning of shortages, it was as much as she could do not to stuff the doughnut in her mouth whole and ask for more, and some to take home for the family. It was no wonder the Americans were so generous with their goodies; they could afford to be.

When she finally stopped going into raptures about the doughnuts and the deliciously sweet coffee, they sat and talked, eager to know more about each other. He told her that he was twenty-two and from Minnesota, where he worked as a truck driver in the family business. Her own background seemed boring in comparison, but he didn't seem to think so. In fact, he seemed to find her extremely fascinating, and told her she was very beautiful and had a cute accent.

By the time they danced the last waltz together, she was positively floating. When he asked her if he could see her again the following night, she couldn't believe her luck. He explained that the nature of his work meant he was often on duty in the evenings, but he currently had a few nights off. She barely heard what he said, she was so thrilled to be seeing him again.

Pete was very attentive to Nancy on Saturday night. They jitterbugged and smooched, and sat upstairs in the cafeteria in the interval and talked. She learned that his parents lived in Kent and he'd worked in a bank before the war. He was an only child and his father was something substantial in the civil service.

He seemed more interested in talking about her, so she told him a little about the family, and her job.

'A railway porter, eh?' he said, as though that was the most fascinating employment in the world. 'That must be interesting; you get to meet all sorts in that job, I bet.'

She made a face. 'You can say that again. But I enjoy the work. It's certainly taught me how to handle people. It's hard graft, though.'

'I bet you look snazzy in uniform.'

'I don't know about that, but I am rather proud to wear it.'

'You'd look good in anything.'

This was getting better by the second. 'Thank you,' she said graciously.

He held her hand across the table and looked at her as though she was the most beautiful woman he'd ever seen. 'I expect you're used to receiving compliments, a woman with your looks, that stunning hair and such gorgeous blue eyes.'

Actually, she couldn't remember the last time she'd been complimented about her appearance, but she just said modestly, 'Well . . . we all get nice things said to us from time to time, don't we?'

After the interval they danced every dance and could hardly have got closer when they played 'Who's Taking You Home Tonight?' He insisted on seeing her home right to her door. He didn't have to go back to camp until the next day so wasn't worried about the time and seemed unconcerned about how he would get back, since there would be no buses or trains by the time he'd been to Ealing with her. He told her he'd walk if necessary, as though Northolt was just around the corner. What a gentleman!

When they arrived at her place, the spot outside the front door was occupied by Jean and Ed, getting as close as was possible in a public place without breaking the laws of decency, so Pete kissed Nancy goodnight at the gate. There wasn't much of a moon, so privacy wasn't a problem.

'I'd better be off, then,' he said eventually, having arranged to see her again.

Without any prior intention, she blurted out, 'I can't let you walk for miles in the blackout. You can hardly see a thing tonight. You're welcome to stay here until the morning if you don't mind sleeping on the sofa.'

'That's very kind of you,' he said, smiling. 'But will it be all right with your father?'

'He'll be in bed, but it'll be fine,' she assured him. Dad was not the easiest of men, but he was very patriotic and wouldn't turn anyone in uniform away.

As it happened, there were two strange men in the Sparrows' living room when Arthur came down the next morning to get an early cup of tea. Jean had taken her lead from Nancy and Ed was in the armchair, Pete on the sofa. The sisters had managed to find a few blankets for them, and the men used their heavy coats for extra warmth.

Much to Nancy's surprise, her father took an instant liking to Pete. She'd thought he might be too sophisticated for

Arthur's taste, and he'd feel awkward in the company of such polished manners, but he was very impressed.

'They're brave boys, our pilots,' he said after the men had gone, having been given breakfast, albeit that porridge and toast was all they had to offer. Jean had gone to tell her gran all about her amazing American, and Leslie was playing out in the street, so they were on their own. 'They've done wonders for this country in the war, absolute wonders.'

'He hasn't said much about what he does,' Nancy said. 'He seems proud to be a pilot, but hasn't given any details.'

'Military people have to be very careful what they say, especially with all these "Careless Talk Costs Lives" and "Walls Have Ears" posters everywhere.'

'I'd be interested to hear about such an exciting job, though.'

'What he does is so dangerous he probably doesn't want to think about it when he's off duty,' her father suggested. 'War pilots are under tremendous pressure. Up there in the sky, exposed, just them against the enemy. It's a very daring occupation.'

'I'm sure.'

'You've found yourself a good 'un there, Nancy,' he effused. 'A real gent. You want to hang on to him. Don't let him slip through your fingers.'

'He isn't a bar of soap,' she chuckled.

'You know very well what I mean. That's a man who'd know how to treat a wife. He's a good catch, an' all. He's in the professional classes. You wouldn't go hungry if you were married to him.'

'Steady on, Dad. This was only our second meeting,' she reminded him.

'If you've any sense you'll make sure there's a third and fourth and plenty more after that,' he advised her.

'There is going to be a third next weekend, but who knows what will happen after that?'

'He seems very keen on you,' her father observed. 'He couldn't take his eyes off you.'

'Yes, he does seem to like me, but it's very early days. Let's just see how it goes, shall we?'

But she was looking forward to seeing Pete again. His charm and obvious admiration gave her a terrific boost. She was cautious, though. Someone like him could easily sweep a girl off her feet.

Whilst taking an instant liking to Pete, Arthur was rather more circumspect in his judgement of Ed, purely because of the reputation the GIs had where women were concerned.

'You watch your step, my girl,' he lectured Jean later. 'The Yanks are sex mad.'

'Not all of them,' she defended.

'Of course they're not.' Nancy backed her up. She'd thought Ed was an absolute sweetheart when the four of them had been talking last night before bed. He was warm, generous and funny, and seemed very taken with Jean. 'I thought he was a smashing bloke.'

'I'm not saying he isn't a nice enough fella,' Arthur made clear. 'But there are plenty of our girls finding themselves in trouble by the Yanks. So make sure you don't become one of 'em, because they don't stay around to accept their responsibilities after they've had their fun.'

'Do you have to be so crude, Dad?' objected Jean.

'If I need to make a point, yes.'

'Give Ed a chance, Dad,' urged Nancy. 'Don't judge him on hearsay about the Americans in general.'

'I'm just spelling out the situation as it really is, not how it seems to an impressionable young woman like Jean.' He looked at Nancy. 'There's no point in her having her head filled with lovey-dovey rubbish. Everyone knows what the Yanks are like. They're young, away from home and having a good time when they're off duty.'

'I'd marry him tomorrow if he asked me,' announced Jean in a serious tone.

'If he did mention marriage, it would only be to have his way with you.'

'I would be very upset by that remark, Dad, if I didn't know that what you say isn't true.'

'I'm a man of the world and I know what I'm talking about.' Although Arthur had taken no part in his children's lives when they were growing up, he was more involved with them now and instinctively concerned for their welfare. His views on this issue were coloured, however, by the general view shared by British men about the GIs.

'Perhaps it might be an idea for you to get to know him better before you start making plans for the future,' advised Nancy. 'You *have* only just met him.'

'That makes no difference to the way I feel,' she stated categorically. 'I know he's the right man for me.'

'You've felt like that before,' Nancy reminded her.

'No. Not like this.' Jean was adamant, but unusually subdued. 'Ed is the only man for me and I have a strong feeling that it's the same for him.'

'Are you sure you're not just in love with the idea of love, not to mention the stockings and chocolate and other goodies that'll come your way?'

'That's a horrible thing to say, Dad,' she objected strongly. 'How can you think that about your own daughter?'

'Come on, Jean. You used to say that yourself,' Nancy reminded her. 'You were always going on about getting a Yank for what you could get out of him.'

'Originally, yes, but it's different now that I've met Ed.' She was ardent about it. 'I know how I feel and no one can take that away from me. It doesn't matter what you say to try to put me off, it won't work because I know my own mind about this.'

'Let's wait and see what happens, shall we?' suggested Nancy in an effort to defuse the situation.

But somehow she knew that neither her father's views on the subject of Ed, nor anyone else's would make any difference to her besotted sister.

Chapter Ten

Spring was definitely on the way, thought Bobby cheerfully, noticing how light it still was as he strode through the Acton streets on his way to Irene's flat one blustery evening in March 1943. The government's extension of summer time had made a big difference to the hours of daylight, and would be even more significant next month when the clocks went forward a second hour for double summer time.

He was home on a weekend pass and had been working in the shop all day. Now it was time to make arrangements for some relaxation with Irene this evening. They always managed to have a few laughs, which was just what he needed during a break from army life.

Immersed in thoughts of light relief ahead, he almost collided with a man in a trilby hat and raincoat who was standing in the middle of the street, peering towards the houses with a puzzled expression.

'Can I help you, mate?' offered Bobby. 'You're looking a bit lost.'

'I'm looking for number thirty and I'm buggered if I can

find it,' the man explained, referring to a book he was holding. 'I haven't been to this street before and a lot of the houses aren't numbered.'

'It's a wonder the doors haven't gone, as well as the numbers,' remarked Bobby, nodding towards the cavities on the other side of the road. 'This street has taken quite a battering.'

'It's the same everywhere you look,' the man said, with a sad shake of the head. 'London's like a ruddy bombsite.'

'Battered but not broken, eh?'

'Break us! Never!' agreed the man spiritedly.

Bobby looked towards the houses, which were small and old and terraced. 'Let's see if we can find one with a number on it and you can work it out from that,' he said companionably, moving along, studying the front doors. 'Ah, here's number twenty and twenty-two so it's a few doors down to the right.'

'Thanks, mate,' said the man, looking at Bobby properly for the first time.

Bobby reeled from a blast of recognition. He would know that face anywhere, even though time had marched all over it since he'd last set eyes on it. But Nancy had said both her parents were dead. 'Mr Sparrow?' he blurted out disbelievingly.

'That's me.' Arthur studied the other man's face, looking blank.

'I wouldn't expect you to remember me. I was just a boy the last time you saw me.' He paused. 'Bobby Collins . . . ?'

Arthur's eyes widened slightly and he fixed his studious

gaze on Bobby's countenance, his expression hardening. 'Your face doesn't look familiar, but I remember the name. It's one I'm never likely to forget.'

'It was all a long time ago,' said Bobby, wishing now that he'd remained anonymous, and moving on swiftly. He was deeply affected by this meeting because seeing this man again reminded him of Nancy, whom he'd tried so hard to forget over the past months. 'So, how are you keeping, Mr Sparrow?'

'Not so dusty.'

'What brings you to these parts?'

'I'm working. Doing my insurance round. I've got a few houses to call on around here. There aren't enough collectors, with so many people being away in the forces, so I have to go out of my own local area.'

'Oh.' Bobby was surprised by the nature of his employment. 'You work on dry land these days, then?'

'Hobson's choice,' Arthur replied. 'My health got buggered when my ship went down, and I had to come out of the merchant service.'

'Sorry to hear that,' said Bobby in a sympathetic manner. One thing he did remember clearly about Nancy's dad was his love of the sea.

'Sailing the high seas is a hell of a lot different to doing an insurance round,' he went on to say. 'Still, someone's got to do it and it suits me.'

Bobby nodded politely.

'Have you seen any action?' enquired Arthur, acknowledging the fact that Bobby was in uniform.

'Yeah, I was in the Western Desert earlier in the war. They brought me back to Blighty when I got wounded and I've been at Aldershot ever since, for some reason best known to the army. How much longer I'll be there, I've no idea. But I am expecting to get posted abroad again at some point soon.'

'The war's certainly dragging on longer than anyone expected.'

'That's a fact.' Bobby hesitated, looking at Arthur. 'How's Nancy?' he asked, hungry for news of her.

'She's very well,' her father replied with a note of triumph in his voice. 'In fact, she's never been better. She's courting strong. An airman – a pilot, as it happens.'

Bobby felt like he'd been punched in the stomach, but he did his best to appear unfazed. 'A pilot, eh! A touch of class.'

'He's a very decent chap and thinks the world of her. We're expecting them to get engaged at any time.'

'Good. I'm glad she's happy.' Bobby's smile was strained.

'She certainly deserves it,' said Arthur pointedly. 'She didn't exactly have a good start as far as that sort of thing is concerned, did she?'

'No.' Bobby was determined not to be dragged into an argument.

'She seems settled at last.'

Bobby detected the warning in his tone, even after all these years, and needed to get away before his true feelings became apparent. 'Well, I'll let you get on with your work.'

'OK, then.'

'S'long then, Mr Sparrow.'

'Ta-ta,' replied Arthur.

As Bobby carried on down the street, he was aware of a drastic change in his mood. It had shifted from happy and hopeful to desolate in a split second, and all because of an unexpected meeting with someone he'd thought was dead. He wished he hadn't seen Mr Sparrow. He'd have been better off not knowing about Nancy's new man. She'd made it clear to Bobby that there could be no future for them, but there had always been that lingering hope. Now that he knew she was with someone else, even that had gone.

'What's up with you?' asked Irene when she opened the door to him, her eyes resting on him adoringly. 'Have Hitler and his army landed on our beaches or something?'

'They'd have a job.'

'You look as though you could do with some cheering up, whatever put that miserable look on your face,' she said, ushering him inside. 'And I'm just the person to do it.'

'Good. Let's go out and have some fun tonight, shall we?'

'I've an even better idea. Instead of going out, why don't we have a quiet night in here?' she suggested meaningfully. 'I know just what you need to put the smile back on your face.'

He found himself grinning in spite of himself. She really was good company and did seem to think a lot of him. 'I'm all in favour of that,' he enthused.

'Why not stay now?' She made a face. 'Though I'm a bit low on rations.'

'Mum will be cooking a meal for me, so I'll have to go home and have that,' he explained. 'Mustn't waste food, must we?'

'I'll see you later, then.'

Bobby felt better as he made his way home. Nancy was getting on with her life, and maybe it was time he did the same and made a proper commitment to Irene. What did it matter if he wasn't in love with her? She was very keen on him, and he would be good to her. Once committed he wouldn't let her down. It wasn't as if he was ever going to get over Nancy, but maybe marriage to Irene would help him to finally move on.

Perhaps he should begin to think in terms of proposing to her at some point. It was a shame, he thought as he reached his front door, that the idea didn't fill him with excitement.

It was Easter Sunday and Nancy and Pete were walking in Hyde Park hand in hand. As shabby as the park was, with parts left untended, sheep grazing here and there and an area turned over to allotments in the 'grow more food' campaign, an element of normality survived, with a few indomitable tulips and daffodils providing a welcome splash of colour, and people queuing for rowing boats by the Serpentine.

The West End was heaving with people; everybody, it seemed, was out and about, despite the government's plea for them to stay at home, and warnings of overcrowded public transport. The expected return of the Blitz hadn't happened and people were making the most of it, knowing that they could be driven back into their Anderson shelters at any time.

'It'll be absolute chaos at work tomorrow, being Bank Holiday Monday,' mentioned Nancy casually. 'The trains were crowded like you wouldn't believe yesterday and the day-trippers will be out in force tomorrow, so it'll be all hell let loose on the station. It's a good job I managed to get today off. At least I've had a chance to recharge my batteries.'

'I'm glad you got the day off too,' Pete said, slipping his arm around her. 'If you hadn't, I'd have sat in Paddington station all day and watched you at work.'

'Aah, that's sweet, but I can't think of anything more boring for you,' she said, smiling at him.

'It wouldn't be boring, not as long as I could catch a glimpse of you.'

'You say the nicest things.'

'I mean them too.'

She believed him. He really was the most charming man she had ever come across, and he hadn't put a foot wrong since the day she'd met him. He and Ed were now regular overnighters in the Sparrows' living room, and took it turn about with the sofa and the armchair. Pete couldn't get a pass every weekend, but they had had quite a few together and, in between times, he sent her the most loving of letters.

Now they sat down on a bench in the sunshine, idly chatting and watching the world go by. After a while, he suggested that they walk up to Marble Arch for tea, if they could get in anywhere. On the way, they saw that a jolly crowd had gathered in Park Lane and joined it to see what all the laughter was about. The cause of the merriment was a sheep that had taken advantage of the lack of railings – which had been removed for the nation's scrap-metal pile – and strolled into the road. The animal was sitting down in front of a jeep full of bewildered Americans. It was quite content and showed no sign of moving. Eventually, one of the GIs managed to stir it with some gentle persuasion and led it back into the park to loud cheers from the crowd. The holiday spirit was very much alive and kicking, despite all the obstacles.

They joined the crowds in Lyons and had toast and currant buns. Nancy was trying to squeeze another cup of tea each out of the pot when Pete said, 'I'm going away to Norfolk in a day or two on a special course, and there won't be any leave until I get back, so I won't be able to see you for a while.'

'Oh.' Surprised by this unexpected news, Nancy put the teapot down on the table and looked at him. 'How long is a while, exactly?'

'Could be as long as a few months or even more,' he replied. 'I honestly don't know. It's all very hush-hush.'

'I'll miss you,' she said frankly.

'Likewise.'

'We'll just have to put up with it.'

He seemed distracted. 'Actually, Nancy, there's something I want to say to you.'

He's going to end it, she thought, the energy seeming to drain out of her. He's going to give me the push.

'The thing is . . .' he began. 'Well, you know how I feel about you, don't you?'

'Do I . . . ?' She was confused now.

'I'm sure you must know that I love you.' He paused, looking at her adoringly. 'So . . . will you marry me, Nancy?'

Nancy was speechless. She supposed she shouldn't have been surprised, since Pete had seemed smitten with her since the day they'd met. But she hadn't expected a marriage proposal! Not yet, anyway.

'I know we haven't known each other long, but I know that you're the only woman for me,' he continued when she didn't reply. 'Marry me, Nancy, please, as soon as we can.'

Her head was spinning. He inspired her with happiness and desire; he pressed all the right buttons. Yes, all of that. But she didn't feel as if she really knew him. Their relationship had never been the stuff of real life. That was part of its charm – the surreal and ephemeral feel to it. They only saw each other for a few hours on a Saturday night, if he could get a pass, and part of Sunday morning. That wasn't long enough to know anyone beyond a superficial level. He'd probably been on his best behaviour, too, as people were when it was all so new.

She suspected that she'd never seen the real Pete. She'd never heard him say a word out of place or lose his temper. Their conversations were always casual and jokey. Were these lightweight meetings enough of a foundation for a lifetime together? Plenty of people got married on less, especially these days, she reminded herself.

'I know it's a bit sudden,' he was saying, obviously worried by her silence. 'But who knows what tomorrow will bring? We have to seize the moment these days.'

'Yes, yes, of course,' she said, unsure about her feelings for him, but anxious not to hurt him. Disturbingly, she couldn't stop thinking about Bobby at this crucial moment and struggled to push him out of her mind. 'I'm a bit taken aback, that's all, especially as we won't see each other for ages after we part today.'

'Exactly. If we were married, it would be a comfort to us both when I'm away,' he went on eagerly. 'If we could get married today, I'd do it. But we both know that isn't possible, so let's do it on my next leave.' His enthusiasm was almost childlike.

'We can't get married just like that,' Nancy replied. 'It's a huge step to take.'

'People don't hang about in wartime,' Pete pointed out. 'They just go ahead and do it, with no frills or fuss. Big weddings are out of fashion, with everything being in short supply and people being on the move.'

'Hey, slow down, Pete,' she urged him. 'People usually get engaged first. You haven't thought it through properly.'

'It isn't a spur of the moment decision.' He took a small box out of his pocket and opened it to reveal a diamond ring. 'And here is the proof.'

She gasped, her hand flying to her chest. 'Oh, Pete, I don't know what to say.'

'Just say that you'll wear it.' He seemed keen to the point of desperation. Her mind was in a whirl. But then he gave her one of his most irresistible smiles and added, 'Please say you'll wear my ring. It would make me so happy.'

Somehow his ardour swept her along, and she held out her left hand. 'In that case, I'd be honoured,' she heard herself say.

'Thank you,' he said, slipping the ring on to the appropriate finger. 'Thank you so much.'

'It's beautiful,' she said, studying the small solitaire diamond and watching it sparkle in the light.

He leaned forward and kissed her across the table while people around them smiled. Although she managed to conceal it well, Nancy was disconcerted by a sudden and unexpected shudder of fear . . .

The family were all delighted for her when Nancy told them the news later. Pete had had to leave her at Ealing Broadway to get the bus back to camp so wasn't with her.

'You didn't waste any time, did you?' said Jean with good-humoured envy. 'You got him hooked double sharp. You've certainly made up for lost time.'

'I didn't get him hooked, as you put it,' corrected Nancy. 'He thought it up all on his own.'

'Lucky you. I wish Ed would do the same,' said Jean wistfully. 'Still, perhaps this news will give him a nudge in the right direction.'

'Ed will do it when he's ready, without any prompting, given time,' suggested Nancy. 'Anyone can see that he's dotty about you.'

'I'll say he is,' piped up Leslie disapprovingly. 'He's always slobbering over her when he thinks no one can see them. Ugh, it's horrible. It turns my stomach.'

'That's enough of that sort of talk, Leslie,' warned his father. 'You shouldn't speak like that about your sister and her boyfriend.'

'You wouldn't be so pleased if Ed did pop the question, would you, Dad?' suggested Jean, moving on. 'Given your opinion of Americans.'

'I'm not so dead-set in my opinion of them now,' he told her. 'Ed's a very nice bloke when you get to know him.' Ed was a hard man to dislike and Arthur had failed miserably, won over by the young American's warm heart, generosity and the occasional bottle of whisky from the Post Exchange, or PX as it was usually known, the US equivalent to the British NAAFI. 'I just don't want you to get your hopes up too high about him taking you back to America with him. It's one thing taking a girl out dancing or to the pictures, and quite another taking her halfway across the world as his wife.'

'I realise that. But what makes you so sure he won't want to do that?' she asked.

'I'm not sure that he won't,' he was quick to assure her. 'I hope he does if that's what you really want. I don't want you to get hurt, that's all. Anyway, I'm not so sure if it isn't just the glamour of going to America you're really after.'

'How many more times must I tell you that I love Ed for himself?' Her voice rose with fervour as she struggled to convince them. 'I've changed since I met him. And yes, I do want to go to America because of the glamour of the place.

It's my dream and I'm not ashamed of that. But if Ed wanted to stay here after the war or go to Timbuktu to live, I'd be happy with that, as long as I was with him.'

'I believe you,' said Nancy. 'And I'm sure Ed will ask you soon.'

'I'm sure he will too,' responded Jean. 'No matter what Dad says. I know Ed better than you lot and I know how he feels about me.'

'You girls and your love lives,' tutted Arthur. 'I'm going down the pub for some men's talk.'

'And I'm going to see Gran to tell her my news.' Nancy paused, remembering an arrangement she had made with her sister earlier. 'Did you look after Evie for a while this afternoon so Gran could have a rest, like you promised?'

'I wouldn't dare not to, knowing you'd be on my back if I didn't,' she said. 'Ed didn't have to go back to camp until teatime so we took her over the park.'

'Thanks. I owe you. I'll take your turn the next time you want to go out on a Sunday afternoon.' Nancy walked towards the door with a spring in her step. 'See you all later, then.'

The fact that Leicester Square was dirty, shabby and bomb-damaged didn't keep the crowds away. It was teeming with people one Saturday afternoon in May when Nancy and Ruby were queuing at the Empire Cinema to see *Gone With the Wind*. They'd both been on early turn at the station, and had come here straight from work. They'd been spending more time together lately, since Polly had gone.

'Will you be moving far away when you get married?' enquired Ruby chattily.

'No, of course not,' said Nancy, alarmed that such an idea had even occurred to her. 'Whatever makes you ask that?'

'People do sometimes move away to another area when they get married, don't they?'

'I suppose some do.' She hadn't considered this at all. 'But not many, especially in wartime, with all the men away in the forces. They stay where they are to be near their families.'

'You won't be going into married quarters, then?'

'I hope not. I don't want to move away. But I must admit, Pete and I haven't even talked about that side of it yet. It's much too far into the future. Anyway, I can't move far because of my job.'

The real reason she needed to stay close to home was to keep Evie out of Dad's way, and help Gran with her as much as she could. But she kept quiet about that because Ruby hadn't been taken into her confidence about the Sparrows' dark secret. She'd been given the same story as everyone else, that Evie lived with Gran because they were all out at work for long hours, and it gave the child more stability if she was housed at her grandmother's.

'That's one good thing to come out of the war,' remarked Ruby. 'At least there can be no argument from the men about their wives going out to work, since they are obliged to do so now by law.'

Nancy was thoughtful. 'I think Pete might be the sort of

man who wouldn't want his wife to work in normal times, when there's a choice.'

'You only think? Don't you know?'

'No, I don't as it happens. We've never discussed anything like that,' Nancy replied, reminded of how little she knew her fiancé. 'It all happened so fast. We only had a few hours together after he popped the question. We didn't get around to talking about actual married life.'

'What about in your letters to each other?'

'Oh no, we don't touch on anything as practical as that. It's all very lovey-dovey.'

'How romantic.' Ruby thought for a moment. 'You could always bring up the practical side of it, though.'

'I could do.' Nancy paused thoughtfully. 'But I'd rather wait until he comes home.'

'You're not overly anxious to get the wedding arrangements underway, then?'

'I'm not, as it happens. I'd like to just enjoy the fun and excitement of being engaged for a while, before we get weighed down with practicalities,' she confided without any prior intention. 'It's all happened a bit too fast, to tell you the truth, Ruby. I think we ought to get to know each other better before we rush into marriage. I haven't even met his people yet.'

'Doubts?' queried Ruby.

'No, not at all.' Nancy refused to let any of those take root. She was doing the right thing and everything was going to be all right, she had convinced herself. 'It will all be fine when he comes home on leave. It's not seeing him that makes him seem like a stranger.'

Ruby looked wistful. 'It must be nice to have a sister to talk things over with.'

'I haven't talked to Jean about my relationship with Pete,' she told her.

'She's there if you want to, though, isn't she?'

'Oh yes, she's there, in the flesh anyway,' Nancy said with a wry grin. 'If not always in spirit. She's very taken up with her American boyfriend at the moment.'

'I wish there had been someone for me to talk to . . . about things.'

'Boyfriends and stuff?'

'Not especially that. Just things . . .'

'Is something the matter, Ruby?' asked Nancy kindly, noticing a terrible sadness descend on her suddenly. For a moment, Nancy thought her friend was going to burst into tears.

But she just said; 'No, I'm all right.'

'You sure?'

'Yeah, I'm fine.' She spoke in such a way as to discourage further enquiry, and looked towards the entrance of the cinema where people were beginning to come out. 'At last. The early performance must have finished, so we should be going in soon.'

Taking the hint, Nancy said, 'About bloomin' time too. I hope the film will be worth the wait.'

They weren't disappointed. Three hours and forty-eight minutes later they emerged, feeling refreshed and uplifted, having sat through dramatic battles and passionate love scenes, all in glorious Technicolor, the war and all their personal problems forgotten. They talked of nothing but the film all the way home on the train.

When Nancy got in, she immediately detected a peculiar atmosphere in the house.

'What are you doing at home on Saturday night?' Nancy asked her sister. 'Ed can't have stood you up or you wouldn't have that soppy great grin on your face.'

'Of course he hasn't stood me up. He wouldn't do that,' Jean was keen to point out. 'He's just popped down the pub to see if he can get hold of something to celebrate with.'

'Celebrate? Why? What's happened? Has he proposed? Is that it?'

'No, it isn't that.'

'What, then? And what's tickling you, Leslie?' Her little brother was giggling and her father smiling. 'What's the matter with you all? Has the war ended while I've been out, or something?'

'You'd have known about it wherever you were, if it had,' grinned her father.

'But we do have a surprise for you,' announced Jean.

'Surprise? What's going on?'

'Close your eyes,' instructed Jean.

'Why? What for?'

'Just close your eyes and shut up,' came Jean's typical reaction.

Nancy finally did as she was asked, and heard the squeak of the kitchen door opening, then footsteps and some whispering and chuckling.

'All right, you can open them now,' said her sister.

Wondering what on earth she was about to see, she opened her eyes.

'Micky!' she whooped with delight, seeing her brother standing in front of her. Tears of joy streaming down her face, she threw her arms around his neck and smacked a kiss on his cheek. 'Oh, Micky. It's so good to see you.'

'You too, sis.'

'I can't believe it. How . . . ?'

'They've brought some of us back for some sort of special training down in Hampshire,' he explained. 'Don't ask me what or why because I haven't a clue. They're keeping us in the dark, as usual. Anyway, I'm long overdue some leave, so they've given me ten days before we get started.'

'What a wonderful surprise,' she said, hugging him again and feasting her eyes on him, taking in every inch of his face, his freckles, his ginger hair. He was thinner than he used to be and looked a little gaunt, but seemed fit enough. 'We thought you were in some god-forsaken corner of Italy.'

'I was, and I will be again soon. After a few weeks at the camp in Hampshire we're going straight back overseas.'

'You've nearly given me a heart attack with the shock, but it was worth it,' she said.

'I thought my heart was going to give out when I saw that Dad was alive,' he confessed. 'I thought I was seeing a ghost when I saw him sitting in the armchair.'

'I did write and tell you,' said Nancy.

'Yes, Jean said you did, but I didn't get the letter.'

'How do you think we all felt when he came strolling in

the front door as though he'd never been away?' she smiled. 'It's a wonder we didn't pass out cold.'

They had a do for Micky at the Rook and Raven on the Saturday night a couple of days before he was due to go back. Ruby sat with Evie so that the Sparrow women could all go together, and Leslie stayed at his pal's house a few doors down.

'Enjoying yourself, Gran?' asked Nancy, while Micky was busy talking to his father, Uncle Wilf and Ed. Jean, completely disregarding the fact that some people fiercely disapproved of women who went out with the 'oversexed Americans', was busy extolling Ed's virtues to some neighbours.

'Yes, love, I am,' replied Gladys. 'It's ever so nice of Ruby to look after Evie for us. She's very good with her. She has a way with kiddies.'

'She does seem to be very fond of Evie and jumped at the chance of sitting with her.'

'Evie loves her, too.'

'Mm.'

Gladys cast her eye around the room. 'It's a pity none of Micky's pals are around to see him before he goes back,' she mused.

'I suppose we can't expect the army to take that sort of thing into consideration when there's a war to be won,' said Nancy. 'It's just wonderful to have him home, even though it isn't for long.'

Predictably, Nancy was asked to take her place at the piano, and she played the usual favourites. She'd just come to the end of 'Bless 'em All' when she noticed something that caused her to decide it was time to take a break.

'All getting on top of you is it, Micky?' she asked, finding her brother standing outside alone, smoking a cigarette in the dusk. He was looking morose, until he saw her, when he immediately forced a smile.

'What are you doing out here, sis?'

'I saw you slip away and thought I'd come out and find out what's the matter.'

'Why should anything be the matter just because I've come outside for some fresh air?' he asked.

'You haven't just come out here for fresh air. You've come out to be on your own because something is bothering you. I don't know what it is, but I know there's something on your mind. Would you rather have had a quiet leave? With a little less fuss. Is that what it is?'

'Of course not. I'd think you were all ill if you didn't organise a party of some sort.'

'Well, something's troubling you. I've seen it in your eyes ever since you've been home.'

He drew hard on his cigarette, staring blankly ahead of him. 'No, nothing's wrong, Nancy. I'm fine, honestly. I just came out here for a bit of a breather.'

'I understand,' she said. 'I just wanted to make sure that you're all right.'

'You always were the family mindreader, but you've got it wrong this time.' He exhaled slowly to make a smoke ring. 'I can't be laughing and joking all the time, you know.'

'You've done plenty of that since you've been home,' she

said. 'But only for our benefit. The laughter hasn't come from your heart.'

'Leave it, sis, please.'

'We're all so proud of you, Micky,' she told him.

It was as though she'd physically struck him. He stiffened visibly, his jaw tightening. 'Thanks.'

'Well, don't sound so pleased about it,' she said with irony. 'We're your family. Of course we're proud of you. You deserve it.'

He stared at her and she thought for a moment he was going to slap her. But he said stiffly, 'It's nice of you to say so but, you know me, I'm not one for pretty speeches.'

'Yeah, I do know that.'

'Didn't you ought to go back inside before they send out a search party for the pianist?'

'I'd rather stay out here and chat to you for a while, even though you can't wait to get rid of me.'

'If you're going to stay, stop talking about me,' he said. 'Tell me about this pilot fella of yours.'

She didn't have a chance, as it happened, because Uncle Wilf came looking for her. 'There you are, Nancy,' he said. 'What are you doing out here?'

'Talking to Micky.'

'Can't you do that later? They're all asking for you to get back on the piano.'

'OK. I'm coming.'

Wilf disappeared inside.

'Go on, then,' urged Micky. 'You heard what the man said.'

'See you later, then,' she said and went inside.

It was quite some time before she saw Micky come back into the pub. That is one very troubled young man, she thought worriedly.

Evie was two years old. She was bright, loquacious, loveable, had more energy than the National Grid, and little fingers that found their way into everything. She was also extremely determined. She had decided that she didn't want to go to sleep yet and there was nothing Ruby could do to persuade her otherwise.

'Wanna get up,' said the little girl, her huge blue eyes resting persuasively on Ruby through the bars of her cot.

'You have to go to sleep now, darling,' tried Ruby. 'You've had your story. It's time to settle down.'

She pointed to the door. 'Another story. Other room,' she said, her lower lip trembling.

'Now don't start that lip-wobbling thing,' said the power-less Ruby, struggling not to weaken. 'It's sleep time for a little girl like you. Come on now, settle down.'

'Story . . . please.'

'You've had lots of stories,' Ruby reminded her.

But Evie didn't give up that easily. She certainly knew how to turn on the waterworks and Ruby was no match for her when she was in full flow, despite the fact that Gladys had warned her that she would need to be firm on the bedtime issue.

'Oh, all right then, just five minutes,' she said, lifting her out of her cot. 'But that's all.'

The crying stopped instantly.

'You're a fraud, do you know that, Evie Sparrow?' Ruby said affectionately, carrying her into Gladys's living room. 'A proper little con artist.'

In reply, Evie put her arms around her neck and gave her a wet kiss.

'You'll get me shot if your gran finds out I've let you stay up,' Ruby told her, doing her best to sound stern, even though she was completely in thrall to her.

As she settled down with Evie on her lap, Ruby thought how very lucky Nancy was to have siblings, Evie in particular. Oh, well, that was just the way things were. You had what you were given in life and got on with it. She opened the book and began yet another reading of *Goldilocks and the Three Bears*.

The five Sparrow siblings were in the garden in the sunshine the following afternoon. Their father was inside, their grandmother having her Sunday afternoon rest.

'You'll make Evie sick, throwing her up in the air like that, Micky,' warned Jean from a kitchen chair in the sun.

'She loves it,' said Micky, as Evie screamed with laughter and begged for more.

'That doesn't mean she won't bring her dinner up all over you,' said Leslie, who was at an age to enjoy any talk of an unwholesome nature.

'She wouldn't do that, would you, Evie?' said Micky fondly. 'She has far too much respect for her big brother.'

'Piggyback, pease,' she demanded, lifting her arms.

'A piggyback it is,' he said, lifting her on to his back and running around the small garden with her.

'You'll be worn out before she is,' warned Nancy who, with Leslie, was weeding the vegetable patch that had once been their lawn. She was pleased to see Micky smiling, and seeming to mean it. He was really enjoying Evie, who had only been a small baby when he last saw her.

'I'm exhausted already,' he puffed.

'You've a way to go yet, mate,' his sister chuckled. 'She's hardly started.'

He gave Evie a few more turns around the garden, then handed her over to Leslie, who put her on his shoulders and walked around with her. He had now been told that she was his half-sister and seemed to love her no less for that. The truth about her origins hadn't seemed to shock him, perhaps because he wasn't old enough to fully comprehend such things.

'Phew! I see what you mean,' said Micky, flopping down on a chair beside Jean. 'She's got more energy than the Flying Scotsman.'

'Oi! Jean!' called Nancy. 'You can stop sunning yourself and give me a hand with this weeding.'

'In a minute.'

'I'm not supposed to be the only one in this family digging for victory, you know.'

'Dad'll do it,' said Jean without any interest. 'He enjoys a spot of gardening.'

'He can't do it all,' Nancy reminded her. 'It's too much for him with his dicky lungs. You help to eat the stuff we grow, so you should help with the work. It's only fair.'

'I'll give you a hand,' offered Micky.

'No, you don't have to help. We'll let you off, as you're going back off leave tomorrow.'

He got up and went over anyway, getting down on to his haunches beside her.

'Isn't Evie allowed in the house at all?' he asked in a low voice, because the doors and windows were open and he didn't want their father to hear.

'Only when it can't possibly be avoided. Christmas, that sort of thing. She has wandered in there on the odd occasion, but Dad went berserk so we try to make sure it doesn't happen again by keeping a careful eye on her.'

'I suppose you can see his point in a way. I mean, it must have been one hell of a shock for him, coming home to find Mum dead and Evie here. And he isn't obliged to accept her,' he said. 'But it does seem a shame, for both of them, because she's such a little sweetheart.'

'As you say, he's quite within his rights, and we have to respect his wishes.' She pulled out a weed from among the cabbages. 'But I feel the same way as you do about it. He's missing out as much as she is.'

'What are you two whispering about?' Jean wanted to know.

'Come and do your bit over here and you'll find out,' challenged Nancy.

'I'm not that eager to know,' she chortled.

Nancy felt a sudden surge of emotion. It was lovely, the five of them here together, talking, teasing, laughing. She was so glad Micky would have the memory of this Sunday afternoon to take back to the battlefields with him. For the first time since he'd arrived home, he seemed to have relaxed a little. There was something tormenting him, though, she was sure of it.

That night Nancy woke up with a start, wondering what had disturbed her, and realised at once that it was the sound of footsteps on the stairs.

Slipping out of bed, she crept from the room in her pyjamas, careful not to wake Jean, not even stopping for her dressing-gown.

Micky was sitting on the sofa in the living room, smoking a cigarette.

'Can't you sleep?' she asked.

'No, and I didn't want to wake Leslie with all the tossing and turning,' he explained in a low voice.

'Fancy a cuppa?' she whispered.

'I was going to make one, but didn't want to use the tea ration.'

'I think we can spare a few tea leaves for a soldier,' she said. 'I'll have one with you.'

'You go back to bed,' he urged her. 'You've got to get up early for work in the morning.'

She sat down in an armchair opposite him, leaning forward slightly, with her lower arms resting on her knees. 'Is it the thought of going back that's worrying you?' she asked.

'Who says I'm worried?'

'I do.'

'You always were a nosy cow.' He tried to make a joke of it, but it fell flat.

'That's what sisters are for, isn't it? To poke their nose into their brother's business.'

'Look, I know you mean well, Nance, and I appreciate it,' he said, knocking the ash off his cigarette into the ash-tray, 'but you can't help.'

'So there is something?'

'There was,' he admitted. 'But not now, because I've solved the problem.'

'Really? You don't look as though you have.'

He looked at her through a pall of smoke. 'There's no point in pumping me, Nancy, because I'm saying nothing more.'

'Why are you being so mysterious?'

'I don't want to implicate you.'

'Implicate me? What are you talking about? What have you done?'

'Nothing. Just leave it, will you, and go back to bed.'

'You're scaring me, Micky, with all this secrecy and talk of implication,' she told him. 'You can't leave me not knowing, and worrying like this.'

He was silent, twisting his cigarette end in the ash-tray.

'Micky, what's going on? Please tell me.'

He looked at her, his facial muscles pulled tight with tension. 'All right, you asked for it, but you won't like it,' he said in a hard tone, lowering his eyes. 'I'm not going back. When I leave here tomorrow I won't be reporting back for duty, but as far as the others are concerned, I've gone back in the normal way.'

'What . . . what do you mean?'

271

'What do you think I mean?'

'Oh Micky, you can't be a deserter!' she gasped. 'They'll hunt you down. They won't rest until they've caught you. Your life will be a living hell.'

He shrugged. 'At least I won't have to kill anyone else,' he said grimly. 'I can't do it any more, Nance. I can't stand to be a part of any more mass murder; the smell and feel of it, the whole bloody business.' Tears came into his eyes and his voice was ragged with emotion. 'Do you know what it feels like to kill a man, a young, strong man who just happened to have been born in another country? Can you imagine what that feels like?'

'Terrible, I should think. I'll never know,' she replied. 'But Micky, you're doing it for your country, for all of us. So that we can be free.'

'Don't you think I know that? It makes it even worse that I don't have the stomach for it.' He looked into space, remembering. 'It's ironic really. I was so keen for action; couldn't wait to do my patriotic duty.' His hand trembled as he lit another cigarette. 'So much for all that now.'

Realising that he needed to talk, she let him go on without interruption.

'There's a look in their eyes the moment before you let 'em have it,' he went on. 'They're as scared as I am. And boy am I scared!' He paused, and moistened his dry lips with his tongue. 'All that stuff people keep saying about me being a brave soldier, out there at the front. It's all a load of rubbish. I'm not brave at all. I'm just a snivelling coward.'

272

'How can you say that when you've been out there fighting, doing your bit?'

'I can say it because it's true.' He was sobbing now, his words distorted with anguish. 'I haven't got the bottle, Nance. I don't have the guts.'

'But you are doing it, even though you're scared,' she reminded him.

'Not any more,' he wept. 'I don't care what happens to me, as long as I don't have to go back to the fighting.'

She went over and sat down beside him, putting her arms around him. Initially he pulled away, but eventually succumbed and cried in her arms.

'Shush, let it all out,' she said soothingly.

'I've proved my point now, haven't I?' he said when he was calmer. 'I mean, what sort of a man cries like a baby in his sister's arms?'

'A good and caring human being; a man with compassion and humanity.'

'A man without guts, you mean.'

'Surely courage is what you do, not what you feel?' she suggested. 'You've never shirked your duty, even though you've hated what you've been doing.'

'Oh, God, now I've gone and got you involved.' He was full of self-castigation. 'They'll come here looking for me when I don't report back. They'll ask questions. You'll have to lie to them, and say I said nothing to you, or you'll be in trouble. You won't know where I am so you won't have to lie about that.'

'Where will you go?'

'God only knows,' he replied. 'Anywhere but back to the army.'

'I know you, and I know that you'll never be able to live with the shame.'

'I'll throw myself under a train, then. I'd rather do that than go back.'

'Oh Micky, don't talk like that, please,' she entreated, brushing the tears from her eyes with the back of her hand.

'You should have let me be,' he admonished. 'I'd have gone off tomorrow and you'd have been none the wiser.'

'We'd have known when the military police arrived on the doorstep. Just imagine what that would have been like.'

'That's the sort of evil git I am,' he said. 'I don't deserve to be a part of this family. You're better off without me.'

'Oh, Micky, now you're just being melodramatic.'

She was at her wits' end. She knew in her heart that if he did desert, he would take his own life before the military police caught up with him. He wouldn't want to live as a traitor. There seemed to be no way out for him. How cruel this awful war was.

'Sorry.'

'That's all right.' She wanted to get down on her knees and beg him to report back for duty tomorrow, because the other way would be hell for him. But she had no right to remind him of his duty to his country and send him back to unimaginable human slaughter. She turned to him and took his hand. 'Look, Micky, I'm not going to tell you to go back. I have no right to do that. I'm not the one who has to go and face what's out there at the battlefront. Only you know how you feel and you must do what you have to. But I want you to know that I'll stand by you whatever happens. I'll love you whatever you do, and you will always be a hero to me.'

He stared at the floor, looking shamefaced. 'Thanks, sis,' he muttered in a thick voice.

'I'll go and make that tea now,' she said and slipped from the room.

Nancy barely slept for what was left of the night. She and her brother sat together for a long time after she'd made the tea, talking about the family and their childhood. When Nancy finally went back to bed, all she could think about was Micky on the run. Every time she closed her eyes, she had terrible images of him being taken away by the military police, who would show a deserter no mercy. She tried not to disturb Jean with her restlessness, but the tension knots in her stomach were pulling so tight, it was hard to lie still.

She dozed off for short periods, but was fully awake even before the alarm went off. Micky was already up and downstairs in the kitchen making tea when she went down.

'You'll be dead tired at work today, thanks to me,' he said. 'Sorry about last night, Nance.'

'Don't be sorry. You needed to talk to someone and I was glad to be there for you,' she assured him. 'I'll get through the day, don't worry. The air raids have taught us all to get by with very little sleep.'

'It isn't quite so bad for me,' he remarked. 'I might manage to get a bit of kip on the train to Hampshire, if I'm ever so lucky.'

She looked at him. 'You mean . . . you're going to report back for duty?'

'I suppose I'll bloomin' well have to, won't I?' he groaned, making light of it in his old way, but she guessed it was just a front. 'I can't be a quitter, can I? Us Sparrows weren't brought up that way.'

'Oh Micky, please be careful.' The thought of the horrors he was going back to face seemed suddenly too awful for her to bear.

'Hey, come on, Nance,' he said, seeing her face crumple. 'Don't you start cracking up as well. I did enough of that last night for the both of us.'

'Sorry,' she sniffed.

'Come here,' he said, opening his arms to her. 'I'll be back home again before you know it. Just you wait and see.'

'Yeah, I know you will,' she said emotionally as he held her close.

Jean came sailing into the kitchen in her pyjamas, curlers in her hair, remnants of yesterday's make-up lying on her face in patches.

'What's going on? Are you two saying your goodbyes in advance or something?' she asked, yawning. 'I wondered what on earth was happening when you weren't in the bed to turn the alarm off, Nance. I nearly jumped out of me skin when that thing started clanging in my ears.'

'I just fancied an early start and Micky had the same idea,' fibbed Nancy.

'You must be mad, getting up before you have to.' Jean was far too self-absorbed to suspect that Nancy might not be speaking the truth, or even to notice that she'd been crying. 'Ooh good, you've made some tea. Lovely.'

Nancy and her brother exchanged a look. Her eyes made it clear to him that what had happened last night would never go any further.

Chapter Eleven

'You'll get yourself talked about, the way you're carrying on,' Mabel Collins warned her son over breakfast one morning later that month.

'My back's broad, Ma.'

'This isn't only about you, though. It's about Irene too. What must her neighbours be saying about her, with you coming out of her place with the milkman?'

Bobby sipped his tea slowly, looking at her. 'Nothing, because nobody sees me leave; they're all still in bed.'

'Someone's bound to have spotted you.'

'I'm very discreet. I'm away from there well before people are up and about. Anyway, it's only now and again, when I manage to get a weekend pass.'

'I know that moral standards aren't so strictly upheld in wartime, but the rules are still there, and that sort of thing is bound to set tongues wagging.'

'Irene and I are both adults. She's been married and I've been round the block a time or two, so we're both a bit past a goodnight kiss on the doorstep. Anyway, she's always very keen for me to stay over at her place.'

'I've no doubt she is. She'll do anything to get her claws into you and your money.'

'You're wrong about her, you know.'

'I hope I am, for your sake.'

His mother's comments set him thinking. Bobby was no angel, but he was basically an honourable man, and treated women with respect. He shouldn't have risked Irene's reputation by staying overnight at her place so readily. The fact that it was always her idea and she was very persuasive was no excuse; he should have been more aware of the potential damage to her good name. He'd have a chat with her about it this evening, and make sure that she was fully aware of the consequences.

Irene had first suggested that he stay the night a couple of months ago; the same day he'd run into Arthur Sparrow and had arrived at her place looking very down in the mouth. It was also the day he'd begun to consider the possibility of taking his relationship with Irene to a more serious level. But he still hadn't made a commitment; he just couldn't bring himself to do it, somehow.

Later that same day, Nancy was halfway up a ladder with a broom and a bucket of paste, sticking a poster on to a platform wall at Paddington station. It was a government advertisement which urged the population to help the war by being frugal and not taking 'the squander bug' with them when they went shopping.

'What's all this, then? Have they given you a promotion?'

asked Ruby waggishly from below. 'I see you've got your foot on the ladder.'

'Oh very funny,' laughed Nancy, intent upon trying to ensure that the poster was correctly positioned. 'This isn't as easy as it looks, you know. It might not be brain surgery, but there is a special knack to it. If I'm not careful it'll be skew-whiff. I want it right so as not to give old Perce any cause for complaint.'

'He'll probably find something wrong with it however well it's done,' Ruby suggested lightly. 'You know what he's like.'

'Don't I just. But he'll have a job to find fault with this by the time I've finished.'

'You're a Jill of all trades today, then?'

'That's right. Variety is the spice of life, as they say,' Nancy returned cheerfully.

'I had to help out over in the ticket office for a few hours yesterday,' mentioned Ruby. 'It was ever so hectic and confusing. I didn't know what I was doing most of the time, but it made a change.'

'Turning your hand to anything is what it's all about in a place like this when there are staff shortages and we need to keep the service running.' Nancy leaned back and squinted at her work. 'Does that look straight to you?'

'Perfect,' her friend said.

'Good.' Nimbly, Nancy came down the ladder, carefully managing the bucket and broom. 'You certainly get to try a lot of different jobs when you're working here, apart from the routine tasks. Just think of all the new skills and experience we'll have gained by the time the war is over.'

'At which time we'll hand the jobs back to the men and go back to women's work.'

'No doubt about it,' agreed Nancy. 'It's been made very clear to us that our positions here are only for the duration of the war. It'll seem funny going to work in civvies and staying clean instead of getting covered in station dust and grime.' She looked thoughtfully towards the platform. 'This isn't the easiest or most glamorous job, but it's grown on me and I'll miss being part of all the hustle and bustle. I'm absolutely worn out when I go off duty, but it's rewarding somehow.'

'The most rewarding part of the job *is* going off duty,' said Ruby with a wry grin. 'But, seriously, yes, I do know what you mean.'

'Working in a dress shop will be like a holiday after this.'

'You won't be going back to that, though, will you?' queried Ruby.

'I haven't given it much thought, but yeah, if they want me back, I'll go.'

'But you'll probably be married by the time the job here finishes, so you'll be at home keeping house, won't you?' her friend suggested.

Nancy gave the matter some consideration. 'Do you think pre-war rules will apply after the war, as far as married women are concerned, and they'll be expected to stay at home as a matter of course?'

'If they are, there'll be a lot who won't be happy about it,' replied Ruby. 'Not after learning new things and earning their own money.'

'I don't see how things can ever completely revert back to how they were before,' Nancy observed. 'Women have spread their wings and shown what they can do. They won't want to give it up.'

'It might be nice having a man keep you so that you don't have to go to work, though.'

'Maybe,' said Nancy doubtfully. 'Anyway, let's get the war behind us before we start worrying about what will happen afterwards.'

'Are you still not anxious to get married too soon?' Ruby enquired.

'I'll be happy to leave it for a while.' Plagued by uncertainty and stubborn thoughts of Bobby, Nancy was hoping that when she saw Pete again, she'd be reassured that she'd done the right thing in accepting his proposal. 'It would be nice to get to know Pete a little better.' Fortunately, before she could be asked to elaborate, the conversation ended abruptly when she spotted Percy Wellington striding towards them with his clipboard. 'Look out, here comes trouble.'

'Is this a private discussion or can anyone join in?' he asked with typical sarcasm.

'You can join in if you like, Mr Wellington,' said Nancy cheekily. 'We wouldn't want you to feel left out.'

'Nancy,' warned Ruby in a hushed tone.

'Don't worry about it, Miss Green,' he said. 'I'm used to insubordination from your friend here. It's water off a duck's back to me.'

'He loves me really, don't you?' Nancy teased him. Since he'd begun to show her some respect, she had felt able to push her luck with him a little, on the odd occasion. But she was careful never to take it so far as to belittle his senior position.

'That's enough of your cheek, Miss Sparrow,' he said, deadpan, eyes fixed on his clipboard.

'I've just finished putting up the last poster,' she informed him, nodding towards it.

He looked at it only briefly. 'It seems to be all right,' he said, seeming preoccupied and going on to say, 'I've come over to ask you both if you can do some overtime tonight.'

Nancy groaned. 'Don't you think we spend more than enough time here already?'

'We *all* spend far too much time here,' he replied. 'I don't want to work late any more than you do, but there isn't a choice. Several late-shift staff have phoned in sick and someone's got to keep the station running. It can't be helped, I'm afraid.' He paused, probably remembering that the two women belonged to the union, Nancy guessed. 'However, if you really can't do it, I'll see if I can find someone else.'

'I'll do it,' said Nancy.

'Me too,' added Ruby.

'Good,' he said, writing something down. 'I'm glad you realise how important our work here is. The country simply couldn't do without us.' He looked from one to the other. 'Now that that's settled, back to work, please. And I mean work, not standing around yapping.'

'Yes, Mr Wellington,' they chorused respectfully, and he turned and marched off down the platform.

'He isn't nearly so much of a tyrant as he used to be, is he?' remarked Ruby after he'd gone.

'He's had to face up to the way things are now, instead of hanging on to how they were before the war. He knows there's no point in throwing his weight about, because women will be needed here until the end of hostilities and there's nothing he or anyone else can do about it.'

Nancy had heard through the grapevine, however, that there was still prejudice in other areas of the station, such as the engine sheds. Some of the men there felt genuinely threatened by the way the 'weaker sex' had proved how strong and capable they really were.

'I'll see you later, Ruby,' she said now, hurriedly picking up her broom and bucket. 'I'd better go and divest myself of this stuff and get ready to meet the next train.'

Irene wasn't in the least bit bothered about the possibility of gossip, and insisted that Bobby stay the night with her whenever it suited him. He said he would leave earlier to avoid being seen.

'I appreciate your concern, but there's no need for it,' she assured him, over a watered-down gin and orange in her local pub, which was packed to the doors. 'It's very sweet of you to consider my reputation but, honestly, life *really* is too short.'

'I don't want you getting a bad name on my account,' he told her.

'Before the war that sort of thing might have bothered me, and even now I don't deliberately set out to offend people,' she explained. 'But if the way I live upsets anyone, then that's their problem. I can't live my life to suit them. I've no children, and my husband is dead, so there's no one close to me to be hurt by it. I wouldn't let you stay if there was. You know me, Bobby, I'm no shrinking violet. If I didn't want you to stay you'd soon know it.'

He gave her a mock salute. 'All right. You're the boss.' He thought how fetching she looked this evening in a low-cut blouse and floral skirt, her lustrous brown hair falling to her shoulders. 'I'll let you make the rules as far as that's concerned.'

Just then a sound they hadn't heard in a while rose above the hubbub in the bar. The siren's miserable wail produced instant silence.

'They're back again, then,' moaned Irene, as some people hurried out of the pub to the safety of their own air-raid shelters.

'Probably just a false alarm,' said a man at the next table.

'Well, Hitler is *not* going to make me rush my drink,' declared Irene. 'I might not be able to get another drop o' gin for months, so I want to savour this.'

The pub did empty to a certain extent, but some indomitable punters refused to be budged.

'Come on,' said Bobby after a while, with Irene's safety in mind as the bombers got closer. 'Finish your drink, love. There's no point in taking unnecessary risks. I'll take you home to your Morrison shelter.'

'I suppose we'd better make a move,' she agreed reluctantly.

As they stood up to leave, the building shook from an

almighty crash. Instinctively, he grabbed Irene, shielding her with his body and taking a sharp blow to the back of his head from flying timber as the door was smashed in and the windows shattered. The force of the blast threw him forward.

'Irene,' he muttered when he'd gathered his wits sufficiently to realise that he was on the floor, 'are you all right?'

'I think so,' came a muffled voice from beneath him. 'Apart from the fact that you're lying on top of me and squashing me half to death.'

'Sorry,' he said, rolling off her.

'No need to apologise for protecting me,' she told him. 'You all right?'

'Yeah. Apart from a bump on the head.'

The landlord of the pub hurried over to offer them assistance.

'We're all right, mate. Get down,' Bobby urged as there was another earth-shattering explosion close by.

'Flipping heck,' said Irene, lying on her stomach. 'That was a close one.'

People were terrified, screaming and crying, some sounding hysterical. 'We've had it this time,' someone was sobbing nearby. 'The siren was too late, we didn't have time to get to the shelter.'

Gradually the explosions lessened. The ghastly drone of enemy planes grew distant and was replaced by the clang of fire engines and ambulance bells.

Although everybody in the pub was shaken, no one was seriously hurt, though there were plenty of cuts and bruises. But when Irene and Bobby emerged on to the street after the all clear they were greeted by the most heartbreaking devastation. There was smoke and debris everywhere. A row of houses opposite had been completely demolished and firemen were working with hoses to extinguish a cluster of fires. The area was already cordoned off and rescue teams were working to get people out of the rubble.

When Bobby tried to help he was told by an official that the emergency services had things under control and additional help could be dangerous.

'Somebody up there must be watching out for us,' said Irene shakily as she and Bobby walked through the smoky streets to her flat, the grief and destruction of their city weighing heavily on them both. 'If the bomb had been a matter of yards nearer, we would have had our lot.'

'Yeah.'

They were both too upset to say much. When they got to her front door, she said, 'Sweet tea is supposed to be good for shock.' She gave a nervous laugh. 'In the absence of anything stronger.'

'I won't stop if you don't mind. Will you be all right on your own?' He looked concerned. 'Only I need to go home to see if Mum's all right.'

'Of course. You must go right away,' she urged him, fiddling to get her key into the lock in the blackout. 'I'll be fine.'

'Sure?'

'Certain. The raid's over now. Anyway, I'm on my own in the air raids when you're away at camp,' she reminded him. 'Thanks for looking after me back there, though. I would have been the one who got the crack on the head when the door came in if you hadn't got behind me. You're a real smasher, do you know that, Bobby Collins?' Their narrow escape had made her more emotional than usual.

'Flattery will get you everywhere,' he said with false levity. The incident had sharpened his emotions too. It had brought his protective instincts to the fore and made him acutely aware of his masculinity.

'See you tomorrow, then,' she said. 'Hope your mum is all right.'

'Before I go,' he began, on impulse, 'I have something to ask you.'

'Spit it out then and get off home to your mum,' she urged him. 'I'm dying for a cuppa.'

'Will you marry me?' he heard himself say, to his utter astonishment. 'I know it's a bit sudden, but I'd be very honoured if you'd be my wife.'

Her immediate reaction was delight, but then she gave him a slow smile, and said, 'Oh, I get it. This is all about my reputation, isn't it? Honestly, Bobby, you don't have to go to such drastic lengths to save that. I don't need the grand gesture.'

'And you're not getting it,' he told her gravely. 'I'm not that much of a gentleman.'

'In that case, the answer is yes,' she beamed, wrapping her arms around him, and seeming to need no further assurance. 'Yes, yes, yes! I would love to marry you.'

'Wonderful.' She felt warm and desirable in his arms.

'As much as I'd like to continue along these lines,' she chuckled, never one to mince words, 'you must go home to your mum.'

'Yeah, I know. G'night.'

'G'night.'

In his own bed later that night, having raced through the smouldering streets of Acton to find his mother safe but unnerved by the sudden return of the bombing, he looked back on his proposal to Irene and wondered what on earth had possessed him to do such a thing when it was the last thing he'd intended.

It must have been the raw emotion of the moment. He'd been high on adrenaline after the raid and it had made him impulsive. He wasn't in love with Irene and knew he never would be. But the two of them were very compatible, so why not? he tried to convince himself. He'd been thinking in terms of commitment to her for a while and instinct had made the decision for him, so perhaps now was the time to finally accept that what he'd had with Nancy was never going to come his way again. No matter how hard he tried to forget her, his feelings for her just wouldn't go away. Maybe it would help if he was to do the same as her and get on with his life with someone else.

Anyway, he didn't have a choice now, because the proposal had been made and he wasn't going to hurt Irene by retracting it. He would stand by his word. It was the only decent thing to do. Maybe when he saw Irene tomorrow it would seem all right. He'd get her an engagement ring as soon as he could to make it official. That might make it seem more real.

But for all his efforts to persuade himself that it was the

best thing, he still couldn't sleep, so he got up and went downstairs. He sat in the armchair mulling it over until his head ached, then lit a cigarette and tried to concentrate on the positive aspect of sharing his life with Irene. But all he could think of was what might have been with Nancy, and it made his heart ache. Dawn was breaking before he finally went back to bed.

A few weeks later the residents of Ealing found themselves under heavy attack from the bombers once more.

'I do hope Arthur will be all right on his own up at the house,' said Gladys worriedly, sitting next to Evie, who was wrapped in a blanket and fast asleep on the bunk in the Anderson shelter.

'So do I,' said Nancy, who was next to Leslie on the opposite bunk. Jean and Ed – who had just happened to be at the house when the siren went – were squashed together next to Gran. 'But if he's determined not to come down into the shelter, we can't force him.'

'He just can't bear to be closed in, underground,' said Gladys. 'Probably stems from being at sea.'

'Or his nearly drowning,' added Nancy.

'He should have been here during the Blitz,' said Jean unsympathetically. 'That would have cured him of it, because he'd have been driven down here by sheer terror.'

'Shall I go and see how he's doin'?' offered Ed in his broad American drawl.

'Don't you dare,' warned Jean. 'I don't want you getting yourself killed.'

'And never mind what happens to your father,' admonished Gladys.

'Dad won't come down here whatever Ed says to him, so what's the point in Ed risking his life as well?' Jean replied stubbornly.

'We can't leave the poor guy up there on his own,' persisted Ed, already easing his way towards the hole at the end of the shelter. 'I'll just go up to the house and see if he's doin' OK.'

'Dad's being selfish, if you ask me,' Jean complained after Ed had gone. 'Staying up there in the house and having us all worry about him.'

'He can't help it,' defended Nancy. 'Don't forget he's been wounded, and breathing is difficult for him under normal circumstances. He probably thinks he won't be able to breathe at all down here.'

'I suppose so,' Jean conceded grudgingly. 'But if anything happens to my Ed because of him . . .'

'That's enough, Jean,' warned her grandmother. 'You'll frighten the children.'

'I'm not scared,' announced Leslie, somewhat unconvincingly.

'You'll be all right, Les.' Nancy noticed how pale and pinched with fright her brother looked in the flickering candlelight. He'd been away in the country during the Blitz so wasn't as used to air raids as the rest of them. It occurred to her, too, that the shelter's claustrophobic atmosphere might bring back bad memories of his imprisonment in the coal shed at the farm. 'You can lie down if you like. Put your head on my lap and try to go to sleep.'

'With that racket going on out there!' said Jean as the drone of the enemy planes grew ever closer. 'He doesn't stand a cat's chance in hell.'

'And talking of the cat . . .' mentioned Nancy. 'Where is Smudge? We came down here in such a rush, I didn't have time to go looking for him.'

'He'll be all right,' said Gladys. 'He's got nine lives, remember.'

'Which is eight more than Ed has,' Jean pointed out crossly. 'And he chooses to put the precious one he does have at risk because of some silly phobia of Dad's.'

At that moment Ed climbed back into the shelter, with the good news that Arthur was fine and sitting under the living-room table with the cat. 'Sorry, guys, but I can't persuade him to come down here. He says he just can't; he'd sooner take his chances up there.'

'Thanks for trying, anyway,' said Jean, cuddling up to him as he sat down.

The roar of the planes got louder, as did the bangs, bumps and crashes. They could hear an enemy plane directly over-head. Everyone held their breath. Nancy was always paral-ysed with fear as they waited for the bomb to drop. She froze; couldn't think or move.

When the bomb did hit its target, the ground shook so violently Nancy thought they must have taken a direct hit and was astonished to find that they were all still alive. It had been very close though. Everyone was too shocked to speak in the immediate aftermath.

'Oh my God,' said Nancy at last, through dry, trembling

lips. 'It was so near it could have been our house.'

'I'll go and take a look,' offered Ed.

Jean was crying now. 'You can't go out there again, not until the all clear has gone,' she sobbed. 'Don't do it, Ed, please.'

'I have to go, honey,' he told her in a gentle tone. 'I can't just sit here doing nothin' when your dad's up there on his own.'

'No!' she shrieked, clinging on to his arm. 'You're not to go, I won't let you.'

'Pull yourself together, Jean,' urged Nancy. 'He'll only be gone a minute.'

Evie had woken up and was whimpering. Nancy lifted her on to her lap and rocked her.

The planes grew distant even as Ed left the shelter. A few minutes later, Nancy heard voices and was filled with relief, for Ed was talking to her father.

'Hold on to Evie, will you please, Gran. It's quietened down so I'm going out to see what's going on,' she said. 'Dad sounds all right, but I want to know if the house is still standing.'

Thank God, she thought, as she climbed into the garden and saw the dark silhouette of the terraced house against the sky in the moonlight. But as she looked around at the broader horizon, her heart lurched at what she saw . . .

'Homeless at my age,' said a grim and grey-faced Gladys, after the all clear had gone and they were all in the house, having been to see the smoking pile of rubble that had once been her home, and established that nothing could be saved. One half of the small block of flats had been completely demolished – the half with her flat in it.

'You're not homeless, Gran, and you never will be while we're around,' soothed Nancy, sitting on the sofa with her arm around her grandmother. 'You can move in here with us. There'll always be a home for you here, you must know that.'

'Course there will be.' Even Jean was full of compassion for her grandmother. 'It'll be lovely having you here. It'll save on shoe leather too, because we won't be running to and fro to your place all the time.'

'It'll be smashing,' said Leslie.

'You'll be very welcome,' added Arthur.

'Thanks, everyone. I don't know what I'd do without you,' she said tearfully, resting her hand on Nancy's.

'You'll never have to, because we'll always be here for you,' Nancy assured her.

'Everything I owned was in that flat,' Gladys said bleakly. 'It's all gone, nothing left. All my personal stuff, things you can't replace, like photographs and letters and other precious bits and pieces of sentimental value. All our clothes have gone. Evie doesn't have a stitch to wear now.'

She looked so forlorn, Nancy could have broken down in tears for her. Being bombed out was traumatic enough when you were young and strong. When you were getting on in years it must be even more crippling. Her grandmother was entitled to an easier life at her age.

'We'll take care of everything, don't worry, Gran,' said Nancy kindly. 'We'll all rally round.'

295

They were sitting in the Sparrows' living room, drinking tea. Everyone was shaken to the core by what had happened. Evie was in Arthur's double bed, which had now been allocated to herself and Gran, while Arthur was going to sleep in Micky's bed in the boys' room. It wasn't ideal, but new sleeping arrangements had had to be worked out with speed to accommodate their unexpected visitors – temporarily, at least.

'I think you might be able to apply for extra clothing coupons if you've been bombed out and lost all your clothes,' said Jean. 'So that'll help.'

'About the only positive thing I can think of to say is that at least all the residents of the flats were taking shelter, so no one was killed,' said Nancy. 'You and Evie are still here. That's the most important thing to us.'

'Yeah, I suppose when you look at it like that, it isn't so bad,' was Gladys's gloomy response. 'When you think of what's happened to some poor devils.'

'I suppose I'd better try to force myself to go down the shelter in future if we get any more raids like that,' said Arthur, who was extremely distressed for Gladys and was still trembling slightly.

'We'd all be a lot happier if you could manage it,' said Nancy.

'You need some strong liquor to steady your nerves before you go down there,' suggested Ed. 'I'll see if I can get you some to keep for that purpose.'

'That's very kind of you,' said Arthur.

'That's my Ed for you,' praised Jean, looking at him adoringly. 'Kind-hearted to the tips of his toes.'

'Meanwhile, we need to get you settled in for the night, Gran,' said Nancy.

'At least I don't have to do any unpacking,' said Gladys, her eyes brimming with tears, but her sense of humour shining through.

'That's the spirit,' encouraged Nancy. 'It'll take more than Hitler's bombers to get our gran down for long.'

A moment of stark realism nudged into Nancy's emotional state of mind, and she couldn't help wondering how her father was going to cope with having Evie in the house in the long term. Obviously, he wasn't cruel enough to refuse the two of them shelter under these dreadful circumstances. But what was going to happen when the shock and initial goodwill had worn off and the little girl was around the house for the indefinite future? There was trouble ahead, Nancy was sure of it.

Chapter Twelve

At the time, it didn't seem possible that anything positive could come from the loss of Gladys's home and all her possessions. But the outcome of the disaster was that it brought her back to where she belonged, at the centre of the family.

They returned to communal meals, shared enjoyment of wireless programmes, noisy discussions, idle chatter, and the general feeling of family unity they had lost when Gladys had been effectively banned from the Sparrow household along with Evie.

Gladys positively thrived in the role of chief cook and bottlewasher. Naturally, the rest of the family were more than content to come home to hot meals and the bliss of not having to wade through a backlog of domestic chores after a hard day's work, though the girls didn't leave it all to her, and helped out when they could.

They had all done their very best to make the rehabilitation of Gran and Evie as smooth as possible for them. As well as rolling out the welcome mat, Nancy also trawled through secondhand shops and market stalls, and visited the

WVS in search of clothes for the two bomb victims. Joining forces with her gran, she threw herself into 'make do and mend'. They dyed some old curtains blue and made them into little frocks for Evie, even managing to get a plain dress for Gran out of the same material. They also knitted like mad for the winter.

Even Jean – who couldn't sew to save her life and was a reluctant knitter – set to work on a jumper for the little girl. Leslie's contribution came in the form of errands run for Gran without complaint, and increased levels of patience with Evie when her inquisitive little fingers found their way into his things.

Ed managed to get some extra blankets for them. He also came up with a bottle of whisky for Arthur, to encourage him into the shelter during air raids.

'You can say what you like about the Yanks,' Arthur was often heard to say, 'but they're generous to a fault. Young Ed is a credit to his country and a pleasure to have in the house. I'm proud to know him.'

With respect for Gran's feelings, her father managed not to complain about losing his bedroom, Nancy was pleased to observe. He grumbled a bit about Leslie's untidy ways and noisiness in the bedroom they now shared – all the singing and whistling and comics and cigarette cards strewn all over the place – but he was kindness itself to Gran and did everything he could to make her feel at home.

His way of dealing with Evie was to pretend that she wasn't there – not an easy feat with a child like Evie, who was omnipresent about the house and exuded love to all and sundry. She still adored him and trotted around after him everywhere. His rejection of her was painful to watch. Nancy could hardly bear to see her climb on to his lap only to be immediately removed and told firmly not to do it again. Her bottom lip would tremble and she would dissolve into tears, but she always came back for more.

Dad's most well-known cry became, 'Will somebody please take this child away from me.'

In August, Pete returned to Northolt and was given some leave. He was even more good-looking than Nancy remembered. But he had only one thing on his mind: marriage to Nancy *during this leave*. And to this end he showed Nancy the extent of his tenacity.

'Be realistic, Pete. How on earth can we do it that soon?' she asked, keeping her voice down because they were at the front gate saying goodnight and the windows were open due to the warm weather. Preferring being near to Nancy to spending his leave with his parents in Kent, Pete was staying at a forces' club in central London. It was more convenient and comfortable than dossing down in the Sparrows' armchair every night.

'By special licence, of course,' he replied breezily, as though her concern was beyond his comprehension.

'But weddings take a lot of organisation.'

'Not these days. Speed is of the essence now.'

Indeed it was. A typical wartime wedding was arranged in a hurry and lacked all the usual trimmings, including a honeymoon. There was an urgency in the air; people wanted to be officially united in case the worst happened. Nancy was trying not to be influenced by the current live-for-today climate. She wanted her marriage to have solid beginnings. 'Wouldn't it be more sensible to wait a while? We hardly know each other.'

'I know you well enough to know that I love you,' he said. 'So what's the point of waiting?'

'And what's the mad rush?'

'If you have to ask that, you can't feel the same as I do.'

'It's just that there are other things to be considered,' she said, trying to hang on to her common sense in the face of his powerful persistence. It wasn't in her nature to be irresponsible. 'Weddings cost money and that isn't abundant in my family, because we haven't had time to save up.'

'I'll take care of the cost.'

'The bride's people are supposed to be responsible for that.'

'I've just changed the rules.' He smiled at her. 'So that problem's solved. What's next? You keep them coming, I'll keep knocking them down.'

'It isn't a good time for me to leave home, with Evie still being so little . . .'

'Nonsense! Your gran is running things now, so you're free to fly the nest,' came his prompt reminder. 'And we'll live near enough for you to call in on a regular basis.'

She laughed. His supreme confidence was hard to resist. 'You wouldn't want me to move into married quarters with you, then?'

'Married quarters are hard to get, with so many men

being in the air force,' he explained, to her utter relief. 'So, we could live around here somewhere, but I'd have to stay at camp when I didn't have a pass.'

'I could stay on here then, and you could stay here with me whenever you could get away,' she suggested impulsively.

'With me in the armchair and you upstairs in bed? Not likely. We'll need a place of our own, even though I'll be away a lot of the time.'

'We won't find a place with the housing shortage as it is in London.'

'We will if we're willing to pay over the top for it,' he stated categorically. 'Even in wartime everything has a price. I know that accommodation is in short supply, with so many houses being bombed, but a lot of people have fled to the country and rented their houses out. We should be able to get a couple of furnished rooms if we don't mind paying well over the odds.' He looked towards the house and lowered his voice even more. 'As much as I like your family, we need privacy. Snatching a few minutes alone with you when everyone's gone to bed just isn't enough for me.'

'How can we afford to pay the earth? I don't earn a fortune.'

'I'm not reliant on my pay from the RAF, you know,' he informed her. 'My father's pretty generous in his allowance to me.'

An allowance from his father! This was a whole new world to Nancy. Her dad could only just afford a pint down the local after he'd paid his share of the housekeeping.

'That's one of the perks of being an only child,' Pete went

on. 'There's no competition for affection and no one else for the parents to spend their money on.'

Where Nancy came from, you paid your way as soon as you left school and started work. No further financial support was expected. The only allowances she'd experienced were the ones you made for someone when they behaved badly.

'Lucky you.' It must be nice, she thought, to have that sort of security, but she always felt rather sorry for people who didn't have siblings.

'Yes, I am. The old folks aren't too bad at coming up with the dosh,' he said, with the casual air of someone who's never known anything else. 'I'll consider myself even luckier if I can get you to marry me before I go back off leave.'

'There's so much we don't know about each other, considering we're about to take the most important step of our lives. I don't even know if you want to have children,' she blurted out.

'That's easily rectified. I don't.'

'Not ever?'

'It isn't something I've ever given any serious thought, to tell you the truth,' he said. 'Maybe later on I might fancy the idea.'

'I really do want to have kids.' Nancy thought it was important he knew where she stood on this issue. 'I mean that.'

'All right, don't get yourself in a stew over it. If that's what you want, eventually we'll have them,' he said, as though to pacify her. 'But for the time being it needs to be just us.' He reached over and touched her face. 'Don't spoil the romance by talking about kids. We'll have them, all in good time. Right now I need to know if I can go ahead and look for a place for us to start our married life in. I'm on leave, so I've plenty of time to look into it while you're at work. But I'm not going to waste my time searching for a place if I'll have to live in it on my own. So, are we getting married this leave or not?'

His self-esteem was so dazzling, his personality so strong, he made anything seem possible. So what if he wasn't the love of her life? Her feelings for him would probably grow stronger when she got to know him better. She had to cut the ties with the past sometime.

'You might find furnished rooms in one of the side streets near Ealing Broadway station,' she suggested with a smile that put a huge grin on his face. 'A lot of the big houses around there are rented out as rooms.'

They got married at Ealing register office one sunny Saturday a week or so later, and despite the haste and the shortages, it was a very happy occasion for Nancy. She didn't have enough clothing coupons to buy a fancy outfit, but she managed to get a pretty blue summer dress and a little white feathery hat. Everyone said she looked lovely.

At first glance, the wedding cake was an elaborately decorated, traditional two-tiered affair, but inside the fancy cardboard frame they'd borrowed from the baker there was just a jam sponge, lovingly created by Gran. Arthur had collected some little rounds of paper out of the hole-puncher at the insurance office he worked from to use as confetti, and they had a finger buffet at the Sparrows' house. Pete told her his parents couldn't make it at such short notice, but all the immediate Sparrow family, apart from Micky, were there, as well as Ed. Ruby managed to get the day off work to attend and some of Nancy's other friends from the station added to the celebrations. Polly was invited but couldn't get leave. Amazingly, Nancy had talked Percy into letting her have Monday off, which meant she could have a long weekend with Pete.

His best man was another pilot, called Rex, who spoke highly of Pete's courage and skill in the air, but didn't say much about the man himself. The wedding presents weren't lavish, because of the lack of time and the shortage of everything, but most people gave them a small gift, and the family pooled their coupons and bought them a full set of bedding.

One thing they didn't have time to arrange was a hotel for their wedding night, so they went straight back to the attic rooms Pete had found for them in a rooming house near Ealing Broadway station. But having done all their courting under the Sparrows' watchful eyes, just having a place of their own was as good as any honeymoon away. Ever the romantic, Pete carried his new wife over the threshold.

'At last,' he said, setting her down inside the door and slipping his arms around her. 'I've wanted this so *very, very* much.'

'Me too, Pete,' she said. 'Me too.'

★　★　★

'I know it isn't exactly a palace, but it isn't a bad little place, is it?' remarked Pete the next morning over toast spread thickly with the peanut butter Ed had got them from the PX especially for their first breakfast as a married couple. 'It'll do as a temporary measure, anyway. Just until we can get something better.'

Nancy didn't reply.

He waved his hand in front of her eyes. 'Hey, dreamer. Am I talking to myself here?'

'No, no. I'm listening.'

'So, what do you think of the place, then?'

'It's fine,' she said at last, casting her eyes around the room which was lit by the morning sun. It was a living room and bedroom combined, with a small kitchen leading off it. There was a sofa and two armchairs and a small dining table and chairs, with the bed situated at the far end. The room was large, with high ceilings and flowery wallpaper, stained here and there with damp patches. All the basic essentials were supplied, except the bedding. The furniture was well worn, but clean and comfortable. There was a communal bathroom for the tenants on the floor below. 'Quite comfy really.'

'So, why are you looking so sad, then?' he asked. 'You should be feeling radiant this morning.'

Radiant? Was he kidding? Bruised, used and bewildered was how she was feeling. Was he really going to pretend that nothing unusual had happened?

The brutality of his lovemaking had shocked her and left her hurting all over. Initially startled by the rough way he'd approached her, she'd instinctively drawn back. He'd flown

307

into a rage, accused her of being frigid, then physically forced her to submit to his will. She'd never seen him utter even a cross word before.

Afterwards, as she sat trembling and exhausted in the armchair while he slept, she was plunged further into confusion when he sat up shouting, crying and punching the air, seeming to be only semi-conscious. She'd held him in her arms until he was calmer, then he went back to sleep, leaving her worried, lonely and wondering what on earth she had got herself into. Where was the charming man she thought she'd married?

Now she said, 'Well, it was quite a night, one way and the other.'

'Yes, wasn't it?' he said proudly.

'With you having that funny turn, I mean.'

'Funny turn?'

'You remember.'

'I don't know what you're talking about.'

'You were very troubled about something; you sat up shouting and carrying on.'

'You must be mistaken.'

'I assumed you must be having some sort of a nightmare.'

'A nightmare! Me!' He was furious at the suggestion. 'Don't be so ridiculous. I've never had a nightmare in my life. Rock solid stable, that's me.'

'I wasn't suggesting any lack of stability,' she corrected swiftly. 'I'm just telling you what happened. Something must have been playing on your mind for you to be so disturbed.'

He looked at her with such hostility, her heart pounded and her palms dampened as she feared he was about to lose his temper again.

'Nothing was worrying me and I don't want to hear anything of that sort mentioned again – ever,' he said, through gritted teeth.

'All right, all right,' she objected. 'There's no need to lose your rag over it. I don't need to be spoken to like a naughty child.'

'No, no, of course not,' he said, sounding more controlled. 'I don't know what's got into you.'

'Look, I'm sorry.' He gave her one of his boyishly persuasive looks. 'I'm just a bit tired, that's all. So, am I forgiven?'

She considered the matter. 'Well, all right,' she said, trying to stifle her new fear of him. 'But I'd rather you didn't fly off the handle like that.'

'Don't accuse me of having nightmares, then.' His mood hardened again. 'And don't you dare mention it to anyone else.'

'What's so shameful about having a bad dream?' she asked.

'I'm a fighter pilot, for Godsake,' he reminded her aggressively. 'That sort of thing might suggest to certain people that I'm losing my nerve.'

'I don't see why.'

'You know nothing about the world I move in, so you'll have to take my word for it.'

She shrugged. 'No one will hear about it from me, I promise you.'

'Good.' He finished his toast and sipped his tea, while

she barely ate a morsel. 'So what would you like to do today?' he asked, smiling and seeming to revert back to the man she'd known before they'd shut the door behind them last night.

Still in pain from his lovemaking, what she most wanted was time alone to think, and maybe have a bath if there was any hot water. But instead she said, 'We could go to the West End later on. See a film maybe.'

'Or,' he began, a salacious gleam coming into his eyes, 'we could do what everyone is supposed to do on honeymoon. We could stay in bed all day.'

'I think we should go out at some point,' Nancy said quickly.

'We got married so that we could be alone together,' he reminded her. 'Why would we want to go out where there are other people?'

'We can't stay in this room all day.'

'I don't see why not.'

She looked towards the window. 'It's a lovely day, for one thing. Some fresh air will do us good. Anyway, it's nice to go out.'

He narrowed his eyes at her. 'Don't go all frigid on me again,' he warned.

'I'm not and I wasn't last night. You were very rough, that's why—'

'I was *not* rough.'

She looked at him for a moment, then pulled down the top of her dressing-gown to show the bruises on her arms. 'That's how gentle you were,' she told him.

'It was your own fault,' he muttered, without so much as a hint of remorse. 'What do you expect if you play games with a man?'

'I was not playing games,' she asserted, pulling her dressing-gown around her again. 'You didn't give me a chance. I didn't like the rough treatment.'

'Grow up, Nancy,' he said nastily. 'We're married now. That's what married people do.'

'Not like that.'

'Stop pretending to be so naive.'

She looked at him, hardly able to believe that this was the same person who had proposed marriage to her. 'What's the matter with you?' She wanted to understand his attitude. 'Why are you being like this with me? You weren't like this at all before we got married.'

'You can't expect me to be on my best behaviour all the time now that we're married,' he said.

Nancy had a sinking feeling in the pit of her stomach as she realised the magnitude of the mistake she'd made in marrying him. Hot angry tears filled her eyes. Why had she been so stupid as to let herself be talked into it when she'd known in her heart that it wasn't right? She'd been flattered by his lavish attention, swept along by his magnetic person-ality when she was old enough to know better.

'Why did you marry me, Pete?' she asked.

'What a question to ask your new husband. Because I love you, of course.'

'It doesn't seem much like it at the moment.'

His face softened slightly. 'I am a bit bossy, but I do love

311

you,' he said, reaching over for her hand. 'And there's nothing I won't do for you.'

She still wasn't reassured. She felt on edge, as though she didn't know him at all.

'Right now I want to show you how much I love you by going back to bed.'

'I haven't finished my breakfast yet.'

He looked at her in such a way as to make her want to get as far away from him as possible. But she'd married him and she wouldn't break her vows. 'I don't really want any more breakfast anyway,' she said.

Jean thought Ed seemed rather quiet and preoccupied that same Sunday, so when she walked to the bus stop with him in the late afternoon, she asked him what was the matter.

'Nothin',' he replied moodily, which was most unusual for him, because he was the most even-tempered of men.

'You've been a bit odd all day, come to think of it,' she observed.

'You're imagining things.'

'I'm not,' she denied. 'What is it? Have you gone off me or something?'

'No.'

'You have,' she said, far too besotted with him to keep her feelings under wraps. All the clever tactics she'd learned over the years for manipulating men deserted her completely when she was with Ed. 'I can tell from your voice that something's wrong.'

He smiled his wide smile, his teeth protruding slightly. 'I

haven't gone off you, honey,' he said, his tone becoming tender. 'You know I'm crazy about you.'

'Why are you being so peculiar with me, then?' she wanted to know.

'Bin thinkin', I guess.'

That sounded frighteningly ominous. Perhaps he'd been thinking it was time he gave her the old heave-ho. Maybe she'd been too eager and scared him off. Oh, please don't let it be that, she prayed. 'Thinking?' she said, through dry lips. 'Am I allowed to know what you've been thinking about?'

'Not now. This isn't the right time.'

He *was* going to ditch her. She knew the signs. He'd remembered that he had a girl back home he suddenly wanted to be faithful to. Bracing herself for the worst, she said, 'Well, you may as well tell me what it is, as you've admitted that there is something on your mind. It won't be fair if you don't.'

'It isn't the sort of thing I want to talk about when there isn't much time,' he said. 'And I have a bus to catch.'

'You had plenty of time to tell me earlier, mate,' she told him heatedly. 'So for Godsake spit it out now. Don't mess me about.'

'OK. It's just that, well . . . I've been thinkin' that now Nancy and Pete have taken the plunge and got hitched, maybe it would be kinda nice if we did the same.'

'Oh my God, I don't believe it. Oh, Ed.' She was ecstatic. 'Were you really thinking that? Are you saying that you want to marry me?'

'I guess I am,' he said, smiling. 'But I was going to do it properly when we had more time.'

'Oh, Ed,' Jean said again, throwing her arms around him and covering his face with kisses.

'Hey, slow down,' he urged. 'It isn't as simple for us as it is for them.'

'Why not?'

'Because you'd have to come to America to live after the war,' he reminded her.

'You think that's a problem?' she said in a tone of disbelief. 'Are you crazy?'

'I know a lot of English girls want to come to the States because they think it's glamorous. But it's a big thing, Jean, moving halfway across the world,' he pointed out gravely. 'Sure, it's a great country and it sounds like fun to be going there, but the US is a long way from your folks and your usual way of life. Things are different there and you could get awful homesick.'

'I'll risk it,' she told him without hesitation. 'I'll have you by my side. I'll live anywhere as long as it's with you. I know some women see the GIs as a ticket to paradise and set out to get one with that in mind, but I'm not one of them.' She paused, wanting to be completely honest with him because he meant so much to her and had paid her the ultimate compliment of asking her to be his wife. 'I admit I had something like that in mind before I met you. But not any more. Once I clapped eyes on you, everything changed. I changed. Honestly, Ed, if you said we were going to live at the North Pole I'd go with you happily.'

'Would ya, really?'

'The answer is most definitely yes, yes, yes!' she said excitedly. 'I'd love to marry you.'

'I should have got down on one knee.'

'We'll skip the formalities. You've said you want to marry me,' she grinned, hugging him tight. 'That's good enough for me.'

His bus was approaching. 'I'll see you at Oxford Circus station as we arranged, on Saturday.' They'd arranged to meet there because they were going to see a film in the West End. 'We'll talk about it properly then.'

'I can't wait.'

'Me neither,' he said, kissing her and holding her close as the bus drew up.

She waved to him through the window, smiling and feeling as though her heart would burst. She couldn't remember ever feeling this happy before.

'So, how are the newly-weds?' beamed Gladys, when Nancy and Pete went to Sycamore Road to visit one evening a few days later. 'How's married life treating you?'

'We're loving every minute,' replied Pete. 'We can't get enough of it, can we, Nancy?'

'That's right,' she responded dutifully.

'You're going back off leave tomorrow, aren't you, son?' said Arthur.

'That's right,' he confirmed. 'We've just called round so that I can say cheerio.'

'You managed to drag yourself away from your love-nest, then,' Jean put in.

'It wasn't easy,' replied Pete.

'You're quiet, Nancy,' commented Gladys.

'She's exhausted,' said Arthur crudely, letting out a chuckle. 'If she isn't, she ought to be.'

'Don't embarrass the girl with your pub talk, Arthur,' tutted Gladys.

'It'll take more than that to embarrass me, Gran,' said Nancy with false levity. 'I'm used to Dad's vulgarity.'

Nancy was in no mood to be coy. Her father was right. She was exhausted. But not in the way he meant. It was from coping with Pete's mood swings, brutally enforced sex and being woken in the middle of the night by her husband's nightmares, which he continued to deny having. The only thing that was keeping her going was the thought of him going back off leave tomorrow.

It hadn't been all bad these past few days. Sometimes he was tender and loving, just as he'd been before they'd moved in together. Then she could understand why she'd fallen for him. But the slightest thing would at first irritate him, then send him into a fury; it could be something as small as a comment she might make about the war, a dropped 'h', or even the food they were eating. If he was in the mood, he would find any excuse to disagree with her. He'd started to physically abuse her too. She'd been slapped and punched more times than she cared to remember these past few days. And often when he'd finished hurting her, he would beat himself around the head in temper.

His nerves must be stretched to breaking point for him to behave as he did, and Nancy thought he might need

316

professional help, but any suggestion of this made him angrier than ever.

Seeing him now, being so friendly and warm to everyone so that no one would guess what lay behind the act, it was easy to see why she'd been fooled. The man was irresistible when he behaved like this.

Piloting Spitfires was known to be one of the most dangerous and stressful jobs of the war and it had obviously taken its toll on him. Of course, he would never admit it, for fear of being grounded. Flying was the one true love of Pete's life – that was the one thing about him she was sure of.

He was a very complex individual, though, and a calculating one. He'd proved that by the control he'd had over his behaviour before they were married, right up until they'd closed the door on the world outside of their rooms. Also, no matter how sexually eager he was, he always took precautions. He was almost paranoid about avoiding pregnancy. He said he didn't want that sort of responsibility yet.

Thank goodness he was going back tomorrow and she would get some breathing space. Of course, the easiest thing would be to leave him, but she wasn't a quitter. She'd made promises in the register office and would stand by them. She couldn't help remembering how gentle Bobby had always been, though, and that made her feel even more trapped and miserable.

One thing she wasn't going to do was worry the family with it. They would be after Pete's blood if they knew what he'd done to her. This was her problem and she would deal with it.

She was brought out of her reverie by the sound of Jean's cheery tones.

'I've got the most amazing news, Nance,' she chirped. 'You would have to be on your bloomin' honeymoon when something so wonderful happens to me. I've been absolutely bursting to tell you.'

'Sorry to have put you out,' quipped Nancy.

'She'd have been round your place like a shot if I hadn't stopped her,' said Gladys. 'She's been that excited.'

'Tell me then, before I die from the strain of waiting,' smiled Nancy, and was delighted to hear about Ed's proposal because she knew how much Jean had wanted it. She was also very fond of Ed and was glad he was joining the family.

'Seems as though you've started a trend,' said Gladys, nodding towards Nancy.

'Yeah, it does seem that way,' she said, hoping that her sister was a better judge of character than she herself had been with Pete.

Nancy was on duty at the station until late on Saturday, so she didn't call in to see the family that day, but arrived for lunch on Sunday as planned. Arthur had gone to the pub for a pre-prandial pint, Gran was in the kitchen, cutting swede to add to the potatoes to make them go further, and Leslie and Evie were in the living room. The latter's eyes lit up at the sight of her adored Nancy, who picked her up and smothered her with kisses.

'Where's Jean?' asked Nancy after a while, noticing that her sister wasn't around. 'Out somewhere with Ed?'

'She's still in bed,' replied Gladys.

'Blimey, it's nearly two o'clock, and that's late even for her.'

'She's sulking,' Leslie informed her.

'Nothing new there, then,' grinned Nancy. 'Who's upset her this time?'

'Ed's ditched her,' her brother announced.

'Now, Leslie, we don't know that,' admonished Gladys. 'Take no notice of him, Nancy.'

'Jean thinks he's chucked her, anyway,' Leslie told them. 'I'm only repeating what she said herself.'

'What's happened between them, Gran?' Nancy enquired. 'Did they have a row?'

'No. Nothing like that. But Ed didn't turn up for their date last night,' explained Gladys. 'She waited for hours for him at Oxford Circus station, so she was none too pleased when she got home.'

'Perhaps he couldn't get away,' suggested Nancy. 'Military establishments aren't holiday camps. He must have had to go on duty at the last minute or something for him to have let her down.'

'That's what I said. I told her she'll probably get a letter from him next week with an explanation. But she's upstairs moping and calling him everything under the sun. She's acting hard, but I think she's shed plenty of tears too. She really does think the world of Ed.'

'I'll go and talk to her.'

'Trust her to go and ruin everything when it was all going so well,' grumbled Leslie. 'Now Ed won't come here any more.'

'Don't tell me you've started to approve of Jean's love life,' said Nancy lightly.

'Is it Ed, or the chocolate and chewing gum he brings with him that Leslie approves of, though, I wonder?' suggested Gran with a wry grin.

'Well . . . the chocolate is nice,' admitted Leslie.

'You mercenary little horror!' rebuked Nancy.

'I like Ed as well,' he declared hotly. 'It isn't just because of the chocolate and stuff that I like him coming here.'

'We all like Ed,' said Nancy, setting Evie down on the floor. 'You stay down here with Leslie, poppet, while I go and have a chat to your sister.'

'He's obviously had second thoughts about proposing to me,' said Jean, lying back against the pillow looking gloomy, her eyes puffy from crying. 'I feel such a fool, Nance.'

'Jean, he missed one date and there could be any number of reasons why.'

'He left me standing there like I was on the game,' she said, as though Nancy hadn't spoken. 'That's just downright cruel.'

'Now, come on, we all know Ed well enough to know that he doesn't have a cruel bone in his body.'

'We thought we knew him, you mean.'

'I think you should give him a chance to explain before you judge him,' her sister advised. 'He'll probably be here next weekend as large as life, with a perfectly good explanation. Either that or you'll get a letter telling you why he let you down.'

'I hope so, but it seems too much of a coincidence to me. You know, he asks me to marry him – though he's very quick to make a big thing of all the problems – then he stands me up on our very next date. He's never done either of those things before, so it speaks for itself. You add the two things together—'

'And come up with a wild assumption,' Nancy cut in.

'I wish it was just that,' Jean confessed thickly. 'But it seems too much to hope for. I mean, when a fella stands a girl up on a date it usually means that he doesn't want to see her again.'

'Not when you've been as close to someone as you've been to Ed.'

'That makes it even worse, somehow. I never tried to play it cool with Ed or hide how much he meant to me. My heart was an open book to him. I was straight with him from the start, because I couldn't help myself. Now, I'm not just humiliated, I'm really hurt, aching inside. I really love him, Nance.'

'Yeah, I know you do.' Pity wasn't an emotion Nancy normally associated with Jean, but she felt very sorry for her now. 'But Ed's a good man and obviously thinks a lot of you. He wouldn't just leave you in the lurch for no good reason.'

'My heart tells me that, but my head says different.' She brushed her hair back from her brow, her face blotchy from weeping. 'Oh, why did he let me down?'

'He'll turn up,' encouraged Nancy. 'This time next week you'll be wondering what all the fuss was about.'

321

Jean blew her nose and seemed to perk up. 'Anyway, what about you? Are you going to tell me any juicy bits about married life?'

'Not likely,' said Nancy, forcing a light tone.

It might take Jean's mind off her own problems if Nancy was to spill the beans about hers, and the idea of sharing her troubles was tempting, but she resisted the temptation. It was, after all, a very private matter.

'Spoilsport,' said Jean, trying to sound cheerful and failing miserably.

Ed didn't appear with a plausible explanation the following weekend. Or the one after that. There was no letter either. Sadly Nancy had to admit that it was beginning to look as though Jean might be right and he had had a change of heart.

She suggested that Jean write to him at the barracks, but her sister was dead set against the idea. 'If he wanted me, he would have been in touch by now,' she pointed out. 'It's been over two weeks and there hasn't been a word, so he isn't going to contact me now. That's what he was telling me when he didn't turn up. I'm not so dim-witted that I can't get the message.'

Nancy guessed that Jean was still hoping in her heart that he would turn up. You could see hope flicker in her eyes every time anyone knocked at the door. Then, on the third weekend, her fighting spirit returned.

'I'm not staying in another Saturday night, fretting for a bloke who didn't even have the guts to tell me to my face that he didn't want to see me any more,' she announced. 'I'm going up the Palais with the girls from work.'

Halfway through the evening, she came home looking devastated, eyes swollen, mascara smudged on her cheeks.

'The lying, cheating pig,' she said to anyone who cared to listen, which in this case was Gladys and Nancy, who happened to be visiting for the evening.

'What's happened now?' asked Gladys.

'Ed's been transferred,' she explained, seething with fury. 'And he didn't even have the decency to let me know he was going. Some of his mates were at the dance. I heard about it from them.'

'Oh dear.' Her grandmother was very sympathetic. 'Where's he gone to?'

'They didn't know. There's all this stupid secrecy in the military. Bloody Yanks.'

'It's just as hush-hush in our forces, I think, love,' said Gladys.

'Anyway, what does it matter where he is? He couldn't care less about me, that's obvious. All that stuff about wanting to marry me was all codswallop; he knew he wouldn't have to follow it through.' Jean looked utterly forlorn. 'You hear all these stories about the GIs moving to another base and never getting in touch again because they're too busy with the girls in the new town, don't you? But I never thought Ed would do that to me.'

'He did seem to be a very nice young man,' ventured Gladys. 'So we were all taken in.'

'Leading me on like that, pretending he wanted to marry

323

me,' she ranted. 'It was all just words, all of it. Still, at least now I can stop hoping every time someone comes to the door. I can stop looking for the postman.'

'Oh Jean,' said Nancy. 'I'm so sorry. I really am.'

'Don't make it worse by pitying me,' she sobbed, tears streaming down her face. 'I'm fine. Absolutely fine. There are plenty more fish in the sea.'

She went upstairs, leaving her words echoing with a false ring.

'The rotten bugger,' fumed Gladys when Jean was out of earshot. 'I know what I'd like to do to him. I really trusted that bloke.'

'Me too,' said Nancy, knowing from recent experience just how easy it was to misjudge someone's character.

It seemed that the Sparrow sisters had both got it wrong this time.

Chapter Thirteen

A thick, sooty mist lay low over the streets of Acton as Bobby walked to Irene's one autumn evening. The fog, added to the blackout, resulted in almost no visibility and expletives echoed into the vapour as he collided with walls, lampposts and other people stumbling along in the opposite direction. But nothing could dampen his spirits tonight, because he hadn't been home for a while and it was so good to get a break from the camp.

After his initial misgivings, he'd accepted his engagement with good grace, and begun to rather enjoy the sense of commitment, albeit to the wrong woman. They hadn't set a date for the wedding yet, but he intended to change all that tonight, because an overseas posting was almost certainly imminent and he felt duty-bound to make everything legal before he went abroad.

He hadn't heard anything official, but things had been said to make him believe that something was in the offing. When the much awaited second front did finally get underway, he was bound to be sent back on to active duty.

So there were practicalities to be taken into account. As his wife rather than his fiancée, Irene would have the status that would entitle her to a marriage allowance and – if the worst happened – a widow's benefit. As unromantic as these things were, they had to be considered. He was a responsible man. Having made a commitment to her, he wanted to make proper provision.

He was smiling as he approached her flat. He hadn't had a chance to let her know he was coming, so she was in for a nice surprise. He could hear voices as he approached her door, which was ajar. Someone was obviously on the way out.

'He's a good catch and well worth the effort,' said a woman's voice he didn't recognise. 'You'll never want for a few bob once you're hitched to him. A part-owner of a well-established pawnbroking business. Phew! I should say so. I wouldn't mind some o' that myself.'

'That's why I went all out to get him,' he heard Irene say, to his horror. 'I've no intention of working behind the counter in a grocer's shop for the rest of my life. He'll be a nice juicy meal ticket for me.'

'You need to get him properly hooked a bit sharpish, though,' said the stranger. 'You never know what'll happen these days. If you've nothing in writing you'll get bugger all.'

'That's worrying me too. I want it made legal as soon as possible. But if I rush him, it might frighten him off.'

'Come on, Irene, a woman like you can show him the way.'

'Yeah, course I can. I'll make a few subtle hints when I see him next. So subtle he'll think it was his idea and we'll be spliced before he has the chance for second thoughts.'

'That's the stuff,' said the stranger, cackling. 'Us girls have to look after ourselves, don't we?'

'Not half. The men think they're the clever ones, but we run rings around 'em,' chuckled Irene. 'Flatter 'em, give 'em plenty of loving and you can get what you like out o' them.'

He'd heard enough. He pushed the door open and said grimly, 'Not out of this one, you can't, Irene. Not any more.'

'Bobby . . .' Irene stared at him aghast, while her visitor made a hasty retreat without another word. 'We were just joking around.'

'Joking around, my arse,' he said. 'I've been on the other side of that door for long enough to know what you're really like. A hard-hearted gold-digger. Well, you won't find a meal ticket in me.'

'But Bobby, please . . .'

'Save your breath,' he ground out. 'The engagement's off and I never want to see you again. You can keep the ring. You might get a few quid for it to help you get by until you find another sucker who might actually be fooled into going the whole way and marrying you.'

As she realised that she wasn't going to win him over, her attitude changed. The eyes that were usually so soft and inviting were now cold and hard. 'All right, so I was after a bit of security,' she said icily. 'What's wrong with that?'

'Everything when you lie and cheat to get it.'

'It wasn't all lies.'

327

'Oh, spare me more fairytales.' His dark eyes were almost black as he fixed them on her face. 'People say I have a kind heart, but I'm not so daft that I'll allow myself to be taken for a ride.' He turned towards the door. 'Goodbye, Irene.'

'Bobby, wait . . .'

'No. No more,' he said, swinging round to face her with a cold stare. 'You concentrate on finding your next victim, because it isn't going to be me.'

And with that he marched off down the street, and headed for the nearest pub. What a mug he'd been, he thought, over a pint of weak wartime beer. Why hadn't he had the nous to see through her? He'd been warned enough times by his mother. Maybe he hadn't wanted to see the truth, because Irene was a diversion from his memories of Nancy. Oh well, whatever the truth of the matter, he'd had a narrow escape.

'From what you've said, it sounds to me as though Jean needs taking out of herself,' said Ruby.

'She needs something,' agreed Nancy. 'I've never known her to be down like this before. Jean likes a good time. Boyfriends come and go with her as a rule. She's given the elbow and had the same thing done to her. She usually picks herself up and gets back out there. But not this time.'

'She must have been really smitten.'

'She was. Absolutely. But it's turned out not to have been the same for Ed, so she has to face up to it and get on with her life. I know she's hurting, and I feel for her, I really do, but she must drag herself out of the trough she's got herself into or she'll just sink ever deeper. I'm really worried about her. She doesn't want to go out anywhere after she gets home from the factory.' Nancy and Ruby were on the Tube on their way home from work. The train was packed and they were strap-hanging. 'All that talk about there being more fish in the sea, and how she was going to get out there to hook one of them was just that – talk. She just stays at home being fed up. It's as though all the life has gone out of her.'

'She used to love going out dancing, didn't she? Especially to the Palais.'

'She won't go near the place now.'

'Can't you ask her to go with you?'

'I don't go there.'

'Perhaps you could go with her just once, to get her back into the swing of it,' suggested Ruby. 'You could pretend that you need cheering up with Pete being away. It's Saturday tomorrow and you're not on late turn, so you could do it then. The sooner the better.'

'I can't go up the Palais,' Nancy stated categorically. 'I'm a married woman.'

'There is that.' Her friend paused thoughtfully. 'But you'd only be going to keep Jean company, not to look for a man.'

'That isn't how it would seem to other people.'

'It was just an idea. I remember you saying once that you really enjoy dancing and the music and everything.'

'I love it, especially the jitterbug, even though I'm not very good at it.'

'Well then, give yourself a night out and help your sister at the same time,' Ruby persisted.

'I suppose I could stay upstairs and watch the dancing

from the balcony. There's a cafeteria up there.' She pondered for a moment. 'I doubt Jean would come, though, the mood she's in.'

'It's worth a try.'

'If you're so keen to help Jean, and think this is such a wonderful idea, why don't you come along too?' suggested Nancy, warming to the idea. 'I'll do it if you will.'

'I've never been to a dance hall in my life.' Ruby looked terrified. 'I can't dance.'

'Now's your chance to learn. You're young and single. So why not?' said Nancy.

'I'd be like a fish out of water.' Ruby was totally fazed by the prospect. 'I'll be the Queen of the Wallflowers.'

'Don't be too sure of that,' advised Nancy. 'Anyway, we can sit upstairs and watch the dancing from the balcony. Once we get Jean there, she won't need us. Believe me, once she hears the music and feels the atmosphere she'll soon get into the mood. She never has any shortage of partners.'

'I don't have anything to wear,' came Ruby's next excuse.

'I'm sure you can find something. You don't need a ball-gown. This is the Hammersmith Palais we're talking about, not the Dorchester,' Nancy reminded her. 'A skirt and blouse or jumper will do.' She cast her eyes over her friend's pale face and limp, greasy hair. Ruby never made any effort with her appearance, but there was definitely potential for improvement. 'A bit of make-up wouldn't go amiss if you've got any.'

'I never use it.'

'So make an exception,' suggested Nancy. 'I'll lend you

some of mine. And I don't make that offer lightly, as it's in such short supply. It'll make you feel good; give you confidence.' Nancy was beginning to think that perhaps she could kill two birds with one stone, that she could bring Ruby out of herself, as well as remove Jean from the doldrums. 'Please say you'll come to keep me company. It'll be easier if there are two of us.'

'Something tells me I'm going to regret this,' sighed Ruby. 'But all right. If you can talk her into it, I'll come.'

'That's the spirit. I'll go home and put the idea to her tonight and let you know tomorrow at work.'

'I wish I'd kept my big mouth shut now,' admitted Ruby gloomily.

'It's too late to change your mind now, girl,' Nancy grinned. 'You've committed yourself.'

'Well, stone me, if it isn't Gordon Rawlings!' greeted Bobby, giving a warm handshake to a soldier, an old school pal, at the bar of one of the local pubs. 'I haven't seen you for yonks. How's life treating you, mate?'

'Not very often, but I'm all right. Yourself?'

'Not so dusty. How long are you home for?'

'Ten days.'

'You jammy sod. I'm only on a forty-eight.'

'I've had a long spell overseas,' Gordon explained. 'We've been brought back for some special operation, so I reckon I'm entitled to a spot of leave.'

'Course you are. I was only kidding.'

'I heard you'd got wounded earlier on in the war,'

331

mentioned Gordon. 'Mum heard about it through the local grapevine.'

'Yeah, I did get a bullet in me, but it's a while ago.'

'Did they send you back into action?'

'No, not yet. I reckon they must think that my wound has affected my responses and that could put other people in danger.'

'Could be. Who knows what goes on in the minds of army officers?'

Bobby bought him a drink and they got talking about old times.

'Those were the days, eh?' Bobby reminisced. 'Football in the street, cricket in the alley.'

'And beatings up against the wall,' put in Gordon, who had less fond memories.

Bobby frowned, remembering. 'It was no bed of roses growing up around our way, was it?' he said. 'There were some real hard cases about.'

'I've still got the scars to prove it.'

Through the mists of time, Bobby recalled that Gordon had been a natural target for bullies when they were children, mainly because he was physically weaker than the other boys and never had much to say for himself. He was still rather odd-looking – tallish and thin, with a long nose and pointed chin. 'Yeah, they were rough on you for a while,' Bobby said.

'You and your tough mates soon put a stop to it when you found out what had been happening, and I'll always be grateful to you for that.'

'Those thugs just needed a taste of their own medicine,' said Bobby. 'Bullies soon change their tune when someone stands up to them.'

'I didn't have it in me to do that then,' admitted Gordon.

'I bet you have now, though. You have to in the army and it gets to be a habit.'

'Oh yeah, I can look after myself now, all right.'

They spent a little more time down memory lane before moving on to other things.

'You married?' asked Bobby.

The other man shook his head. 'No, I've never even come close. You?'

'Not married. But I was engaged, up until yesterday, as it happens,' said Bobby, finding it surprisingly easy to talk to Gordon, even though he hadn't seen him for years. 'I found out she only wanted me for what she could get.'

'Blimey, that's rough.'

'I was none too pleased, I can tell you.'

'You're in here drowning your sorrows, then.'

'Not really, though I suppose I will if I stay in here long enough,' he said. 'I came down here because I'm at a loose end and didn't fancy sitting indoors on a Saturday night.'

'Same here,' Gordon told him. 'All the blokes I know from round here are away.'

'It isn't often your leave coincides with your local pals', is it?'

'I don't think it's ever worked out that way for me.'

'As we're both on our own, we may as well join forces for the evening, then. We could have another drink here, then go on somewhere more interesting, if you like,' suggested Bobby.

'Suits me.'

'Good. We'll have one more in here, then go and find some action,' said Bobby.

'I'll get these,' insisted Gordon, looking for someone to serve them.

Arthur was ensconced in his armchair, reading the newspaper and enjoying the fact that it was a Saturday night and he didn't have to go out on his round.

Gladys came into the room with her coat and headscarf on. 'I'm going down the road to see Flo,' she announced, referring to an elderly widow who lived in the street. 'She's in bed with a nasty attack of bronchitis and I need to make sure she's all right and get her anything she needs before she settles down for the night.'

'Mm,' he grunted, paying little attention.

'The girls have gone out dancing and Leslie is staying the night at his pal's house, so I'd appreciate it if you would listen for Evie.'

He took heed now. 'Not likely,' he objected. 'I'm not doing that.'

'She's fast asleep and there's unlikely to be a peep out of her,' she told him in a brisk, determined manner.

'You know how I feel about that wretched child,' he reminded her.

'This isn't about you. This is about a friend and neighbour who's sick and on her own. Us women are taking it in turns to call in on her and it's my turn now, so I have to go.'

'You've no right to go out and leave me on my own with her,' he complained. 'You took her on. She's your responsibility. Nothing to do with me.'

'Yeah, yeah, I know all about that, but I didn't realise the girls would both be out,' Gladys explained. 'It won't hurt you to help out for the sake of a sick neighbour. I doubt you'll even have to get out of your armchair. Look on it as a favour to Flo. I mean, how would you like to be ill and alone?'

'I don't like it,' he moaned. 'I don't like it at all.'

'Then you'll just have to bloomin' well lump it, because I'm needed elsewhere,' she blurted out. 'So for once in your life stop thinking about yourself.'

Before he had a chance to say more, she turned and walked away. Listening to her closing the front door carefully so as not to wake Evie, he went back to his newspaper. It was just as well the nipper was asleep in bed, because he wouldn't look after her otherwise. What was the world coming to when a man wasn't master in his own house?

'There's no one I fancy here,' said Jean, eyeing up the talent around the dance floor. 'Nothing worth a second glance among the lot of 'em.'

'Don't be so horrible,' admonished Nancy. 'They're all perfectly presentable.'

'Not to me.'

'That doesn't matter, anyway, because we've only come

335

for a night out and a laugh and not to look for men, so cheer up, will you?' said Nancy. 'You're spoiling it for Ruby and me.'

'Sorry, I'm just not in the mood.'

'You will be once you start dancing . . . which is going to be any minute now by the look of it, because there's a GI on his way over.'

She was right.

After Jean was swept on to the dance floor to jitterbug to 'Deep in the Heart of Texas', Ruby said wistfully, 'I never thought I would ever say this, but I'd love to be able to do that.'

'Let's give it a try, then,' suggested Nancy.

'Don't be daft.'

'I'm not brilliant, but I did learn a few steps from Pete,' she told her. 'We could have a go.'

'I'd be too embarrassed.'

'Who's going to look at us? The floor is so crowded no one will pay any attention to what we're doing, they're all too busy enjoying themselves,' Nancy pointed out. Indeed, the whole area was a swirling mass of couples, jiving, jitter-bugging, and the more conventional doing the quickstep.

Ruby – who looked a whole lot different with a spot of lipstick and rouge on her face and a shine on her freshly washed hair – still wasn't convinced.

'We'll pick it up as we go along.' Nancy grabbed her arm. 'Come on, let's have a go.'

Neither of them had much of a clue. Nancy didn't go dancing often enough to be proficient. But once they were out on the dance floor, Ruby lost some of her inhibitions and began to have fun and Nancy soon caught her mood. Copying the others, they began to get the hang of it, pausing every so often because they were helpless with laughter. It had been quite a while since Nancy had had a really good laugh and it was very uplifting.

Arthur had dozed off in his chair, the newspaper resting on his lap. He came to with a start, his eyes snapping open, and wondered what had woken him. He turned the wireless off and listened. Then he heard it, the fearful sound of a child crying upstairs.

She can get on with it and cry herself back to sleep, he told himself. I am not going up there. Absolutely not! Her grandmother will be back soon, and she can deal with it. The wailing grew louder and he felt his stomach tighten and his heart pound. He tried to ignore it, but the noise played on his nerves. Muttering a few choice words, he stamped up the stairs and put the bedroom light on.

She was sitting up in the big double bed she shared with her grandmother, sobbing her heart out, ginger curls wet on her brow, her nose running, face soaked with tears.

'What's the matter with you?' he asked sternly, forced by the state of her face to wipe it with his handkerchief. 'What's all this noise about?'

'Wanna come downstairs,' she said, crying and hiccuping by turns.

'Well you can't,' he told her firmly. 'You must lie down and go back to sleep.'

Her breath came in little gasps as she worked herself up. For one alarming moment he thought she was going to choke.

'Does it hurt anywhere?' he asked, panic rising.

'Me go downstairs,' she wept.

'Have you got a pain?' he enquired.

'Wanna go downstairs,' she repeated.

'You're just trying it on,' he admonished. 'Well, I'm not having it. So just stop that silly noise and lie down. I'll leave the light on for you.'

Her cries were enough to wake the dead and he was really frightened. How on earth was he going to stop her? He'd never been involved at this level with his own children when they were small, let alone someone else's brat.

'I want my gran,' she stuttered, through shuddering breaths.

'Your gran's gone out.'

'I want Nancy.'

'Nancy isn't here either.'

Her screams reached new heights.

'They'll be back soon,' he told her.

This did nothing to comfort her. She was beside herself, her whole body racked with sobs, her face crimson, eyes red raw. She'd got herself worked up into a state and couldn't get out of it. What was he going to do? He couldn't let her carry on like this; she'd make herself sick or pass out or worse . . . Oh well, there was only one thing for it. Inwardly trembling, he reached down and lifted her out of the bed, expecting her to turn up the volume and fight against him.

But while she didn't stop crying altogether, the noise did subside a little. Her head felt hot and wet as she rested it against his shoulder.

He carried her downstairs and sat her on the sofa, then wiped her face with a damp flannel and dried it. She was still making funny little breathing noises in the aftermath of the tantrum and her face was blotchy, her eyes all puffed up, but she was quieter. Thank God for that!

'Do you want a drink of water?' he asked.

She shook her head.

'Well, you'd better sit there until your gran comes home.' He daren't risk setting her off again by putting her back to bed. He supposed he ought to get something to put over her, in case she got cold. He'd never hear the last of it from the women of the family if he allowed so much as a draught to blow on her, they were all so besotted with her. Where the hell was Gladys?

Having covered Evie with the eiderdown from one of the single beds, refraining from suggesting that she lie down, for fear it would restart the waterworks, he sat down in his armchair and stared unseeingly at the paper. How was he expected to concentrate on anything when he was alone in the house with a screaming machine? In full flow, she was enough to send the entire German army into retreat, and his nerves were in shreds.

The way she was staring at him now was unnerving too. She seemed to be trying to work him out, her huge blue eyes resting unwaveringly on his face with a puzzled expression. It was a peculiar thing that he was so frightened. Arthur, a man who had lived with danger at sea for most of his adult life, was scared stiff of a two-and-a-half-year-old child. The sea and all its perils he could cope with. His wife's child by some stranger? Not in a million years!

He hid behind his paper, praying for Gladys to return and hoping that the child would go to sleep. But no such luck. He felt something touch his knee and before he had a chance to object, she had climbed on to his lap. The newspaper fell to the floor as she shifted about, trying to get comfortable. He didn't want some stranger's brat cuddling up to him, but couldn't bring himself to remove her. It wasn't so easy when there was no one else here to attend to her.

He needed to stop her wriggling, though, so altered his position so that she was snuggled into the crook of his arm, her head resting against his shoulder. After some more restless movement, she became still and her breathing was soft and even. She was sleeping peacefully in his arms.

He supposed he ought to carry her upstairs and put her back into bed. But he daren't risk waking her and have her yell the place down again. It was far too damaging to his nervous system and enough to give a man of his age a heart attack.

Just as he was wondering what his next move should be, something astonishing happened. An unexpected sense of tranquillity came over him as they sat there together in the silent house. All he could hear was the sound of her gentle breathing and the clock ticking; she felt warm and soft against him and smelled of soap and clean pyjamas. It felt so good, so right. Smudge padded into the room and settled down on the mat at Arthur's feet, and for the first time since he'd been home he felt really at peace.

Gladys was both astonished and moved at the scene that greeted her on her return, her little granddaughter asleep in Arthur's arms. She had rarely seen two people so much at peace and it brought tears to her eyes.

Her son-in-law carried Evie upstairs and together they put her to bed. She didn't stir as – with infinite gentleness – they covered her over.

'Thanks, Arthur,' said Gladys when they were back downstairs. 'I didn't expect her to wake up, but you seem to have managed all right anyway.'

Reality hit him like a fist in the face and he was furious with himself for letting down his guard against the manifestation of Lily's unfaithfulness.

'I didn't manage, I didn't manage at all,' he told her. 'It was a bloody nightmare.'

'But she was asleep in your arms. The two of you looked so right together,' she said.

'She fell asleep from sheer exhaustion after damaging my eardrums with her screaming,' he told her forcefully. 'It's a wonder I wasn't out cold too.'

'You obviously calmed her down.'

'I had to bring her downstairs or we'd have had the neighbours banging on the door, complaining about the noise,' he muttered. 'She climbed on my lap of her own accord. I didn't want her there, but I daren't put her down for fear she'd start that bloody noise again.'

341

'Oh dear. I am sorry. She's usually so good. Must have been some sort of a tantrum.'

'Oh, I'm going to the pub,' he said, walking purposefully across the room. 'And I hope they've got some beer in, because I need a drink to settle my nerves after what I've just been through.'

'You've been in the war and you can't cope with a harmless little child!' she challenged.

'She isn't just any child though, is she?' he reminded her bitterly.

'No, she's a very special one.'

He didn't reply, just left the house, collecting his coat from the hall stand on the way. As he walked to the pub in the blackout, his stomach was churning and he realised that he was shaking all over. That bloody kid was getting under his skin and he was furious with himself. Gladys had no right to shift her responsibility on to him, not even for an hour.

'It hasn't been as bad as you thought, has it?' said Nancy to Ruby. 'In fact, I would even go so far as to suggest that you're enjoying yourself.'

'Well . . . maybe just a bit.'

They were upstairs, looking down at the dance floor from the balcony.

'It'll soon be time for the last waltz,' Nancy commented. 'That's definitely one I shall sit out. It can get a bit too smoochy for me, and if some bloke you don't know asks you, it can be horrible.'

'I'll stay with you, then.'

'We'll get the coats as soon as it starts,' said Nancy. 'The queue is always miles long at the end. I've got Jean's cloak-room ticket.'

'OK.'

'Jean has found herself a new admirer, by the look of it,' remarked Nancy, looking down. 'She's dancing with that GI again. He's been after her all night. I doubt if she'll be coming home with us.'

'Our plan worked, then.'

'Yes, it seems to have done,' Nancy agreed, looking pleased. 'It's so good to see Jean out and about again. And *you* have to take the credit. It was your idea.'

'I shall think twice about the consequences for myself before I come up with any more bright ideas, though,' said Ruby, turning and sitting down at a nearby table. The majority of people were on the dance floor or flanking the edges, and most of the tables were free.

Nancy turned and sat down opposite her. 'Go on with you. You've had a whale of a time,' she smiled.

'Yeah, all right. I admit it. It has been a bit of fun.'

'It's been a good laugh for me too,' smiled Nancy. 'Just what I needed.'

'Well, we haven't exactly had the women falling at our feet, have we?' said Bobby.

'How can they, when we haven't even asked anyone to dance yet?' Gordon pointed out. 'We've been sitting up here talking since we got here.'

'Which wasn't until after the interval.'

'It'll be too late if we don't get down there soon,' said Gordon, looking over the balcony. 'It must be nearly time for the last waltz.'

'I'm not bothered about getting fixed up,' said Bobby. 'Women are more trouble than they're worth.'

'Just because you've had one bad cherry, it doesn't mean you should lose your appetite for the rest on the tree.'

'You know me better than that,' chuckled Bobby.

'We might as well go down there and have a dance,' suggested Gordon. 'Seeing as we've paid for a ticket.'

'All right, all right,' said Bobby as the music ended. 'I'll just finish my drink and we'll go down . . .' His voice tailed off and a huge smile lit his face.

'What the bloomin' heck have you seen to make you look so happy?' asked Gordon. 'You look as though you've just lost a farthing and found a five-pound note.'

'Better than that, mate, much better,' said Bobby, looking beyond Gordon to a table nearby where his beloved Nancy was sitting with a friend. He mustn't go over; he'd promised when he last saw her that he'd stay away. Anyway, her father had told him that she was getting engaged, so she'd be married by now. He had to leave now before she saw him. But he couldn't do it. He just couldn't be this near to her without saying hello.

Nancy was rendered speechless when, responding to a tap on the shoulder, she found herself looking up at Bobby Collins. 'I know I shouldn't be doing this,' he said nervously, 'but I couldn't leave without asking you to dance.' Nancy looked around anxiously. She had to get away quickly; she couldn't trust herself to talk to him, let alone dance with him.

'Er . . . we're just leaving actually, Bobby,' she stuttered at last. 'Sorry.'

'Ah, what a shame.' His disappointment melted her heart.

'We have to get away promptly, I'm afraid.' She forced the words out. 'We're just going to get our coats before the rush, aren't we, Ruby?'

'We can get them after this dance. It doesn't matter if there's a queue,' said a beaming Ruby, about to descend to the dance floor with Gordon, who was also smiling fit to bust. 'See you later, Nance.'

'Well . . . those two obviously like the look of each other,' observed Bobby, staring after them as they joined the masses of people on the floor.

'It does seem that way, doesn't it?' agreed Nancy, astonished that her plain, socially inadequate friend seemed to have blossomed in such a short space of time.

'So . . . why not come and dance with me while you're waiting for her?' he suggested, smiling in the way she remembered so well. 'You don't want to be standing around on your own, do you?'

She knew she should listen to her head and say no, no, no. But she *so* wanted to be with him, just for a few precious minutes.

'Thank you, Bobby,' she said graciously. 'I'd love to.'

345

Chapter Fourteen

Nancy had often wondered what it would feel like to be this close to Bobby again, had thought about it endlessly when she was younger. Over the years, she'd hoped to find that special something with other boyfriends, and later with Pete. Now she knew why it hadn't happened.

As she'd grown up and matured in her outlook in the years following those heady days, she'd reflected on her love affair with Bobby as a thing of youth, unrepeatable now that time had passed. But the feeling was still there, stronger than ever, something so indefinable and profound she knew with absolute certainty that she would never find it with anyone else. The sheer wonder of it was tinged with sadness in knowing that it could never follow its true course, because she was married to someone else.

'So . . . what's a respectable married woman like yourself doing in a place like this?' he asked lightly, moving his head back, tilting it to one side and looking at her with a smile in his eyes.

She gave him a knowing look. 'You didn't miss the ring, then,' she said.

'Oh no. A plain gold one has "off limits" written all over it as far as I'm concerned.'

'So why am I here with you?'

'There's no harm in a dance for old times' sake, is there?' He grinned. 'Our first and last waltz, you might say.'

She chuckled, her blue eyes sparkling into his. 'We weren't old enough to go out dancing then, were we?'

'Not to proper dances.'

The last time they'd met she'd sent him away because of the painful memories he evoked. Now she realised that all she wanted was to be with him.

'Sorry I was so hard on you last time we saw each other,' she said, looking up at him with remorse. 'Dragging up the past again hurt so much, I just couldn't take it.'

'No need to apologise. I understand.'

They indulged in light conversation, exchanging details about their current circumstances. She explained why she was there tonight.

'So I have your sister to thank for this dance with you, then,' he said lightly.

'Yep. She's the reason I'm out on the town instead of at home like a respectable married lady,' she said with a wry grin.

He looked at her with unmistakable tenderness. 'It's so good to see you again, Nancy.'

'It's lovely to see you too.' She wanted to sink into his arms and stay there for ever.

'So . . . are you happily married?'

She longed to pour her heart out to him about the miserable state of her marriage. But somehow it didn't seem fair to him, or to Pete. 'Yeah, course I am.'

Bobby noticed her hesitation, and said, 'Sure?'

She nodded.

He gave her a shrewd look. 'Treats you right, does he?'

'What is this, the third degree?' she snapped, because seeing him again had made her feel even more trapped with Pete.

'No. Of course not. I care about you, that's all. We go back a long way.'

'I know,' she sighed. 'I shouldn't have bitten your head off.'

'I forgive you.'

'The dance will be ending in a minute, so let's just enjoy it,' she said in a jokey manner, to ease the tension and lighten the mood.

'You always were a bossy cow,' he reproached her affectionately.

Wanting to squeeze every last morsel out of this brief respite from the hardship of the world outside and her disastrous marriage, she leaned her head on his shoulder and succumbed to the sheer joy of being with him. It felt so good, so right, as though they were made for each other.

When the music ended, they stood facing each other in silence. She could hardly drag herself away, but knew she must. What they had was never meant to be.

He didn't want to leave her either, but said in a voice ragged with emotion, 'Well, I suppose that's that, then. Maybe our paths will cross again one of these days.'

She needed to remove herself from temptation with all possible speed. 'I'm sorry, Bobby, I must fly. I have to find the others. I've got their cloakroom tickets.'

With a huge amount of self-control, he didn't try to detain her. He just said, 'Take good care of yourself, Nancy. All the best. Be happy.'

'You too.'

Bobby watched as Nancy turned and disappeared into the crush of people heading towards the exits and the cloakrooms. He was in so much turmoil that he had to physically restrain himself from going after her. She was married, *end of story*, he told himself. His heart aching, he went to find Gordon.

Much to Nancy's surprise, Jean went home on the train with herself and Ruby.

'We thought you'd be going off with that GI you were dancing with all evening,' she remarked, forcing herself to be sociable, when all she really wanted was to relive those few special moments with Bobby. 'He seemed very keen.'

'I think he was rather, but I'm not interested,' she told them. 'He was nice enough to dance with, but that's as far as it went for me.'

'You're getting choosy, aren't you?' Nancy obseved, still putting up a front. 'A hunk like that and you turned him down!'

'I'm off men, the lot of 'em.'

'That won't last.'

'Probably not, but I'll never trust another Yank, and that's definite.'

'You can't damn a whole nation just because Ed let you down,' reproved Nancy. 'That isn't fair. Anyway, you seemed to be thoroughly enjoying yourself with him.'

'It was just a question of getting through the evening, really,' her sister explained. 'As you two had forced me into coming, I thought I'd better stick it out or I'd never hear the last of it.'

'At least it got you out of the house,' said Nancy, turning to her friend. 'And Ruby enjoyed herself, didn't you?'

'I certainly did,' she replied dreamily.

Two pairs of eyes were fixed on her now.

'You certainly came out of your shell in a big way, didn't you?' remarked Nancy. 'I couldn't believe it when you sailed off with that soldier for the last waltz.'

'Me neither,' she admitted. 'But I'm very glad I did. His name is Gordon and I think he's smashing.'

'So when's your first date?' prodded Jean.

'Tomorrow,' Ruby announced with delight. 'I'm meeting him in the afternoon.'

'You're a dark horse,' smiled Nancy. 'I've never seen anyone transformed in such a short time.'

'That's the magic of the Palais,' put in Jean. 'It works every time.'

'Well, it certainly didn't take Ruby long to get the hang of it,' joshed Nancy.

'What about you and that dark-haired soldier, Nancy?' Jean enquired.

Nancy tensed. 'What about him?' she replied with feigned indifference.

'You were all over him.'

'No I wasn't!' Oh dear. Had she really behaved so irresponsibly as to let her feelings show in the joy of the moment?

'Phew! Not much! You should have seen yourself,' Jean grinned. 'Just count yourself lucky that it was only us who saw you and not your husband.'

Consumed with guilt, Nancy said, 'I only danced with the man. It was a waltz. I couldn't very well do it without touching him.'

'And, boy, did you make the most of it,' joked Jean. 'You looked as though you wanted to drag him outside and have your wicked way with him.'

'Don't be so stupid,' retaliated Nancy sharply. 'You're taking it too far now.'

Jean narrowed her eyes at her sister. 'Your dark-haired lover-boy looked vaguely familiar. Is he the one you were talking to in the Rook and Raven that time?'

'You did already know him, didn't you, Nancy?' remarked Ruby casually. 'I remember that you called him by his name when they first came up to us.'

'I knew him a long time ago,' she explained.

'Quite well by the look of it,' teased Jean.

'Watch what you're saying, Jean,' warned Nancy. 'You'll get me a bad name.'

'You're the one who was wrapped around the soldier, so if you get a bad name it won't be down to me,' she defended herself. 'Anyway, I'm only kidding, so you can stop getting your knickers in a twist.'

'Calm down, both of you,' intervened Ruby. 'We've had

352

a good night out. Don't spoil it now. I can't make you two out. You're always arguing, so how is it you never actually fall out permanently?'

'Dunno,' said Jean with a casual air. 'Because we're sisters so we're stuck with each other whether we like it or not, I suppose.'

'You're very lucky to have each other, though.' Ruby sounded envious.

'Lucky isn't the word I'd use.' Nancy was joking now.

'Cursed would be nearer the mark,' added Jean, also joshing.

'Especially for me, having a man-eating sister.'

'You were the man-eater tonight, mate, with that soldier,' laughed Jean.

'See what I have to put up with Ruby?' said Nancy with mock umbrage.

Ruby was wise enough not to take sides, so just laughed it off.

There was a good atmosphere between the three of them, Nancy observed. The evening had been a success. Jean seemed more cheerful and Ruby had got herself a date. So, mission accomplished!

Now, as the other two chatted together, Nancy lapsed into her own thoughts, going over every wonderful second of the dance with Bobby, wishing she hadn't had to leave him.

They each went their separate ways when they came out of Ealing Broadway station. Nancy was still feeling low as she walked home.

Reaching the top floor of the house where her room was situated and seeing a light under the door, she reproached herself for forgetting to switch it off before she went out. She should know better in these times, when it was downright unpatriotic to be wasteful with electricity, which ate into the coal reserves. 'Cut Your Gas and Electricity,' the government posters urged, adding, should anyone be in any doubt, 'They both come from coal.'

Opening the door, she realised that she hadn't been careless after all.

'Pete!' she gasped, her eyes widening with shock. 'How lovely to see you.' Hiding her sudden tension, she went over to the armchair where he was sprawled out, to give him a welcome hug. 'I wasn't expecting you home.'

'Obviously not,' he said, pushing her away, his face like thunder.

'Sorry I wasn't here,' she apologised, her nerves jangling. 'If I'd known you were coming . . .'

'Just as well for me that you didn't.' His voice was low, so as not to attract the attention of the other tenants, but his tone was harsh and threatening. No matter how much of a rage he was in, he never took the risk of being overheard. He was far too artful for that. 'At least I know what's going on behind my back now.'

'What on earth are you talking about?'

'Don't insult me by denying it, since I've caught you redhanded.'

'All I did was go out for the evening with my sister and my friend.'

'It's where you went I'm referring to,' he informed her brusquely. 'I went round to Sycamore Road looking for you. Your dad was out at the pub, but your gran told me you'd gone to the Hammersmith Palais.'

'That's right.' She did actually understand why he was angry; it was for the same reason she'd had doubts about going when Ruby had first suggested it.

'At least you remembered to put your wedding ring back on before you got home,' he said, in a tone of savage accusation. 'That's something, I suppose.'

'I didn't take it off.' She was horrified at the suggestion. 'I wouldn't do that. It would never even occur to me.'

'Don't make me laugh,' he scorned. 'A wedding ring would cramp your style. How could you cheapen yourself like that?'

'I've only been up the Palais to cheer my sister up. Not out soliciting on the streets,' she reminded him.

'You're a married woman. People go to the Palais on a Saturday night for one thing: to get fixed up with someone,' he stated in an uncompromising manner. 'It's a recognised fact.'

'But that wasn't why I went there tonight. Absolutely not! I went because of Jean.'

'You're just a cheap little tart.'

'Oi! That isn't fair,' she snapped back at him. 'All right, perhaps I shouldn't have gone out dancing. I wouldn't have gone out anywhere if I'd known you were coming home.'

'I didn't think I had to book an appointment to find my wife at home.'

'Normally I would have been here, or at Dad's . . .'

355

'But you weren't, were you?' he persisted nastily. 'I come home looking forward to seeing my wife, and where is she? Out bloody dancing.' He got up and began to pace about. 'You couldn't even go somewhere respectable like a concert or even the pictures, could you? Oh no! You have to go out to the most fertile hunting ground in London.'

She remembered the last waltz with Bobby and her cheeks burned. She couldn't even begin to contemplate what Pete would do to her if he were to ever find out about that. Seeing something in his eyes that she had learned to fear, she said, 'I'm sorry to have upset you, Pete. I really am.'

'You will be sorry,' he said, lunging towards her and throwing her against the wall. 'You know how I hate it when you step out of line.'

'Pete, no, please . . .'

'Scream and you'll get worse,' he reminded her, pinning her against the wall, his grip bruising her arms. 'You should know that by now.'

Frightened for her life, she was helpless against his superior physical strength as his fist beat into her stomach, her chest and her legs. Sobbing quietly with the pain of the blows, all she could do was wait until his temper was finally spent.

Early the next morning – after a sleepless night – she lay next to him feeling sick, exhausted and miserable. He'd been more brutal than ever last night, beating her so violently she'd thought, at one point, that her end had come. Then there was a grotesque sexual act with no hint of tenderness or love. This was what he did when he was angry, and he'd been especially furious last night.

She really felt she couldn't take any more; she *didn't want* to take any more. She'd vowed at the start that she would stand by him and never tell a soul about the beatings, because she'd married him for better or worse. But the situation had become impossible. His leaves were a blight on her life, rather than the blessing they should be. He was a dangerous man. One of these days he was going to go too far and she wouldn't live to tell the tale.

Her instinct was to slip from the house before he woke up, for fear of what he would do to her when she told him. But he would only come after her and cause a scene at home. Anyway, she wasn't going to be a coward about this. She had to tell him to his face that she simply couldn't stay under these dreadful conditions.

An hour later she was dressed, had a small bag packed and was ready to leave; she even had her outdoor coat on in case she had to make a hasty exit. She hadn't packed the rest of her things, with the idea of coming to collect them when he'd gone back to camp. She'd made tea and toast, and was about to wake him when he stirred.

'Hello,' he said, yawning and stretching. 'You're up and about already, then?'

'Breakfast in bed,' she said, handing him a tray.

'You're spoiling me.'

She didn't say anything, or sit down, just stood stiffly by the bed.

He sat up and leaned against the pillows, which he propped against the iron bedstead, the tray on his lap. 'Aren't you having any?'

It was barely believable that he could half murder her, then carry on afterwards as though nothing untoward had happened, so convincingly that she began to think she must have imagined the whole thing. The ache and throb of her bruised body, however, assured her she hadn't.

'I'm leaving you, Pete,' she blurted out. 'I can't take any more violence.' She hesitated for only a moment, her gaze resting on him; she was poised ready to make a run for it. 'You're a bully and if you lose your temper and start on me now, I'll report you to the police, who will in turn inform the RAF, I should imagine. Assault is a criminal offence, even for heroes of the sky like you.'

'Leaving me! The police!' He sounded astonished. 'What's all this about?'

'You know perfectly well what you've done to me, so don't act the innocent.'

She was ready to make a dash for it the second she saw any sign of his temper rising. But to her astonishment, he was contrite.

'Nancy, I'm so sorry,' he said, putting a hand to his brow. 'It's the stress of the job. I get these blind rages and take it out on you.'

'Not any more you won't. I've had enough.'

'Please don't leave me, Nancy,' he begged, his eyes brimming with tears. 'You're the only thing in the world that matters to me. I love you so much.'

'Love!' she snorted. 'You don't treat someone you love the way you treat me.'

He lowered his eyes. 'It's this wretched temper of mine,' he tried to explain with a sob in his voice. 'It takes over. I don't mean to hurt you.'

'But you do hurt me, very much, and I'm fed up with being treated like a punchbag.'

'I'll change,' he said ardently, his velvet eyes meeting hers. 'I'll do anything you ask, anything at all. But please don't give up on me. I love you and I don't know how I'd get through life if I didn't have you. I live for the times when I come home to see you.'

This was the Pete who cried in her arms after a bad dream; this was the vulnerable, almost childlike side of his nature.

'I still have to go,' she said, shaking with emotion. 'If I stay, you'll end up killing me, and getting yourself hanged for murder.'

'I'll get medical help for my temper.' He clutched his head, his breakfast uneaten on the tray. 'I get this burning anger that I can't seem to control.'

'You controlled it before we were married,' she said. 'There was no sign of it then.'

'We didn't live together then, so it was easier. But I'll change, I promise.' Tears were flowing now. 'I'll do anything you ask if only you'll stay. I'll go and see the quack, get him to give me something for the stress.'

'How do you get on with the other chaps in your squadron?' she enquired, realising that for the first time they were talking about it in a relatively civilised manner.

'I don't have any close friends, but I'm pally with them all,' he told her. 'We're all under stress. Tempers get frayed. I'm not the only one to lose mine. We all live and work together, there are bound to be things about each other that rankle.'

'You don't get violent with them, though?'

'I've had a couple of brawls,' he admitted, looking sheepish. 'But I wasn't reported. The chaps know I'm a good pilot and they respect me for that. There's a code between us. We accept each other's faults and live with them.'

'They're a match for you physically, though,' she pointed out. 'I'm not. That's why I have to go. Before any serious damage is done.'

'Nancy, please don't leave me.' He was sobbing loudly now, forlorn and pathetic. 'I need you so much. I have to know that you're there for me. No matter how tough things are, you're there. Just give me one more chance ... please. I'll never lay a finger on you again, I swear.'

She didn't want to stay with a man she feared and didn't love. But she was a compassionate woman and he looked so vulnerable and in need of her, she couldn't turn her back on him. 'All right, I'll give you one more chance,' she said, much against her better judgement. 'But only on condition that you get some medical advice about your violent temper.'

'I will, I promise,' he assured her. 'I'll go and see the MO as soon as I get back. If they ground me, they do. I'd sooner that than lose you.'

'Surely you're too valuable as a pilot for them to ground you over something like that?' She paused, thinking about it.

360

'The last thing I want is to put your career in jeopardy. I know how much it means to you,' she said. 'But I'm not prepared to stay unless you get medical advice. It's too dangerous.'

'I'll do it as soon as I get back.'

She heaved a sigh of resignation. 'All right, I'll stay.' She had terrible doubts about it, but just couldn't bring herself to desert him.

'Thank you, Nancy,' he said, putting his arms around her. 'You're a saint and I don't deserve you. This means so much to me.'

'I hope it does,' she said worriedly.

It was seven a.m. one chilly autumn morning on platform six on Paddington station. Shivering with the cold and wearing mittens, enormously grateful to the railway company for allowing women porters to replace their navy serge skirts with trousers to match their jackets, Nancy and Ruby were working together with a motorised tractor, more commonly known by station staff as a 'mechanical horse'. They were hauling several trolleys piled high with heavy luggage that had been sent on in advance.

'Isn't it a treat, working with one of these?' remarked Nancy, who was standing at the front controlling the levers, while Ruby was riding behind her on the small platform and would help her to load the luggage on to the train.

'An absolute dream compared to the hand trolleys,' agreed Ruby.

'Just think of the staff muscle power it would save if we used them for shifting everything.'

'Phew, I'll say,' agreed Ruby. 'But staff muscle is cheaper for the company than modernisation, so I think we'll be using hand trolleys for a long time to come, if not indefinitely. Bags I get to drive it back.'

'That's only fair,' agreed Nancy.

She brought the device to a halt at the luggage compartment and they began lifting the cases, trunks and packages on to the train.

'Gordon went back off leave yesterday,' Ruby mentioned gloomily as they lifted a large trunk between them on to the train. 'I won't half miss him. I saw him every day while he was on leave, even if only for a short time after work.'

'You'll write to him, though.'

'Oh yeah, we're both keen to do that.'

'Funny that, wasn't it?' said Nancy. 'The way the two of you hit it off at once.'

'It was amazing. I liked the look of him as soon as I set eyes on him, and I could tell he felt the same.' She paused, staring into space and luxuriating in the memory. 'It was so good between us. I felt sort of warm and safe, but excited too. I've never felt like that in my life before. Do you know what I mean?'

Didn't she just? 'Yeah, I know exactly what you mean,' Nancy said.

'I'd given up hope of ever finding anyone,' her friend went on to confess. 'I've never felt even remotely comfortable with a man before. But Gordon and me, we're two of a kind. Neither of us is smart or good-looking, but I feel as though I'm special when I'm with him. We have the same ideas about things, we laugh a lot, and just feel right together. It's such a wonderful feeling.'

'It's incredible how your life can change in an instant like that,' Nancy remarked.

Ruby nodded, sighing. 'It's going to seem very lonely now that he's gone back, though,' she said. 'We didn't have long together – it was only just over a week – but I got used to having something to look forward to after work. It's just me and Mum and the wireless again now.' She shrugged. 'Still, I mustn't complain, because it's the same for everybody. I mean, you have to put up with Pete being away, don't you?'

In Nancy's case it was a blessing and at that moment she longed to say so, to be truthful about her marriage for once. She could never confide in the family, because they were too emotionally involved with her and would be upset on her behalf and out for Pete's blood. The urge to blurt it out passed. 'You get used to it after a while.'

'I suppose you do. It isn't as though I was used to having him around before.' Ruby was far too engrossed in her new-found happiness to notice the terrible sadness in Nancy's eyes. 'I'm still a bit raw from the parting.' She paused, mulling something over. 'Fancy coming round to my place tonight for a nice long natter? Mum'll be out at her Townswomen's Guild, so I could use the company.'

'I'd really like that,' replied Nancy, as they put the last suitcase on to the train. 'Meanwhile, do you want to play drivers on the way back?'

'You bet,' she laughed.

★   ★   ★

'I owe an awful lot to you,' said Ruby that evening, as she and Nancy sat in the Greens' living room drinking tea.

Nancy had only ever been here before to call for Ruby and had never been further than the hall. Now she noticed how immaculate everything was, shiny and neat, with nothing out of place. The furnishings were of good quality, on account of Ruby's father having had a good job. The Sparrow home was chaos in comparison, littered as it was with Evie's toys, Leslie's comics, catapults and cigarette cards, and the knitting bags, newspapers and other family articles.

'Because I forced you to go up the Palais and you met Gordon?' she said now.

'I'm in your debt for a lot more than that,' Ruby told her earnestly. 'You befriended me and made me feel different about myself. You didn't give up on me, even though I was horrible to you.'

Nancy sipped her drink, remembering. 'I must be a glutton for punishment.' She thought back on it. 'You certainly weren't the easiest person to make friends with. Talk about aggressive.'

'Aggression was a habit I couldn't shake off,' Ruby said. 'I didn't know how else to behave. It was a defence mechanism, I suppose.'

'Why did you always feel the need to defend yourself?' Nancy wondered.

Her friend shrugged. 'People didn't like me,' she said, as a fact, rather than a whine of self-pity. 'I'm not a likeable person, I know that, so I rejected them before they got a chance to do it to me.'

'That's really sad, Ruby.' Nancy was sitting in an armchair

with her feet curled under her. Ruby was in the other chair. 'Didn't it ever occur to you that if you were nicer to people they would reciprocate?'

'I did know that, sort of, but I couldn't do it. I just didn't know how,' she explained. 'Not until you came along and drew me out of myself. I'll never forget that feeling of having a friend, that first time we travelled home together on the train. It was just a small thing, but it made me feel a part of things, and that made all the difference.'

'It took you long enough to come round to it.' Nancy gave a wry grin. 'All those elaborate stories you used to make up to avoid my company on the train.'

Ruby rolled her eyes in self-reproach. 'I know. Wasn't it silly? I can see now how stupid I was, but I was afraid . . . afraid of upsetting you somehow, and turning you against me as I always had with everyone else in the past.'

'Where does it all come from, Ruby?' Nancy was genuinely interested, rather than just curious. 'I know it must go back a long way, because I remember you were always in trouble at school for fighting and quarrelling. If there was a skirmish, it was a pound to a penny you were the cause of it.'

She made a face. 'I can hardly bear to think about it. The more alienated I became, the unhappier I was and the angrier I got and the more I did it. It was a vicious circle and I couldn't break out of it. I was desperately lonely and miserable throughout my childhood. I longed to be popular, to have friends.'

'Most of us do,' said Nancy. 'But you were turning people against you the whole time.'

'I couldn't stop myself. It was just the way I was.'

'What about your parents? Didn't they give you any guidance?' Nancy asked. 'I'm sure the school must have contacted them about your behaviour as you were always in so much trouble.'

She nodded. 'Mum was always having to go to the school to be told about my latest escapade. She used to give me a bit of a telling-off, but she was always too busy quarrelling with my father to worry too much about me.'

Nancy tutted. 'That couldn't have been very nice for you,' she said.

'It was awful, especially as I had no siblings for company. That's why I've always longed for a sister or brother, and why I think you and Jean are so lucky.'

'Ah, now I understand.'

'Mum and Dad's rows used to make me feel sick, all the shouting and screaming. I used to put my head under the covers in bed and stuff my fingers in my ears, but I could still hear them.'

'How awful.'

She nodded. 'I don't know if living in an atmosphere of aggression and hostility had anything to do with the way I was.'

'I'm sure it must have done.'

'When you're a kid you accept things as the norm, because you don't know anything else, do you? It's only lately, since things have got better for me, that I've begun to wonder why I was so dreadful.'

'I should think your miserable homelife had everything

to do with the way you behaved,' Nancy opined. 'If aggression is all you know at home at a formative age, it's bound to have an effect.'

'Even when Mum and Dad weren't arguing, they were very preoccupied with each other. I always felt outside of them; not a part of a family.'

'Were they not suited?'

'I wouldn't say that exactly. Looking back on it, I can see that there was plenty of passion around, though I didn't know what it was then, of course. When I was in a room with the two of them together, I always felt as though I shouldn't be there, because they wanted to be on their own.'

'What were all the rows about?' asked Nancy.

'Dad was a bit of a lad with the ladies, though I didn't realise that until I got older,' Ruby explained. 'He just couldn't leave other women alone. Mum used to find out he was playing around and all hell would break loose. She always forgave him and took him back, though. He was always the love of her life and still is, even though he's dead. She talks about him all the time to people. She just goes on and on. It's embarrassing when you can see their eyes glazing over, especially as she carries on as though he was a model husband. She's blanked the other stuff out.'

'It's her way of coping, I suppose.'

'I don't blame her for it. If she's happier that way, then good luck to her,' she said. 'It just surprises me how anyone can be so self-deluded.'

'She probably isn't in her dark moments, when the truth

forces its way in,' suggested Nancy. 'She's just trying to get through life with the least possible pain, I should think.'

'Mm, I expect so.' She paused. 'Anyway, that's enough about my life history. I don't know what made me come out with all that stuff.'

'Probably did you good to get it off your chest.'

'Could be,' she agreed. 'But all I intended to do was to say how much you've changed my life.'

'Glad to have helped.'

'If there's anything I can do for you at any time, you only have to ask,' she offered.

Nancy was sorely tempted to bare her soul to Ruby about her marriage. She knew instinctively that she could trust her confidentiality, and it would be such a relief to share the worry with a good friend. But before she could succumb to temptation, Ruby's mother came in, explaining that her meeting had finished early.

A small, thin woman with sharp features and brown hair peppered with grey, she was a friendly soul, and insisted on making more tea. Having administered this with some wartime biscuits, she then proceeded to give Nancy a breathtaking display of the loquacity to which Ruby had just referred.

'One of the ladies at the Guild has just heard that her son has been killed in action,' she told them.

'Oh dear,' said Nancy politely.

'I feel for her, I really do,' Mrs Green went on. 'I know what it's like to lose a loved one. I was devastated when my dear husband Tom was killed.' She shook her head, sucking in her breath. 'I couldn't have felt worse if a bomb had hit me.'

'I'm sure it must have been—'

'I carried on as best as I could, of course,' continued the older woman, seemingly unaware that Nancy had spoken. 'But I'll never get over it. *Never.* He was the most wonderful man who ever walked the earth, the only man I ever loved, and I shall worship him until the day I die.'

'That's lovely,' Nancy said diplomatically, though knowing the true story of the Greens' marriage, she understood why Ruby was wearing such a pained expression.

'What we had was very special,' Mrs Green continued. 'I doubt many people find what we had in the whole of their lives.'

Nancy gave a courteous nod.

'He was an absolute darling. He adored Ruby and me. We were his life, isn't that right, dear?'

Ruby exchanged a look with Nancy, then, with a mixture of affection and irritation, said, 'Yeah, that's right, Mum. But I'm sure Nancy doesn't want to hear the details.'

Nancy felt rather sorry for the older woman, who obviously drew comfort from inventing her own version of history. It was harmless enough. 'You go ahead, Mrs Green,' she invited. 'I'm in no particular hurry.'

It was just as well she wasn't, as it happened, because there was no stopping Ruby's mother now that she had a captive audience.

'Not a day goes by when I don't think of him.'

'I'm sure . . .'

'You become like one person when you've had a long and happy marriage.'

Nancy began to forget that she was listening to a work of fiction, because its creator was so convincing. She really must have loved the man to lose herself so completely in this fairytale. She let her go on . . . and on . . . and on, until she eventually paused for breath, then went over to the sideboard.

'I've got something to show you,' she announced, her voice rising excitedly.

And out came the family album.

'M-u-m,' tutted the squirming Ruby. 'Nancy doesn't want to look at old photos of people she doesn't even know.'

'It's all right, Mrs Green,' assured Nancy, full of pity for this sad, deluded woman. 'I'd like to see them. I enjoy looking at photographs.'

Ruby gave an exasperated sigh, then sat back and let her mother do her worst.

Mrs Green put the book on Nancy's lap and sat on the arm of her chair, slowly turning the pages and offering a detailed explanation of each one. There were sepia pictures of Ruby's grandparents, more recent family groups featuring Ruby, and her parents' wedding photographs, over which Mrs Green positively drooled.

'I was so happy that day,' she breathed. 'It was absolute bliss.'

'He was a handsome man,' commented Nancy, looking at the black and white images of a dark-haired man with finely carved features and a neatly trimmed moustache topping a smile that looked to be carefully staged for the camera. She fancied he had a rather self-satisfied look about him, but thought she was probably biased, knowing what she knew about him.

'He was indeed. All my friends were envious when he chose me,' the older woman said proudly. 'He was such a charmer too. Not only did he have good looks, but a sharp brain as well, and such a lovely way with words.' Turning to the back of the album, where there were some loose photos, she picked one up and studied it, lapsing into thought for a while. 'He gave me this when we were courting.' Her voice trembled with emotion. 'I want to weep every time I look at it, because they were such happy times . . . and they've gone . . . for ever.' She took a handkerchief from the sleeve of her jumper, blew her nose, and handed the picture to Nancy. 'See what he's written on the bottom? Isn't it beautiful?'

As Nancy's gaze moved down the head-and-shoulders picture of Ruby's father, her eyes popped. She blinked, then stared hard again, incredulously. A chill crept over her as she remembered seeing a similar message written in the same sprawling handwriting.

'My darling Ann. You light up my life and I love you so much.' It was the signature that really made Nancy's head spin. It was signed, 'Your ever-loving Blue.' It even had the same squiggle under the B as the signature on the letter she'd found in her mother's pocket.

'Something wrong, dear?' Mrs Green enquired. 'You've gone very quiet.'

'You're ever so pale,' added Ruby. 'Have you come over poorly?'

'No, I'm fine.' She cleared her throat, struggling to compose herself. 'Blue is a very unusual name.' She feigned a casual air. 'I thought you said your husband's name was Tom.'

'It was. Blue was a nickname he acquired as a schoolboy – some of the kids thought it was funny to call him "Blue" rather than "Green". It stuck, as these things often do. I found it rather childish, so always called him Tom. But he liked his nickname, so preferred to use that.' She smiled affectionately. 'He thought it was snazzy, being a bit out of the ordinary.'

'I see.'

'Mind you, I'd give anything to be able to call him by either name now,' Ruby's mother said, sinking back into melancholia. 'But that's life. Here today and gone tomorrow, as they say. He went out for a drink one night and never came back. The pub was bombed with him in it.'

One of the few things her mother had told Nancy about Evie's father was that he'd been killed in a pub bombing. Reeling from the shock, Nancy felt as though she might be about to pass out.

'Are you sure you're all right?' she heard Ruby ask, as though from a distance. 'You don't look well.'

'I do have a bit of headache, actually,' she fibbed, seizing the opportunity to escape. 'So I think I'll make tracks.'

As Ruby saw her out into the blackout, Nancy was relieved to get away so that she could collect her thoughts in the aftermath of this bombshell.

★　★　★

372

Nancy's hands were trembling as she fumbled for the letter which was now hidden at the back of her underwear drawer at the bedsit. She needed to make sure she wasn't mistaken. One look confirmed that she wasn't. The signature on her mother's letter was identical to the one on Mrs Green's photograph!

So much pain had been caused by her mother's affair, and it was now obvious to Nancy that the man hadn't had any real feelings for her at all. Nancy wanted to weep at the sadness of it all. But, having stumbled upon the identity of Evie's father, she found herself with an awesome responsibility, and she had to work out what to do. Unless she handled the situation with care and sensitivity, people were going to get hurt.

Chapter Fifteen

By the next morning, Nancy knew exactly what she must do about the staggering information that had come into her possession so unexpectedly.

She suggested to Ruby that they go for a walk in the dinner hour, after they'd finished their meal in the canteen.

'A bit chilly for a stroll, isn't it?' Ruby frowned. 'I don't fancy it at all.'

'A nice brisk walk in the fresh air will do us good.'

'I'd rather stay here and rest my aching feet, if you don't mind. We walk miles as it is in this job.'

'Look . . . I've got something important to tell you and I'd rather not do it against the clatter of a railway staff canteen. It's a private matter.'

'Blimey, I hope it isn't bad news.'

'Let's get out of here and I'll tell you.'

'So Evie isn't your father's child, then,' said Ruby, looking somewhat bemused as they walked through the war-torn streets towards Paddington Green. The urban landscape was drab beneath dismal grey skies, and there was bomb damage everywhere, many shops and houses reduced to rubble. Even the autumn trees failed to add much colour on this cloudy day. But a small, homemade Union Jack flew on top of one pile of debris, illustrating the mettle that still existed among the people of this battered island.

'That's right,' Nancy confirmed. 'You are the only person outside of the family to know about it. It's our most closely guarded secret. It has to be to protect Evie.'

'I can understand that, but I'm blowed if I know why you've told me.'

'Because something has come to light that means you have every right to know.'

'This is beginning to sound really scary.'

'There's nothing to be scared of, but I think, perhaps, you'd better sit down,' Nancy suggested as they came to a dilapidated bench on the edge of the green.

'Right. Out with it,' urged Ruby, sitting down. 'I'm nearly having kittens with the worry of what I'm about to hear.'

'Well, you know you've always wished you weren't an only child . . .'

'Yeah . . .'

'You're not,' Nancy said quickly. 'You have a sibling.'

'Don't be daft, Nance. Stop messing about.'

'I'm not messing around, kid.'

Ruby looked at her, her face turning scarlet, then draining of colour. 'I don't know where you got that idea, but it can't be right. I would have known.'

'You told me your dad was fond of the ladies,' Nancy reminded her.

'Oh, oh I see. The old devil had a child with someone else, did he? I suppose I shouldn't be surprised, but it's still a shock.' She shot Nancy a look. 'But how do you know?'

'I found out by accident.' She paused. 'Little Evie is your half-sister.'

Ruby was speechless. 'You mean your mum and my dad . . .' she muttered at last.

Nancy nodded. 'I was just as shocked as you are, I can tell you.'

'But how did you actually find out?'

Nancy explained and went on to tell her everything, and showed her the incriminating letter. 'Mum told me she was only ever unfaithful to my father with one man, so your dad was definitely Evie's father. Anyway, you can see something of you in Evie, even though she's the spit of Mum.'

'I can't believe it.' Ruby was radiant. 'I've adored Evie from the moment I first set eyes on her. To know that she's my own flesh and blood. Oh, Nancy! It's like a dream come true!'

'It isn't going to be that simple, though,' said Nancy, staring at the ground.

'No?'

'No. I've given it a lot of thought and come to the conclusion that, in everyone's best interests, the only thing we can do is keep it to ourselves. I felt duty-bound to tell you, but no one else must know.'

'Because of my mum and your dad?'

377

'Exactly. I can't stop you saying anything, of course. It must be your decision. But knowing how your mother still feels about your father, I think she'd be better off not knowing, though that may not be possible when Evie's old enough to care about such things. Obviously, later on Evie will have a right to know the truth. But not now. As for my dad, it would be a mistake to drag the whole thing up again. He doesn't need reminding that Evie isn't his child.'

'It would break my mum's heart, probably send her into a complete decline,' said Ruby, with a sigh of resignation. 'Maybe one day she'll face up to the truth about Dad and stop being so soppy about him. But there's no sign of it yet.'

'It'll probably come with time.'

'I want to be a proper sister to Evie, though,' Ruby confessed. 'I'd like to do things for her, like big sisters do. Knowing what I do, it'll be hard to continue being an unofficial aunt.'

'She loves you as things are,' Nancy pointed out. 'You've looked after her enough times.'

'I want more now, though.'

'You can see as much of her as you like without anyone suspecting a thing,' said Nancy. 'You're always welcome at the Sparrow house.'

'Thanks, Nance.' She paused thoughtfully. 'It's odd really that you and I share a sister, but we aren't related.'

'It is a bit weird.'

Ruby tutted, rolling her eyes. 'My dad's still causing trouble, even from beyond the grave.'

'He provided you with something you've always wanted, though,' Nancy reminded her.

'Yeah. Despite the complications and the reminder of what an old bugger he was, I have a sister and that means so much to me, especially as it's Evie.'

'I'm so pleased for you. She's very special to me too.'

As they walked back to the station, Nancy could feel a new depth to their friendship now that they shared something so precious to them both.

As chilly autumn hardened into raw winter, the bitter cold days brought with them a virulent flu epidemic. Londoners who had worried about the health of Mr Churchill – who'd been taken ill with pneumonia in the Middle East – found themselves rather more concerned about their own well-being as the disease swept across Britain, disabling entire households.

Fingers were firmly crossed in the Sparrow family for Arthur, since even the mildest attack could be dangerous for a man with such fragile lungs, primarily because of the vicious cough the illness left in its wake. His luck seemed to hold, but Nancy went down with it good and proper. Her temperature was so high she was forced into bed, feeling so ill she could do nothing but lie there, sweating, shivering and aching all over. After a few days of aspirin and her own company, she was sure she was no longer contagious and ventured out to Sycamore Road one morning to see how the rest of the family were.

'Your dad's still managing to avoid it, but Jean and Leslie have both been in bed with it since yesterday, which is where you should be, by the look of you,' Gladys observed, putting the kettle on for tea, and getting the cups out of the cupboard.

'You look shocking, Nancy. You shouldn't be out of doors in that state.'

'I wanted to know if you lot were all right,' she explained. 'Anyway, I couldn't stand another whole day in that room on my own.'

'You should have come round here as soon as you started to feel poorly, and I'd have looked after the lot of you together,' said Gladys, pouring milk sparingly from a bottle into the cups. 'If I'd known you weren't well, I'd have been round your place like a shot to bring you back here, or at least given you a bit of looking after.'

'You've got quite enough to do, without my adding to it,' Nancy said, erupting into a coughing fit.

'The others are barking like dogs too,' remarked Gladys, as her granddaughter was rendered helpless against the raucous, hacking cough. 'You'd swear you were in Battersea Dogs Home when they both get going.'

'You look after yourself, Gran,' advised Nancy when the coughing finally abated. 'We don't want you running your-self ragged, looking after the others.'

'I'm as strong as a horse,' she assured her, adding with a grin, 'Mind you, if I catch the flu myself, I'll get my own back and have you all running around after me.'

'Gladly will we do it, and welcome the chance to give you a bit of spoiling.' She poked her head into the empty living room. 'Is Dad out on his round?'

She nodded. 'And Evie's playing with the little girl across the street, so we can have a nice quiet chat, just the two of us.'

'I might as well make the most of the time to chat,' Nancy replied. 'I'm going back to work tomorrow.'

Gladys frowned. 'Isn't it a bit too soon, love? You don't look at all well.'

'I'm still a bit weak, but my temperature's down and the aches and pains have more or less gone, so I think I'll be able to cope,' she said. 'I need to be at work. They'll be short-staffed with so many people off with the flu.'

'Still, as half the population has got it too, there'll be fewer passengers,' Gladys pointed out.

'There is that, I suppose. But I still think I should go back.'

'If you really feel well enough, then you must do what you think best, love.' She looked towards the stove as steam began to rise from the spout of the kettle. 'Have you heard from that lovely husband of yours lately?'

Nancy nodded. 'I had a letter yesterday, as it happens.'

'Will he be coming home for Christmas?'

'He isn't sure,' she replied. 'If he does get away, it won't be for long, but he says he might be able to make it for a few hours on Christmas Day. He'll have to cycle over, as there's no public transport.'

'He won't mind that, if it means seeing you, he's that potty about you.' Gladys poured boiling water in the teapot and swilled it around. 'I bet you're looking forward to seeing him, aren't you?'

'You bet.' With a great deal of trepidation, was the true answer to that, but Nancy couldn't bear to shatter her gran's illusions; she thought Pete was a 'lovely fella', and a 'real gent'. To be fair to him, the last time he'd been home – the only time since she'd agreed to give him another chance – he'd been charm itself, amiable and loving the whole time. He'd been noticeably evasive when asked about his promise to seek medical advice for his temper, which probably meant he hadn't done it, but she hadn't pressed him on the subject. He was making an effort and that was a step in the right direction.

But no matter how civil he was, she couldn't relax in his company because she was always expecting him to turn on her at any moment.

'Let's hope he does make it, though Gawd knows what we're going to have to eat,' Gladys was saying now. 'They reckon that poultry will be in even shorter supply this year. I doubt if even Wilf will be able to get us a bird.'

'We'll still have a good time, Gran. Us Sparrows are experts at making the best of things,' Nancy reassured her. 'As long as we manage to get a few toys for Evie, and create the Christmas spirit in the house, that's the important thing.'

'I can't help remembering how Christmas used to be before the war, though.' She looked wistful.

'It will be again. The war won't last for ever,' Nancy reminded her. 'All the good times will come back when it's over.'

'I bloomin' well hope so.'

Gladys had just poured the tea when they heard the clunk of the letterbox.

'The postman's late this morning,' she muttered as Nancy went out to the hall to collect the mail.

'That's peculiar, Gran,' said Nancy, coming back into the room with a puzzled expression. 'There's a letter from America for Jean.'

'Blimey, I wonder who that's from,' said Gladys, equally curious. 'Ed's the only American likely to write to her, and he's away with the war somewhere, so it can't be from him.'

Nancy turned the envelope over and her hand flew to her throat. 'Carter's the name of the sender,' she announced. 'That's Ed's surname, so it is from him.'

'No!' gasped Gladys, turning pale. 'Well, he's got a flamin' cheek, getting in touch with her after all this time; he's no right after breaking the poor girl's heart. The least he could have done was let her know he was going back to America.'

'I'll take the letter up to her,' said Nancy, already heading for the stairs.

'Well?' enquired Gladys, a few minutes later when Nancy reappeared. 'What did he have to say for himself?'

'I don't know. She wanted to be on her own while she opened the letter.'

'That's understandable. We'll just have to wait until she's ready to tell us, then.' She shook her head worriedly. 'This will bring it all back to her, just when she might be beginning to get over him. I hope he hasn't made any promises he won't keep and given her false hope.'

'Yeah, I hope so too,' said Nancy in a grave tone.

Bobby was very afraid as he sat beside his mother's hospital bed, watching her fight for her life. A neighbour had phoned his camp with the news that his mother had been rushed into hospital with pneumonia, and he'd been given compassionate leave.

There were screens around the bed, isolating her from the rest of the ward and reminding him how critically ill she was. He'd been told that it was touch and go. She looked so tiny, lying there with her eyes closed, as frail as a baby bird, her face white and beaded with sweat, cheeks flushed an unhealthy red and sunken through loss of weight. Although she was a woman of petite proportions, she'd always enjoyed robust health. He couldn't remember her ever being sick before, apart from the odd cough or cold, and it was unheard of for her to take to her bed. This current crisis was a direct result of the flu bug that was incapacitating people in droves. His mother had had a particularly severe attack and there had been complications.

Thank God for her caring neighbours, who'd realised how ill she was and got her into hospital. She wouldn't have got a bed had it not been an emergency, because London hospitals were grossly overcrowded and chronically under-staffed, due to deaths from air raids and doctors being called up into the services.

Bobby wasn't much of a churchgoing man, but he had a faith of sorts and he prayed now as never before, unashamed of the tears streaming down his face. His mother was the most precious thing in the world to him and he couldn't bear to lose her.

Jean looked really ill when she came downstairs in her old, red woollen dressing-gown, ashen-faced and trembling.

Clutching the letter, she sank down weakly on to the sofa in the living room.

'You shouldn't be out of bed in your state of health,' warned Gladys.

'You do look a bit rough, sis,' added Nancy.

'I feel it too,' she said. 'I shan't stay down here for long.'

'So . . . what did Ed have to say?' Gladys was naturally wary.

'He says that he loves me and wants to marry me,' she said dully. 'He's sorry he wasn't able to let me know that he was being transferred.'

'Oh, Jean, that's wonderful!' whooped Nancy, wondering why Jean looked so grim, having just received such good news. 'Did the US military send him back to America? Is that why he's there?'

Her sister shook her head. 'He isn't there. His letter was sent on to me by his mother,' she explained, her voice trembling now. 'It was in among his personal effects, which the US army sent on to her. She found it in his wallet, apparently, and thought I ought to have it.'

The other two women looked baffled.

'His mother? What's she got to do with . . .' began Nancy, her eyes widening with horror as the truth began to dawn. 'Oh no, you don't mean . . .'

'Yeah, I'm afraid so. Ed is dead.' Her voice was high and tight. 'He was killed somewhere in Kent soon after he proposed to me. He was keeping order among the GIs stationed in a nearby camp when the jeep he was in was blown up by a stray German bomb. None of the men survived.'

385

'Oh, Jean,' cried Nancy, going over and sitting beside her sister. 'I'm *so so sorry*.'

'Me an' all, love,' added her gran.

Jean's face was bloodless, her lips red and swollen with cold sores from the flu. 'Everything goes to the next of kin when one of the men is killed,' she said sadly. 'I didn't exist as far as the US army were concerned. It's lucky for me that his mother was kind enough to send his letter on to me, along with one of her own, explaining what had happened to him. I'd never have got to know otherwise.'

Wet-eyed, Nancy and Gladys nodded.

'I misjudged him in the worst way possible,' Jean continued, her voice flat and lifeless. 'He didn't let me down at all. He was transferred without any warning the day after he proposed to me, and didn't have a chance to let me know that he was going. It's all there in the letter which the poor love didn't get the chance to post.'

'Poor Ed,' said Nancy.

'Yeah, poor Ed,' echoed Jean. 'All this time I've been so wrong, saying terrible things about him, and he's not even been able to defend himself.'

'We've all said a few choice things about him,' Gladys reminded her, sitting down on the sofa next to her. 'We weren't to know the truth.'

'But I loved him, so I should have trusted him,' Jean said, her voice thick with emotion. 'I should have known there was an explanation, instead of immediately thinking the worst of him. I'll never forgive myself. *Never!*'

Nancy was at a loss to know what to do to ease her

sister's pain. What could anyone say or do that would make her feel any better?

'At the back of my mind I always had a tiny glimmer of hope that I was wrong about him and that one day he would just turn up.' Jean's eyes brimmed with tears. 'Now I know he never can. I won't get the chance to make it up to him for the awful things I said and thought.'

Her body crumpled and her cries were like those of a wild animal; ugly, guttural wails. Nancy and Gladys sat with her until she was too exhausted to shed another tear, then helped her upstairs to bed.

'I know it isn't much of a consolation, but at least she can begin to grieve for him now,' Nancy suggested to her grandmother when they were back downstairs.

'I was just thinking the same thing myself. Eventually she can get over it, instead of going through life thinking he let her down.'

'As long as she manages to let go of the guilt for thinking the worst of him.'

'Jean isn't one to dwell on things for long.'

'Not normally, she isn't. But I think Ed stirred feelings in her she didn't even know she had.'

Nancy hoped that in the months and years ahead, the fact that Ed had loved Jean after all would be a comfort to her. Her sister was often selfish and manipulative, but never with Ed. He had definitely been the love of her life, there was no doubt in Nancy's mind about that. It was so damned tragic.

*　　*　　*

'Oh, so you're awake now, are you?' joshed Bobby the next morning with his mother, who was looking better, but was still very frail. 'About bloomin' time, too.'

'Is that any way to talk to your sick mother?' she returned weakly.

'No. But if I'm too nice to you, you'll think you're about to breathe your last,' he kidded her.

'Ooh Bobby, don't say such awful things.' Her voice wasn't strong, but her spirit was shining through. 'It could so easily have come to that.'

'But it didn't, and you're going to get better with some decent care and attention,' he assured her, holding her small, bony hand. 'I've had a few words with the doctor.'

'Did he say when I'll be going home?'

'It's too soon for that. You've got some serious recovering to do first.' He looked down the ward, from which there was a continuous explosion of coughing and wheezing; there were extra beds and every one was occupied. 'They've moved the screens away, so at least you'll have company.'

'I'd be better off at home.'

'They won't keep you here a moment longer than they have to, because they are so short of beds and doctors.'

'I shouldn't be here at all, when the hospitals are under such a strain. Not to mention the expense to us.'

'It's worth every penny, and thanks to the business, we can afford it.'

She nodded. 'I feel sorry for the people who can't afford to pay to go into hospital. They won't let you on the ward until you've been means tested, no matter how sick you are,' she said. 'Someone could die while they're waiting. That isn't right, is it?'

'Maybe one day free medical care will be everyone's right,' Bobby suggested. 'There's been talk of some sort of National Health Service in Parliament.'

'It's high time they did more than just talk about it.' His mother paused. 'Anyway, son, I'm sorry you've had to come all the way home.'

'I wouldn't have missed it for the world.' His eyes twinkled. 'You being so quiet, I mean.'

She tutted and rolled her eyes in mock disapproval.

Tears welled up in Bobby's eyes. 'All joking aside, Ma, you gave me a real scare,' he said, unable to hide the raw emotion in his voice. 'Thank God it was just a scare.' He looked at her with affection. 'I know I don't often talk like this to you, but you mean the world to me.'

'I *must* have been ill for you to talk so soft,' she responded thickly.

'Anyway, now that you're feeling a bit better,' he said, clearing his throat, 'we can make plans for your convalescence. I think you should go and stay with Auntie Rose in Brighton for a while. A spot of sea air and some rest is just what you need to put you back on your feet.'

'And what's going to happen to the shop if I go away?'

'The same as is happening to it now. George has stepped up his hours and is looking after things,' he said, referring to the man of advanced years who normally worked a few hours a week for them and knew the pawnbroking business inside out. 'So you don't have to worry about that.'

'I know you mean well, son, and yes, I will accept George looking after the shop until I'm well enough to take over again.' Her eyes glinted with determination. 'But I'm not going away anywhere other than my own home when I'm discharged from here. The Blitz didn't drive me out of London and I'm damned sure a hiccup in my health isn't going to either.'

'But you might not feel up to cooking and looking after yourself,' he suggested carefully.

'If I don't, my neighbours will do it for me, the same as I do for them when they're ill,' she told him. 'We look out for one another round our way. The one good thing this war has done is bring us closer to our neighbours.'

'Yeah, you're right about that,' he agreed, remembering how concerned and helpful her neighbours had been.

'There will come a time when you and I will swap roles and you'll be the one giving the orders,' she told him. 'But that time is still a very long way off.'

'OK, you win.' He reached into his battledress and produced a bar of chocolate, which he handed to her in a jokey manner to hide his serious mood. 'I thought I'd never hear the last of it if I came to visit empty-handed.'

'Too right, you wouldn't. But ta very much.' She grinned. 'You can smuggle me a bottle of Guinness in next time you come. It's full of iron and will help me to get my strength back.'

'You'll be in big trouble with the matron if you're caught with booze in here.'

'I'll have a smile on my face though, won't I?' She gave him a shrewd look. 'Which is more than you've got now. That smile you're putting on for my benefit isn't at all convincing.'

'I've been worried about you.'

'Yes, I'm sure you have, but . . . there's something else on your mind.' She studied his face. 'You still not over that Irene business?'

'I'm over it and glad to be out of it,' he replied. 'She was never the one for me.'

'Well, I'm not going anywhere if you want to talk about whatever it is that's troubling you.'

This was neither the time nor the place to bare his soul about his feelings for Nancy. But he was overwhelmed by the need to do so, and out it all came. The pain of the past, the anguish of wanting to be with her in the present.

'Are you sure it isn't just because she was your first love?' suggested Mabel, having listened patiently to what he had to say.

'No, it's more than that. She's the only woman I'll ever really love, Ma,' he replied. 'I can't get her off my mind. Even when I was with Irene, Nancy was never far from my thoughts.'

'You know your own feelings, son,' she said, with a sad shake of the head. 'But there's no future for you with her if she's married. You've no choice but to steer clear.'

'I know that, and I won't go near her.' He was leaning forward with his elbows on his thighs, his head on his fists. 'But it's so hard, because I know there'll never be anyone else like her for me.'

'You'll meet someone else, son,' she consoled. 'You may

391

not be able to forget Nancy, but you can have a decent life with another woman.'

Suddenly ashamed of his weakness in burdening his sick mother with his own problems, Bobby said cheerily, 'Yeah, course I can. It'll all work out. Sorry to have worried you with it.'

'That's what mums are for.'

He took her hand again, focusing his mind on her. He worried about her being on her own, especially as there were more rumours about the second front coming, and he was almost certain to be going back on active service. That meant he wouldn't get home to see her for goodness knows how long. Thank God for friends and neighbours, he thought again, as they went on to talk about other things.

Despite Pete's doubts about getting home on Christmas Day, he arrived, red-faced and breathless from cycling, just in time for dinner at the Sparrow home.

'That proves how much he loves you, Nancy.' Gladys was full of admiration for him, as usual. 'To ride a bike all that way to see you on a bitter cold day like this, when he has to cycle back again tonight.'

'What us men do for love, eh?' remarked Wilf lightly.

'Don't make me laugh,' teased his mother. 'I can't imagine you even walking round the corner for love, let alone cycling from Northolt to Ealing and back all in one day.'

'I've had my moments,' he grinned, tapping his nose. 'Sons don't tell their mothers everything, you know.'

The meal passed pleasantly, albeit that corned-beef hash replaced traditional Christmas fare. It was supplemented by plenty of vegetables, and they had managed to get hold of some sherry so drank a toast to absent loved ones – Lily, Ed and Micky, who'd been somewhere in Italy the last time they'd had word from him. Nancy had been relieved that his letter was quite upbeat, considering he had been so close to deserting on his last leave.

Jean was still rather subdued over the news of Ed's death, but made an effort to be cheerful, Nancy noticed approvingly. Evie was the saviour of the occasion, with her excited chatter and pleasure in the special day. They all made a fuss of her, except Arthur, who did his best to ignore her in his usual studied way.

As soon as lunch was over, Pete got Nancy alone and suggested that they go to their own place for a while. This seemed a natural enough request for any husband to make, so they left, missing the traditional games the Sparrows always played on the afternoon of Christmas Day. Nancy's tacit reluctance to leave was a painful reminder to her of the difficult state of her marriage. A loving wife should be only too eager to be alone with her husband.

'I'd rather we'd had Christmas dinner on our own at our place,' he complained, as soon as they were away from the house and walking home through the cold streets, the light already beginning to fade. He was wheeling his bike.

She was immediately on the defensive, sensing a storm brewing. 'But I didn't know if you were coming,' she reminded him. 'You were doubtful about being able to get away. Anyway, Christmas dinner is a family occasion and I like us all to be together.'

'I'm your family now.'

She had learned to recognise the irritated tone of voice that almost always heralded trouble. A horrible dragging sensation pulled her down.

'So are they,' she reminded him.

'They're just relatives,' he stated.

'They're not *just* relatives, they're family and they mean the world to me.'

'And I'm your husband,' he persisted, increasingly disgruntled. 'You shouldn't have arranged to go there. Surely it isn't too much for a husband to ask to be on his own with his wife on Christmas Day?'

For fear of enraging him further by pointing out that he was being unreasonable, she tried to placate him. 'We're going to be on our own *now*,' she said, increasingly suffocated by his attitude.

'Yeah, but for how long, eh?' he questioned, his voice rising. 'I've got to go back tonight.'

'Look, I'm sorry that I've upset you by being with my folks for dinner today. Apart from not wanting to be on my own if you didn't make it, it just didn't occur to me that you wouldn't want to be with them too.'

'You should have known better. It's quite a way on a bike, you know.'

She halted in her step and looked at him, a stunning figure in RAF uniform, his flying jacket giving him a sporty air. 'Is this conversation leading where I think it is? Because if so, I'm not coming back with you.'

'All I'm saying is—'

'What you're doing is working yourself up into a temper, and I am not going to be on the receiving end of it,' she cut in. 'Not this time. We've had all this out and you made a promise to me.'

'A promise I have no intention of breaking,' he came back at her.

'That's all right, then.' She slipped her arm through his, determined to lighten the mood. 'Cheer up. It is Christmas, remember.'

'Yeah, Christmas, and tonight I'll be sleeping in a barrack room full of blokes, instead of with you.'

'All the more reason to make the most of this afternoon, then.'

'Well, if you put it like that.'

He did cheer up and didn't lose his temper. But Nancy felt just a whisper away from a beating every second of the time, most of which was spent in bed at his demand. After he'd pedalled off into the night, she walked back to Sycamore Road and recaptured the Christmas spirit in the warm and cheery company of her family.

'Will you read me a story from my new book please, Nancy?' asked Evie, who was in her pyjamas.

'Course I will, love.'

'She's worn the rest of us out this afternoon and she's still showing no sign of slowing down,' smiled Gladys.

'Come on, then,' said Nancy. 'Let's take your lovely new book upstairs and I'll read it to you in bed.'

The little girl handed Nancy a book of fairytales and headed up the stairs. Nancy followed her, feeling happy and at ease in the homely atmosphere of the Sparrow household. She knew instinctively that she would never feel like this in any home where her husband was present.

No matter how hard she tried to make the marriage work, she didn't think any woman could please Pete for any length of time. He was too self-absorbed, and had too much of a depressive personality. But while he kept his promise to her, she would keep trying.

A feeling of regret came over her as she wondered how Bobby was spending his Christmas, and wished she could be with him at this emotive time of year. But it wasn't to be, so she would bask in the warmth of her family, and enjoy telling her little sister a story.

Watching Evie grow and develop made Nancy ache for a child of her own, something she knew she would never have with Pete. She wouldn't risk exposing her children to his cruel temper so it was just as well he didn't want to start a family.

There was a general mood of optimism among people as the new year got underway. The main topic of conversation was the much hoped-for invasion of Western Europe by the allies that had been expected for so long. Every day the newspapers were full of prophecies and hints.

But the end of January brought only a resumption of the air raids.

'So, here we all are again,' said Gladys as the family gathered in the Anderson, with the exception of Arthur, who still couldn't bring himself to venture down there, and remained in the house, drinking the whiskey Ed had acquired for him. 'We've got right out of the habit of sheltering. I'd forgotten how dismal it is down here.'

'I'm glad I was here and not at home when the siren went,' said Nancy.

'Have they got an Anderson at your place?' Gladys enquired.

'They don't need one, because they use the cellar, though there hasn't been a raid since we've been there,' she explained. 'It's probably quite safe down there, but I'd sooner be with you lot.'

An ear-splitting explosion rocked the ground. Evie began to cry.

'You'll be all right, darlin',' reassured Gladys, holding her close. 'Everything's going to be fine, I promise you. We're all here together.'

Comforted, the child stopped crying. 'Where's Smudge?' she asked. 'Where's that pussy?'

'Don't worry about him. He'll have found somewhere safe,' Nancy assured her. 'Cats are very good at looking after themselves.'

'I wish he was here,' she said tearfully.

So did Nancy, as it happened; she always felt uneasy if their much loved family tabby was missing during a raid. 'We'll see him soon,' she assured the little girl.

Sitting hunched over, with her fingers in her ears, Jean felt as though her stomach had turned to water. She didn't remember being this terrified in earlier raids, not even during the Blitz. Probably because she'd usually been out dancing and had let it all happen around her. She'd been too busy enjoying herself to bother much about danger.

Maybe it was Ed's death that had changed her, in that it had made death more personal. She'd been heartbroken when she'd lost her mother, of course, and still missed her every single day, but nothing in her life had affected her as profoundly as hearing that Ed had been killed. She'd ached almost to the point of physical pain every minute since the awful news had come from America.

But through all the grief and the torturous guilt at having misjudged him, something else shone through: the warmth of knowing that she'd been loved by him. Although he wasn't there, that feeling embraced her and lived on within her. It was so very sweet. She didn't need anyone else while she had that.

Clenching her teeth so hard her jaw ached, as another bomb exploded somewhere close by, she decided that if she was spared tonight she would do something she should have done weeks ago, she would write to Ed's mother to thank her for sending his letter on to her. Then, somehow, she would start to live her life again.

Chapter Sixteen

By mid-February London was a blitzed city again. The raids were shorter and faster than those of earlier blitzes, but had an intensity that was harder on the nerves because there was no lull in activity, no breaks during which your insides could settle down.

'They're early tonight,' observed Arthur one evening, as the siren wailed over the neighbourhood sooner than usual. 'Hoping to catch us all on the hop, I reckon. Off you go down the shelter with your gran, Leslie. Chop-chop.'

Donning his coat and scarf, and grabbing his copy of the *Beano* and a torch, the boy stood at the bottom of the stairs, shouting up. 'Come on, Gran. Dad says we've got to go to the shelter straight away.'

'You go on,' urged his father, standing by the back door, anxious to see him on his way to safety. 'Your gran will catch you up in a minute.'

'Why don't you come too, Dad?' suggested Leslie. 'I know it's smelly and 'orrible down there, but it must be better than being up here on your own.'

'I'll be all right, son. Don't worry about me. You just get yourself underground, sharpish.'

Arthur let him out and shut the door behind him swiftly, to minimise any escaping light. He was about to give Gladys another call when she appeared in her outdoor clothes.

'Honestly, you can't even have a wee in peace these days,' she complained. 'The buggers are early tonight, too. I haven't even had a chance to make tea to take down the shelter with us.' She poked her head into the living room, and seeing it was empty, called out, 'Evie, come here, love. Evie . . .' The lack of response produced an increase in volume. 'Evie, come on now, there's a good girl. Don't mess me about.'

Her calls went unanswered.

'That's funny,' she frowned. 'Where the devil has she got to?'

'I thought she'd gone to bed. She was running about in her pyjamas the last time I saw her.'

'I always let her have time to play when she's ready for bed,' she reminded him. 'She was down here with you and Leslie when I went upstairs.'

'That's right, she was.' He thought back on it. 'But she went off somewhere. I just assumed she'd followed you upstairs and you'd put her to bed.'

With rising alarm, they searched the house, calling Evie's name and looking into every room and cupboard, in case she was hiding as a prank.

'She isn't here anywhere,' concluded Gladys, breathless with anxiety. 'Perhaps she followed Leslie to the shelter.'

'She couldn't have done, because I let him out and shut the door after him.'

'If she isn't in here, she must be outside in the garden somewhere.' Gladys was frantic now. 'Oh Arthur, we must get her to safety in the shelter quick. The bombs will start dropping at any minute.'

The two of them tore outside into the night, the bitter wind whistling around the houses, fences and across the top of the Anderson shelter. Leslie confirmed that Evie wasn't in there with him, and there was no sign of her in the back garden either.

As the moan of the siren died away, a creaking, then a banging sound caught Arthur's attention and he saw in the moonlight that the old wooden side-gate was open.

'Bloody hell!' he gasped. 'The kid's got out! There's no front gate, so she can get out into the street.'

'Oh my Lord.' Gladys was already running towards the gate.

'How long has she been gone, do you reckon?'

'No more than a few minutes,' she replied. 'She'll have gone looking for the cat, I bet; you know how much she adores that bloomin' animal.'

'You go down into the shelter with Leslie, and leave me to find her.' He was very definite.

'I can't do that when she's out there somewhere,' she sobbed. 'The poor little thing might get killed.'

'I'm going to look for her.' He was in command now and was brooking no argument. 'It doesn't need the two of us, and young Leslie will need you for company as Jean is working late. Anyway, it's too dangerous for you to be out on the streets.'

'It's just as risky for you, Arthur.'

'Yeah, but I've got the luck of the devil. I must have, or I wouldn't still be here, would I?' he pointed out. 'You stay with Leslie while I go looking for the nipper. I won't be long. She can't have gone far.'

'Hurry up, Gran,' urged Leslie, poking his head out of the shelter.

'Coming, love,' she said and climbed down under the corrugated iron, her heart knocking the hell out of her ribs and her mouth so dry she could barely swallow.

Never in his entire life – not when vulnerable to the elements and the bombs at sea; not even when his ship had been hit and he'd clung to life in the water for so long – had Arthur been this frightened. Not for himself, but for Evie, and that was much worse, because he felt out of control. He'd tried his best to shut her out, but now the thought of her out there alone and unprotected all but pulverised him.

He hesitated where the front gate would have been had it not been taken away for the war effort, looking both ways and staring hard into the moonlit street for a sign of movement. He shouted her name as loudly as he could. There was no sign or sound of her. All he could hear was the rasping wind and the distant drone of enemy bombers. She could have gone in either direction, and he had no way of knowing which one. The bombers drew closer, and the explosions began, the sky already becoming tinted with the familiar red glow, symbolic now of death and disaster.

Deciding that she'd probably turned left, because the family usually went that way to the main road, he made his way along the street, his eyes darting from side to side.

Anxiety manifested itself in a flash of rage at the carelessness that had created this situation. Then he heard the voice of his own conscience. Gladys and the family did a good job with Evie, but they couldn't watch her every second of the day. He had been downstairs with her; he should have noticed what she was doing. He didn't want her in his life but, as a responsible adult, he shouldn't have let a child, *any child*, wander off into the street in these dangerous times.

Where was she, for God's sake? He was hoarse from calling her name, smoke already creeping down his throat, burning his chest and making him short of breath. Then, at a bend in the road, he spotted her in the moonlight, a tiny figure wandering along the pavement, lost and alone in the biting wind. He couldn't hear her above the roar of the planes and the gunners on the ground, but he knew instinctively that she was crying.

He ran towards her, uttering her name, but it was drowned out by the racket all around him. Desperate to reach her and very nearly there, he found himself suddenly knocked off his feet by the blast from a nearby explosion, the tinkling of broken glass sounding terrifyingly close.

Scrambling to his feet, he saw huge orange flames leaping from houses further down the street. Then he spotted what looked like a bundle of clothes in the road just a few yards away from him. Looking more closely, he saw that it was Evie, lying motionless on the ground.

Tears rolled unchecked down his cheeks as he got down on his knees beside her. He put his head to her chest to see if she was breathing. She let out a whimper. Oh, thank God!

'Shush, sweetheart, you'll be all right now,' he soothed. 'I've got you. We're going home.'

With infinite gentleness, he lifted her up and carried her back towards the house. As she lay in his arms, quivering and weeping from fright, his head rang with the sound of her endless chatter, her laughter, her tears, her out-of-tune singing of nursery rhymes. He had vivid images of her walking, running, skipping, and was imbued with the sweet essence of her that filled the house.

That split second when he'd thought she might be dead had been a defining moment. All this time he'd tried to fight it, had refused to admit that he was becoming fond of her. He hadn't wanted to love her, so had forced himself constantly to remember the origins of her existence, and rejected her time after time.

He'd blinded himself to the joy she brought to the family; *his family*. All right, so he wasn't a part of her biology, but he could be a part of her life. God knows she'd shown how much she'd wanted it, until he'd finally driven her away with his cruel indifference. What did it matter whose blood she had in her veins? She was here with him, a living, breathing blessing. They could so easily have lost her just now, and the thought of that was hardly bearable.

'Oh, you've got her,' wept Gladys as he carefully lowered her down into the shelter. 'Thank the Lord for that.'

'She was knocked over by a bomb blast, the poor little thing. Some houses down the street have really caught it,' he explained, transferring her to her grandmother's waiting arms. 'She's had a hell of a fright, but I think she's all right apart from that.'

'Where's Smudge?' With typical childish resilience, Evie was already beginning to recover, though she was still very tearful. 'I couldn't find him. He ran away from me.'

'He'll be back when he's ready,' Arthur choked out, physically weakened with relief that she was alive and well. 'He's a law unto himself, that moggy.'

'You ran away from us, too, didn't you?' said Gladys, too overwhelmed with relief to reprimand her too sternly at this stage. She stroked her hair from her brow and kissed her gently. 'You know you're not supposed to do that, darlin'. It's very, very naughty.'

'I was only looking for Smudge.' Her bottom lip began to tremble. 'But I didn't like it out there in the dark. I was cold and I wanted to come home, but my house had gone away like that pussy.'

'That's because you're too little to go off on your own in the dark,' said Gladys thickly. 'You mustn't ever do that again, Evie. You promise me now.'

'I promise, Gran.'

'I'm going up to the house,' muttered Arthur, and Gladys was far too preoccupied with Evie to remark on the fact that he'd conquered his claustrophobia sufficiently to bring Evie into the safety of the shelter.

Alone at ground level, Arthur could hold back his

emotions no longer and was sobbing unashamedly when he got back into the house. He'd been through a life-changing experience and was emotionally drained. They'd have to make damned sure that Evie didn't go wandering off into the street in future. He couldn't bear to go through that again. She was far too precious to him.

As the explosions continued to bang and blast all around, he sat under the table. He'd gone down into the Anderson because of Evie and would do it again if it was necessary for any of the family. Meanwhile, he preferred to take his chances up here, and would occupy his mind planning what he would do to welcome Evie into his life. From now on, she was going to know what it was like to have a dad. He hadn't been much of a father to his own children when they were little. But he would be to Lily's daughter, from this moment on . . .

One evening a few days later, Nancy got home from work to find her husband sprawled in one of the armchairs.

'Hello,' she said, going over and kissing him dutifully. 'Did you manage to get an overnight pass?'

'I've got two weeks' leave.' He made no attempt to embrace her, which was most unusual. Normally he couldn't wait to get her into bed when he first arrived home. 'They've told me to take time off to relax.'

'That's considerate of them,' she remarked pleasantly, though inwardly dreading the next two weeks. 'So why are you looking so narked?'

'Because it probably means I won't be flying again,' he

snapped. 'I shouldn't be surprised if I find myself with a desk job when I go back. They say I'm stressed and need to calm down, which is as good as saying I'm not up to the job.'

'Not necessarily . . .'

'Of course that's what it means.'

'Did something happen to bring all this about?' she wondered.

'Some chaps have been saying things about me to the powers that be. A pack of lies about me losing my temper too often.' His voice rose with every syllable. 'A disruptive influence is how the squadron leader put it. Told me to take time off to get myself sorted out.'

'That seems fair enough.'

'That shows how much you know about how these things work.'

'I wouldn't know how they work, would I, as I'm not in the air force,' she pointed out boldly.

'So don't give your opinion, then.'

She took a deep, calming breath. 'You get very bad-tempered when you're tense, Pete,' she ventured. 'Maybe something a bit less taxing might be a good idea for a while.'

'That's right, you turn against me as well.' The malice in his eyes was a chilling reminder of just how spiteful he could be. 'It's a bad show when a man can't even rely on his wife for support.'

'I'm not turning against you,' she tried to assure him. 'But I find it comforting to know that the RAF pay enough attention to their men to notice when someone needs a break from flying. Surely an excessive amount of stress would impair your judgement, wouldn't it?'

'Everybody's nerves are overstretched when they're on ops.' He was very dogmatic. 'Nerves get the adrenaline flowing, sharpen your concentration.'

'There must be a certain point at which stress levels are a destructive element, though,' Nancy suggested. 'The air force must think so to have given you some leave. I think it can only be a good thing.'

'I'm a fighter pilot,' he reminded her with seething irritation. 'It's what I do and want to continue doing.'

'Well, it's only for a couple of weeks,' she reminded him with determined cheeriness. 'And you're probably worrying unnecessarily about what will happen when you go back.'

'I'm on the slippery slope,' he went on mournfully. 'Once they get the mistaken idea that my nerves are a bit shaky, who knows what might happen?'

'I'm sure it won't happen, but if they do ground you for a while, it isn't the end of the world.'

'It will be the end of *my* world,' he corrected. 'Flying is in my blood and I'm a damned good pilot. I don't want to waste my time pushing paper about.'

'You'll just have to make sure that you don't give them any cause to make you do that, then,' she advised him. 'By staying in control and not losing your temper.'

'My temper's no worse than anyone else's,' he claimed. 'Everybody gets irritable at times.'

His behaviour at camp had obviously been as unacceptable to the RAF as it was to her, or they wouldn't have given him special leave. He'd probably given one of the other chaps a good hiding.

'If they were to ground you for a while, they'd give you something useful to do,' she ventured. 'Something of value to the RAF.'

'Pen-pushing for a skilled pilot like me!' he said in a portentous manner. 'Surely even you can see that that would be a waste of my special skill and talent?'

'All I can see is your arrogance, at the moment,' she blurted out.

'The last thing I need from you is a lecture.'

'Let's drop the subject and enjoy the fact that you've got leave.' She moderated her tone and clung tenaciously to her self-control. 'You might as well make the most of the time off.'

He didn't reply, just leaned back in the armchair and stared miserably into the distance. 'I don't want to be stuck in this lousy room,' he said suddenly.

'Let's go out then,' she suggested. 'We could go to the flicks.'

'No thanks.'

'What about me?' she asked impulsively. 'Perhaps I might like to go.'

'Go then. I'm not stopping you.'

'As if I would go out without you when you've only just come home,' she said. 'I thought it might be nice for us to go together.'

'Not for me, it wouldn't,' he informed her gruffly. 'I don't want to watch a load of poncy actors pretending to be other people.'

The two extremes of his personality were hardly believable. At times he'd suffocated her with his possessiveness. Now his indifference was equally distressing, because she never knew what to expect next. She could hardly bear to imagine what he would be like if the RAF did give him a desk job.

'As you don't fancy the cinema, I'll get us something to eat and we'll have a quiet night in, then,' she suggested.

'I'm not staying in here all night,' he came back at her. 'I'm going down the pub when I've had some food. And if the local doesn't have any booze I'll keep looking until I find a pub that has.'

Nancy's heart sank. He was difficult enough when he was in one of his dark moods. With alcohol inside him, he would be a hundred times worse.

'Do you want a hand with that, Nancy?' asked Ruby as her friend struggled to load some luggage on to a trolley for a passenger who'd gone off to buy a newspaper while her cases were being dealt with. 'You look as though you could do with it.'

'I can manage, thanks,' replied Nancy. 'You'd better get on with your own work, or you'll have his lordship after you.'

'He won't notice if I spare a few minutes to help you with this lot. Anyway, what's up?' asked Ruby, seeing Nancy wince as she struggled to lift a suitcase. 'You look as though you're in pain.'

'I'm all right.'

'You don't look all right to me,' stated Ruby, lifting a case on to the trolley. 'You look as though it hurts to move. Did you take a tumble in the blackout or something?'

If only it was that simple. Pete had been home for ten days and the evidence of it was hidden beneath Nancy's uniform in various shades of red, purple and black. But she said with feigned buoyancy, 'No, nothing like that. I'm fine, honestly.'

Ruby gave her a close look. 'No you're not.' Concerned, she bit her lip. 'What is it, Nance? There's obviously something wrong.'

Finally driven by despair to say more than she'd intended, she blurted out, 'Yeah, you're right. There is something wrong.'

'Well, you know what they say about a trouble shared . . .'

A booming voice interrupted the conversation. 'Oi! You two!' said Percy, appearing out of the crowds in the waiting area. 'This is a railway station, not the local branch of the Women's Institute. You're not paid to stand around jabbering. There are passengers to deal with and a train to get out. It doesn't need two of you to load one trolley.'

'We'll talk in the dinner hour,' Nancy whispered to Ruby out of the side of her mouth as the two women got back to work.

'Oh, Nancy, how awful for you,' was Ruby's reaction to the truth about Nancy's marriage, told to her over sausage and mash in the staff canteen.

411

'It is pretty horrible.' Nancy was close to tears, but just about managing to stay in control.

'Pete seems such a nice sort of bloke, too,' said Ruby. 'It just goes to show that you never know what goes on behind closed doors.'

'Don't tell anyone, will you, Rube?' urged Nancy. 'It's vital that no one else knows.'

Ruby didn't look happy about this. 'I won't say anything, but surely someone should know what's going on? I mean, the man must be stopped.'

'If the family get to know, Dad and Uncle Wilf will go after him and probably end up getting hurt themselves. Pete's a strong man.'

'Mm, I can see your point.' Her brows met in a frown. 'But someone has to sort him out. Assault is a criminal offence. You should report him to the police. Let them deal with it.'

'I have threatened to do that in the past, but it isn't so easy when it's your own husband.'

'Well, something needs doing.' Concern for Nancy was making Ruby assertive. 'The first thing you must do is get away from him. It's far too dangerous for you to stay.'

'Yeah, I know.' She looked up, the shadows under her eyes almost as black as charcoal. 'I should have done it that first night of his leave when he came home drunk from the pub and beat me up. I warned him I would if he started knocking me about again.'

'So, why are you still there?'

'Oh, I don't know, Ruby,' Nancy sighed. 'He tells me he's sorry, swears he'll never lay a finger on me again, and I end

412

up giving him another chance, even though I know in my heart he'll never change.'

'It isn't like you not to be strong.'

'No, it isn't. But . . . somehow the violence weakens you, drains your confidence. Sounds pathetic, I know, but . . . it's hard to explain if you've not been through it.'

'I understand.'

'Anyway, he's going back to camp early the day after tomorrow,' she told her. 'So there's only one more day to get through.'

'But he'll get leave again.'

'I'll make sure I'm out of there by then.'

'You need to get out of there before then, Nancy. Another day could be too late,' said Ruby. 'From what you've said, I think your life is in danger.'

Nancy knew she was right. 'I'll try to get away tonight,' she said.

'Better still, don't go back there after work.'

'I'll have to, to get my things. I'm not going to let him frighten me to that extent.'

'I'll come with you. We'll collect your things together.'

'No. It's kind of you to offer, but I don't want to get you involved. It's best if I do it on my own. I'm working late tonight, so he'll be out at the pub when I get in. With a bit of luck, I'll be out of there before he gets in.'

'Let me come with you,' Ruby persisted. 'Just in case you need some support. I really do want to help.'

'You've already helped by listening to me and giving me the strength and determination to get out of there.'

413

Suddenly Ruby's kindness and the relief of having shared her secret was too much for Nancy and she burst into tears. 'Oh Ruby, you're such a good friend. You've made me feel strong again.'

Ruby passed her a handkerchief. 'You only have to say if you change your mind and want me to go with you tonight, and I'll be there.'

'I know, and thanks.' She wiped her eyes and reached across the table and touched Ruby's hand. 'I feel as though you're like a sister to me now,' she confided. 'I think our mutual bond with Evie has brought us closer together.'

'That's the nicest thing anyone could ever say to me.' Ruby was almost in tears now. 'Now, promise me you'll get out of there tonight.'

'I promise. Anyway, enough of my troubles,' said Nancy, wiping her eyes and composing herself. 'How are things with your love life? Is Gordon still in the picture?'

'Very much so,' her friend beamed. 'We write to each other all the time. He's stationed in Devizes now; some sort of special training.'

'It's probably got something to do with the second front we've been waiting for for so long. I'm glad it's going so well for you.' Nancy was genuinely pleased for her, despite her own problems.

'Me too. I can hardly believe how much my life has changed. I feel like a different person.'

'That's what love does for you, kid.'

As they went back to work and Nancy was reminded of her own troubles by the pain in her body every time she so much as moved a muscle, she knew she was going to have to keep her promise to Ruby and leave . . . tonight!

She was in the middle of packing her case when the siren went. Almost immediately, she heard the other residents trooping down the stairs to the cellar. She stuffed a last few things into the case and closed it, and had just put her coat on when Pete came in, looking the worse for drink.

'Where are you going?' he asked in a slow drawl.

'The cellar, of course,' she replied hurriedly, eager to be on her way. 'Where else would I be going when the siren is wailing its head off?'

'What's this?' he asked, swaying as he pointed towards the suitcase on the bed. 'If you think you're leaving, you've got another think coming.'

'We'll talk about it later,' she said quickly. 'Right now, we need to go to the cellar.'

'I'm not going to sit in some damp, miserable cellar with a load of strangers, just because of Hitler's thugs.'

'That's a stupid attitude,' she came back at him, her stomach in knots. 'We have to go to the cellar for our own safety.'

'I'm not bothered about the Luftwaffe. Let them do their worst.'

'You might not care if you live or die, but I do, and I'm not taking any chances by staying here. We won't stand a chance if the house is hit. We're sitting ducks up here.'

'I'm not going and neither are you. If I die, you'll die

415

with me. I'm not letting you go. You're never going to get away from me, Nancy.'

'Pete, please . . . let's just get through this air raid.'

The siren had stopped and the planes were getting closer. Nancy was terrified. The two of them were so vulnerable up here in the attic.

'We'll get through it together, here,' he said, his voice slurred. 'I'll show you that I've got bottle. I'm used to being in the sky, face to face with the enemy. An air raid is nothing to me.'

'Bottle!' she blasted at him in a rage born of fear. 'You're not proving you've got bottle. You're just proving how selfish you are. You might be a hero of the skies, but there's nothing heroic about your behaviour as a human being. Not content with beating your wife if the mood takes you, you won't even let her get to safety in an air raid. Too selfish to think of anyone but yourself. *You, you, you*, that's all you ever think about.'

His fists came at her so hard across the chest, she fell to the floor. Managing to get to her feet, she made a dash for the door, but he dragged her back and punched her so hard in the stomach that she crumpled and slithered back down on to the floor, sobbing now with pain and terror.

As she tried to get up again, there was a crash that shook the house and knocked her back down. She watched in horror as the roof came down directly on top of Pete, who disappeared under the rubble, just seconds before bricks and mortar came down on her. She felt herself falling as the floor gave way.

Hurting all over, she tried to call for help, but nothing came out. Her throat was full of dust, and she felt as though she couldn't breathe. There seemed to be no air. Panicking, she desperately gasped and panted. The bangs and crashes outside and the clanging bells of the emergency services were muffled by the wreckage. Then more debris came down, there was a blow to her head, then nothing . . .

Chapter Seventeen

'Come on now, Evie. Make up your mind, love. We can't keep the lady waiting all day.' Arthur was holding Evie up to see the glass jars lined up on the shelves behind the counter in the sweetshop. The purchase was proving to be a lengthy process because she was indecisive to the nth degree when it came to choosing her sweet ration, and had already changed her mind several times.

Now she pointed to a jar of enormous pear drops.

'Ooh, I think they might be a bit too big for a little 'un like you to manage,' Arthur suggested wisely. 'You might swallow one whole and choke yourself. What about something smaller?'

'Those, please,' she said, pointing to the Dolly Mixtures.

'You're sure, now?'

She nodded vigorously, eyes bright with anticipation, red curls bouncing.

'Two ounces of Dolly Mixtures, please,' Arthur said to the elderly assistant.

The red hair swung from side to side now, as the little

girl shook her head. 'Can I have those, please?' Evie stabbed her finger at the fruit drops.

The long-suffering assistant paused, holding the jar of Dolly Mixtures in mid-air.

'Sorry,' he said, with a sheepish look. 'She'll make up her mind in a minute.'

'It's all in a day's work for me, love.' She put the jar back on the shelf and waited for confirmation of the latest choice. 'She isn't the only one, believe me. All the kiddies take ages to decide, and change their minds half a dozen times before they're through. It isn't all that surprising, as they get so few sweets, and as long as I haven't actually weighed them out, I don't really mind.'

Arthur turned to Evie. 'So you definitely want the fruit drops then, do you? You're not to mess the lady around any more. There are other people waiting to be served.'

She gave him a wide smile, nodding her head slowly.

'Fruit drops it is then, and no more mucking about.' He put her down while he got his money and the ration book out. Bringing Evie to the sweetshop had become a joy to him since he'd taken her to his heart a couple of weeks ago. Pleasures he'd denied himself with his own children, by staying on the periphery of their upbringing, were now being enjoyed with Lily's daughter – small, ordinary treats, like reading her stories and taking her to the park. Being involved in her life uplifted him. And he particularly needed a boost to his spirits today after what had happened last night.

Completing the purchase and leaving the shop, he met Wilf on the way in, wearing a grave expression.

'I've just been round to your place and Mum said you'd brought the little 'un down here,' he said grimly. 'Trying to take your mind off it, are yer?'

'Yeah, I suppose so,' Arthur replied. 'It's sweetshop day for Evie anyway, no matter what dramas are happening around her. But I did think a walk might help to calm me down.'

'I've come down here to get some fags to calm my nerves,' said the other man. 'I really need a smoke after the news I've just had from Mum. I hear they've got some ciggies in here. I hope they haven't sold out.'

Arthur tutted, looking solemn. 'What a bloomin' awful thing to happen to our Nancy, eh?'

Wilf nodded. 'Shocking, mate. Shocking,' he agreed. 'The poor thing.'

'I'll say. Losing your husband and your home all in one go is a hell of a crushing blow. Still, she didn't lose her own life as well, thank Gawd.'

'My thoughts exactly.'

'It's nothing short of a miracle that she didn't, you know,' Arthur went on to inform him. 'The debris hit her as well as him, but he had serious head injuries and was dead by the time the rescue people got to him. It depends whereabouts on your body it catches you, I suppose. She was lucky not to get badly injured, with all that stuff coming down on top of her. She's got plenty of cuts and bruises to show for it, and was unconscious for a while, but there's no life-threatening damage, apparently.' He dashed forward as Evie wandered towards the kerb. 'Don't go near the road.' His tone was stern, and he clasped her hand with a strong grip.

'We've had enough bad news for one day. We don't want you getting run over as well.'

Wilf smiled affectionately towards the little girl, who was wearing a blue winter coat and matching knitted hat, her hair spilling out beneath it. 'Nice to see the two of you happy together, mate,' he mentioned to Arthur in a confidential manner. 'She's given you a new lease of life, by the look of it.'

'Cor, not half. It took me long enough to come round to the idea, but I'm tickled to bits now that I did.' He paused. 'But I'd better be going. It's cold for her out here, and I've got to go and do my insurance round when I've taken her home to her gran.'

'I'll walk back with you,' said Wilf. 'Hang about while I pop in the shop to get some ciggies. Won't be long.'

A minute or two later, the two men walked along the street with Evie between them – ostensibly a happy little girl out with her father and uncle, the latter puffing on his much needed cigarette. No stranger could begin to imagine the real story behind this ordinary family scene.

'You home on a forty-eight?' Bobby asked Gordon when he happened to meet him in the pub one Sunday lunchtime in March.

'Yeah.' Gordon made a face. 'Back to spit and polish tonight.'

'Same here,' said Bobby. 'I'm going back to camp this afternoon.'

'Still, we might as well make the most of these weekend

422

passes,' Gordon pointed out. 'There won't be any of 'em when the big push gets underway.'

'True.'

'I can only stop for a quick one,' Gordon told him. 'I'm meeting Ruby.'

'Still going strong, then?'

'We sure are.'

'You seem dead keen,' grinned Bobby, since Gordon's beaming smile was impossible to miss. 'No wonder I haven't seen you in here lately.'

'I've got better things to do with my time now,' his friend told him cheerfully. 'And it's all thanks to you. If you hadn't dragged me along to the Palais that night, I wouldn't have met her.'

'I'm a fool to myself then, because I've lost one of my best drinking pals,' joked Bobby. 'But good luck to you. I hope it goes from strength to strength.'

'Me an' all. But thanks, mate.' He sipped his beer. 'Ruby and I have often said that our meeting must have been fate, because she didn't want to go to the Palais that night either and only went because her friend twisted her arm,' he said. 'So we are both in debt to the two of you.'

'Glad to be of service.'

'Shame about Ruby's friend, isn't it?' Gordon's mood became sombre.

'Which friend?' Bobby didn't give him a chance to reply. 'Do you mean Nancy?'

Gordon gave him a look. 'You obviously haven't heard,' he said.

Bobby's heart lurched, fear whipping through him. 'Heard what? What's happened to her?'

'She was bombed out, a few weeks ago,' the other man informed him sadly. 'The house next door to the one where she and her husband had attic rooms took a direct hit and brought some of the adjoining property down with it. The two of them were in the attic, of all the daft places to be during an air raid.'

'Bloody hell . . . is she . . . ?'

'She's alive.'

'Oh, thank God for that.' He felt quite shaky with relief. 'Is she all right?'

'She's out of hospital and recovering well, but she hasn't been too good, according to Ruby,' he told him. 'Cuts and bruises mainly, and a bump on her head from the debris which knocked her out. Nothing serious, but it must have been a very traumatic experience for her.'

'What about her husband?'

'He was dead when the rescue people found them.'

'Blimey, that's tough. Poor Nancy.'

'Widowed and made homeless in one fell swoop,' said Gordon. 'Bloody Germans.'

'Where's she living now, then?'

'She's moved back in with the family,' he replied. 'They've rallied round, as families do at times like this. Almost everything she owned was lost in the bombing.' He finished his beer slowly. 'Anyway, I'd better shoot off. I don't want to keep the love of my life waiting.'

'See you, mate,' said Bobby.

Alone at the bar, he sipped his beer, immersed in his own thoughts. Finally he knew what he had to do.

That same day, Nancy decided to go for a walk in the afternoon. Jean was busy writing to Ed's mother, who'd become something of a pen-pal since Jean's thank-you letter to her. Gran and her father were enjoying a Sunday afternoon snooze in their armchairs, Leslie was playing football in the street, and Evie had gone to play with a neighbour's child. So, thankfully, no one had offered to keep Nancy company. She needed some time on her own. As much as she loved them all, family life could be suffocating in the large doses she'd had of it while home on sick leave.

Hands sunk deep into the pockets of her bottle-green coat, and wearing a thick headscarf against the lively March wind, Nancy headed for the park and sat down on her favourite bench, luxuriating in her own company. It was sheltered slightly from the wind here and the weak warmth of the sun felt comforting on her face.

She tried not to dwell on the actual bombing, because the memory set her nerves jangling. Instead, she concentrated on the fact that she had been blessed with survival. Pete's death was a tragedy, of course, but one of his own making. There had been no need for him to die and almost take her with him. All the other residents of the rooming house, who had sheltered in the cellar, had been unhurt after the raid. It was ironic that a man who'd done so much for his country, and proved his immense courage in the air on a regular basis, had died as a result of arrogance and inebriation under the debris of an attic room.

No one but Nancy knew why they had still been in the attic after the siren had gone, and had not taken shelter in the cellar. The assumption was that they hadn't had time to get there before the bombing had started, and she had no intention of enlightening them. Ruby remained the only other person who knew about Pete's violence towards Nancy and that wasn't about to change either. She saw no point in shattering people's illusions about him and destroying his reputation, when there was nothing he could do to put things right or defend himself. The man was dead, the whole thing over. An episode in her life she would not like to repeat and wanted to forget.

Oddly, it felt almost as though her marriage had never happened. She hadn't even been involved in his funeral, which had been taken care of by the RAF. Still in hospital at the time, she'd been unable to attend. There had been no contact from any of his relatives and she suspected that none of them even knew of her existence.

Now that she was living back at home, everything was much the same as before she'd left, except for the wonderfully improved situation between her father and Evie, which made for a happier atmosphere altogether. But while things hadn't changed there, Nancy had altered within herself, which was hardly surprising after everything that had happened. She felt older and wearier, but definitely not wiser. She'd been vain enough to be taken in by the flattery and attention Pete had lavished on her, and stupid enough to marry a man she didn't love, with disastrous consequences. In all honesty, she couldn't claim to be grief-stricken by Pete's death, given the pain and anguish he'd caused her, but she was sad that he'd died. He'd been a young man with a long way to go.

Occupation was what she urgently needed. Being on sick leave had given her too much time to brood. Had it not been for the bruising and torn muscles that meant she'd barely been able to lift a newspaper, let alone heavy luggage, she'd have gone back to work sooner. But now that she was feeling stronger, she was determined to be busy again, to feel that there was some purpose to her life.

As always, she felt soothed by this park, as changed as it was. Vegetables were now growing where there had once been grass, and the only flowers were a few wild daffodils growing in a cluster near the bench.

Someone sat down beside her.

'I called at your house. Your gran said you'd gone for a walk, so I thought I might find you here,' said a familiar voice.

'Bobby!' She could have wept with the joy of seeing him.

'I heard from Gordon what happened,' he explained, looking tenderly into her eyes. 'I'm so relieved that you're safe and well. My heart almost stopped beating when Gordon said you'd been bombed.'

'I had a narrow escape.'

'Thank God you did,' he said emotionally. 'Sorry to hear about your husband, though.'

'Thank you.'

'How are you feeling now?'

'Much better. I'll be glad to get back to work.'

Searching his face for something of the boy she'd known, she found it in his eyes. Although now topped by heavy, well-shaped brows, they still had that special bold sparkle and the sense of immeasurable depth she remembered so well. The contours of his mouth had altered with manhood, but not the warmth of his smile. She knew that his being here was right. She wanted him to stay.

'I'm so glad you came looking for me, Bobby.'

'I couldn't stay away when I heard what had happened. You've had a tough time.'

'Haven't we all in this awful war?' she replied. 'I'm one of the lucky ones.'

Silence fell. He felt as nervous as a young boy. But what he had to say could wait no longer. 'Nancy,' he began, looking at her worriedly, 'I know you've only just been widowed, and this may not be a good time, but I can't hold my feelings back any longer. I still love you. I never stopped. I've been miserable all these years without you.'

His words seemed to soothe away all the pain and misery she'd been through lately.

'I know you'll still be grieving for your husband,' he went on in a fast anxious tone, 'and if you tell me to go away, I'll never come near you again. But I'm going back to camp this afternoon, then being posted overseas, and I can't go away leaving these things unsaid.'

She didn't answer right away, just sat there looking at him. 'I'm not grieving for my husband, Bobby,' she said at last. 'My marriage was the second biggest mistake of my life.'

'And the first?'

'My going along with my father all those years ago and shutting you out of my life.'

'You mean . . . ?'

'Yes, Bobby, you're the only man I've ever loved, the only one I've ever felt safe and right with. I've tried to forget you. Even got married in the hope that it would stop me loving you. But it was no use.'

'I want us to start again,' he said, excited now. 'I can't bear not having you in my life.'

'I want us to be together too, Bobby,' she said, looking into his eyes. 'But you're going away.'

'But I'll be back. You know me, I always turn up. And when I do, will you marry me?'

'Yes, Bobby,' she said, slipping her arms around him and kissing him. 'I want that more than anything. It would be a dream come true.'

'Oh no! That's all we need, a bloody snow blizzard,' complained Private Micky Sparrow as he trudged wearily over marshy ground in the foothills of the Italian mountains with the rest of the platoon, the bitter, howling wind blowing snowflakes into his face like icy pin-pricks.

'Oh well, we've been soaked to the skin for weeks on end in the autumn rains, so we might as well have the snow as well,' said his pal Syd, marching beside him.

'Someone up there must have thought we were having

it too easy,' remarked Micky. 'Must have thought a snowfall would toughen us up some more.'

'As if we need it.'

'Exactly.'

Following the tanks, they plodded on, the snow beginning to settle and make the ground even more slippery, their packs weighing heavily across their shoulders. Micky was tired, nauseous with cold and hunger, every bone in his body aching, his feet sore and wet. Discomfort was the norm; the men were used to it.

'Roast beef and Yorkshire pud,' said Syd suddenly.

'Fish and chips,' responded Micky. It was a game they played to help protect their sanity in the relentless terror, interspersed with periods of boredom, and the sheer physical misery of their lives under the present conditions. It was as though they had ceased to be human beings and were merely part of the war machine.

'With salt and vinegar.'

'And brown sauce.'

Food, home comforts and women were the main fantasies of the many men in the allied armies in Italy, who had suffered many losses and felt forgotten by a world taken up with the Normandy landings in June.

'Churchill ought to come out here and see us,' said Syd, referring to the Prime Minister's visit to the troops serving in Naples. 'He'd soon stop the rumours about us being D-Day dodgers.'

News had come down the line to them about a song, popular back home, to the effect that the troops in Italy were having a wonderful time, drinking wine and dodging the danger of the D–Day landings.

'I wouldn't mind some of what they're accusing us of having, would you?' said Micky.

'Just a taste would do me, mate.'

'I'm more of a beer man, myself,' Micky told him. 'A pint in my local would do me.'

'Me an' all. That and a warm bed to go home to,' said Syd, who had a wife and kids he adored. 'The missus in it, waiting for me.'

'One day we'll get back to Blighty.' Micky had learned that optimism and a robust spirit were essential if he was to stay sane during this dreadful existence. 'We might not have to wait much longer, you never know your luck.'

'We've still got a few Germans to see off.'

'That's true,' he agreed. 'There'll probably be some to deal with in the village we're heading for.'

'Let's hope we get there before nightfall, so we can get rid of the Jerries and find a barn or something to sleep in,' said Syd. 'I don't fancy kipping in the open again tonight.'

'Me neither.'

Micky had never got over his horror of war, and still constantly doubted his own courage. He had a permanent knot in his stomach and sometimes thought he'd rather be dead than have to endure another day in the pursuit of destruction of human life. But the survival instinct always prevailed, and somehow he dragged something from deep inside of him and did what he had to, again and again.

Haunted by what he considered to be a flaw in his

character – in that he was in a constant state of fear – he made up for it by trying to be an exemplary soldier. His role model and hero was their leader Captain Parks, a man of immense courage and humanity. He never once showed that he was afraid, faltered in his duty or lacked understanding or care for his men. There wasn't a man serving under his command who didn't both like and respect him.

But now the sound of gunfire and shelling filled the air suddenly.

'Oi, oi. Sounds as though we've run into trouble before we've even reached the village,' said Micky, throwing himself on the ground along with everyone else, rifle pointing ahead, eyes scanning the landscape, which was bleak in the falling snow, the trees bare of leaves, the snow-covered mountains rising awesomely in the background. 'Looks as though they're shooting at us from behind that hill.'

'Some of 'em are advancing down towards us,' observed Syd. 'We'll soon see about that.'

As a knot of enemy soldiers came down the hill, Micky could see that their numbers were quite small. The order for Micky's group to advance came from the front, so he and the others got up and moved forward with speed and stealth.

'Bloody 'ell, the Captain's been hit,' spotted Syd.

Micky stared ahead at the man he so admired lying in the snow. He was still alive, though. Micky could see him trying to pull himself back. From here, it looked as though he'd been shot in the leg. But he was about to get finished off by the approaching German soldiers.

Fired with fury against the enemy on behalf of his Captain,

Micky ran towards him, undeterred by the bullets winging around him. Moving swiftly, he reached the officer and grabbed him by the shoulders, pulling him out of the line of fire and out of sight in a small forested area.

'Good man,' said the Captain.

'I'll go and get the medics to come to you, sir,' said Micky, noticing blood seeping through the other man's trousers.

'Don't worry about me, I'll be all right,' he said. 'It's just a flesh wound. You get back to the others.'

Whatever his own feelings on the matter, it wasn't done for a private to argue with an officer, so Micky just said, 'Yessir.'

However, on the way back to the platoon, he took a slight detour to the medics' vehicle and told them where the wounded Captain was before heading back to the gunfire, almost tripping over someone on the way.

'Syd! What the hell are you playing at down there? You nearly had me over.'

'I slipped on the ice and did my ankle in,' he replied. 'Feels as though I've broken it.'

'Blimey, that's torn it.' Micky leaned down. 'Here, grab my hand.'

He managed to heave his pal into a vertical position, but Syd cried out in agony as he tried to put weight on his foot, and slithered back to the ground.

'You go, Micky.' Syd's face was screwed up with pain. 'I'll sort myself out. Get out of here, quick.'

'You'll be a sitting duck here.'

'So will you, if you hang about,' said Syd. 'I'll be all right. You get yourself back to the others, sharpish.'

But that wasn't Micky's way. Syd was a mate and a married man with children. Micky couldn't leave him here to die. Managing to drag him to his feet again, he half carried him to the safety of the wooded area where the Captain was. The medics were already there, administering first aid to the officer. Micky handed Syd over to their care and prepared to head back to battle.

The sound of gunfire was relentless. There were bodies in the snow everywhere. But for the first time since he'd been in action, Micky felt as though he'd done something worthwhile, in getting the men to safety.

Turning to leave, he spotted a German soldier peering from high up in a tree, his gun aimed at the Captain and the others. Darting forward to act as a diversion and a shield, Micky aimed his rifle and pulled the trigger. The enemy soldier fell out of the tree, but not before firing a shot at Micky, who dived to the ground and missed the bullet by a whisper.

'Private Sparrow,' came the Captain's commanding tones.

'Sir,' replied Micky warily.

'Well done! You're a brave man and a bloody fine soldier.'

'Sir,' he said again, getting to his feet.

As he headed back towards the main battle, he knew that this was his proudest moment.

After the news came through on the wireless that Hitler was dead on 1 May 1945, everyone expected peace to be declared right away. Instead, they waited and waited, the tension palpable.

'It's nearly three o'clock. Mr Churchill will be speaking to us from Number Ten, Downing Street any minute,' said Gladys excitedly on the afternoon of Tuesday 8 May, as the family clustered around the wireless set.

'He's bound to officially declare peace,' said Nancy. 'They wouldn't have made today a national holiday otherwise.'

'I bloomin' well hope he does,' said Jean. 'All this waiting's killing me.'

'Shush,' said Arthur. 'He's coming on.'

There wasn't a sound in the room, apart from the Prime Minister's deep and distinctive voice speaking against the hiss and crackle of the wireless reception. Leslie knew that he uttered a word at his peril; even Evie managed to stay quiet.

'The German war is therefore at an end,' Winston Churchill said in conclusion. 'Long live the cause of freedom. God save the King.'

Everyone stood in silence for the national anthem, then there was uproar as they all hugged and kissed each other in turn, laughing, crying, dancing around the room.

'All we want now is our Micky back home,' said Gladys.

There was a general roar of agreement. Nancy hoped with all her heart that Bobby would be back too. She hadn't heard from him for a while and prayed every day for her sweetheart's safe return.

'Our days here are numbered now,' said Nancy, as she and Ruby stood on platform one waiting to meet a train when they returned to work after the victory holiday. 'The men will soon be doing the jobs again.'

'Yeah,' said Ruby, with a hint of wistfulness. 'We've had some fun, haven't we?'

'I'll say.'

'I'll miss working with you.'

'Same here,' said Nancy. 'But we'll still be seeing a lot of each other, as we're practically sisters.'

'Too true.'

'Anyway, you'll have far more exciting things on your mind than our days together here at the station,' smiled Nancy. Ruby and Gordon were planning to get married as soon as they could after he got home.

'I'll never forget them, though,' she said. 'It was while working here that my life changed, thanks to you.'

'Uh-oh, here comes the man himself,' said Nancy, catching sight of Percy heading towards them. 'Even he's smiling today.'

'Morning, ladies,' he said.

'You're looking happy today,' said Nancy, having greeted him respectfully.

'Of course I am. The war is over. Peace at last. It's enough to make a cat laugh.'

'You won't have to put up with us women for much longer, either,' she said. 'That's an added bonus for you.'

He stared at his clipboard for a moment, then cleared his throat. 'You haven't been too bad, really,' he said gruffly. 'In fact, you've done a good job.'

'Thank you. Praise indeed, coming from you,' grinned Nancy.

'Don't let it go to your head,' he said, trying unsuccessfully to return to his normal, sterner persona. 'There's still plenty of work to be done. I don't want to see you standing about yapping. The train's on its way in, so get to your positions. Chop-chop!'

They were both smiling as they said in unison, 'Yes, Mr Wellington.'

It was August and the early evening sunshine emphasised the shabbiness of everything in Sycamore Road. The bomb damage, the houses left unpainted because of lack of materials, the boarded-up windows waiting to be reglazed along with thousands of others. It was going to take a long time for the ravages of war to be put right, but at least the children could play safely in the streets now, and the adults could live without fear of the bombs.

Three months into the peace and Nancy still thanked God for it every day. The shadow of danger that had blighted everyone's lives for six years had gone and it was the most wonderful feeling. The shortages hadn't got any easier, but were more endurable when you knew you were safe.

Standing at the front gateway, beneath the red, white and blue bunting strung across the road, she looked back on the victory celebrations.

VE Day had been unlike any other day she'd ever known or was likely to again. The enormity of knowing that they were free was indescribable, and the outpouring of national joy and patriotic fervour was something she would never forget. The residents of Sycamore Road had rushed into the streets after the official peace broadcast, cheering and doing the hokey-cokey.

Later on, the Sparrow family had joined the crowds in central London, singing, dancing, laughing, everyone glad to be alive. With Evie on Dad's shoulders, they'd walked to Buckingham Palace, floodlit and magnificent, the balcony adorned in crimson drapes with a yellow and gold fringe. When the King and Queen and the two young princesses had appeared, the crowd had erupted. The only thing missing on that wonderful day had been the men who had made it all possible, many of whom wouldn't make it back at all.

The Sparrows had been blessed; they'd welcomed Micky home a few weeks ago. Oh, what a party that had been! Jean was in especially high spirits at the moment, having been invited to visit Ed's folks in the USA. She was planning a trip to America later this year. Dear Ed; he'd been such a sweetheart.

Watching Leslie having a kickabout in the street with his dad, and Evie giggling mischievously as she ran off with the ball, Gran looking on from the window, Nancy wished so much that her mother could be here to see them all together like this.

Looking up the street for a sign of what she had been waiting for all day, and seeing none, she decided to go back indoors. Then, taking one more hopeful look, she saw a handsome soldier turn the corner. Bobby was here at last! Smiling fit to bust, she ran towards him.